Penitence

Penitence

Penitence

A NOVEL

Kristin Koval

CELADON
BOOKS

NEW YORK

To Bea and Bernie, my mother and father

———— ••• ————

PENITENCE. Copyright© 2025 by Kristin Koval. All rights reserved.
Printed in the United States of America. For information, address Celadon Books,
a division of Macmillan Publishers, 120 Broadway, New York, NY 10271.

www.celadonbooks.com

The Library of Congress Cataloging-in-Publication Data is available upon request.

ISBN 978-1-250-34299-7 (hardcover)
ISBN 978-1-250-34300-0 (ebook)

Our books may be purchased in bulk for promotional, educational,
or business use. Please contact your local bookseller or the Macmillan Corporate
and Premium Sales Department at 1-800-221-7945, extension 5442,
or by email at MacmillanSpecialMarkets@macmillan.com.

First Edition: 2025

10 9 8 7 6 5 4 3 2 1

Each of us is more than the worst thing we've ever done.

—*Bryan Stevenson*

Prologue

N ora Sheehan sits in a jail cell in Lodgepole, Colorado, surrounded by three cinderblock walls and the kind of steel bars she's only seen on television, gray and cold. She's thirteen, the woman she might become still a shadow even though she's ready to discard her childhood. A longing for her stuffed penguin—a gift on her fourth birthday from her older brother Nico—grips her with an intensity she doesn't understand, and she twists her thin arms around her shoulders, a featherless bird warming herself with naked wings. She doesn't look like the sort of girl who just shot her brother.

The two cops in the adjoining room, arguing about what to do next, don't stop to think about whether or not Nora is cold. Lodgepole, a three-hour drive from the nearest small city, is not equipped to handle a murder or a murderer, and not equipped for a thirteen-year-old criminal of any kind. The older cop is thinking of his fourteen-year-old daughter, sleeping at home under a polka-dotted comforter, and her upcoming quinceañera, when she thinks she'll become a woman. The younger cop is thinking of how quickly the life drained out of the three holes in the dead boy, how quickly a human body pales without its blood. Both wring their hands, at times squeezing so hard their fingertips blanch. This kind of thing doesn't happen in their town. It only happens on the news. It can't be real.

Angie Sheehan is at home, in the purple house on Pine Street with chipped paint, staring at the crime-scene tape covering the door to her son's room. The same tape covers the door to her daughter's room. Nico's bed lies empty, and she wishes she could sink into the faint imprint his body made on the mattress, smell the sweetly masculine body spray he convinced her to buy to mask his burgeoning teenage odor. Angie shivers, not from shock or terror but because when her husband David left to find a lawyer, he left the front door cracked, and a cold draft winds through the house. *I should go close that door*, she thinks. *We can't afford a higher heating bill, not now.* She's alone with the noises of an empty home, noises that will rattle around the rest of her life. She closes her eyes against the crime-scene tape, the cold, and the leaden dawn leaking through the window at the end of the hallway.

Across town, David pounds on Martine Dumont's door. He's here because Martine didn't answer her phone—why would she, at 5:25 a.m.?—and he's already pressed the doorbell once, twice, three times. He stood behind her yesterday in Bea's Market when he bought ginger molasses cookies, Nico's favorite, so he knows she's in town. He's always felt a slight distaste for Martine because she handles the ugly divorces and represents criminals like the girl two counties over who left her newborn baby in the trash behind the high school. And because she's Julian's mother. When he watched her answer questions about that girl's trial in a press conference, cool and collected, his distaste morphed into a revulsion that brought bile to his throat—How could a mother throw away her child, and how could Martine defend that mother? But now he needs her. He needs cool and collected. He pounds harder.

Martine, still blissfully asleep, not yet a part of the unfolding tragedy, is on the left side of the bed even though her husband Cyrus has been gone for more than a year. She fell asleep to the hoots of a great horned owl echoing through the house's metal chimney, *hoo-hoo-hoos* cascading into each other in a gentle reverberation she felt rather than heard, a synesthesia pattering up and down her limbs. When the pounding finally wakes her, she jolts. Someone has died, that's the only reason for a knock on the door at this hour. *Julian*, she thinks wildly, but only momentarily.

He wouldn't have named her as an emergency contact, not after all this time and not when he lives in New York. Someone warning of a fire, maybe, but it's late in the season. Snow already blankets town, a dreary layer of heavy white slop that blew in from the northwest two nights ago and caught the snowplows by surprise. It cheered early-season skiers but depressed everyone else. The pounding is probably just a bear knocking over a trash can, searching for food to fatten up before hibernation. She puts on a pair of sweatpants, hopping to pull up the left leg, and stubs her toe on the nightstand. When she yells "Shit!" and leans on the edge of the bed to rub away the pain, her then-living husband, her younger self, and the little-boy versions of Julian and Gregory stare at her in a two-dimensional reproach from a silver picture frame on the nightstand.

Julian, who can't remember the last time he spoke to his mother, is two time zones away and already at work. He's a criminal defense attorney working in Manhattan, unaware the consequences of his long-ago actions have blossomed, an efflorescence he never anticipated. Martine will be on the news by tonight, her tight-lipped quote about her newest client repeated again and again in soundbites parsed by journalists to attract a schadenfreude-obsessed world. When he sees the headline, sitting in the back of an Uber on his way home at midnight, he'll stop scrolling to skim the article, partly because the murder took place in Colorado and partly because it's similar to cases he sometimes takes *pro bono*. When he sees Martine's name, he'll slow down and read more carefully. And when he sees the name of his hometown and the killer's mother's name—Angie Sheehan—he'll turn his phone over and look out the Uber window, not seeing or hearing the honking cars crowding a blocked intersection.

And Nico? Nico is in the morgue.

Chapter One

Martine is fully awake by the time David finishes explaining what happened, or what he thinks might have happened. Not because he took a long time in the telling and gave her time to make the morning coffee but because he spat out the whole story in one breath and this shock eclipses the shock of her stubbed toe from moments before. She can't process it as a murder so much as a blight, yet another on poor Angie, who was already sandwiched between caring for a mother with Alzheimer's and a sick son—Nico, only fourteen, had recently been diagnosed with juvenile Huntington's—even before *this*. Angie wore the strain of her life with grace, but Martine hasn't seen her smile in a long time.

They're standing in the foyer, frigid air sneaking past the door David left cracked behind him, snow from his boots melting onto the warm floors. He's wearing shorts and a T-shirt even though the weather already qualifies the season as winter, and Martine looks up, embarrassed by the intimacy of the wiry hair on his calves. He's a law enforcement ranger for the National Park Service and should be used to being outside, to feeling hot in the summer and cold in the winter, but the bare legs covered in goose bumps seem like a crack in his armor, an admission of how desperate he is. A gap in the floorboards sucks up the water pooling next to his right foot, absorbing it into the innards of her Victorian house.

"I'm sorry," she says idiotically, because what does that really mean? That she'll bring over a casserole? That the *sorry* could somehow ameliorate what happened? The words, emptier than they usually are, hang in the air between them.

David shifts his weight and dislodges another clump of snow from the top of his boots. More water to warp the already warped oak floor. His auburn hair, streaked with fading red on his temples, sticks up in greasy clumps, but his eyes lock on to hers like a too-firm handshake, unwilling to let go. "We need you. They took Nora to the jail."

Martine looks at him silently, trying to maintain her poker face. It's always been one of her best features as a lawyer: no one ever knows what she's thinking.

"She's only thirteen," he says. "A kid. There must be different procedures for kids."

"David, I'm retiring in a couple of months. I can refer you to a lawyer who will do a better job than me. I've just done one case like this, and it was only attempted murder." She can't take on new clients. She's seventy-two and tired, tired of mean divorces and bitter custody cases and lawsuits for missed rent, tired of writing wills for worried parents and drafting contracts for the new liquor store and defending ski bums for public intoxication. The past few years she's felt like a sin-eater, defending her clients for all their wrongs, keeping their secrets. Somewhere along the way, the magic of being a lawyer, of representing each person to the best of her abilities, of arguing and positing and compromising, wore off. She's slowly been transferring her clients to another attorney in town who bought her practice, a younger woman still hungry for work, still building her client list. She knows David knows this because Lodgepole is a small town. Everyone knows everything about everybody.

David returns her look with his own poker face. "Angie said you'd say that. But Nora needs a lawyer."

Yes, thinks Martine. *But not me*. Especially not for this family. Still,

Nora is just a kid. She shouldn't be in a jail cell. And the woman who bought her practice doesn't do criminal defense work. She's part of that new generation that only does what they want to do, as though they're too good to get their hands dirty, and sends all those cases to a law firm in Waring, over an hour away.

"Angie said you should do it because of Diana. We can't afford anyone else. We already took out a second mortgage to pay for Nico's medical bills. You're it, or she ends up with a public defender."

She knew that was coming and nods her head once, not wanting to seem enthusiastic, or worse, like she knows she's caught and has to do it. "Wait here. Give me five minutes to get dressed."

He nods back and folds his arms across his chest, wrapped in his own layers of hell, impervious to the wind now surging through the open door, and she decides to not ask him to close it.

As Martine and David cross the empty parking lot in front of the jail, she's grateful for one thing: the town is still asleep. When it wakes up, there will be a firestorm of attention, and not just from nosy neighbors in Lodgepole. She hated dealing with the media when she represented the sixteen-year-old who abandoned her baby, all those reporters looking for a story, looking for someone to blame. What, why, how. Whose fault. The teen mother's fault. The teen father's fault. The state's fault, for not advertising its safe haven laws. Your fault, for representing a criminal. The mother's mother's fault. All those pointed fingers will now be pointed at Nora, at Angie and David. Maybe, once again, at Martine. She hesitates just a moment, then opens the glass doors leading into the lobby and steps inside.

It's not much of a lobby, given that the jail is only an extension of Lodgepole's small police department, built in the sixties next to the then-new red brick courthouse. The glass doors do little to keep cold air out. Angie at least has a coat, but like David, she wears shorts and a T-shirt, maybe what she slept in, and the unzipped puffy jacket hangs off one shoulder. Julian once loved Angie and Angie once loved Julian—decades ago, when they were in high school—and an unexpected tenderness for her overwhelms Martine, eclipsing her uncertainty about taking this case. Angie seems unaware she's shivering, and Martine pulls the jacket all the way onto her shoulder and zips it, gently sweeping her uncombed hair to the side. The fluorescent ceiling lights give Angie's face a sallow hue, and Martine feels like she's seeing a future version of her, old Angie or about-to-be-interred Angie. For a moment, mired in the impossible pain Angie must feel, Martine forgets she's here to work.

"I'm so sorry." The empty words erupt from Martine's mouth again before she can stop them, but Angie doesn't hear her because she's already moved toward the two cops sitting behind the desk.

"I want to see my daughter."

The older one, Ignacio, clears his throat. In Martine's experience, he's gruff but fair. He seems baffled, though, unsure of the rules for a young teen who shot and killed her brother. "I don't know if that's allowed, Mrs. Sheehan."

"Of course it's allowed," snaps Martine. "Nora's thirteen."

"The sheriff said she'd be back as soon as she showered. She's in charge."

"My daughter shouldn't be in a jail cell." Angie's voice wavers and she looks at David for support. He grips her hand but doesn't say anything, perhaps afraid his own voice might waver and betray his uncertainty about where his daughter belongs.

"That's all we have. We don't have another secure location for a kid who—" Ignacio stumbles, then stops. He seems unwilling to say the rest of it out loud.

"There's a procedure for this," the younger one, Colin, says, nodding his head as if it will support what he's saying. "There must be. Mrs. Dumont is right. We can't keep a kid in there."

Ignacio pffffts, exasperated or frustrated or uncertain like David, and Martine steps forward, because this is ridiculous. "She can see her lawyer." She taps her fingers on the desk and stands up as tall as her shrinking body allows. "Let me see her, or I'll call Judge Castro and let him know what's going on in this police department."

Ignacio finally nods at Colin, and Colin leads Martine behind the desk and down a hall. The linoleum squeaks under her wet boots, and it's hard to tell whether the dingy floor is gray or just coated with a layer of grime. The sound grates on her, and she tries to erase the noise from her steps by setting each foot down quietly, by making herself smaller and lighter, but before she can succeed, they've left the hallway and moved into the cell blocks with cement floors.

"You can talk in her cell." Colin unlocks the door and motions for Martine to enter.

Nora stares at the floor. Goose bumps cover her bare arms the same way they covered David's legs, tiny hairs protruding from each one, searching for heat or comfort or something other than this reality. Her hair, redder than David's, hangs in strings down her back like yarn. Her shoulders barely fill out her T-shirt, as though they're nothing more than a hanger in a closet.

"Get her a blanket, or a sweatshirt, or something," Martine calls after Colin, hoping he hears her.

She sits on the edge of the hard bench facing Nora. She only took that case with the abandoned baby because no one else would, and her knowledge of criminal defense law is too basic for her to be defending a homicide. She has no idea where to start, what to say.

"Do you remember me, Nora? My name is Martine Dumont. I'm a— I'm a friend of your mother's, and she asked me to talk to you. I'm going to be your lawyer." Friend, is that what she is to Angie? She used to be friends with Angie's mother, and together they broke up Angie and Julian after Diana died. Saying *I am your mother's ex-boyfriend's mother* would not be comprehensible, or even matter, to Nora. *Friend* will have to do.

Nora's eyes, still aimed at the floor, dart back and forth, as though she's searching for something in the cement.

"Are you okay?" asks Martine, her voice softening. Her history with this family shouldn't matter. Nora is just a girl. She takes her jacket off and drapes it over Nora's shoulders.

"You won't have to stay here much longer. As soon as the sheriff gets back, she'll drive you to Pinyon County Juvenile Detention Center— that's the detention center where delinquent kids from western Colorado go while they wait for their trial to start. You'll be with other kids there. You shouldn't be in this jail cell." Martine winces at the word *delinquent*. It's the correct legal term for what Nora is, but it sounds both worse and better than it should. What kid wants to be called a delinquent? But also, Nora is much more, much worse, than a delinquent.

"She'll be here soon, and I won't be able to talk to you again until tomorrow, so we need to talk now," Martine continues. "I know you were awake all night and you're tired, but I need to ask you some questions, okay? Everything you say to me is subject to attorney-client privilege. That means I can't talk to anyone about it, and what you say is safe with me."

Nora holds perfectly still, her darting eyes now locked in a numb gaze at nothing. Martine has represented kids before, but always older teens, ones caught selling weed or alcohol, or driving under the influence. What could a thirteen-year-old understand about attorney-client privilege? What could Nora understand about what she'd done, about the consequences of killing a person?

"Can you tell me what happened last night in your house—what happened with Nico?"

Nora looks like an unfinished statue, a marble figure frozen in place by a sculptor who forgot to add life to his creation. Martine keeps her face still, but the silence between them grows, and she shifts her weight on the bench.

"Would yes-or-no questions help? Let's try that. Did you call 911 last night to report that you shot Nico?"

Nothing.

"What did you say to the 911 operator?"

Nothing again.

Somehow Martine has already veered away from yes-or-no questions. Shit. She tries to reset.

"Does your dad keep his work gun in the house?"

Not only is Nora not speaking; she isn't shaking her head yes or no. She's almost catatonic.

"Did you shoot a gun last night?"

"Did the gun go off by mistake?"

Martine feels her voice getting edgier, and she forces herself to stop asking questions and think through what she does and doesn't know. Nora might need a *guardian ad litem*—her parents will be conflicted out because they're the parents of both the killer and the victim—and she'll definitely need a juvenile psychiatrist. Nora shot Nico point-blank three times: once in the eye and twice in the chest. It would be almost impossible to argue in court it was an accident. And if it was intentional, Nora must be having a mental health crisis. Otherwise, a thirteen-year-old could not have done this. Would that mean she could argue "not guilty by reason of insanity" and get Nora sentenced to a psychiatric facility where she could get help? She's heard those arguments are hard to win, but perhaps the mere existence of a mental health issue would mitigate Nora's eventual prison sentence, reduce it to something less than life. Then again, how will she argue anything if Nora won't talk to her?

She closes her eyes and tries to remember the last time she saw Nora in town, to remember any shred of information that might help this conversation, but a jumble of images, mostly of Nico, appear instead. Nico before he was diagnosed, all knees and elbows as if his body was growing in uncoordinated spurts, racing to be tall before he was ready, smiling on the front page of the *Lodgepole Ledger* as the winner of the Juniors' Slalom Skier of the Year award. Before that, Nora and Nico in town, giggling as seven-and eight-year-olds at the ice cream shop. And long ago, Nico as a toddler, whooshing down a slide in the playground, just a couple of years after Angie and David got married. She banishes Nico from her thoughts, refocuses on Nora, and says the first thing that comes to mind.

"I live across town from you, near the cemetery. I walk there in the morning with my dog, Jack."

Nothing.

"Sometimes I see owls. Last night there was a great horned owl on my roof when I came back from my walk." Martine opens up a photo on her phone and enlarges it so Nora can see the owl on the eaves, partially hidden by the cottonwood branches towering over her house.

Nora recoils from the photo, then closes her eyes, and Martine puts her phone away.

"I'm sorry," she says, the words no longer empty, and lays her hand on top of Nora's. "This is going to be hard."

"The cops took a bunch of stuff," says David, "and we're not allowed in their rooms right now. They're coming back for one more look later this morning. They took my work gun, too."

He shoves open the door to Nico's room and leans in without setting a foot inside. The bed is stripped, and the mattress, bed frame, and floor are splotchy with the remnants of last night's violence. If Nico had been a girl, the stark red on the white mattress could have been a period stain, a sign of a normal life cycle instead of proof of an early end. The rest of the room is orderly, with books in their place and dresser drawers closed.

"Nico was in bed when—when it happened." Angie's voice breaks, and she looks down at the hallway carpet. David makes no move to comfort her, doesn't take her hand or rub her back. He's either stoic or stunned, and Martine, somewhat stunned herself, looks away uncomfortably and focuses on the bedroom.

Typical fourteen-year-old-boy decorations—a Ferrari poster, a skiing poster, and a Messi soccer shirt—cover one wall. But there's also a row of old stuffed animals on top of a bookshelf, all birds: a rainbow-colored parrot, an ostrich whose plush neck can't hold up its head, a bald eagle draped in an American flag. More birds, the two-dimensional kind, perch in a tree painted on one wall. Bark-covered limbs coated in green leaves stretch from the trunk and curl onto the ceiling and adjoining walls. Whole families of birds sit on branches and babies' beaks gape in twig nests, hoping for a painted worm to drop into their mouths. A humming-bird flutters into a blue sky, only a faint whiff of wings visible, its perpetual motion barely arrested by the artist's paintbrush. And on top of the tree: a misshapen owl. Now Martine understands Nora's reaction.

"Nico liked birds?"

David nods. "It started with *Sesame Street* when he was little, you know? Because of Big Bird. When he started reading, he checked out every bird book he could from the library. We thought he'd outgrow it, but eventually it morphed into him loving birds of prey, because he once skied on a mountain called Birds of Prey. He was saving up to go to a falcon-hunting camp next summer."

"Angie, you did a beautiful job painting this," says Martine. Angie was a talented artist in high school, and Martine had heard she won a scholarship to the Rhode Island School of Design and then worked in a gallery in Soho after graduation.

"Nora helped, too," says David. "Or tried to, anyway."

Angie's jaw tightens. "I painted this for Nico when he was little, then added to it for his birthday every year. When he turned fourteen, I added a falcon, but Nora snuck in one day when we were at a doctor's appointment with Nico and tried to make it bigger. It ended up looking strange, and I transformed it into an owl as a temporary fix. I promised Nico I'd turn it back into a falcon when I could."

"She was only trying to *help*. If you'd let her when she asked, that wouldn't have happened," mutters David. Angie glares at him, and he turns to Martine. "Nora loved to paint, too. Loves, I mean. She loves to paint."

"And she loved Nico," says Angie. "That's why none of this makes sense."

"Can I see Nora's room? I need to see if there's anything in there to help with her defense," says Martine.

Angie looks down the hallway, but her eyes are glazed and filmy, focused on nothing as though she's anywhere but here. "She loved Nico," she says again.

David turns and opens the door to Nora's room across the hall, again stopping on the threshold, barred by the crime-scene tape. "We can't go in here, either."

Nora's room is nothing like Nico's. A wrinkled duvet lies on the floor next to the unmade bed. Paintings and drawings, mostly of rivers and mountains, cover the walls and the sides of a small dresser, and T-shirts and jeans hang out of open drawers, like a clothing bomb had exploded. Crumpled papers, soda cans, and empty bags from Bea's Market overflow the small wastebasket.

"She doesn't like to clean her room," says David.

Martine nods. "No teenager does."

"I never painted her walls because once she was born, I had two babies," says Angie, crossing her arms across her chest. Her voice, devoid of emotion, contradicts her defensive posture. "There was no time to paint. And even as a toddler, she wanted to hang her own art."

"They took her tablet and phone, and everything from her backpack. But her brushes and paints are still in here." David points at them, stuffed onto a bookshelf in the corner.

"Once they've finished the initial investigation, I'd like to come back and look around more closely," Martine says.

"Do you want some tea?" asks David. He takes Angie's elbow and guides her to the kitchen.

"We can talk about Nico while it brews," says Angie.

Nora, thinks Martine. *We can talk about Nora. That's the child you have left. The daughter you hired me to defend.*

While David boils water, Angie and Martine look out the kitchen window at an aspen, its limbs full of golden leaves crinkled brown around the edges, a real tree full of real birds. Bird feeders stuffed with seeds hang from two branches, and robins and chickadees dive in, then skirt off when threatened by a raven.

"This was Nico's favorite place in the house, other than in front of the Xbox. He sat here to do his homework, getting distracted by those birds." David hands Martine and Angie steaming mugs, and they sit down at the oak kitchen table. Scratches and dings cover the surface, and in one corner, Angie's name is etched into the wood. It's Angie's childhood kitchen table, a hand-me-down from her mother Livia, the same table in the same kitchen where Martine and Livia used to sit and drink coffee—when they were still friends. "The only time he didn't was early summer, when blue jays came and stole the robins' eggs, or if the eggs had already hatched, the babies. The jays ate them. The babies, I mean. Nico liked birds of prey, but for some reason he hated the blue jays for eating baby robins. He was sensitive, for a boy."

He spoons three teaspoons of sugar into his mug. "Personally, I never feel bad for the robins. They have a whole forest to hide their nests, but they always choose to build a nest here."

Martine sips her tea while David babbles but declines the sugar when he pushes it toward her. Twenty-five years have passed since she was last in this house, and she's having heartburn from the awkward déjà vu. Martine never wanted to be in this house again, with or without Livia.

"What can you tell me about Nora?"

Angie and David look at her blankly, then David, as if he wasn't listening to the question, says, "We told you what happened."

"Yes, but I need to know about Nora, so I can figure out how to defend her. It's not a question of whether she did it. She called 911, said she shot her brother. That's a confession and it'll be admissible in court." David nods his head, jaw slack, and Martine continues. "We'll have to figure out the best argument for her legal defense so we—"

"It was a mistake," interrupts Angie. "They must have been playing with David's gun."

David sets a hand on top of Angie's. "Let's listen to what Martine has to say."

"Well, the DA might try to argue it was intentional, since three shots were fired, and since those shots were aimed at Nico's heart and head, he might be successful." Martine says this as gently as she can, and phrases it passively so she won't upset Angie and David any more than necessary. Stating outright the DA *will* argue the shooting was intentional because Nora shot Nico point-blank three times would only make things worse. "So if we can't argue it was a mistake, we also need to know about Nora's mental state, whether she's fit to stand trial or whether her mental state can be used to mitigate the time she'll serve."

"The time she'll serve," repeats David, as though he's trying out the words.

This is Julian's area of expertise, and Martine wishes she could swallow her pride and call him, but he's rebuffed her too many times. They aren't estranged, not exactly, but asking for assistance on behalf of the girlfriend he hasn't seen since high school probably won't help reestablish their mother-son bond. She gives the best answer she can think of.

"She's going to serve time somewhere because it was a homicide. With the right facts and a best-case scenario in court, and depending on how she pleads, maybe we can get her sentenced to a mental health facility that can help her. For me to do that, I need to know everything you can tell me. What Nora liked to do in her spare time, how she did in school. What her personality is and has it changed recently. Whether she got along with Nico."

David cups his hands around his mug and silence fills the room. Martine clears her throat but waits, and once he starts talking, he doesn't stop for an hour. She takes notes on a yellow legal pad: Nora loved Nico, he wants to make that clear. Martine stars "Nora loved Nico" every time he says it, and by the time he finishes talking, there are ten stars, the blue ink smudged on most. It's a hodgepodge of information: The two of them were Irish twins, only eleven months apart, and they did—or used to do—everything together. They loved fantasy, especially the Marvel movies and the Harry Potter movies. They played video games with their friends. Nora listened to rap and pop but hated country. They were on the ski team, but Nico was the better skier. They played soccer. Nora was—is—a good kid. That sentence gets seven smudged stars. Nora loved—loves—painting, just like Angie. She was on medication for depression because last year she started spending a lot of time in her room and stopped hanging out with the family. This happened right after Nico was diagnosed—here, Angie interrupts David and says, "We assumed that was what was making her sad."

David agrees. "She and Nico figured out enough about Huntington's to know what it meant for him. The doctors said that when it progressed, it would be like having muscular dystrophy, bipolar disorder, Alzheimer's, Tourette's, schizophrenia, and Parkinson's all at the same time, and it scared all of us."

"But Nico wasn't that sick, not yet. It could have been normal middle school blues," says Angie. "From girl drama. It's hard to be a kid that age. Her depression could have been that."

The two statements—the litany of symptoms Nico would eventually experience and the fact that he "wasn't that sick, not yet"—bewilder Martine. And yet, maybe the two statements aren't inconsistent. Isn't that the way with every disease, that sometimes you're fine until you're not? The discordance in the conversation rubs like sandpaper on her skin, and even though she can't ask the question, she wonders how long he had left.

"Maybe," says David, in a tone that's not quite brushing Angie off but also makes clear he doesn't agree. He pulls a framed photo from the windowsill and hands it to Martine. "This picture is from two years ago, before Nico was diagnosed, when the doctors still thought his dropping grades and strange behavior were Asperger's or ADHD. Nora had just gotten braces because of some spacing thing in her mouth."

Nico is in the center of the picture, surrounded by David, Angie, Nora, and Livia. Nora is smiling, an open-mouthed, toothy grin, and the camera flash glints off her braces. Her hair is woven into a thick, shiny french braid slung over her shoulder. Her posture, hunched shoulders, mirrors David's. In fact, everything about her comes from him, the sharp cheekbones, the arched eyebrows, the pale skin. Nico is smiling, too. He doesn't look like David or Angie, and Martine wonders if that was another early, hidden sign of the juvenile Huntington's. She knew a thinning face could be one of the symptoms for some neurodegenerative diseases because Cyrus had treated a couple of afflicted patients. But then again, maybe the face of who he might have become was simply hidden behind the sweetness of a little boy, behind the dimpled chin and hairless cheeks. Livia, body and head shrunken down to a fraction of their former size, like she'd been caught by an ancient headhunter, clutches her arm around Nora, as if to protect her granddaughter from some unseen danger.

When Martine finally gets home, she's relieved Jack hasn't peed in the house. If he makes a mistake, it's always on Cyrus's old Persian rug under the dining room table, and it's getting harder and harder to get rid of the smell. Overseeing Nora's transfer to the juvenile detention center, talking to the Sheehans, and responding to inquiries from the press had taken longer than she thought it would. Jack's tail wags hopefully and she smiles at him as if he can read her face.

"Okay, Jack. Good boy." Thank God for dogs. He's happy to see her every time she comes home, no matter how long he's had to wait. She ruffles the scruffy fur around his ears. "Let's go for a walk."

They end up in the cemetery, Jack's favorite place to play and Martine's favorite place to think. There's a chain-link fence enclosing the huge swath of grass and graves, and the caretaker doesn't mind if dogs run around off-leash. Martine and Jack usually run into one or two neighbors, humans and dogs, and the playtime keeps Jack from getting lonely. She winces when Jack lifts a leg and pees on Ethel Sweeney's gravestone—it's one of the oldest in this historic graveyard, and Ethel might not approve—but before she can scold him, he takes off toward a yellow lab he loves.

The thought of talking to anyone about her day, about Nico and Nora and what this means for Angie and David, is overwhelming, and she wanders off to the left of the main path, trying to avoid the lab's owner. The woman is a spinster gossip in a middle-aged body and would wheedle as much information out of Martine as she could. *Where were the parents? Is Nora crazy? Did Nico suffer? How could she have shot her own brother?* She'd somehow know just enough to make Martine wonder if there was a leak in the police department, and anything she learned would fly through the town's gossip mill and end up in the news. The media has already latched on to the shooting, and the last thing Martine wants to do is reveal a detail a reporter might use to mold a story, to turn what happened into something it wasn't or render Nora the villain in the public eye, all dependent on their mood. The district attorney is up for reelection, so what the public thinks will matter. She might not be an expert on juvenile homicide cases, but she knows she needs to carefully control the narrative on Nora.

She ends up by Diana's gravestone, right next to an almost-identical one for Roberto, Livia's already-dead husband. There's a space on the other side for Livia, but none for Angie, reflecting either a belief in their eldest daughter's immortality or the assumption she'd eventually rest in the Sheehan plot next to David.

"Diana Alessia DeLuca, age 7

JULY 19, 1983–FEBRUARY 28, 1991
OUR ANGEL IN HEAVEN"

Nineteen ninety-one, ancient history that still won't loosen its grasp on her. How had she been coerced into representing Nora, when she'd spent all the years since then doing the best she could to avoid everyone in the DeLuca family? She avoided eating in DeLuca's, their Italian restaurant, and crossed the street if she saw Livia or Roberto on the sidewalk. Eventually, Roberto died and Livia got Alzheimer's. By then, Angie was married to David and teaching high school art, caught up in being a mother and living her own life, and Martine relaxed and assumed she could forget the past.

When she'd seen Angie around town, she'd focused on her as she was then—an adult with her own life rather than Julian's ex-girlfriend. Nico and Nora spent a lot of time at a playground Martine passed on her walks, and occasionally she watched them. They were, after all, Angie's children. Nico was boisterous and loud, always running and laughing, full of the mischievous energy she'd loved about Julian and Gregory when they were young, and a tow-headed blond like Julian had once been. Nora was quieter, the kind of kid who sometimes climbed a tree to read in a comfortable nook, but she spent most of her time at Nico's side. If Julian and Angie had stayed together, these could have been her grandchildren, and sometimes she imagined playing with them, riding on the rickety seesaw with Nico or pushing Nora in a swing. Even then, Martine already suspected she might never have her own. Julian had finally married, but he and his wife Mayumi were old enough that it might not be possible, and Gregory, a journalist with wanderlust, was always traveling, reporting on genocide in Myanmar or drought in Somalia or wildfires in Australia, so she kept her dreams of grandchildren to herself. She waved to Angie from across the park but never stopped to say hello.

As the kids got older, Martine saw the family around town less and less. When she did, David was never with them—he worked in the Black Canyon of the Gunnison National Park and must have spent hours every day commuting. Some rangers spent weeks at a time up there, and she assumed he did the same. She sometimes saw Nora along the trail by the river, painting landscapes on an easel, and Nora usually smiled and waved, probably with no idea of who Martine was other than a lady she saw around town, but today in jail was the first time she'd seen Nora in months. At some point, Nora had morphed from the happy little girl who ran around a playground attached to her brother into the pubescent young teen who shot him.

Reconstructing the past in a way that might make sense of any of this feels insurmountable. The day's pressure wells up in her chest, as if the devil himself is sitting on it, breaking her sternum, forcing her to feel everything she doesn't want to feel. After Cyrus had his first heart attack, he told her the pain was like an elephant sitting on his ribs. After his second one, the one that killed him, her heart felt like it was breaking, but today she feels the pain Cyrus described. She should feel relief, because it's not a heart attack and not an elephant, but she can't, because this pain comes from the whole world, crushing her lungs with the weight of all its tragedies. It's the stress of solving an unsolvable puzzle, of making sense of the nonsensical. It's Nico and Nora and David and Angie. Above all, Angie.

Angie feels this, too, only she can't articulate it. She's in her house with its chipped purple paint, sitting on a couch bleached by time and sun, barely breathing. The lungs and heart are born to work independently of the brain, to function automatically, but she finds she must now tell them what to do. Breathe in, breathe out, breathe in, breathe out. Beat, beat, beat. If her mind wanders and she forgets to concentrate, when she returns to the tasks of her heart and lungs, she realizes she hasn't been breathing, and the thump of her heart has slowed to an echo.

David, sitting at the kitchen table, copies the important dates Martine gave them onto the calendar pages he printed out:

Day 1 (October 13):	Arrest
Day 3 (October 15):	Detention hearing
Day 6 (October 18):	Petition in delinquency filed
Day 36 (November 17):	Preliminary hearing
Day 51 (December 2):	Entry of plea
Day 111 (February 1):	Adjudicatory trial
Day 166 (March 28):	Sentencing

He's methodical and organized, using blue pen for the day and green for the action on that day. Martine said it wasn't all set in stone, that these dates only apply in the juvenile system, and if the DA charged Nora as an adult instead of a juvenile, the dates would change. Everything would change. When he pointed out what he thought was obvious, that Nora, at thirteen, *was* a juvenile, Martine looked at him, looked at Angie, and shook her head. He could see the pity in her eyes, and he knew what she was thinking: he and Angie couldn't take any more. He hadn't protested. They would cross that bridge when they came to it. He would focus on these dates for now. The detention hearing on day 3 would confirm that Nora would be held in a juvenile detention center. Martine was clear: there was no way the judge would grant bail and release her for home detention, not with a homicide. It was hard to catch everything Martine said because his ears were still ringing, either from the shots they heard in the night or just because, but he'll google the meaning of *petition in delinquency* and *adjudicatory trial* later. The acrid smell from the discharge of his Sig Sauer .45 still lingers in his nostrils even though Angie says she doesn't smell anything. He blows his nose so hard his nostrils pop, then returns to the calendar. When he finishes, he recaps each pen and stands to hang the next six months of his life, of Nora's life, on the refrigerator, but finds he can't walk. He stares down at his feet, still in the boots he wore that morning to Martine's house.

Chapter Two

Angie can't prevent her mind from returning to that night. One moment, she was going to bed, thinking of the week ahead. A week she thought would look like all her weeks since Nico got sick last year: doctor's appointments; therapy appointments, physical and emotional; driving Nico to those appointments; finding time to drive Nora to soccer or school, or encouraging her to find her own rides. Laundry, cooking, and cleaning. Visiting her mother. Driving, more driving, always driving. Helping Nico with his schoolwork so he didn't fall further behind. Food shopping, if she was lucky enough to have time to herself; otherwise, David did it. Tending to the depression Nico developed after he googled "juvenile Huntington's disease" and figured out he'd eventually develop dementia—"Like Grandma Livia?" he'd asked, terror in his eyes—and die within five to ten years. She tried to be positive in the face of a prognosis that wasn't positive, but at the end of every day, she sank into bed, drained.

The next moment, she and David woke to shots, loud bangs that jolted them out of a deep sleep. At first, they thought someone had thrown a rock through a window. But when they rushed out of their bedroom, there was Nora in her sweats, the same ones she'd been wearing for three days, standing in the hallway on her cell phone.

She had David's gun in one hand and red splatters on her face. For a moment, Angie wondered why Nora was painting in the middle of the night, but there was blood, so much blood, in Nico's room. She heard David barking orders at someone—it must have been her, it couldn't have been Nora—but she was frozen in place and couldn't do anything other than watch him stuff towels into Nico's wounds. The police and EMTs were there in minutes, pushing them out the bedroom door and into the hallway. Blue-and-red lights flashed in the driveway and a group of neighbors huddled outside. The ringing in her ears echoed into a roar that overwhelmed all other sounds, a jet taking off that never stopped throttling its engines. The rest of that night is obscured, like an ugly watercolor covered by angry broad strokes of black. She can't remember the last time she saw Nico, whether she turned to look at him one last time or didn't get the chance.

Since then, she's asked David over and over what happened next. Each time, he says the same thing, expressionless, his emotion below the surface the way it always is. They talked to Sheriff Nelson on the front lawn while Ignacio and Colin talked to Nora in a police car. They took Nico away in a zipped black bag—*her child, in a body bag*—a bigger version of the evidence bags holding Nora's bloody clothes, and took Nora away in handcuffs.

"I remember from here," Angie always says at this point in the retelling.

But she doesn't want to. She felt, still feels, imprisoned in an alternate reality, in a narrow tunnel, suffocated by walls contracting around her. Maybe that's why she keeps asking David to repeat the story of that night. This feels like a nightmare, the kind she used to have every few years, when she'd wake from someone dying, knowing it wasn't real but with the palpable sensation it was. She'd break away from the terror with a jerk, as if someone knocked the wind out of her, heart racing and sweat gathering under her breasts, half-aware she only needed to wake up all the way to make it disappear, and in the morning call whoever her brain thought had died so she could hear their voice. What she really wants during David's retelling is for him to say *this* is the nightmare, to wake and comfort her, then let her peek through the children's doors to lay eyes on their sleeping bodies, chests rising and falling synchronously with their breath.

This reality persists, though. Every day she wakes up *into* the nightmare. The police finally tore down the crime-scene tape blocking the children's rooms, but the doors are still closed and one torn corner of tape remains embedded in a groove in the wooden doorframe, a yellow reminder she can't scrape off because she can't bring herself to touch it. David took Nico's mattress to the dump and ordered a new one. Angie cleaned Nico's room, scrubbing the blood splatters out of the carpet and off the walls with chemical cleaners that induced a splitting headache. She reorganized the shelves and stuffed his school backpack into the closet without opening it to see what was inside. There was no blood in Nora's room, but she tidied the shelves, made Nora's bed, washed the dirty clothes strewn on the floor and put them in drawers. David tried to take some of those clothes to Nora, and they fought about that, bitterly, because Martine said the kids were required to wear state-issued sweats. What use was taking clothes to Nora she couldn't wear, it was pointless, but he insisted, then returned after the visit and stuffed the jeans and T-shirts back into the wrong drawers. She wasn't sure what bothered her more, the idea of Nora in a prison uniform or David thinking he could—or should—bring her new clothes. Nora killed Nico. Her brother, their son. Didn't he understand that?

Their children's rooms (Is a dead child still "her" child?) are both on the first floor, one on the left side at the front of the hallway, the other on the right of the back, the hallway an umbilical cord connecting two children who never shared a womb but seemed to live in attached worlds. Every day Angie paces the length of the house, from the front door through the TV room to the kitchen and down the children's hallway to their bathroom at the end and back again, over and over. David is gone, either at work or visiting Nora, and the pacing is the only thing Angie can do to keep her racing heart from exploding, to keep her frothing thoughts from bubbling over. She feels her pulse in her face, in her hands, in the bulging vein in her neck, and counts the steps in each direction. When she talks on the phone to David or Martine, the only people she's willing to speak to, she's dimly aware she's speaking too quickly, tripping over her words the same way she's tripping over her thoughts, but she can't slow down. Her pants have begun to hang from her hips and David makes her drink a cup of water when he gets home, but food hardens in her mouth like concrete drying in the sun and she can't convince herself to swallow anything. The pants hang because of the not-eating or the pacing or the heart that won't stop racing, who knows, and each time she says this to David, he frowns and begs her to eat a piece of toast with peanut butter, to sit next to him on the couch and take deep breaths, but all she can think about is the new mattress he ordered, and she always turns to him and repeats the same question.

"But who will sleep on it?"

The funeral is small, because Angie is unwilling to face a world of people who know one of her children killed the other. When she googled Nico's and Nora's names, something she knew she shouldn't do but did anyway, articles from across the country popped up. The dangers of guns in the home, the violence of today's teens because of video games and movies. Other articles speculated: drugs, maybe, or mental health. Because Nora is a minor, most identified her only as Nico's "thirteen-year-old sister" but he only had one sister, one sibling, so it was clear who the media meant. The *Lodgepole Ledger* was the kindest, sticking to facts, writing only about Nico and his accomplishments as a young skier before he got sick, but she made the mistake of reading the comments and cried at what she saw: trolls condemning Nora as evil or blaming her and David as parents. In the days since, she's avoided eye contact if she leaves the house, always studying the ground or her feet or the sky.

Inside St. John's Catholic Church is a safe space, though, with only Father Lopez, David, David's parents, and Martine. No Nora, because the state wouldn't allow her to leave the juvenile detention center for the funeral. And no Livia, because Angie hasn't told her about Nico's death and the funeral would only confuse her. Angie's mother hasn't recognized Nico or Nora in a long time, and most days she doesn't even know who Angie is. And even if Livia was still Livia, Nora was her favorite. A funeral for a forgotten grandchild shot by a favorite grandchild would be too disturbing.

The service is closed casket. Even though the undertaker mended the holes in Nico created by the gun wielded by Nora, he couldn't fully repair Nico's face. David said this to Angie last night using those carefully chosen words, as though he, too, was afraid to say the real words, the uglier ones, aloud, and Angie nodded in response, grateful for the solidarity of their fear. It was the only solidarity she felt with him, the only thing that kept her from saying what she believes: this funeral is his fault, the gun in the house is his fault, it's all his fault.

She's been to other funerals, of course. Her own sister, her father. She cried at both. And she was weepy at the fire chief's funeral four years ago when he died not fighting a fire but in a car crash, even though she barely knew him. She won't cry today, though. Not because she doesn't want to. She can't. She feels every emotion, a whole carousel of emotions, except the one that would elicit tears.

Angie glues her eyes to the casket during the funeral mass. It's larger that it should be for a child because Nico was big for his age, and the size feels like an insult: an adult-sized casket for someone who never got to be an adult, for a child who never got to live his life's dreams. When Nico's behavior first went haywire, and the doctors diagnosed him with Asperger's and ADHD, she adjusted the dreams she had for his life. Maybe he wouldn't go to Middlebury or the Rhode Island School of Design, but they'd help him find the right college, the right job. Maybe he'd work outdoors as a park ranger or a ski coach, where his differences wouldn't impact his success. Then, when they said the first diagnosis was wrong, that he had juvenile Huntington's, she adjusted her dreams again. She thought they had a few good years left, years where he could still be a normal kid—attend school, ski with the family even if he couldn't race anymore, or go on vacation to Disney or the beach—they'd find a way to squeeze in as much life as possible before the disease took over, when the dementia would steal who he was even before the disease stole his life. Now the remainder of those dreams lie in a wooden box. Inside this box lies her son, flat on his back, arms laid out by his side or perhaps folded across his chest. The lines in the light wood pucker into swirling imperfections at the corner, just past the metal handle someone will hold when they lower it into the ground. *We begin our lives in one container*, she thinks. *A uterus. And we finish in another. A box.*

Is she really supposed to leave him alone in that dark container? To abandon him?

Her stomach rebels against the cloying incense burning by the alter, and she breathes in through her mouth and out her nose to quiet the nausea. When she was little, she thought that smell was God, but God must be absent today or this wouldn't be happening. Unless—and now her heart somersaults—this is a mistake, a joke. She looks around, waiting for a sign. A sign from God, a God her mother believes in but Angie doesn't. Or better than a sign from God, a message from her son. *I am right here, Mom.* Now she listens, not to Father Lopez but for the sound of Nico's voice, the emphasis he used to put on the words *right here* during hide-and-seek when she couldn't find him. He would spring from his spot, usually inside his wicker hamper, eyes sparkling with laughter. *I tricked you. I got you.* His pudgy four-year-old fingers would wrap around her cheeks and squeeze a smile out of her. She remembers the softness of the skin on those fingers, the sometimes sticky feel if he'd been sneaking honey from the jar in the pantry.

Now she waits, holding her breath. She hopes.

But nothing. Nico is not here. Nico is not anywhere.

The only sound in the church is Father Lopez's nasal intonation of Our Fathers and Hail Marys.

God is not here. God is not there. God is not anywhere.

A mirthless hysteria she almost can't control threatens to froth up and bubble over. Dr. Seuss is rhyming and chanting during her son's funeral service. Not here, not there, not anywhere.

Questions spin in her head. She's mostly blamed David for what happened, because of the gun, but now she turns on herself. What had she done, what kind of mother was she, to let this happen to Nico? How had she ended up as the mother of the children that appeared in that Google search? Maybe the media trolls who pointed fingers at her were right. Maybe she was a bad mother. Maybe this is her fault.

Lint on her black dress catches her eye, and she picks it off, then picks at an imperfection in the seam, pulling at a thread until she tugs it loose and unravels it entirely. She starts on a second thread, but David nudges her and shakes his head like she's a small child misbehaving in mass. A desperate imperative to unthread and rethread the dress, as if she were Livia fixing a ripped shirt with a sharp needle, engulfs her.

For a brief moment, she wishes she were burying her mother instead, because at least life would be happening in order, the way it's supposed to happen. She slaps her own face at this thought, hard, the hand rising of its own volition and smacking her cheekbone, the pain soaking her skin like rain, because this is what her mother must have felt when Diana died, only maybe Livia had wished for Angie's death, had blamed her the way Angie now blames Nora. David pulls her hand from her face and squeezes it when his parents turn, shocked, to the percussive clap of her palm and cheek colliding.

How is she to comprehend Nico's death, the death of her child?

Warmth spreads across her cheek, the warmth of violence, of physical pain, something she welcomes because at least she understands it, and later she'll be able to see the mark of her hand, the fingerprints fanning out on her cheek like bloodstained lace.

After the funeral, they leave the church separately: David to visit Nora, and Angie to visit Livia. In the empty parking lot, him with one hand on the door of his black pickup truck and her shivering next to the minivan, he looks at her expectantly.

"You should be visiting Nora, not your mother," he says. His voice strains, either from the effort of saying those words or to stop himself from saying others. He hasn't shaved in days, and the brick-colored scruff on his cheekbones only magnifies how haggard he looks, like red buds on a blanched aspen at the end of winter.

"I can't," says Angie. The drive to the nursing home in Waring is only one hour and the drive to the juvenile detention center in Rimrock Junction is three, but that's not why she chooses to visit Livia instead of Nora. She hasn't been to visit her daughter yet because she's not sure what to say, how to *be* when she's with her. She worries she'll lose control of her anger, let it run freely through Nora's misery, stampeding past and over the guilt and sadness she can plainly see during Nora's court appearances—and intellectually understands, but can't bring herself to sympathize with. Nora stole more than a life when she shot Nico. Who knows how long he had left to live, five or eight or ten years, but all anyone wants is more time. That's what Nora stole. Time.

"I'm not ready," she adds flatly. She doesn't know if she'll ever be. Seeing Nora, looking into the same eyes that looked down the barrel of David's gun and lined it up with Nico, that must have watched David when he unholstered that gun and locked it in the safe, registered the combination so she, too, could unlock it—she'd have to meet those eyes and forgive those eyes, that face, that child. A mother is supposed to love her daughter, but Angie tingles with fury at Nora, a fury she's not sure she could control in person. A fury that might dip into hate.

Something like pain crosses David's face, and she wishes she could reach out and hug him, or that he would reach out and hug her, but neither of them moves toward the other.

"You're the adult here," he says. "You need to be ready. You have to be there for your daughter."

"She's not the victim," says Angie. "No one has to be there for her." That sounds cruel, even to her own ears, but it's satisfying to throw some of her pain in David's direction. She climbs into the minivan and the door slides shut quietly, a nondefinitive end to a conversation they've had three times. Someone does have to be there for Nora, but she feels tangled in the absurd paradox of how to keep loving Nora without betraying Nico. She pulls away without looking back at him.

Maybe she's right; maybe she is, and always has been, a bad mother. David visits Nora whenever he can, driving three hours each way without complaining. He brings things—not just clothes, but candy, chips, stuffed animals—even though he's never allowed to give them to her, no matter how much he begs, and instead can only give her snacks from the detention center's vending machines. Nora still hasn't spoken, but David says he talks about television shows or what he saw in the forest when he was working. What would Angie talk about? Is she supposed to say *Hey, Nora, you're grounded for shooting your brother?* Or how about *Hey, Nora, we just went to the funeral for the brother you killed and it was a beautiful service?* Or what she really wants to say: *I will never be able to forgive you.* She already knew there was no how-to guide for being a parent—that became clear when she realized she'd eventually need to provide the same caretaking to her son she was already providing to her mother, when she learned he'd be left with less mental capacity than an old woman with Alzheimer's—but there's definitely no guide for this. And even if there were, she clearly violated it. Otherwise, Nora never would have done what she did. She, Angie, must have somehow caused Nora to turn into a monster. Maybe she, Angie, is the monster.

It's easier to visit Livia. If Angie does or says the wrong thing, her mother will forget about it before Angie leaves.

The road snakes down the valley and out of the box canyon, then up and onto the Waring Mesa. As the lodgepole pines and spruce give way to aspens and then scrub brush, she turns the volume up on the radio and focuses on the view. Eventually the blaze of autumn will fade and the leaves will wither, dropping to the ground before being buried by a white blanket, but for now the aspens still hold their leaves and the chokecherries hue a deep red. The minivan isn't great on the curves, and she could easily end up in the San Moreno River, but she leans in and doesn't let up on the gas. The loud music is a barrier against the angry voice in her head, and she sings along, belting out the lyrics without caring who can hear because the volume is so loud she can't hear the voice outside her head, either.

At the front desk, Angie refuses to meet the receptionist's eyes, as if she hasn't known her for years now, hasn't seen her each time she checks in to visit Livia. Angie knows everything there is to know about her life. But the receptionist also knows about Angie's life, and that's the problem. The receptionist is one of the good ones, and the kindness of her pity would hurt more than the cruelty of internet trolls. Instead, she walks straight to her mother's room.

"Hi, Mommy," she says, as brightly as she can. "I'm here."

Livia's on the couch, her body enveloped by plush cushions, clutching rosary beads. Her face lights up the way it does for every visitor, and she claps her hands, dropping the beads on the floor. Over the past few years, as her memory clouded, the anger and grief that seized her after Diana's death lost their grip and she softened into a different person, more like the mother Angie remembered from early childhood. She wished her father could have seen the change, because his last years were dominated by an angry and hard wife. When Angie once complained, tired of how stoic Livia seemed even as he lay dying of cancer, he'd sighed. *You have to be a hard person to survive a hard life,* he'd whispered. *She had her own life, a history in a small Italian village you know nothing about and can't understand.* Then he'd turned over and fallen asleep.

Angie sinks into the couch next to Livia and sets the rosary back into her hands. Alzheimer's has done nothing to diminish Livia's memory of her Our Fathers and Hail Marys, even if she has no idea why she says them. The beads and cross are wooden, worn to a silky smoothness. She's had them restrung at least five times, though sometimes the number of restringings stretches out in Livia's current versions of the story.

The skin covering her talon-like hands is like velvet, prone to damage if rubbed the wrong way, and Angie reaches for the peppermint lotion on the side table and rubs it into the backs of Livia's hands. An ache wrenches her gut and tears wallow up through her throat. More than anything, she wishes her mother could comfort her, wrap her in the kind of hug she used to get from Roberto as a child. Livia was never an easy mother—and Diana's death sucked away what little softness she once had—but Angie would take any bit of her old mother now, because at least she understood what it was like to lose a child.

When Livia first moved here, she was still occasionally herself, but as the Alzheimer's advanced, the lucid periods retreated. Now Angie must shift conversations away from the present and into the past, the only place Livia still lives. As her awareness of the present has faded, so has her reluctance to talk about her history. Her memories of forty, fifty, sixty years ago have reemerged like mittens found at the bottom of a melting snowdrift. They have whole conversations about when Livia came to America to marry Roberto, the sisters and brothers Livia left behind in Calabria, and the aunt, not much older than Livia herself, who raised them, sometimes skipping meals so the youngest siblings could eat. The stories shift sometimes, their shapes pliant, obedient only to the whims of Livia's tangled neurons, but the characters are always the same, and Angie wonders if Livia's constant writing and rewriting of her history is what softened and transformed her into a mother Angie wants to remember.

"Do you want to go outside to see the aspens? The leaves are still yellow."

"I can see them from here," says Livia.

Angie tugs her mother up and transfers her into a wheelchair, supporting almost all of her weight with one arm. Her mother is lighter and easier to help than she used to be, and Angie settles Livia into the chair, then wheels her over to the window. Sometimes Angie feels like all she does is sit at windows and watch what's going on outside, separated from the real world by a pane of glass, something so thin she could break it by punching her fist through it, if only she had the energy. Today, though, the glass pane is a welcome respite, a giant screen allowing her to spectate with no pressure to do anything other than watch leaves flutter to the ground.

"Look!" Livia says. "It's—it's that guy with the mask. There! Do you see him?"

"Yes, Mommy. It's a raccoon. I think he's confused about what time it is, because they usually come out at night." She says this gently, always careful not to speak to Livia like a small child who can't understand what's being said, even if that's sometimes the case. "He's probably trying to eat a lot before winter, like the bears."

Livia nods, as if she does understand. Sometimes Angie brings watercolors so they can paint, and that's easier than keeping up conversations about what's on the other side of the window, but she has something she wants to talk about, something she hopes happened long enough ago that Livia might still remember. The first few days after Nora shot Nico, Angie thought only of her own pain. But her recognition today at the funeral—this was what her mother felt, all those years ago—dismayed her. Before then, she'd only ever thought about Diana's death from her own point of view, but now she needs to remember it in a way she's always avoided. Maybe understanding Livia's pain over losing a child will subdue her own.

"Mommy, I want to talk to you about Diana," she says, then waits to see what part of Livia is here today. She shouldn't push, she knows she shouldn't, but Nico's funeral, his everyday absence, his forever absence, gnaws at her.

Her mother's eyes brighten at the mention of Diana, the way they always did for Nora. "Diana. Such a beautiful child. She has green eyes, like my mother. We made cannoli together last week, did you know that? It was for her fifth birthday party. They were perfectly shaped, and Diana dipped the ends in chocolate chips."

Angie nods, hoping Livia stays in the moment. She doesn't remember this story and wonders if it's her own memory failing or if this is her mother confabulating. It's not lying, Dr. Bartlett says. She's just filling in memory gaps with whatever she can come up with.

"And then Angela came in and . . ." Livia slows down and looks right and left, as if she's checking the room. Her eyes, milky with cataracts, leak yellowed fluid, not quite tears but not quite nothing.

"What next?"

Livia lowers her voice to a whisper. "*Li ha rovinati. Mangiò uno, e quando l'ho beccata, ha rovesciato il vassoio e sono caduti a terra.* She ruined them like she ruins everything. She broke them all."

More and more, her mother has been reverting to her first language, forgetting her English. Livia refused to teach Angie and Diana any Italian—after she came to America she lapsed into it only when she was angry or scared—but Roberto taught Angie enough that she understands most of what Livia just said. It's not the first time Livia's softer self has been mean—the personality change is part of Alzheimer's but will always be uneven is the other thing Dr. Bartlett says—but even as she tells herself this, she knows it's not true, not for this. Angie presses her lips together but says nothing.

"*Diana è qui?* Did she come visit me?"

"No, Mommy, she can't come visit you. She died, remember?"

Livia sits up straight. "No."

"I'm sorry, but she did. She was seven and I was seventeen, remember?" Angie says, her voice hardening. For the second time today, she wraps herself in a cloak of cruelty.

Livia's lips quiver and real tears well in her eyes.

"It was a long time ago. You never spoke to me about Diana again, even though I lost her, too. But I need to know something, Mommy. It's important." The made-up cannoli story, blaming Angie for something that never happened, still stings, and she presses on. "I want to know when you stopped hurting after she died."

Livia's eyes glaze over until they're vacant, the brightness draining out of her the way life drained out of Nico. Her mouth slackens, and she looks around, disoriented.

Angie reaches for her mother's pale forearm, for the thin and velvety skin hanging like a decaying sail, sagging and wrinkled, and gathers it all in her hands, the skin and the bone. One of her first memories is of stomping on just-frozen puddles in the early fall, her yellow rubber boots fracturing the thin, glassy ice floating on top of the water. The cracks in the ice spread in a web as she pushed her toe into the glassy surface, then shattered as she smashed her heel down, splashing water and sending ice fragments flying. She squeezes her mother's arm now, gently pushing her fingers into that sagging skin the way she pushed her toe into the thin ice, then walks out of the room without looking back.

Chapter Three

1991

In February 1991, Martine believed her blended family would always be the close-knit unit she'd worked so hard to build. Cyrus was still alive, Julian was eighteen and Gregory twelve. Cyrus's medical practice was thriving. Patients came to see him for every ailment in the book, from delivering babies to setting broken bones to cancer, and no one seemed to care that he spoke with the faintest trace of an accent. Martine's practice had been slower to start—when they arrived from New York City in the midseventies, it was easier for people in this rural part of Colorado to accept an Iranian man as a doctor than any woman as a lawyer—but by that winter, she was busy, too. They were both generalists, forced to do everything as if they were living a century ago when there was no such thing as specialization for doctors or lawyers, because there were so few of them in town. Weekdays were full of work for them and homework for the kids, weekends full of ski races and camping trips. Martine worried about what would happen once Julian left for college—he'd been recruited by Middlebury to race on their ski team—but she knew they'd see each other often because she and Cyrus planned to travel to all his races and bring him home for every holiday.

When Julian called her on February 28 from the town's small hospital, she immediately knew something was wrong, terribly wrong, and that their little family unit would disintegrate even before he left for Middlebury. Her stomach churned as he spoke, his story stumbling and clumsy, not all of it comprehensible. Diana was in the hospital but already dead, Angie was in shock and had been given a sedative, and Roberto and Livia were on their way. Julian sounded out of it, like he, too, was in shock, but Martine knew it was something more.

"It was a tree, Mom. She hit a tree. Angie and I started right behind her, but she was skiing fast, too fast, and went around Big Bend without us. By the time we got there—" His voice faltered. He was on the only payphone in the hospital, the one near the waiting room, and in the background the hospital buzzed with shrill beeps and chattering nurses.

Martine swallowed hard, forcing bitter bile back down her throat. Big Bend was the ski team's pet name for a narrow zig-zag partway down No Way Out, a steep trail leading back to the ski base. Towering spruce and aspens lined the edges of the trail, and once a skier turned the corner, it was true they disappeared from view, but there was no way Diana had been going too fast for Julian and Angie to catch up. She was only seven, still snowplowing on the blacks, barely ready for the junior races. Julian and Angie raced every weekend, and Julian excelled at the downhill. He'd passed six feet a year ago and two hundred pounds that fall, with quads so big the other kids called his legs "tree trunks," the kind of muscles that allowed his legs to withstand sixty miles per hour on fast, icy slopes in races. It wasn't just Julian's voice that sounded off. His story was, too.

"Don't talk to Roberto and Livia," she said. "Don't talk about the accident."

"Mom, I can't not talk to them. They're gonna want to know what happened. And the part about her hitting a tree, that's true. Angie and I, we—"

Martine interrupted before he could finish, afraid of what he would say next. "Go splash cold water on your face, a lot of it, and drink a cup of coffee. I'll be there as soon as I can. You were drunk . . . or high." It wasn't a question, and Julian didn't disagree.

"Mom," he said. Just that. She could hear the fear in his voice, the slight quaver that emerged when he knew he'd done something wrong. It was his tell. He'd had it since the moment he learned to lie, when the worst her sweet-cheeked little boy could do was steal a cookie or forget to flush the toilet.

"I'm talking to you as your lawyer, Julian, not your mother. Keep your mouth shut. Don't say anything more than she was going too fast and hit a tree."

Martine's head spun as she silently raced through the possibilities. She was certain about the alcohol or weed. He was a teenager, the age kids experimented. Maybe they hadn't been watching Diana when they were supposed to because they were high. If so, Julian could be sued by the DeLucas for negligence and prosecuted for possession of weed. But it could also be something worse. What if he'd hit Diana and knocked her into that tree? Martine didn't do much criminal law, but she wondered whether a collision would be criminally negligent homicide or worse, manslaughter. Whatever had happened, it was something that could ruin Julian if she didn't figure out how to control the situation.

It didn't take long for Martine to realize she hadn't done enough controlling. After Diana's funeral at St. John's, the neighbors brought casseroles and cookies to the DeLuca house and served whiskey and tea while everyone milled around, consoling Livia and Roberto, whispering about what happened. But when Martine approached to give her condolences, Livia's eyes blackened. "Get out," she hissed, and then broke into Italian, something she rarely did. "*Vai via*, and take your son with you. I know Julian had something to do with what happened. This wasn't Angela's fault. And it certainly wasn't my Diana's fault." She'd said it quietly enough that no one else heard, and Martine backed up and left as fast as she could without making a scene. She pulled Julian away and left Angie sitting alone on the couch, eyes welling up with tears but shoulders and back erect, as straight as a soldier's.

Livia knew something, Martine just didn't know what, whether Angie had confessed to drinking or smoking weed, or maybe blamed everything on Julian. Julian insisted Angie wouldn't have told her mother anything because it would look just as bad for her, but Martine couldn't be sure. She didn't want Julian anywhere near Livia or Roberto. Or Angie. She still didn't know if Julian had told her the full truth, whether he'd done something more than what he admitted to and Angie was covering for him, or Angie had done something more and Julian was covering for her. Weeks later, when she was still hearing whispers—whispers she'd initially expected, because Lodgepole was a gossipy small town, but that she thought would die down as people went on with their lives—a comment here, a phone call there, everyone wanting to know what really happened, how Martine and her family were holding up, her suspicions were confirmed. Julian had always been a wild child, with a reputation for being the fun kid who would do anything to win a race, or try new tricks—720s or jumps off cliffs—no other kid was crazy enough to try. His ski coach had advised her long ago to calm Julian down and now called to suggest Julian take a short break from the team to gather himself and recover from his involvement in Diana's death. She declined his suggestion—there was only one race left—but she didn't know where the continued gossip might lead, whether it might trigger Livia somehow. Keeping him away from the DeLucas wasn't enough. She had to get him out of Lodgepole to save his future.

Cyrus agreed. He'd seen the autopsy, and parts of it didn't correlate with the usual injuries of a skier hitting a tree. "She had typical tree collision injuries—the dissected aorta and the broken back—and it would be hard to prove something other than what Julian said happened, but I'm worried, too. Both her tibias were broken, and that's more common when one skier hits another."

Martine's mother lived in New York, where Martine and Cyrus had met, and that seemed like the obvious answer. Julian could finish his school year there, find a job that summer, then head to Middlebury next fall. For a couple of years, they'd make sure he found summer internships in New York, and the family could celebrate holidays there with her mother. They'd keep him away from Lodgepole and the DeLucas.

When Martine and Cyrus told Julian he'd be moving to New York,

Gregory was away for the night, sleeping over at a friend's house. Julian sat on the floor and ran his fingers back and forth on the wool carpet, riffling through the tree of life pattern, unable to make eye contact with either of them, hiding his eyes beneath the unruly hair he'd grown out to emulate Kurt Cobain. When he started digging his fingers in the pile, making designs in the only family keepsake Cyrus had from Iran, Cyrus almost chastised him, but Martine laid her hand on his, silently reminding him they had bigger things to talk about.

Julian protested at first. "That's—that's not fair. What about my last race? And off-season training over spring break? I can't miss that. And what about school?"

"You can go to your last race," said Cyrus. "But you'll be settling into Grammie's apartment over spring break. You'll have to find another way to stay in shape for Middlebury's ski team. And you'll go to the high school near her apartment."

"I'll miss graduation." He said this halfheartedly, tracing the designs on the tree with his fingers instead of digging into the pile.

"You'll have a graduation in New York. We'll come out and celebrate with you," said Martine.

Julian didn't say what she knew he was really thinking—*What about Angie?*—because by then Martine had forbidden him from dating her, from even seeing her outside of school and the ski team. And Martine understood his feelings, she really did. Julian and Angie had been together forever. From the day they'd met in first grade, there had been no Julian without Angie and no Angie without Julian. They were like two moons orbiting each other, inextricably bound by an invisible magnetic force. But their love was like a first kiss, nothing more, and its gravity would be subdued by time, relegated to a mere flicker in his mind as he moved on to the main part of his life, the part where he went to college, got a job, and fell in and out of love with other girlfriends. Martine didn't believe in soulmates. Julian's biological father died when Julian was an infant, and she'd married Cyrus less than a year later. They'd had a long and happy marriage, and she loved Cyrus just as well as she'd loved Julian's father. Julian could start an entirely new life once he got to

Middlebury, away from Lodgepole and Angie, away from whatever had happened on that ski slope.

Martine was scared of Livia, scared of what she might do if she figured out the truth, or thought, even mistakenly, Julian was someone to blame. Martine and Livia originally became friends because there were no other working mothers in town and Martine loved that Livia was a tough-as-nails restaurant owner, but Livia had a vindictive streak, something black inside that made her want to squeeze and twist anyone who crossed her or her family. She'd seen it countless times: Livia holding grudges against mutual friends or restaurant employees, even against children, ones who snubbed Angie for a playdate when Angie and Julian were young, or mistreated Diana on the playground. She'd take revenge on the child later, in ways both big and small, dropping that child's slice of birthday cake on the floor or pretending she didn't have a Band-Aid in her ugly yellow purse for the offending child's scraped knee. And after Julian and Angie started officially dating, Livia—a devout Catholic who believed premarital sex was a mortal sin—stiffened against what that implied her daughter was doing with her free time and retreated from the friendship with Martine. She had it in for Julian before Diana's accident, and Martine knew better than to give her the chance to punish Julian for the loss of her favorite daughter.

Julian left a week later. Martine sat with his anger on the flight from Lodgepole's small airport to Denver, then from Denver to New York. He refused to talk to her, refused to eat in the airport or on the plane, and refused to smile when the New York skyline materialized through the window on the Continental flight.

"Look." She nudged him, nodding toward the clouded oval. "There's the Twin Towers, the Statue of Liberty—"

"I know that's the Statue of Liberty, Mom." He said *Mom* like it was poison. "Jesus Christ, I'm not a little kid. I'm eighteen. And I've been here before. I was born here, and we visit Grammie."

"Well," said Martine, trying to contain her hurt, "it's been a few years.

You were thirteen the last time we came here. Usually it's Grammie visiting us. I just thought you might need—"

"No, I don't. I don't need anything. I don't need a reminder of what the
buildings are, a reminder to be excited, or a reminder to be polite at her
house." His flat voice lowered an octave. "I don't need a reminder that you
guys banished me from Lodgepole. From Angie."

Do you need a reminder of why? thought Martine.

He stayed sullen through the taxi ride from Newark, keeping his
eyes focused straight ahead in the Lincoln Tunnel and up the West Side
Highway, through the tour of the bedroom her mother had set aside for
him—Martine's childhood bed frame now outfitted with a navy comforter, the walls emptied to make room for Julian's decorations—and
through take-out Chinese at the small table in the cramped kitchen. A
rehearsed smile emerged when Martine's mother brought out a plate of
chocolate chip cookies.

"Since your grandfather died, I never have anyone to bake these for
anymore," she said, "so I'm glad you're here. I'll take good care of you."

He pushed his chair back, the legs screeching on the floor, and shook
his head. "Thanks, Grammie. Can I save mine for tomorrow? I'm not hungry and I want to unpack."

He hugged Martine's mother but not Martine, then closed the bedroom door just softly enough that she couldn't call it a slam.

"Let him go," her mother said. "This can't be easy on him."

Should it be? thought Martine. She traced her fingers over the grain
of the oak in the table.

"Do you even know if he did anything?" Her mother's voice dropped
to a whisper. "Whether he actually caused the accident?"

"He was drunk or high, Mom, he never denied that. He said Diana
was so far ahead of them they couldn't stop her, but I think there's more
to the story, something he's not telling me." Martine crossed her arms
against her chest, holding in a question whose answer she dreaded—
Had Julian collided with Diana?—because it would forever change the
way her mother thought of Julian. She'd rather her mother be angry with

her than him. "I don't want to talk about it anymore, okay? What's done is done."

"But does your family have to separate? I still don't understand why you and Cyrus and Gregory don't just move back here. Or figure out what happened and deal with it."

Martine ignored the "deal with it" comment. "Because Lodgepole is our home. My law practice is there, and it took a long time to build a full list of clients. Cyrus has all his patients. Gregory has his whole life there."

"And Julian doesn't?" Her mother stood up and tossed the empty take-out containers in the trash can, then wiped down the table. The hands swirling the dishrag were covered in age spots, and Martine tried not to wonder how her mother would handle a resentful teenager.

"Julian was about to leave for college. His life was already about to change. And who knows if he ever would have returned to Lodgepole? Kids don't always move back home after graduation."

"They come home on breaks."

"We'll come here for breaks, or go on vacation together, drive to the Jersey Shore or Florida or go skiing in Vermont. We'll be back for his graduation in June, then back again to drive him to Middlebury in September." Martine said this with as much assurance as she could muster, as though she knew this was the right thing. Every night, she tried to weigh what she was doing for Julian. He and Angie probably had been high—Livia was an idiot if she thought Angie had just been in shock that night, that her unfocused and bloodshot eyes were from a sedative the doctor gave her—and Martine knew Livia was a mother who desperately wanted to assign blame, but it wasn't as though he'd deliberately done it, if he'd done anything at all. Maybe he was protecting Angie, or maybe the accident truly was an accident. Accidents were a part of life, and she didn't want this accident to ruin Julian's.

Down the hall—not nearly as far away in this Manhattan apartment as he would be if he were in his bedroom at home—Julian overheard their conversation and cringed at how easily his mother tossed his life away.

She hadn't even considered the option that the truth didn't implicate him, and even though it did, her disregard for his potential innocence was an insult. He pulled out his Walkman and covered his ears so he wouldn't have to hear anything else she said, then opened the letter that Angie gave him the last day he was in school. He'd read it a dozen times already, maybe more. She'd been accepted into two art schools—NYU and the Rhode Island School of Design—but the scholarship at RISD was bigger and Angie's mother wouldn't let her go to New York anyway. They'd still be close enough to see each other, and they'd have phones in their dorm rooms. They could still be together, and their families wouldn't have to know. No one could keep them apart because they loved each other. He traced the final words, scrawled in Angie's messy handwriting, and wished the paper felt like her skin did after they had sex, warm and thrumming, but it was just paper. No matter—Angie was right.

He kept his door shut the rest of the night, and only emerged to brush his teeth and use the bathroom. After his mother and grandmother went to bed, he snuck out to the kitchen for a cookie, then stood at the window and watched the lights outside.

His grandmother was right about one thing. His mother didn't know the whole story, and she never would. No one would, because Livia would kill Angie if she knew. Maybe not literally, but figuratively. And she would kill him, probably literally.

Angie had been the one to get the weed, from the liftie with a long beard who'd worked at the mountain for as long as both of them could remember, and it was Angie who insisted on smoking it for the last run of the day. They snuck off behind the trees outside the ski team's warming hut, smoked the joint, then stood on their skis in the snow and waited, Angie giggling with anticipation. It was Angie's first time, Julian's second. He disliked being high the first time—he'd felt more anxious than anything else—but hoped it would be different this time. They wrestled while they waited for the high to kick in, and ended up on the ground, skis and poles tangled, laughing. He kissed her, and she shoved snow down the back of his jacket. He wanted, at that moment, for life to never change, for time to freeze so he could stay with Angie forever. He couldn't imagine his life being any different, couldn't imagine wanting it to be any different.

When they finally stood up, Angie complained she still didn't feel high and grabbed Julian's flask from his pocket. Only later would he realize she'd finished all the vodka with her gulps, that somehow she'd swallowed the equivalent of three or four shots. They were late by then—the mountain was almost empty—and they turned and hiked back to the warming hut to get Diana, the juniors' coach fuming about having had to wait.

They decided to ski down No Way Out, because it was steep and fun but intersected by an easier trail, a cat track called Meander, most of the way down. They could keep an eye on Diana as she skied on the cat track, crisscrossing their steeper trail at regular intervals, and they'd wait for her at each intersection. Diana nodded at the suggestion, her hat's yellow pom-pom bobbing up and down, and took off down Meander as fast as she could. Before they could follow, Angie turned green, bent over the side of the trail, and spewed out the vodka. Julian yelled to Diana to stop and then used some wet snow to gently wipe off Angie's face.

"I drank that too fast," she said. "And I guess I forgot to eat lunch."

His head was buzzing and the world vibrating—the weed had definitely hit—and when he looked down the trail, Diana was gone. She either hadn't heard him call out to wait or was mad they'd been late. Angie retched again and he turned back to her.

"Go," she groaned. "I'll catch up."

Time elongates when you're high, stretching out like taffy, occasionally snapping back, and Julian didn't know how long he and Angie had stopped. He aimed his skis straight down No Way Out so he could catch Diana and avoid the trouble they'd get in if Livia thought they let Diana ski alone. He'd never skied high before, but it felt like he was soaring above the trail instead of racing down it. When he raced, adrenaline fueled the occasionally rough ride, helped his quads absorb the speed and his mind focus on going ever faster, told him when to turn to make a gate and helped push his limits as every muscle burned, the skis chattering underneath his feet on rutted-out courses. But now he was floating on the snow, oblivious to the chatter, oblivious to any pain and his real speed, and when he hit the first lip where Meander crossed No Way Out, he launched off it into the air, looking left and right to see if Diana had stopped on the trail to wait. It felt like he hovered forever, hanging like a hawk playing on wind updrafts. He landed, spied movement farther down, and was convinced—lost in a tunnel of bliss—that he'd reach her before the bottom and they'd just wait for Angie to catch up, so he kept going, floating, gliding, the air around him whooshing. That late in the day, the trees to his sides cast deep shadows, but he knew the trail well enough it didn't matter. He didn't see Diana anymore, and at the next intersection, he launched off the lip as hard as he could. He felt invincible, like he might travel twenty, thirty, forty feet on this jump.

The thump when he landed shocked him. She'd been invisible in the dusky light, hidden under the lip like a pedestrian hidden behind a blind hill on a road. When he slammed into her, the collision absorbed most of his speed. He laid stunned on his side and at first didn't realize he'd hit Diana. He could have sworn she was farther down the mountain and thought he'd hit a tree stump or an errant bush, but there was her body, knocked all the way to the edge of the trail against a tree, her body limp and broken like a rag doll, torso bent unnaturally. The impact had knocked off her hat and goggles, and the yellow pom-pom sat forlorn in the middle of the trail. He rushed to her, too bewildered to do anything he was supposed to do. He knew to check for a pulse, knew basic CPR, he just didn't do it.

He didn't know how long he was there before Angie skied down. He waved his arms, yelling for her attention, and she skidded to a stop and gasped. They stood there, Angie breathing *Oh my God oh my God oh my God* over and over, hyperventilating hope in a divine being that in Julian's experience never answered anyone's pleas.

"She hit a tree?"

"I don't—I don't know what happened," Julian stuttered. And he did but he didn't. His heart raced and sweat gathered beneath his heavy jacket, the stickiness making him pinch at the underarm seam. He suddenly realized he hated being stoned, that he never, ever wanted to feel like this again. Did Angie know? Had she seen? The forest lurched around him and he put his hand over his eyes, for now oblivious to the fact that the throbbing in his head was from a concussion and not the weed.

"She hit a tree," said Angie. It wasn't a question this time, and he didn't correct her. "*Shit shit shit.* We have to get help." She looked at him, panic in her eyes.

Julian bent down and pulled Diana away from the tree and back onto the ski slope, swallowing his nausea and pretending he wasn't dizzy. He'd hit her, he knew that now, but why hadn't he noticed her before the collision?

"Wait here. I'll go get ski patrol," he said. "I can get there faster. When she wakes up, she'll want you here." Then he skied to the bottom faster than he'd ever skied in any race, the adrenaline overwhelming the laid-back high. He knew she might not wake up.

Now, in his grandmother's apartment, his heart pounded just re-membering it. He wished for a do-over, to say no to Angie's demand to get high for the last run, for Angie to have not thrown up and stopped up above, for him to have not skied as fast or jumped as high, to have reached ski patrol sooner, even though they said she probably died on impact. But there were no do-overs in life. He knew that now.

He'd never corrected Angie's story of Diana hitting the tree. For all she knew, that was true. They'd agreed to tell the ski patrol investigator they saw it happen, because Angie didn't want to admit to the weed and the vodka and the vomiting, all things that caused Diana to be skiing un-supervised. And when Angie told him how angry her mother was, that she shook Angie's shoulders until her neck cracked and her head spun, he knew with unwavering clarity that he could never tell Angie what had really happened, never even tell his own mother.

Some nights, he blamed Angie for getting them high and drinking so much vodka that she vomited and caused them to lose sight of Diana. Some nights, he blamed Diana for skiing away without them. Maybe she'd been hiding under the lip intentionally, trying to trick them. Or maybe she stopped to rest and didn't know she wasn't visible from above. But most nights, including tonight, he blamed himself, because maybe she would have been visible to someone who wasn't high.

His heart raced, the adrenaline now an unhelpful deluge he couldn't quiet. He finished the cookie, careful to wipe up the crumbs, then opened the cabinet and took a swig of his dead grandfather's whiskey, then another, a bigger one, to slow his racing heart. The city twinkled outside, white and red and yellow lights, in the buildings and on the streets, a sea of humanity above and below his grandmother's sixteenth-floor apartment.

Chapter Four

OCTOBER 2016

Nora is the center of attention in Lodgepole. She's all anyone talks about. But inside Pinyon County Juvenile Detention Center, she's just another kid. Maybe even less than that, because she still isn't speaking. She spent the first week in a locked infirmary, where she received a barrage of medications that may or may not have been necessary and may or may not have helped, but didn't receive her regular medication, a small oval pill she used to take for depression. Now she shares a room with three other girls. They only know her name is Nora because a guard calls it out to another guard when he escorts her to the bunk room.

"Nora Sheehan, juvenile number one-oh-two." When she hesitates at the doorway, he pushes her inside. There are two bunk beds, one on each side of the cinderblock room, and two small desks for four girls to share, molded plastic bolted into the wall, each with a circular, backless stool bolted into the floor. "Upper bunk on the left. Clothes and toiletries go in your plastic bin under the bed."

Nora stands at the precipice of an alternate life, a kind of life she never knew existed, and clutches her belongings: an extra pair of sweatpants, an extra T-shirt and sweatshirt, and underwear and socks, all used, not gently; a toothbrush, toothpaste, and a bar of soap, new. She wears another set of sweatpants, a T-shirt, and a sweatshirt, and a pair of sneakers that close with Velcro straps, all issued by a guard after a strip search. Her ankles and wrists are still raw from the handcuffs and leg irons used to restrain her over the past eight days—when she was arrested, occasionally in the infirmary, and back and forth to Lodgepole for court appearances—and she pulls the sleeves of her too-large sweatshirt over the red parts on her wrists.

"We're bunkmates," the smallest of the three girls says. She's reading a book on the top bunk but sets it down on the wool blanket to examine Nora.

"No," says the biggest girl, "we're cellmates. This is juvie, Jacqueline. It's prison, not camp." This girl, Paradise, lies on the bottom bunk, below the one assigned to Nora. Paradise is too tall for the bunk, almost six feet. In a different life she might have played high school basketball or volleyball, maybe even played in college. Instead, she's here because she keeps getting caught dealing the meth cooked by the aunt she lives with. Both her feet rest on the metal bar at the end of the bed, and she cracks her knuckles when she says the word *prison*.

Paradise is right. Paradise knows she's right because even though she's only sixteen, she's been in juvie three times and her aunt has been to prison too many times to count. When Paradise and her aunt are both free and living in their trailer at the same time, they compare notes. She makes good money selling meth, better than she could make working in her town's Dollar Store, and she's not about to stop; she just has to figure out how to not get caught.

The third girl, Maria Elena, lies on the bottom bunk under Jacqueline, looks at Nora, and narrows her eyes. She's not as tall as Paradise, but she doesn't fit on her bunk, either. Her feet also rest on the metal bar at the end of the bed, and the dirty skin on one heel pokes out of a hole in her sock that's bigger than her entire heel. All the bunks are undersized, and the only girl in this room whose full body will fit on the thin foam mattress is Nora. Nora is smaller and younger than Jacqueline, Paradise, and Maria Elena. Smaller and younger than any other girl currently in this detention facility.

Maria Elena stands and takes the pile of belongings from Nora's hands. It could almost be a nice gesture, a welcoming one, but it's not. The clothes issued to Nora won't fit Maria Elena, but she takes the new toothbrush, toothpaste, and soap and stuffs them in her own bin, then hands her used ones to Nora. Maria Elena, said in the same breath like it's one name and not two, is in for armed robbery even though she was baited into driving the getaway car and didn't do any of the robbing. She's seventeen and this is her first time here. Paradise follows Maria Elena around like a puppy, even though she's been here three times and did do what she's accused of.

Maria Elena and Paradise toss questions at Nora—*Why are you here? What did you do? Is this your first time?*—but lose interest when she won't answer. If she wants to hide her crime the way Jacqueline does, they don't give a shit. Hiding a crime isn't the same thing as burying shame, and nothing she does will provide safe harbor from the consequences of her actions. They turn back to their own conversation and Jacqueline returns to her book, and they all ignore the new girl as she climbs up to her bunk and lies down, facing the wall, curled into a ball like a dog trying to make itself as small as possible.

The girls here sense Nora grew up in a house with her own bedroom, with soccer on the weekends and a minivan-driving mother. Maybe even skiing with a family. When they look at her, they imagine piano lessons and vacations and new clothes for school. She leaves behind a trail of clues about her background every time she moves. Inside her mouth is a set of straight, white teeth, her father visits regularly, and they can almost smell the birthday cupcakes her mother might have baked every year, drifting behind her in a cloud of sweet vanilla. She's had privileges almost none of them had, privileges they scoff at but never would have tossed away as carelessly as she did. When a lawyer shows up to meet with Nora for the third time, a lawyer who clearly is not a public defender assigned by the state but a lawyer her parents must have the money to pay for, this confirms their suspicions.

In here, though, Nora wears the same used sweatpants everyone else does, sits in the same classroom with the same teachers. The ninth graders do basic math and so do the twelfth graders. Science is human health, not chemistry or physics or biology. Nora learned some Spanish in middle school, but that's not taught here. The population of western Colorado is only 20 percent Hispanic, but more than 30 percent of the kids in here, and they already speak Spanish at home. Even if they didn't, the state doesn't pay for foreign languages for delinquents. Art, once a week. Nora's lucky she likes to draw and paint because that's all there is. No ceramics or sculpture or photography because the materials for those classes are too expensive. During free time, the kids watch whatever channel the television is tuned to. There's no Netflix, no Prime Video, no YouTube. The television is locked inside a metal cage, but sometimes a guard will change the channel if a girl asks. This might require a favor in return, usually in the stairwell away from security cameras.

All the girls know that notwithstanding Nora's conformity in the detention center, when it comes time for her trial, her privilege will re-assert itself. Some girls tease her mercilessly, and although she thinks she's being targeted, in reality most of the girls are scared. They are all bullies but they are all bullied. Every day, Nora shuffles from her bunk room with its four colorless walls to breakfast with its crowded tables to classrooms with worksheets she did back in sixth grade. She stares at the floor or the wall. When she walks, she walks with her hands behind her back, like everyone else, thumbs and forefingers folded in a diamond shape so the guards can see she isn't carrying contraband. She doesn't ask for seconds at meals or extra art supplies or for a different television channel. She still doesn't speak. But for her scarlet hair, she might blend into the walls. She is almost invisible.

One of the state's lawyers, a fat man with ruddy cheeks and a high-pitched voice, called Nora uncooperative in front of the judge, but that's not true. She follows the rules, does everything people want her to, ex-cept answer questions. In her plastic bin under the bunk bed, she keeps a piece of paper with a handwritten calendar. She looks at it every morning when she wakes up and every night before bed, wondering when she'll get to leave, hoping the next X she draws through the boxes marking each day will be the last. Usually, juvenile detention centers are tempo-rary way stations on these girls' journeys, but Nora doesn't know she'll remain here far longer than most other girls. Some will be released af-ter a seven-or ten-day hold, either to the custody of their parents while awaiting trial or, for those who have committed minor infractions, re-leased on probation. Others, like Nora and her cellmates, are either too dangerous or repeat offenders and must stay at the juvenile detention center until their trials. This coed youth services center has two halves, one half with this detention center and the other half with a correctional facility for juveniles who've already been adjudicated and incarcerated, but Nora and her cellmates see only one another and the other girls on the detention side. They rarely see the boys in juvie and never cross paths with the kids on the correctional side. What happens outside their small world is a mystery.

During free time, the girls who've earned full privileges due to good behavior are permitted to hang out in the common area of their pod, to watch the caged television or play board games or draw. One day, Nora draws her brother. He has mini-rockets attached to each hip, with fire and smoke spurting from each one. His hair flows behind him, loose and long in the wind, and muscles bulge beneath his superhero costume. His eyebrows knot together as he focuses on catching a villain in the dis-tance. Nora's pencil hovers over the paper, trying to figure out whether he needs a sidekick, something like a Batmobile, or whether some sort of super-speed would be sufficient for this version of him.

"I *said*, is that your brother?" Maria Elena's voice booms, as if she's annoyed. "The one you shot?"

Paradise, standing next to Maria Elena, whispers something in her ear, then laughs at Nora, and the two of them walk away. There was a mix-up with the laundry, and Maria Elena is wearing maroon sweat-pants instead of the blue everyone else wears. They could be from the next pod over, or from the boys' side of the detention center. Maybe even from the correctional facility. She sways as she walks, emphasis on each hip like she's a movie star, maybe because of the novelty of having maroon. Jacqueline, playing solitaire across the table, smiles and says, "I like your drawing," but the spell is broken and Nora's pencil hangs limply from her fingers.

Suddenly, there's a hand on Nora's shoulder, and a squeeze, and she jumps. It's one of the guards, the youngest one. Most guards have mustaches and gray hair, or if they're women, badly dyed hair, but this one has a crew cut because he wishes he could be in the military. His thick arms bulge under a too-small uniform shirt and he probably spends all his free time in the gym.

"Get up," he says. "Your lawyer is here."

He grabs her elbow and pulls her away from the drawing of Nico. None of the girls like this guard. His tiny eyes follow them everywhere, his head swiveling on a thick neck like a lizard. Nora looks back to Jacqueline for reassurance, but Jacqueline points to the bruise on her arm and then looks back at the guard. The girls who've been here long enough know to avoid him, know he's one of the guards who expect a favor for changing the channel, that he sometimes expects favors in exchange for nothing at all.

He doesn't put the belly chain on Nora like when he gets her ready for a court day. On those days, he always makes it too tight, then smiles. Because she's not speaking, she can't complain, but she already knows she can't complain, anyway. She's alert now, more alert than when she was arrested, but she keeps her face blank and hides what she's feeling from everyone around her. When he pinches her elbow a little too hard, she doesn't say anything. She pretends her elbow doesn't hurt and does what she always does: keeps her mouth shut.

Chapter Five

Twelve days after David pounded on her door, Martine walks to the Sheehans' house from her office on Main Street and cringes as she passes St. John's. The memory of Angie slapping her own face replays in her mind, the resounding crack now an earworm she can't banish. Father Lopez's voice had barely wavered as he continued the Lord's Prayer, and no one in the small group of mourners seemed surprised because the grief made sense. No mother should have to bury her own child. Martine couldn't imagine what was supposed to come next, how Angie and David were supposed to move forward. David claimed Nora loved Nico, that they were practically twins and she never would have hurt him. But Nora *had* hurt Nico. She'd done something much worse. And even if Martine tried to argue in court that the shooting was a mistake, she knew—and therefore Angie must know, no matter how gentle Martine tried to be in their initial conversations—that it couldn't have been. Not with three shots, all clearly aimed. Living with that knowledge would be like trying to swim through a dark lake with Nora's shackles, too hard to comprehend even without being the one struggling to stay afloat.

When Martine arrives, she's struck by how worn-down the Sheehans' house is. The Livia she used to know would be mortified if she saw her old house like this. Aspen branches reach up and over the roof, so that if a fire were to sweep through town, it would immediately ignite. Overgrown juniper bushes crowd the walkway and front porch, their poisonous berries discarded on top of the fallen aspen leaves, blue covering brown. The house, a Victorian like Martine's, both vestiges of Lodgepole's mining days in the late 1800s, was never grand, but Livia had always tended it with the same firm hand she used to mother Angie and Diana. Sometimes the haircuts she gave the junipers veered two steps past the trim they needed, but the paint on the wooden siding and welcoming shutters was never chipped, not like this. The houses to either side, both newly built by out-of-town money that razed pieces of the town's history to make way for their once-a-year vacation palaces, dwarf the purple house and make it look that much worse. A tired rocking chair on the porch, the wicker seat torn, sways in the wind, as if rocking a young child from David and Angie's vanished past.

Before she can knock, David opens the door for her. He's in his uniform, an empty holster around his waist, annoyance all over his face. Martine checks her watch to see if she's late, but she's not.

"Did you run here?" he asks.

She tries to laugh; it seems like the polite thing to do, but it comes out as a snort, and she covers her mouth with her hand.

"No, I mean, you seem out of breath," says David.

Martine *is* breathing heavily, and her chest hurts, but that's nothing new these days. The heartburn from all the stress won't let up. She takes a deep breath to calm her lungs. "Just the cold air."

"Right," says David. "So, um, I have to go to work in a few minutes." He leads her to the kitchen table, where Angie sits, lips set in a tight line, hands curled around an empty mug as if it were full of hot coffee and she could warm her hands on it. Martine wonders if she's interrupted a fight; every time she sees them, they seem more than grief-stricken, like they're about to start yelling, or maybe just stopped. She can never tell if they're angry with Nora or each other or her. Or maybe the whole world. David slips on his down jacket and zips it, ready to leave, just as Martine sits down and pulls out the summary of anticipated expenses from her briefcase.

Discussing legal fees is always the worst part of Martine's job, even though she's worked for free on more cases than she's been paid for. Even when she charges her clients, she always charges less than they agreed to pay, especially the ones who look like they can't afford her fees. She can still hear Cyrus's voice in her head, a sound she usually loved, tinged with annoyance, reminding her she wasn't a free legal clinic, she hadn't gone to law school to only do *pro bono* work. She takes another deep breath, this one a steadying breath instead of a breathing breath, because even though she'll work for free on Nora's case, what she's about to say will shock Angie and David. They already know about the first-degree murder charge: the DA filed the official charges last week, the petition in delinquency essentially a formality since he'd made it clear he'd go after Nora with everything he had. A tough-on-crime kind of guy. And yesterday he announced even worse news: he plans on filing to transfer Nora's case out of juvenile court to the district court so he can charge her as an adult. Gilbert Stuckey constantly uses his hulking frame, all six feet four inches of it, anchored by a belly grown from years of whiskey drinking on his cattle ranch, to bully defense attorneys, defendants, and judges. Martine can't wait for him to drop dead of a cholesterol-induced heart attack.

What Angie and David don't know is the following: the typical cost to defend a murder charge is $200,000 to $400,000, money Martine knows they don't have.

"Four hundred thousand dollars," says David. "Shit. We don't—" He sinks down into a chair and his whole body deflates like a leaky balloon. He reaches out to hold Angie's hands, but she recoils from his touch and looks at Martine accusingly.

"I thought you weren't charging us," she says.

"I won't charge you for my time, so it'll be less for you guys." Martine wills herself not to shift in her seat. "But you'll still have to pay court fees,

fees for experts to testify on her behalf, and fees for any other lawyers we have to involve."

"How much less? What other lawyers?"

"I'm not an expert in juvenile homicide cases. I can't do this without some advice. You don't *want* me to do this without advice."

"But how much less?" repeats David.

"I think you'll end up spending one hundred to one hundred and fifty thousand dollars."

"We don't have that," says Angie. "We were barely breaking even before Nico got sick, and once he did, we spent most of our savings on Nico's medical costs. And David doesn't make much, not as a park ranger. He's been a park ranger his whole career."

David withdraws his hands from the table and crosses his arms over his chest. "You haven't worked since Nico was diagnosed."

The two of them glower at each other from opposite sides of the table.

"I'll do my best to keep costs down," says Martine.

Anger flashes in their eyes, and Martine stands, hoping to leave before they erupt, but it's too late. It's hard to know whether this is the pressure of what's happening to their family or simply an unhappy marriage.

"This is your fault. It was your gun."

"It was locked in the gun safe."

"Anyone could see what the combination was when you locked the safe after work. You weren't exactly careful." Angie mashes one hand inside the other, then wrings them together as if she's trying to keep from slapping David the same way she'd slapped herself.

"Was I supposed to send everyone out of the room the second I got home?"

Angie shrugs. "Even if you would have, you used the dates of their birthdays. Anyone could have guessed it."

"Nora never would have done this if you'd paid half as much attention to her as you did to Nico." David's face twitches, like he's trying to dislodge a black fly from his skin.

"Are you kidding? You think I favored Nico over Nora?"

"You know you did."

"And you think she did it because she was mad at me? That she did it on purpose?" Angie says the words slowly, like she's examining each word before she says it, tasting its sound and import.

Martine shuffles her papers and quietly slips them back into her brief-case.

"You always loved him more. You made that clear. Christ, you loved him more than you loved me." David's voice is flat and certain.

"I'm going to go," says Martine, but she's not sure they hear her. "You need some privacy, and we can talk about the fees later. I'm visiting Nora tomorrow, to talk about the charges the DA filed and explain his plan to charge her as an adult."

Angie and David, locked in a glare, don't look at her as she turns to walk toward the front door.

"You think I loved him more because I spent so much time caring for him? Jesus, David. What was I supposed to do? Go teach art and skip driving him to therapy and doctor's appointments?" Angie's words, now a shout, trail behind Martine as she pulls the front door shut.

Outside, the birds in the trees twitter, a furious cacophony of chirping.

Before Martine walks into the detention center, she digs through her purse to find a chewable Pepto-Bismol, pulls out one, then thinks better of it and pulls out a second. She's out of her depth here. When she represented the girl who abandoned her baby, she only took the case because no one else wanted it, not because she was an expert in defending juveniles against attempted murder charges. *It looks bad*, a friend said. *Representing a girl who threw away an innocent baby*. But Martine understood, on some level, what had happened, and knew the girl needed a lawyer. She was barely sixteen, and probably discovered she was pregnant when she was fifteen. She'd hidden it from everyone, including her parents. Martine remembered how overwhelming being a new mother was: one moment you're you, the next you're Mommy, responsible for another life, a tiny, breakable, red-faced being with a constant and irritating cry designed by nature to get under your skin. The girl panicked, like most new mothers do, but she panicked alone in a high school bathroom. She didn't deserve a long prison sentence for attempted murder—she deserved to atone for her mistake, to be rehabilitated and reenter society. Martine doesn't want to live in an eye-for-an-eye world, and she's never understood how the same people who preach about Jesus turning the other cheek can call for bloodlust in the penal system. People who make mistakes don't deserve to be thrown away like garbage, not even a girl who abandoned her own baby.

Not even a sister who shot her brother.

None of that changes the fact that Martine is in over her head, and the stakes are higher in Nora's case. She's charged with actual murder, not attempted murder, and if the DA is successful in transferring her case out of the juvenile system and into the district court, she'll face adult consequences. Although Colorado law clearly allows it, Martine doesn't understand how the system can so blithely treat a thirteen-year-old as anything but a child, and she has no idea how to effectively fight it. And Nora still isn't talking, making everything harder. She seems to listen, but she never responds. She eats, sleeps, follows basic directions, goes to classes. And usually that's it. Today, though, she looks up when Martine enters the meeting room, if the room can be called that. It looks more like an interrogation room, with a metal table and three orange plastic chairs, hard and ugly but the only color in here, the sterility of it as clinical as an operating room.

"Hi, Nora." The thought of another one-way meeting demoralized Martine, so this time she planned ahead and brought watercolors with her. She pours water from her water bottle into a plastic cup and pushes it across the table, along with paints, a brush, and paper. "These are for you. You can paint while we talk."

For the first time, Nora makes eye contact, real eye contact, not the dead, unfocused stare she's had since she was arrested. Martine heaves a silent sigh of relief and pulls out her legal pad, trying for nonchalance. "Go ahead," she urges. "Your dad says you're a good painter."

Nora dips the brush into the cup and uses the tip to wet the black. She drifts the brush back and forth in tiny lines, outlining something.

"We have to talk sometime, Nora. I'm your lawyer, I'm on your side, okay? And you have to talk to the psychiatrist when she comes. She's on your side, too."

The brush keeps dancing around the paper, animated by the ghost of the person Nora used to be, but she doesn't acknowledge what Martine just said. Occasionally she swipes at her head, as if to shoo away a fly, and once she swats her forehead, but there are no flies in this sterile room.

"Let's start with the timeline. The DA filed charges of first-degree murder last week. Your preliminary hearing is November 17. Fifteen days after the preliminary hearing, you have to enter your plea, which means you have to tell the court whether you're pleading guilty or not guilty." Before Martine got here, she decided to not tell Nora about the threats to charge her as an adult. Gil Stuckey announced his intention, but he hasn't filed anything yet, and she hopes to talk him out of it. Presenting Nora with the idea of time in an adult penitentiary would terrify her and only be counterproductive. But this gentler approach doesn't seem right, either. As she explains the timeline of the juvenile justice system, the same timeline now hanging on the Sheehans' fridge, it sounds like *blah, blah, blah,* even to her ears. She starts with a reminder of the timeline in every meeting because she worries Nora didn't understand it the last time she reviewed it, but what could anything she says in these meetings possibly sound like to Nora, a child? She stops and purses her lips—maybe she's going about this the wrong way—but Nora looks up from the painting and nods.

"Thank you, Nora," Martine says, abandoning any pretense of nonchalance. "Does this mean you're willing to talk today?"

Nora hangs her head. Not yet.

"Can you nod for yes and shake your head for no?"

Nora nods.

"Do you remember what happened yet?"

She hesitates, then shakes her head.

"Do you know why you're here?"

The paintbrush swerves, a zig where there should have been a zag, and Nora nods, almost imperceptibly, the movement of her head as faint as the outline of the mountains emerging on the paper.

Martine runs through a list of questions about the night Nico was shot to see if the specifics jog Nora's memory—all questions she's asked before, about the 911 call, where and how she got the gun, whether she remembered being in Nico's room or the jail cell—but none of the questions elicit anything other than a shrug of the shoulders or a shake of the head. She goes backward in time, to see when Nora's memory loss began: Does she remember going to bed that night, having dinner with her family, that day in school? Visiting her grandmother the day before?

Nora hesitates when Martine asks about her grandmother but shakes her head and switches to green.

And then there's the big question, the question the media has asked over and over, the question on the tip of everyone's tongue, the question that might never have a satisfactory answer: *Why?* Was it a mistake? Was it intentional? Was she angry with Nico? The answer would provide the DA with motive. If he finds motive, he'll have intent and maybe premeditation. If he has intent and premeditation, he'll have the elements of first-degree murder and a way to convince the judge to transfer this to district court and charge Nora as an adult. A way to demonize Nora, to convince a jury to send a child to prison for life. Martine needs this answer so she can fight the DA.

But Nora doesn't remember *what* happened and still isn't speaking. There's no way she can explain *why*. She's stopped responding to Martine's questions, is no longer shaking her head or shrugging her shoulders, because she can't—or won't—remember the *what* or the *how* or even the *when*. The brush swirls an ugly mustard yellow onto a moon sliver, strife and discord against the green and black. She probably doesn't remember anything other than what Martine has told her or maybe what other kids here whisper in her ear. She might not even know how many days she's been here.

There was some life in Nora's eyes when Martine set out the paints, but that drained away when Martine asked *why*, and now those eyes drop to the painting. The odd picture is painted not in strokes but in long lines, almost like a Van Gogh. Light from the putrid moon shines on the edges of the mountains, otherwise barely visible. The mountains seem to be the right color, but Nora tinged the dark sky an unnatural pine, a color usually destined for trees clinging to the slopes of those steep mountains.

She looks up and waves the hand holding the brush in front of her face, then swats her forehead again, leaving a blotch of the mustard-yellow paint above her eye.

The next day, Martine does what she should have done from the beginning: swallows her pride and calls Julian. After the disastrous meeting about fees, David called and pushed her to involve Julian—and see if he'd do it for free—and in the end, it's not as hard as she thought it would be. There's no reason for Julian to stay away from Lodgepole, not anymore, and he's the perfect solution to her unease about managing this case on her own. Nora might have mental health issues—what with the catatonia and the swatting at nonexistent flies or whatever it was she thought she saw—and even at thirteen, she could be sentenced to life in prison if Martine mishandles her defense. Although the Supreme Court ruled in 2012 that minors must be given the possibility of parole after forty years, that would be of little comfort to a thirteen-year-old. A mistake in this case would be disastrous. She twirls around on her office chair, the now-worn leather one Cyrus bought her when she moved into the second-floor office of this brick building on Main Street. Her desk faces two empty chairs and a small table, and she half spins back to the window to watch the street below. It's low season, summer long gone, the aspen leaves everyone flocks to town to see either brown or blown to the ground by winds carrying harbingers of winter, and the ski area's opening is still weeks away. The only people on the streets are the ones who live here full-time, walking to Ace Hardware to run an errand or strolling to Fiona's for chicken salad on their lunch break.

She calls Julian's cell, not his office. She hasn't used this number often, but she taps it as automatically as if she did it every day, as if it hasn't been months since the last time they spoke. When she was a young lawyer, writing wills and trusts for a pittance to help pay the bills, she used to wonder about families who were estranged from one another, the ones who said they hadn't spoken to a sister or a father in five years, ten years, twenty years. It hasn't been that long, not yet, but she's wondered more than once if she and Julian are headed in that direction.

"Hi, Mom." He says it as naturally and easily as she dialed his number.

"Julian . . ." Martine had planned out what to say about the case, but not how to start the conversation.

"It's been a while."

"Yes," she agrees. "It has." She doesn't know whether she should apologize or he should. It was his choice to stop calling her, to wait weeks before returning her calls, then stop returning them altogether, but it was her choice to stop trying, to simply give up when he slowly fell out of her life. She's gotten updates from Gregory—the awards Julian won from the New York State Bar Association or the marathons he ran or his vacations with Mayumi—but even Gregory's calls have been thin the past few months because he's on a new assignment, reporting on the conflict in the South Sudan. The silence stretches out between them, and finally Martine clears her throat. Maybe they can avoid apologies and simply move forward. He answered the call; he must have seen the shooting in the news and know why she's calling. And he probably never stopped caring about Angie, even if Angie is now married to David and Julian is now married to Mayumi. "I need your help."

"I'm surprised you haven't called until now." A siren blares in the background; it sounds like he's outside.

"I could say the same about you," Martine says.

"You shouldn't have taken this case. It's all over the news. In the court of public opinion, Angie's daughter has already been convicted, and you're not qualified to defend a murder."

"I know that. Don't you think I know that? But what was I supposed to do? I did that one case, the one where a girl abandoned her baby." She stops twirling in her chair, too weary to keep the movement going.

"It's not the same, Mom." His voice isn't angry or sharp, just matter-of-fact, and Martine knows he's right.

"I'm too old for this, Julian. I'm retiring in a couple of months."

"Gregory told me," he said.

"What was I supposed to do? David practically blackmailed me, said I had to do it because of Diana."

"What do you mean, David? He came to you, not Angie?"

There's more worry in Julian's voice than she would have expected. Diana's death was so long ago that Martine assumed it was firmly in his past. "Yes, but I don't know why," she says. "I don't really understand the two of them. They don't seem very happy."

Julian is silent for so long that Martine wonders if she said something wrong, but eventually he says flatly, "Angie never would have told him what really happened. And he never would have married her if he knew. He's too righteous."

"It doesn't matter what he knows or doesn't know. That was a long time ago. The point is they can't afford another lawyer, and I felt obligated to take the case. It was me or a public defender, and although some public defenders are good, who knows which one they would have assigned to her? Nora's just a kid. She deserves a fair chance in court."

Julian sighs. "Everyone deserves a fair chance, Mom." Silence stretches out between them again. "Have you consulted with someone who knows how to defend a murder charge?"

"This case is going to bankrupt them. They can't afford much. That's why I'm calling you for help."

"You're the one who never wanted me to see Angie again," snaps Julian.

He's right, of course, so she keeps her voice even. "Roberto's dead and Livia has Alzheimer's. I was only ever worried about them blaming you for Diana's accident, and they aren't a concern anymore. And me calling you was *David's* idea. If you're protecting their daughter at their request, I can't imagine either of them dredging up the past."

Julian's quiet for a second, and all Martine can hear is the din of the street behind him, until he says, "Mom—I saw in the news that Angie's son was sick. Did you know? Why didn't you tell me?"

There was no way for Martine to *not* know what was going on with Nico, not with Lodgepole's gossip grapevine. And Angie used to take her art students outside to work all over town, sometimes painting San Moreno peak from Main Street, other times painting cafes or street scenes, and it seemed like every time Martine twirled around in her chair to look out the window, Angie was on the sidewalk below. Or she was with Nico and Nora at the town playground, or running with David on the same mountain trails Martine walked. A year ago, Martine stopped seeing her around town and heard that Nico had been diagnosed with Huntington's and Angie had quit teaching. "Of course I knew. But she had her life here, and you had your life there. What good would telling you have done?"

Sirens blare again on the other end. Eventually he says, "I need to go. I have a meeting in a few minutes. Look, I'll help as much as I can. You had to know I'd say yes. I can fly out for court appearances and some of the work and do the rest from here. Email me the files, and I'll figure out how to manage it."

After they hang up, she feels grateful, then unexpectedly annoyed. How easily he agreed to come help Angie, yet he'd barely returned for Cyrus's funeral. He was willing to disregard everything that happened in the past for a high school ex-girlfriend, but not his father? She spins back to face her desk, opens her purse, and grabs another Pepto-Bismol. She's not sure what hurts more, her feelings or her heartburn.

Chapter Six

David leaves most mornings without saying goodbye to Angie. She knows where he's going because it's written in his small, blocklike print on the calendar of Nora's court dates and because after he hugs her goodnight, a hug she wants and doesn't want, he reminds her, especially if he's going to visit Nora. Twice a week, he drives three hours in each direction to see her. His alarm beeps at 4:30 a.m., and he showers and is downstairs by 4:45. He prepares the coffeemaker the night before, and the scent of brewing coffee drifts into the bedroom when he opens and closes the door, a somnambular comfort until she wakes up. He's quiet, his silent treatment extending through the house like a creeping mouse. The other days, he goes straight to work, even though he's on administrative duty while the National Park Service investigates the shooting. Gil Stuckey has declined to prosecute David, concluding he didn't do anything criminally negligent because his gun was properly stored, but the Park Service has their own process. At least he's still getting paid, because estimates have started coming in for the experts Martine wants to hire, the dollar signs like flashing lights in a toddler's video game, big, bold, and constantly dinging.

They eat dinner in silence: no radio, no television, no smartphones, because neither of them wants to risk hearing about the shooting on the news. They have to speak to each other at the planning meetings with Martine, but not at dinner, so they don't. Angie hasn't mentioned she applied for two jobs—one at Waring Elementary School to teach art starting in January, one in Lodgepole to coach younger kids on the ski team—because she was quickly notified the positions were already filled.

Since she can't work and no longer has children to care for, one morning she tries running to handle the stress. It's a trail that used to feel easy, but by the time she hits the waterfall on Wolf Creek Trail, her chest is heaving. Water cascades down two wide cliffs, runoff from snow-capped peaks above. In December, the falls will freeze into a gelid monolith, the water's descent suspended in time, but this early in the season the ice crystals edging their way across the rock face don't slow the water's flow. Pine and spruce trees shaded the two-mile trail most of the way up from town, but now she's sweating and bends over the pool at the bottom of the falls to splash her face. There was a time when she could beat David up this trail, when she'd tap the weathered sign marking Wolf Creek Falls at 10,715 feet in altitude, turn, and run back to him before he crossed the meadow below the sign. Today she thought her lungs would explode and took five walking breaks, maybe because she hasn't run in a couple of years. Every so often, David used to spend an afternoon visiting Livia or driving Nico to therapy appointments, but Angie always spent that extra time with Nora, not running. She'd go to one of Nora's art shows at school or take her to the movies or watch one of her ski races. It was a respite from being Livia's and Nico's caregiver but not a respite from being a mother. She missed running more than she realized, even if she is out of shape.

Up here, the sky is clear and empty, other than two birds playing on wind currents, one idling high above and the other diving and climbing, reveling in the synergy of air and wings. Hawks, maybe. Nico would have loved seeing them and she can almost hear him correcting her in his pubescent voice, the deepening intonations perceptible only until a fissure appears and shatters them into smaller, crackly sounds that belong to neither child nor man.

They're eagles, Mom. Bald eagles. See the flash when the diving bird turns? That's his white head.

You're right, I see it.

Did you know, Mom—and here his crackly voice would rise again—*the sound you hear in the movies that you think is a bald eagle? That it's actually a red-tailed hawk?*

No! I didn't. Why would Hollywood do that?

Because a bald eagle's call sounds like a million other birds. A chirp, basically. And the chirp doesn't match its tough-guy status, I guess.

"Stop," she orders herself aloud. "Stop."

Her mind arches and bows angrily, trying to wend its way back to a conversation she can't have, but she forces it to reverse course and focus on what her self-help book on grief says about breathing and being in the present. Breathe, the book commands. In and out. The same advice Roberto used to give her. Dawn shimmers over the land saddle connecting the two mountains that frame the falls, Miner's Peak and La Rosa, and she imagines what it would be like to glide on those wind currents, to watch the sun rise and fall each day, to be that free. Breathing and being in the present is harder than the book's author makes it sound, though, and it takes a long time to slow her heart, to stop it pounding from the double whammy of Nico's voice reverberating in her head and the hard run. And before her heart slows, she realizes the burn in her lungs feels good; it makes the world sharper.

Sharp is what she needs. Yesterday she walked their yard's fence line, pacing outside instead of inside. On her fourth turn around the yard, she saw it: on a moss-covered rock in the back corner was a soggy, half-smoked joint.

It shouldn't have been a surprise, not really. The neighbors who moved in a couple of years ago have a big marijuana bush in their backyard, so tall it's visible over the fence, and when they leave it untrimmed, branches

sometimes weave through the wooden slats. Marijuana grows well at altitude, and their neighbors probably weren't the only ones in town growing
their own bud. But why would they have thrown a joint over their fence?
And if someone dropped it, why didn't they come get it? Everyone here
is used to people smoking, so no one would have worried about asking
to hop into their yard for it. But then the anxiety about Nora's case that
dogs her every day—no matter how angry she is—reared up. Her mind
unspooled, sucked into a dizzying whorl that she objectively knew was
anxiety but couldn't control. It might not have belonged to her neighbors.
It couldn't be David's, could it? It wasn't hers because she hasn't smoked
since she lived in New York. And it wasn't Nico's. She was with him all
the time before he died. That left Nora. She wondered how, as a mother,
she could have missed her thirteen-year-old daughter getting high, but a
pit settled in her stomach and she realized—horribly, guiltily—she wasn't
much older when she first tried it herself, with disastrous results.

Could the joint really have been Nora's? If so, that was bad news.
Weed can make you crazy. She read that somewhere. But only if you
smoke a lot of it. More than a lot, and she'd never seen Nora high, not
even once. She would have noticed.

Her mind had spun as she fingered the half joint, almost disinte-
grated from its time under the snow. Nora was depressed. Is that why
she smoked it? If she smoked it? Was she self-medicating? At thirteen?
If Nora's antidepressant wasn't working, she should have said something.
Maybe it wasn't Nora's. Maybe it *was* David's.

It probably didn't matter whose it was. If Gil Stuckey discovered the
weed and believed it was Nora's, he'd use it against her. He'd paint her as
a drug addict. And if he thought it was David's, he'd paint Nora's father
as a drug addict instead. Just because it was legal didn't mean he couldn't
do that. He would find a way to make their family look bad and turn the
jury against them. She'd wrapped the joint up in a wad of toilet paper
and flushed it—no one needed to know what she'd found—but now she
can't stop worrying.

Sharp. She needs to be sharp to handle this.

• • •

Eventually, she turns to run down the hill, then stops. Even if the running feels good, there's no need to hurry home. No one there needs her. She walks the rest of the way, focusing on the crunch of fallen leaves and the snap of dry twigs underneath her sneakers. The self-help book would approve. But when she arrives home, David is pacing back and forth in the kitchen. She left this morning before he woke, pulling on old running shoes in the barely-there dawn light peeking under the blinds. They'd fought again yesterday after dinner and then lay in bed all night like two pieces of wood, stiff and unyielding. They're falling apart, the two of them, when she knows they should be supporting each other, helping the other bear this unbearable weight. Instead, there's a black crack between them, a yawning void with Nico's absence on one side and Nora's guilt on the other. She doesn't know if he wants to reach across the void and touch her, but she feels herself stiffen every time she senses he might. She dressed as quietly as possible this morning because she didn't want him to come running with her, didn't want to give him the chance to apologize or be forced into apologizing herself.

She expects him to bark at her when he turns and sees her, but he shoves his phone in front of her face. "Where were you?"

"Running," she says. "What am I looking at?"

"It's an email from Martine. Did you know? About Nora's mental health?"

Angie scans the email.

This is just a quick email to let you know two things. First, after talking with David, I realized his idea was terrific, and I called Julian. He's agreed to come to Lodgepole to advise on Nora's case. As we discussed, I don't have much experience in homicide cases, and I need advice to ensure we're doing everything we can to get her a fair trial. I know finances are an issue, and since Julian will do it for free, this is the best solution. Second, I've asked for a psychiatric evaluation of Nora, as I have concerns about her mental health. I hope the results will help with her defense, which we can discuss at our next meeting.

"This was your idea? Bringing Julian here?" Angie asks slowly, trying to comprehend what this could mean.

"Did you hear me? Does she need an evaluation to get a prescription for her depression meds, or is this something more? If she thinks Nora has a bigger mental health issue, maybe this could be a way for her to avoid being convicted. This could be good." David's pacing speeds up and he frantically turns back and forth in the small room.

Angie grabs his arms and holds him in place. "Why would you do that? Ask for Julian? I don't want him involved."

"Nora needs the best legal representation she can get, and Julian can help. I googled him. His entire practice focuses on criminal defense, and he's handled lots of juvenile homicide cases through some group called the New York Juvenile Defense Organization. He's perfect."

"No," she snaps. "We don't need him. There are other experts out there. We can find one in Denver. We don't need to use my ex-boyfriend from high school. That's stupid."

David looks at her, his face suddenly placid, and Angie wonders at his lack of concern about bringing Julian, whom he never liked, into their lives. "It's our best option," he says flatly. "Martine already told us she doesn't know enough to do this on her own, and we don't have the money for her to hire a consultant. Julian agreed to do it for free."

"We can find the money," she says with less conviction. She's not sure they can.

"Where?"

She looks away before he can say what he always says—they should sell this house while property values are up, cash out and move down valley where real estate prices and property taxes are in reach for a teacher and a national park ranger—because they've already had this fight. She grew up here. Nico and Nora grew up here. She left once, long ago, and it was a mistake. Lodgepole is home, and if they don't stay in this fully paid-off house her parents gave her, there's no other place in town they can afford to live. Her lungs feel like they're heaving again, as though she's back at the top of Wolf Creek Falls, and she wishes her heart would stop beating so loudly. This is a disaster.

"Answer my question about Nora. Is Martine saying Nora did this because she's mentally ill? Could she go to a hospital instead of prison?" He's pacing again and stops in front of the window and mutters, more to his reflection in the glass than to Angie, "I knew there was something wrong the last time I was there. I knew it."

"I don't know," says Angie. "She's depressed, we already knew that. And she shouldn't have to go to a psychiatric hospital. She shouldn't have to go anywhere at all. The shooting was just a mistake. They must have been playing with the gun. That's all it could be."

Her chin juts out, and she bites her cheek, trying to draw it back in. A memory floods her mind, one she's been trying to suppress. Two weeks—no, one—before Nora shot Nico. It was late afternoon, and Nico sat at the kitchen table, rebuilding an old Lego set, one of his Star Wars Starfighters. Nora wanted to help, but Angie brushed her off because the manipulation of the small blocks was physical therapy for the spastic chorea his hands had recently developed. Nora kept whining, and the whining turned into begging, pestering both Angie and Nico. Nico was struggling, his hands and fingers clumsy, and his cheeks flushed as his frustration mounted. Nora stood behind him, pointing out first one piece and then another, as though it was a puzzle he couldn't solve rather than a model his disobedient hands couldn't build. Nico shoved his chair back from the table, stood, and shouted at Nora, and she shouted back. Without warning, Nico picked up his half-built Starfighter and threw it at Nora as hard as he could. She ducked, and it shattered against the wall, breaking into hundreds of component pieces. By the time David came home, Angie had forgotten it, chalked it up partly to a normal sibling argument and partly to a lack of impulse control caused by the Huntington's. But now—she can't tell anyone about that fight. What if it means something?

"She killed Nico, Angie," says David. "I don't know if it was a mistake or not. And I don't know if the judge will be convinced it was a mistake. But Martine thinks this might be something more than depression, and I want to know what you saw, what you think about how she was acting before all this."

"What *I* saw? What about what *you* saw? You're her father as much as I'm her mother. If we missed something, it's both of our faults." Angie is breathing hard; she wasn't imagining it.

"I was at work all the time, remember? Trying to pay Nico's medical bills."

"I don't know anything more than you. She was a kid, just a regular middle schooler. What kid is happy in middle school?" Nico was the one who wasn't happy, the one who'd morphed from a gregarious little boy with uncontainable energy and a constant smile into an angry, stiff teenager. And when he started falling last summer, he realized something Angie already knew but had been afraid to tell him: he wouldn't be able to race with the ski team again. After that, it was as if his smile had been buried by the burden of what was to come. Angie spent all her time trying to unearth that smile, except how could that have been possible when he knew what Huntington's would do—was already doing—to him? "And also," she adds, "how *could* Nora be happy, knowing what she knew about Nico's diagnosis?"

David's eyes are wild again, all hints of prior calm gone. "You don't shoot someone because you're unhappy. Martine is saying it was something more. We missed it. You missed it."

"You know why else you don't shoot someone? If there's no gun in the house, or if there is, it's locked up correctly." Angie shouts this last bit, then turns and stomps upstairs to hide in the shower. The day Martine told them the DA wouldn't prosecute David, David acted vindicated, like it was a foregone conclusion he'd done nothing wrong. But the vindication must have been a facade, because he's never complained about the Park Service's longer process to clear his name and reinstate his job. He knows he's to blame, and she hopes what she just shouted hits David where it hurts.

Under the hot water, she bursts into tears. She tries but fails to unclench her jaw. She doesn't know if the tears are from the stress of the fight, the worry about the meaning of Nora's psych evaluation, or the knowledge that Julian is coming to Lodgepole.

Maybe it wasn't drugs or retaliation for a fight about Legos. Maybe it was something she'd done as a mother. It could have been something big or something small. Had she loved Nico more, as David claimed? She loved him differently, yes. She knew that. That was unavoidable. But differently doesn't mean more or less. Had she cooked the wrong dinner the night of the shooting? Not gone to enough soccer games? Not gone to the playground enough or yelled one too many times?

The exits from the purple house with the chipped paint are angry. David slams the door behind him and the house shudders as his pickup's diesel engine roars to life. After her shower, Angie climbs into her minivan, hair still dripping, with no idea of where she'll drive. The house key is hidden in a fake rock that sits on a ledge above the porch light—like it is for many houses in Lodgepole—but she leaves the rock untouched and doesn't remember to lock the door or even close it behind her.

That stupid gun. David started out as an interpretive ranger but grew bored of wildlife and land conservation education for tourists—who he claimed didn't really care—and decided to go through law enforcement training so he could try something different. He'd always loved to hunt, and he kept those guns in a storage locker outside of town, but when he became a law enforcement ranger, he bought a gun safe to store his work firearm at home. That was what he called it: a firearm. But a firearm is just a fancy name for a weapon, for an inanimate object that can be used to kill an animate being. She used to love his obsession with the wilderness, his connection to nature, but hates him for it now. She should have said no to the gun, forced him to keep it locked with his hunting rifles, even if it meant another stop on his way home each night. She should have forced him to use a harder combination on the gun safe in the house. But as soon as that thought enters her mind, rage rises in her, because it was his responsibility to do that, and he'd shirked it.

David's fault. Nora's fault. Angie's fault. Nora's fault.

The veins in her neck pulsate, a painful throbbing that's both a physical blow and a pounding bass drum in her ear. *Breathe*, she tells herself. In the nose. Out the mouth. Count the breaths. Up to one hundred. Down to one. Up to one hundred.

Three hours later, the gas gauge flashes red and dings insistently, the chime alerting her just as she approaches a gas station. She knows where she's going now, knows she must. She's avoided visiting Nora for too long. She has to see her eventually, to confront her or comfort her or whatever a mother is supposed to do in this situation. She pulls in and fills up, the insertion of the gas hose into the tank an automated action her arms perform like a robot. In front of her, a young woman in leggings, a puffy coat, and an orange Broncos hat fills the tank of a battered pickup. To her left, a dog sticks its head out a partially open window and barks, the sound shrill and demanding. To her right, a man squeegees his windshield, yakking on his cell phone while two children in the back seat swat at each other, the smaller one crying. All these people, she thinks, living their lives like nothing happened. Coming home from work or going to the dog park or driving with kids to the supermarket like everything is normal. Their ignorance ignites an explosive rage in her and she imagines the gas pumps sparking and blowing them to bits, or the dog jumping out of his car and biting the children or attacking her, then shakes her head to rid herself of those errant thoughts, like she's the dog in the car, shaking off a smack from his owner.

The anger that's been with her every day since Nora shot Nico wells up inside her heart like tears in her eyes, ready to spill over with one kind or hateful word. Both would have the same effect. *Breathe*, she tells herself, trying to quell these emotions she understands but wishes she didn't. *Breathe.*

The first time David visited Nora, he filled out the paperwork for Angie to do the same, then wrote down the address and visiting hours and put the folded piece of paper in her wallet. All she had to do was show up at the right time. The right time is in two hours, so she sits in the juvenile detention center's parking lot, taking sips of bitter black coffee from 7-Eleven.

More advice from the self-help book: *In dark times, try to think of one happy thought per day.* Angie has happy thoughts; she must.

Nico, eight; Nora, seven.

Mexico, the one time she's traveled out of the country since leaving Julian. She and David and the kids drove down to the Baja Peninsula in a borrowed RV and slept next to the beach in the prettiest campsite she'd ever seen. Nora and Nico played in the waves and belly laughed all day, every day. At sunset, Nico used oranges and lemons and drew in the sand with his fingers to teach Nora about the solar system, the sun and the Earth and the moon and how they revolved around one another. He'd learned about it in school, and Nora sat enthralled by the confidence in his voice, even if some of his lesson was a little wrong, a comet orbiting Earth or seven moons for Pluto.

Every day, they bought fresh fish and vegetables from a local market, bright peppers and plump tomatoes and tomatillos she couldn't find in rural Colorado in the winter. One day, Angie and Nora returned from the market with two rafts, fluorescent-green ones with yellow stripes. Nico and David were buried in books about local flora and fauna, David entranced by Durango coyotes and Mexican jaguars and Nico by pelagic birds like albatross and black terns. Angie and Nora blew up the rafts and left the books and boys behind as they ran into the ocean. They interlocked their fingers to keep the rafts together and looked up at the sky, naming the shapes they saw in the clouds. Beneath them, waves rose and fell, pushing them toward the beach, then away, and they played a game where they breathed in sync with the swells, air whooshing in and out of their lungs. The feeling of the undulating sea stayed with her even after the day was over, a lullaby made of motion as she lay in bed imagining she was still swaying on the salty water.

A happy thought, yes. But now she can't remember the lullaby of the undulating sea or the feeling of Nora's fingers interlocked with hers, the sound of Nico's and Nora's laughter as they played in the sand or the tang

of the salsa she made with those tomatillos. She would need a magician
to conjure those sensations.

The coffee's plunge from hot to cold reminds her she's here for a reason,
and when visiting hours start, she walks into the detention center with
her shoulders squared, as if she's done this before, as if she hasn't waited
this long to visit her thirteen-year-old daughter. In the family meeting
room, Angie shivers and wishes she'd remembered to wear a coat; when
she left the house, she'd forgotten everything but her purse. She shifts in
the unforgiving plastic chair, her legs still sore from running.

When a guard leads a visibly thinner Nora into the room, Angie
jumps up. The guard—his stomach bulges over the waistband of his
too-tight pants, and his undershirt is visible beneath an open button on
his shirt—dwarfs Nora, and she's not sure why it's necessary for such a
large man to handcuff such a small girl on the way to visit her mother.
He's clean-shaven, though, and nods at Angie, neither unfriendly nor
friendly, a surprise.

"One hour," he says, then closes the door before Angie can thank
him, if that's what she's supposed to do for her daughter's jailer.

She sits down at the same time as Nora and wonders if they're allowed to touch, whether she's allowed to hug her daughter. She stands
back up and walks around the table to do it anyway, but Nora doesn't
hug her back. Her hunched shoulders neither lean in nor flinch away,
the same way the guard was neither unfriendly nor friendly, and Angie
returns to her side of the table, unsure what to do next. She drove here
with no preparation, no treats to sneak in, no gifts.

Angie should feel compassion for Nora because she's her daughter.
Sympathy or empathy or something, but she doesn't want to feel. She's
only here out of maternal duty and steels herself against softening, because numbness is her armor. If she allows it to melt away, the world and
its daggers will pierce what remains of her. But if she can't feel anything
for herself, how is she supposed to feel something for Nora?

She clears her throat, then says the first thing she thinks of: "Are you
eating?"

Nora stares straight ahead. David and Martine said she looks at them when they visit now, and sometimes nods yes or no, but she's not making eye contact with Angie.

Angie asks everything she can think of: Is the food okay? Do they have chocolate milk? Do you have roommates? Nora's hands are folded on the table in front of her, and Angie reaches across the table to hold them. Her fingers are surprisingly warm, warmer than Angie's, and Angie squeezes them.

"I'm sorry my hands are so cold, honey. I sat in the car outside for a couple of hours before visiting hours began."

For the first time, Nora looks at her, and Angie struggles to read what's in her daughter's eyes. Remorse? Blame? Fear? Anger? She can't help settling on blame, even though, logically, it should be remorse and fear, but she doesn't shy away from the accusation in Nora's eyes.

Nora jerks away from Angie's grasp and stares at her fingers, pale and thin, as though they've been contaminated, then shoves her hands into her lap and out of Angie's view. It shouldn't be Angie saying she's sorry. Or should it?

Martine warned her and David not to talk about the case with Nora because then they could be forced to testify against her, but she's not sure what to say if they can't talk about the reason Nora is here, and the minutes pass painfully. She can't articulate what she feels toward Nora, other than angry, and doesn't know how else she's supposed to feel, or how she *wants* to feel. Eventually, she settles on talking *at* Nora. The weather is bad. Rain a few days ago. Snow only above eleven thousand feet. Falling leaves. Livia's health, the raccoon they saw.

Nora jerks her head toward the door, then to Angie, her eyes wide. "Do you have to go?"

Angie startles at the sound of Nora's voice, the first time she's spoken to anyone since that night. What does it mean that she's speaking again? And that she chose to speak to Angie first? She hides her surprise and says only, "Not yet, honey. We still have a few minutes left."

"But the guard is knocking," she whispers. There's fear, real fear, in her voice.

Angie gets up and peeks through the door's small window. "There's no one there, Nora."

Nora looks at her, eyes wide, and points at the door. "There," she says. "There it is again. Don't you hear it? They're going to make you leave early."

Is this what Martine was talking about? Nora hearing things? Angie strains to hear what Nora hears, hoping to disprove the possibility her daughter needs a psychiatric evaluation because that might mean the shooting was intentional and not a mistake, that something in Nora's head, even if it was prompted by psychosis, told her to point the gun at Nico and pull the trigger, that it wasn't just the tragic result of two kids playing with a gun, but there's only the din of the detention center. A bell chimes in the distance—maybe it's time to change classes, or for exercise time in the yard, or for a meal—and there are voices rising and falling in the next visiting room, but there's no knocking, no guard.

Nora's hands shake, and Angie grasps them again. Nora's skin is dry, as dry and linen-thin as Livia's. "It's okay. No one is there," Angie repeats. She's been holding on to her rage, certain Nora is a villain, furious Nora stole Nico and snatched away his last years. Except now the shaking hands and thin shoulders and plaintive voice reach out, as if to say *have mercy*, and all that fury dissipates, just for a moment, just long enough to alleviate the pressure that's built up and threatened to explode, to allow her anger to leak away, sneak away, a quiet *psss* that's not quite a hiss but a taciturn escape, as though the fury has realized it might not belong in this room, in Angie's heart, in any world.

And then—Nora stiffens and pulls her hands away again, back to her robotic, stoic position. She doesn't say anything for the rest of the visit, stranding Angie once more in the one-way conversation about nothing.

When the guard walks past the window toward the meeting room's door, he taps his watch with his index finger and an unnameable feeling, maybe relief, floods through Angie. The hour is over. She stands as he opens the door, perhaps even before he opens it, and Angie hopes she doesn't appear too eager to leave.

"Goodbye, Nora." Angie hugs her, then whispers, "I love you." Nora's stiff body sags into Angie's, just for a moment, before she straightens her shoulders and pulls away, but Angie holds on, clinging to the crack in Nora's stoicism, clinging to the crack in her own.

The first time Nora returned from a hunting trip with David, her eyes shone. Angie assumed she was on the verge of crying, the shine a product of tears after witnessing David shoot an elk, recognizing the violence of death, but it was something different. It was attention from David, camping in a tent in the woods and heating up hot chocolate over a campfire, setting up with a rifle behind a blind, sitting quietly, waiting, watching, biding time with her father. He'd done the same with Nico the year before, the same with Angie when they first met. It was listening to David talk about the ecosystem and the food chain and predators and prey, and explain how the persecution of coyotes—the song dog, a keystone species and his favorite predator—by way of aerial gunning and poisoning and denning had contributed to the overpopulation of deer and elk, how the death of this elk would help counteract damage to the ecosystem by preventing other elk from starving this winter, how this elk would feed their own family, how his clean shot prevented any suffering. It was a promise to make elk sausage and elk steak and elk lasagna.

Nico hated hunting. Angie hated hunting. Somehow, Nora loved it.

Does that mean anything?

On the way home, Angie stops to see Livia out of habit. Her mother is in bed, already sunsetting and confused, and Angie doesn't bother to move her to a wheelchair or mute the TV so they can talk. She doesn't have the energy to maintain another one-way conversation, and her mother's eyes are closed anyway. Angie's been ignoring the doctor's repeated emails about Livia's declining status because they seemed more like administrative ass-covering than a reference to a real problem, but now she understands the persistence. Even through the covers, it's clear her mother has lost more weight, just like Nora, only for Livia it's the normal progression of the disease, the inability to swallow one of the last steps of Alzheimer's. One of the last steps in her mother's life. The doctor says Angie must decide about a feeding tube.

Angie tilts her head backward into the chair and closes her eyes. Why anyone would choose to prolong life in this condition is beyond her, but she's supposed to think about this from her mother's point of view because she's her agent under a medical power of attorney. She's legally obligated to follow her mother's wishes. The question is, what would those wishes be? They never talked about what Livia would want because Livia never wanted to talk about death. One day, she simply handed Angie a copy of her will and power of attorney and told her to keep them in a safe place. When Livia had to be moved to the memory care home, Angie used the power of attorney to close DeLuca's Restaurant and lease the building to a brewery, then paid for Livia's monthly care costs with that income. Livia would have hated that the restaurant was closed, but Angie knew it was the right thing to do because it was the only way to pay for that care.

She has no such certainty now. Livia is (was?) a staunch Catholic, opposed to abortion, suicide, and euthanasia, but this isn't euthanasia. Where does a feeding tube fit in Catholic dogma? She's not sure she knows and can't help wondering if her mother had understood the reality of end-stage Alzheimer's. There's not even a person inside that motionless body under the covers. The person that lived Livia's life is gone. The body on the bed is not living a life.

"I have to think about it," she taps into her phone, not bothering to thank the doctor or sign the email. When it rains, it pours. She's heard it a thousand times. But this is no longer rain, no longer a downpour. She's been sandwiched between caring for Livia and caring for Nico for too long, forced to make choices no daughter or mother should have to make. Nico is dead. Livia is almost dead. Nora is in jail. This is a maelstrom of shit falling from the sky, the crushing weight and stinking smell more than she can bear. More than any person can bear.

She stands and leaves without speaking to her mother, without rubbing lotion into her hands or even touching her forehead, without saying "thank you" or "good night" to the receptionist, and for the second time that day, without closing the door behind her.

• • •

Nico, eleven; Nora, ten.

Nico crashed his bike. He was riding down Main Street with a gag-gle of kids, including Nora, and tried to do a wheelie. Something went wrong—he claimed he hit a littered soda can and it messed up his bal-ance, but Angie suspected he simply didn't want to admit he didn't know how—and he ended up on the ground with road rash the entire length of one arm. Nora dragged him home for Band-Aids, but Angie only needed one look to know he needed a full tube of antibiotic ointment and gauze, not just Band-Aids. She sat him down at the kitchen table and started to clean the oozing skin.

"Why would you try to do a wheelie?" She was standing next to him, dabbing as gently as she could.

"I saw it on YouTube," said Nico, his grin wide. He winced a little as Angie dug dirt out of the wound, then grinned again. "It looked cool, Mom. I had to try it."

Nora was grinning, too. "It *was* kinda cool."

Angie shook her head. "You should leave that stuff to the bigger kids. You're too young to be doing bike tricks."

Nico protested—he almost had it, he'd get it right next time, you have to start somewhere—and then spent the rest of the day on the couch, watching more YouTube bike videos and pointing out techniques to Nora. His cell phone chimed and dinged all day, not with kids checking to see how he felt but with accolades for his almost-trick. When a girl texted—Angie could tell because his cheeks reddened and he covered his screen with one hand—Nora retreated to the kitchen table with her col-ored pencils and drew a picture of a crowd of kids doing a simultaneous wheelie. Nora was in front, identifiable by her red hair and the zebra-striped sneakers she'd received for her birthday, and Nico was next to her, identifiable by the white gauze wrapped around his arm. Their wheelies were higher than all the kids behind them, and Angie had smiled to herself, knowing Nico would make her erase the gauze. The trick became the stuff of family lore, the wheelie that almost was, or maybe never was, because none of the kids had gotten a video or picture, and Nico, after suffering through weeks of an oozing arm, decided wheelies weren't worth it. When David or Angie or Nora teased him, he teased back play-fully. The wheelie was a success before he fell, or it got bigger and longer, or he'd been spotted by a biking scout and was leaving to join a team.

Nora shooting Nico couldn't have been intentional. They were a happy family. They joked together. They took care of one another. They made s'mores over campfires in the summer, baked chocolate chip cook-ies in the kitchen in the winter. They skied and biked and hiked together. They did puzzles when it rained in the spring and went trick-or-treating together on Halloween.

Maybe it's no one's fault. Maybe it had nothing to do with weed or fighting or hearing voices, nothing to do with a bad mother or a bad father or with looking down the barrel of a gun and aiming at a target. Nora loved Nico; Nico loved Nora. Angie and David loved Nora and Nico.

Maybe Nora was playing with the gun. Maybe, impossibly, it was a mistake.

This is what Angie wants to believe.

By the time Angie arrives back in Lodgepole, the sun has set. She pulls into Bea's Market, making the right-hand turn off Route 22 automatically, like she's done a thousand times. At the meat counter, she asks for four premade cheddar-bacon hamburgers, something Nico used to love, then changes her order to two. As the guy behind the counter wraps them—his bare arms covered in sleeve tattoos, maybe a ski bum here for the winter—she feels eyes on her back. She turns to see two women staring at her, both mothers of girls in eighth grade with Nora. One of them, Jennifer, was a friend before Angie dropped everything and everyone to care for Nico. Michelle is just another mother. They've made their faces soft and empty, as if they haven't just been discussing her.

"Angie." Jennifer steps forward and tries to hug her, but Angie wig-gles free of her embrace. "How *are* you? Are you okay?"

"We've been *so* worried about you," says Michelle. "Can we do any-thing to help?"

It could be kindness but it feels like contempt, and Angie fights a desire to throw their judgment back at them. *As if you aren't blaming me for being the mother of a killer, for letting this happen.*

"We're fine." She grabs the burgers wrapped in brown paper and hurries away, toward the other end of the store. In the cookie aisle, she puts ginger molasses cookies into her cart, for who she isn't sure, then stops because there's Michelle's daughter, with her thick eyeliner and wool knit hat, staring at Angie. Nora always said she went to this girl's house after school when Angie took Nico to therapy appointments. Angie doesn't remember her name. Hannah, maybe.

The girl steps backward, but Angie says, "Wait." She looks right and left to make sure Jennifer and Michelle haven't followed her. "You know Nora."

The girl nods.

"Why did—what did you do together? When Nora came to your house after school?"

The girl looks confused, and her doe eyes blink at Angie.

"Well?"

"Mrs. Sheehan, Nora hasn't been to my house since seventh grade. She stopped talking to me last summer. She stopped talking to everyone." She darts away, her sneakers a flash of white against the market's linoleum.

When Angie gets home, no lights twinkle in the windows and no one waits at the door. David is still somewhere, the house still silent. She unpacks the burgers and cookies from the plastic grocery bag and sits down at the table. Her reflection stares back at her from the darkened window, a middle-aged face distorted by the dirt on the windowpane and the tears in her eyes. Why had Nora stopped talking to her friends? Is it possible Nora shooting Nico wasn't a mistake? She'd assumed Nora was always alone in her room because she was a teen acting like all teens, or because she was depressed about Nico having Huntington's. A psychotic break—the label David thought was a possibility—that was something experienced by people in mental institutions, something the man who'd mugged her in Brooklyn all those years ago had. Not something a kid could be diagnosed with.

Not something *her* kid could be diagnosed with.

Something had happened to Nora, and Angie had missed it. Had it happened slowly, or overnight? Angie once had a friend who'd melted down in front of her, in front of the whole world, maybe, since it happened online. She'd shared a studio with him and two other artists in Brooklyn, lost touch when she left New York, then reconnected on Facebook when he reached out to her years later. His posts seemed normal, initially, pictures of art or food, but gradually transformed into rants about people watching him and close-up, distorted selfies of his puffy face, and finally into incoherent conversations in the comments of his posts, in which he only responded to himself. He never answered the friends who asked in the comments if he was okay, so one day she DM'd him. He demanded she prove she was who she said she was, accused her of posing as the real Angie, of watching him on behalf of the government, then blocked her. She didn't have his cell phone number—they'd known each other before most people had cells—or even have a way to find him, because five hundred Scott Browns showed up when she googled him. He simply disappeared, and there had been nothing she could do about it.

Had the same thing happened to her own daughter?

Angie pulls the framed family picture from the windowsill, the same one David showed Martine during their first meeting. Nico was twelve and Nora was eleven. The before times. When Angie's family was still a family. She'd give anything to go backward in time, to lose herself in that yesterday, to be anywhere but this today. Whether it was a mistake or psychosis or intentional doesn't matter—every answer to *why* hurts.

The hamburger's brown paper wrapping crinkles behind her. David is home; somehow she hadn't heard the front door shut behind him. He doesn't say hello and she doesn't turn around. She hears him thud Livia's old cast-iron pan onto the stove, the click of the gas knob and the ping of the lighter, the sizzle of the meat. Her eyes close, and she moves backward in time, much further back than two years ago, to when the children still wanted books read to them before bed, still colored in coloring books and played with matchbox cars.

Nico, three; Nora, two.

There's Nico, running, breathless with excitement, chasing her on the playground. Tag, she's it, no, now David's it. *Run, Mommy, run, don't let Daddy catch you!* She tags David but trips and falls, and they end up tangled on the ground, tickling each other, laughing as Nico piles on. And there's Nora, running free, but she trips and falls as well. Her lips tighten, she holds her knee and opens her mouth to wail, but Nico's brows pull together with concern, and he helps her up before she can cry. He kisses the knee to make it better, as if he were the parent, because back then a kiss could fix everything, and the game starts again. Round and round they run in that long-ago, and in the now Angie realizes her face is wet with tears, tears as silent as the space between her and that other life. Nostalgia is nothing more than a trick of the mind, she tells herself. A way to turn plain memories into great ones.

She opens her eyes and there's David, his face splotchy and red, sitting across the table. Smeared ketchup, brushstrokes of painted red against the porcelain, is all that's left on his plate. There's a hamburger alone on her plate, no bun, no salad, no fries. He reaches out to hold her hand, but the meat's stench reaches into her nostrils, putrid and rotten, like decay and death, then into her gut, where it twists and turns, wrenching her fortitude. The toast she ate earlier—Was it at breakfast or lunch? Toast or pretzels?—festered all day, and its undigested remnants gurgle. She pushes back from the table and runs to the bathroom, where she watches vomit spew from her mouth, chunks spinning round and round as she flushes the toilet, then collapses to the floor, the tiles cool and welcoming, like snow falling from the sky onto her bare cheek.

As she struggles to catch her breath, she remembers another time she was tangled on the ground, a time further back than the game of tag with Nico and Nora, a time before Nico and Nora, before David.

She remembers Julian.

Chapter Seven

In 1995, Julian's family flew from Lodgepole to Denver, connected to a flight to Boston, then drove almost four hours to Vermont to watch him graduate from Middlebury. Cyrus did most of the driving, occasionally switching off with Gregory, who was sixteen and still swerving when he looked over his shoulder to switch lanes. Martine navigated with a map of New England they'd gotten from AAA during Julian's freshman year. The map was barely creased, barely wrinkled. In the four years since Julian had left Lodgepole, Martine ensured he had no reason to return, and Julian, in turn, ensured they had no reason to visit him in Vermont, an unspoken retaliation she had no right to protest. The blended family Martine was so proud of had separated like milk after a chef squirts lemon into it. The four of them had fun when they were together, but Julian seemed to avoid that togetherness when he could. He'd quit the college ski team the first day of practice, so there hadn't been any races to drive to, and whenever she or Cyrus suggested a visit just for the sake of a visit, he claimed he was too busy. He lived with Martine's mother in New York during the summer or stayed on campus for summer classes; the family spent Christmases together in her apartment or traveled to Mexico or Florida. One time, they visited

Cyrus's family in Tehran and another, the year Julian studied abroad in France, they rented a tiny apartment in Paris. Now Martine and Cyrus barely remembered the route from Boston's airport to Middlebury. Martine double-checked every exit and turn-off, snapping at Cyrus when he drove too fast or too slow but careful not to criticize Gregory. None of them wanted to be late for the event that evening, a special ceremony for seniors who'd majored in English.

The ceremony was held in a brick building with a tall steeple, and as the three of them walked across the quad, Julian and Gregory spotted each other and sprinted to meet under the maple tree in the quad's middle with grins on their faces. Julian's black robe flowed behind him like a cape.

"Dude!" they each yelled, then hugged tightly. Gregory, shorter and stouter than Julian, stood on his tiptoes.

"Mom! Dad!" said Julian. "Thanks for coming." He hugged Martine and Cyrus and smiled at them both. His eyes were bloodshot and he looked like he'd just barely woken up.

"We're so proud of you," said Cyrus.

"Yeah, thanks. Hey, I gotta go inside. I'm a little late and it starts in a couple of minutes. See you after—there's wine and cheese in the library." Then he grinned and punched Gregory in the arm. "No wine for kids under twenty-one, but I'll sneak you a glass."

"Like you haven't already been celebrating." Gregory shoved him back.

Inside, they opened the program and discovered a surprise: Julian's name listed with all the students graduating with honors on the second page. Cyrus and Martine beamed, and Martine ran to grab an extra program and tucked it into her purse. Martine felt relieved—all those times Julian claimed he'd been too busy to visit, he really had been studying—and Julian was still bewildered at his good luck. He thought he'd done too much partying, but here he was, graduating with honors and headed to Columbia Law School. He sat on stage with the other students, and the *D* of Dumont meant he was called up third to shake the department head's hand and receive his honors certificate. Gregory looked embarrassed when

Martine and Cyrus clapped too loud and too hard, but Julian bowed on the stage and the small audience laughed.

The next few days were a whirlwind of other ceremonies, barbecues, and finally, the graduation itself, held outside under a clear blue sky. Martine rushed down the aisle to get close enough to the stage to take a picture of Julian receiving his diploma with her new Canon, and after it was all finished, made Julian pose for even more pictures: first with Gregory, then Cyrus, then her and Cyrus, then with Julian's friends. They all wore cargo shorts under their graduation gowns and pulled cans of Busch Light from deep pockets to guzzle every few minutes, the shorts like clown cars with seemingly endless space. Cyrus looked worried, his brows furrowing into a deep crease every time a new can appeared, but Martine squeezed his arm.

"It's normal," she whispered. "They're just celebrating."

"Okay," he said. "But I hope he's sober enough to help us carry everything."

She shrugged. "How are we going to fit everything, anyway? There's no ski rack on the rental car."

"It'll be like Tetris, one block at a time. I'm a master packer. And I'll tie the skis to the roof rack if I need to," said Cyrus.

Now Martine looked worried, and Gregory laughed at them both, then swiped a beer from Julian and drank it with his friends.

In the end, everything did fit. After all the pictures, all the beers, and all the goodbyes, they tromped up and down the three flights of Julian's social house—Martine smiled when he reminded her a social house wasn't a frat and emphasized they pledged men *and* women—and finished in just a few trips. Julian had sold everything but his clothes and books to the kid taking this room the next year.

"Even your skis?" Gregory's jaw dropped. "How could you?"

Julian wiped his dusty hands on his shorts. "I sold those a while ago. I won't need them while I'm in law school. It's not a big deal."

"What about vacations?" asked Martine. She'd swept the room with a broom whose handle had been broken in half and was bent over trying to get all the dirt into a dustpan.

"I don't know." Julian shrugged. "I guess I'll be studying pretty hard. Everyone says Columbia is stressful. *You* said that, too."

"That's true." Martine stood up and looked at Julian with pride. "But you'll have to learn to relax in your free time. That's important, too."

"Wow," said Gregory. "I wouldn't go to law school if it meant selling my skis."

Martine emptied the dustpan into a trash can and looked at Cyrus with raised eyebrows, but Cyrus just said, "We need to leave soon or we won't get to the city until the middle of the night. Say the rest of your goodbyes and let's get going."

The atmosphere in the rental car as they pulled away was less jovial than earlier that day. They looked like every other family, Cyrus driving and Martine in the front passenger seat, both sons in the back seat with a duffel bag and two backpacks stuffed between them, but their minds were a million miles away from one another. Martine thought of Julian's last goodbye, his departure from Lodgepole and separation from Angie, and assumed this was a better goodbye for him, or at least an easier one. *And maybe*, she thought, *we did the right thing*. He'd left Lodgepole and his past behind and thrived in college. He was following her footsteps, not just into law but attending her alma mater. When she made him leave after the accident, he'd been furious, but wasn't this proof he'd forgiven her? She let her body sink into the soft seat. Cyrus thought of saying goodbye to his old family, the four sisters and one brother he'd left behind in Tehran, his brother just four at the time, sobbing into his mother's skirt, claiming he'd never see Cyrus again. Gregory thought not of goodbyes but of hellos: he was smitten with the younger brother of one of Julian's friends and had discovered they both had dreams of attending Berkeley. And Julian thought of nothing at all. He passed out within minutes of climbing into the station wagon, exhausted from weeks of graduation partying, including that day's beers Cyrus knew about and countless Jack and Cokes he didn't.

Four years at Middlebury had passed quickly for Julian. There was always something to do—classes, clubs, and partying—and when there weren't enough of the first two, there was always more partying. That was what college was for, and just because the social houses weren't technically frats didn't mean there wasn't plenty of beer. Beer was a way to pass the time, but it was also a way to forget the past and the hard left turn his life had taken. When he'd stood at the top of the Middlebury Snow Bowl the first day of practice freshman year, bile gurgling in his throat, he'd suddenly realized he never wanted to ski again. He informed the angry coach before taking even one run, stubborn in his silence when the coach demanded a reason, then sold his skis, boots, and poles. When it became apparent he couldn't dump his past as easily as he'd dumped his skis, he simply drank more. It was an easy out: the drunker he got, the more raucous he got, and even if he was no longer surrounded by his old Lodgepole friends, he still loved being the center of attention. He exchanged ski tricks for rock climbing and led pranks against other social houses, including massive winter snowball fights. And when his parents wanted to visit, he told them he needed to study, though getting decent grades was easy for him. The real reason he kept them at a distance was to avoid any possibility his friends might mention his long-distance girlfriend. Although he tried to shove the thing that tied him and Angie together to the back of his mind, he never wanted to shove Angie herself there. They rarely had enough money to pay for the Greyhound buses to or from Providence, but they spoke often, always careful to avoid the topic of Diana. Julian thought if he could bury that memory deep enough, or at least numb himself to it, life would only get better.

Although college itself had passed quickly, the summer months after graduation seemed endless. He'd spent four years trying to drink away the memory of what happened, and that was enough. At Columbia, he'd start a new life, be someone else, someone better. He'd be defined by his present, not his past. He planned to give up partying—maybe it wouldn't be hard, if all the law students were nerds—and start running to get back in shape. Law school would be his ticket to independence, to life as an adult. Graduates of law schools like Columbia were destined to make money. He'd never be dependent on his parents again, never return to Lodgepole.

Best of all, he'd finally have his own apartment—student housing on Amsterdam and 118th Street, far from his grandmother's apartment, which would give him privacy to meet Angie freely. Angie had also moved to New York after graduation, and although he was sure his grandmother wouldn't care that they'd never broken up, he wasn't so sure she wouldn't tell Martine. All summer, he lied to his grandmother about how often he worked overtime—as a paralegal at a small law firm run by one of Martine's old friends—so he could see Angie for dinner and a movie or spend time in her apartment in the Village. He was tired of having to keep the relationship secret. And since no one else from Lodgepole landed in New York—most of their friends had moved west to California, and neither of them kept in touch with old classmates, anyway—they wouldn't need to worry about running into someone from their past.

The school assigned him a studio on the seventh floor of a building with a rickety elevator. He carried the heavy bags and boxes, and his mother and grandmother brought in the suitcases on wheels and a few bags of groceries from the bodega around the corner.

"Grammie, don't carry any heavy bags. Leave those for me," said Julian. Beads of sweat gathered on her forehead and upper lip, and she wiped them with the back of her hand when she thought no one was looking.

"There's not much, Julian. Just enough to get you started," said Martine, closing the door of the mini-fridge. "I'm sure you'll end up eating pizza for half your meals, anyway." She'd squeezed in milk, apples, juice, and butter on one shelf and pasta sauce and parmesan cheese on the other. The apartment's sole window looked out at a brick wall, but Martine hung curtains from a rod the previous tenant left behind and set two framed pictures on the windowsill: one of Julian and Gregory on the boardwalk in North Carolina during their post-graduation vacation, the other of the whole family on the beach, smiling beneath peeling noses.

When they were done, Grammie took out her camera and snapped a picture of Julian and Martine standing in front of the school-issued couch, arms around each other's waists. "Your first real apartment," she said. "A day to remember."

"Dinner?" asked Martine. "We could grab Chinese at that place on Broadway. Ollies, I think it's called."

Julian shook his head. "Thanks, but there's a thing for One-Ls tonight. I'd like to go meet the other students."

"One-Ls?" His grandmother raised her eyebrows.

"First-year law students. That's what they call us."

Julian walked them to the subway station. They said goodbye on the street, his mother teary, her hug a little too long.

"I'm so proud of you," she said. "You're going to do great at Columbia. You'll be an amazing lawyer."

"Mom," he said, squirming away as gently as he could. "You said that already." And she had, at least ten times. Once, she'd referenced how far he'd come since the accident, as if he were the one who'd overcome a tragedy that happened to *him* when it actually happened to *Diana*, and he stiffened and snapped that he didn't want to get into that, not ever. No matter how hard he tried to remember it as an accident, he would always know that wasn't the whole truth. He'd always feel like he'd stolen a life, and he didn't want to think or talk about it. Now, thankfully, she just referenced a future visit, one he knew he'd stave off with a claim of being too busy. She was flying back to Colorado in a few hours, and with luck, he'd spend Thanksgiving in New York with Angie and maybe a quick solo visit to Grammie. He wouldn't have to deal with his parents until Christmas.

He watched them walk down the subway station's stairs, his grandmother carefully picking her way around a crush of people coming up, Martine holding her elbow, then walked to a bar he'd seen on the way there. Tom's Bar, right next to Tom's Diner. He'd catch a train downtown to see Angie later, after he was certain his mother and grandmother were gone. In the meantime, he sat at the grimy bar, the sticky counter reminiscent of the makeshift basement bar in his old Middlebury house, and ordered a Jack and Coke.

"Actually, no Coke. Just the whiskey."

The bartender, an older guy with dark circles under his eyes and hair that should have been cut months ago, shrugged. "Neat or with ice?"

"Neat." It seemed like something a lawyer in New York would say. Julian swirled the whiskey around and watched the brown liquid coat the sides of the glass, then drank it in one gulp. He had time for one more before he was supposed to meet Angie for dinner. It already felt good, being this free. Tonight he and Angie would be like every other couple. They'd hold hands under the table and on the street, unconcerned about who might see them, and maybe end up back at his new studio, free to spend as much time together as they wanted. He drank the second whiskey more slowly and watched a black fly perched on the edge of the counter rub its hands together, savoring its last meal or getting ready for the next one.

Before he started at Columbia, Julian had always felt like a visitor in New York—coming and going from his grandmother's apartment, sleeping in his mother's old bedroom—but now he felt like a real New Yorker. He bought a bagel and coffee from a street cart on Amsterdam every morning on his way to class in the Toaster, the students' affectionate name for Jerome Greene Hall, an ugly 1960s building with a gigantic window box perched on a platform that resembled the lever used to lower the bread in an actual toaster. He made his way from Constitutional Law to Torts to Civil Procedure during the day, ate a slice of dollar pizza from Koronet on Broadway, and studied in the law library at night. He eschewed study groups in favor of nights alone in his own cubicle. Other students gathered in groups of five or six and handed out assignments to outline readings and prepare flowcharts for finals, but he didn't trust anyone else to do work he could do better on his own, and he couldn't stand their chatter about grades and how to secure an offer from Cravath, Swaine & Moore or Skadden Arps, big law firms he quickly learned carried the most prestige with the highest paychecks.

On Fridays, he packed up his books and headed downtown to spend the weekend at Angie's, a fifth-floor walk-up in the East Village on the corner of Fourth and Avenue A. They never spent weekends at his apartment because it was too far from her art studio—a room at NYU she paid a professor on the side to use—and too much work to pack up her paints and canvases. Traveling back and forth between Columbia and the East Village, Julian belonged to New York and New York belonged to him. He was anonymous in a way he'd never been in Lodgepole or Middlebury. He loved being able to disappear from Columbia's law school bubble into a crowd on the subway, then reappear as a new person in Angie's gritty neighborhood. And Julian did belong there: after all, he'd been born in Mount Sinai Hospital, had lived the first year of his life in a tiny one bedroom overlooking Riverside Park.

As for Angie, she'd transformed herself so completely from a mountain girl into a city girl that it was almost as if she had been born in New York. When she painted, she still wore the same paint-splattered jeans she wore in the art room back in high school—both knees now blown out—but she carried expensive purses she found in thrift shops to her job in a small gallery on Twenty-Fourth Street and draped herself in all black for exhibit openings. She lived with two girls, one a friend from college, the other her friend's sister. Her friend was struggling to make it as an actress, waiting tables at night, always running to auditions during the day wearing four-inch heels. The sister worked as an investment banker and Julian had only talked to her a few times because all she did was work, even on Saturdays and Sundays. Angie felt sorry for her, working harder to prove herself because she was a woman in a man's world, and always threw her laundry in when she did her own.

Everyone knew you made a Faustian bargain when you got a job in that world—either as an investment banker like Angie's roommate or a lawyer in one of the prestigious corporate law firms—but Julian started to wonder whether he wanted to work those hours or even do that kind of work. He wondered what he could do other than be a corporate lawyer or litigator and how he was supposed to figure it out.

Angie just shrugged when he asked. "I don't know, because art is all I've ever wanted to do," she said simply when he asked one Saturday night. "It was an easy choice. I never wanted to take over Mom and Dad's restaurant. I don't like to cook, and Lodgepole is too small. I don't want to live there for the rest of my life."

They'd finished their takeout from the Indian place around the corner, lamb vindaloo so spicy it made their eyes water and noses run, and were sitting on her bed while her actress roommate watched *Groundhog Day* on the VCR in the living room. Bursts of laughter leaked through the closed door every so often, and Angie kept glancing toward the sound, but Julian wanted to talk.

"But, I mean, how did you choose working in a gallery instead of a museum? Or making your own art instead of teaching?"

She shrugged again. "The gallery is more exciting, like an adventure. Teaching would be boring."

"And why painting and not, I don't know, sculpture or photography?"

"Trial and error, I guess. When I paint, I can extract or augment or create beauty by manipulating reality. Or if I want to, I can reflect reality. I feel stuck when I sculpt, almost like everything has already been done. Painting is just—it's what I was meant to do. And I'm at peace when I paint. It's relaxing." She grinned. "Also, I'm a terrible sculptor."

Julian never felt at peace at Columbia. Even though law students spent hours discussing starting salaries at the biggest law firms or how to get the best clerkships, no one actually knew what it was like to work as a junior associate or clerk for a judge. He wasn't sure what he was working toward, other than a job, and he wanted to make money as much as the next guy, but he also wanted to like his job. His favorite class was a criminal law clinic, where he discovered crimes were more than a simple matter of innocence or guilt: criminal law ascribed the nuances of right and wrong on a legal continuum. For the first time, he'd begun to wonder about a career as a defense attorney because he'd realized that for the legal system to work, everyone needed a lawyer. Otherwise, those nuances of right and wrong would be adjudicated as categorical, and there wasn't any justice in that. He had a coveted offer to work for a corporate law firm the next summer even though he was only a 1L—most of those jobs were reserved for 2Ls—but he wasn't excited about it.

"Just take the job, Julian. You won't know what it's like until you try it," urged Angie. "You'd make good money, right?"

Julian nodded and Angie continued: "You can use that money to help pay for tuition next year, so you'd have fewer loans. Or we can go to the beach on vacation. Or both. And then you can try something different next summer." She rubbed his shoulders and he leaned back into her hands, warm and comforting. She pulled his T-shirt up and over his head and kissed the nape of his neck, nuzzling his ear and causing him to collapse into laughter.

"You know I'm ticklish there," he accused.

She dove in again, but he turned and grabbed her arms and tickled her back, career uncertainties forgotten, and they wrestled each other's clothes off. Julian sometimes wondered if the longing ever lessened, if he'd ever not be hungry for her, or she for him.

"Wait," she said and reached into the nightstand drawer to pull out a condom. Her career was important to her, and she always said getting pregnant would be the kiss of death for her job. Julian agreed. Even if he didn't know exactly what he wanted to do, he wanted to focus on whatever it would be without the responsibilities of kids. He wanted a family, and he wanted it with Angie, but that would come later. He liked the freedom they had to roam around the city. They worked hard, but on the weekends they drank gin and tonics in jazz clubs or ate french bread and baked brie in all-night cafes, sat on park benches and read books, and went running in Central Park. Sometimes they even played tourist and went to Coney Island for hot dogs or rode the ferry to Staten Island. He wasn't about to give that up.

One day, they visited the World Trade Center. Both had been to the Empire State Building but neither had been to the Twin Towers. They rode the elevator to the 107th floor of the South Tower and took pictures from the observation deck, and Julian pointed across the way to the Windows on the World restaurant in the North Tower.

"Once I get my first big job—whatever it is—I'll take you there for dinner."

"Aren't there other restaurants we could try?" asked Angie. She stepped away from the edge of the building and shivered.

"Since when are you afraid of heights?"

"I'm not," said Angie. "I'm just cold. Let's go."

Julian put his coat around Angie's shoulders, on top of the coat she already wore. "You'd think someone from Colorado could take a little cold weather."

Angie shrugged. Normally, she loved a city view, the sparkling lights and streets stacked in rows below like a living map, but drizzle had soaked through her jeans and the clouds hanging around the top half of the skyscrapers limited the view. In their prior lives, March would have been the time for them to ski with no jackets, with nothing more than a sweater and gloves. On sunny days, they ditched goggles for Ray-Bans and teased each other about who had the best ski tan: pink cheeks with raccoon eyes because of the sunglasses. The bright blue skies made them giddy, and they could see all the way to the La Sal Mountains in Utah, a hundred miles away. On the warmest days, they skied in bathing suits, just because, and ate lunch at Eagles Nest, the slopeside lodge that set out reclining beach chairs and blasted the Beach Boys. There was plenty of bad weather in Lodgepole in March, but all she could remember now was skiing in a bikini, the warmth of the mountain sun on her skin and the crisp air crackling in the sky.

"No worries," said Julian. "I have something to warm you up." He pulled a flask from the interior pocket of the coat on Angie's shoulders, took a long swig, and handed it to Angie.

She took her own swig. "Thai for dinner?"

Every morning when Angie was getting dressed for work, Roberto called her. He couldn't call at night, because it was the restaurant's busiest time, but he never missed a day, and he'd sent Angie money for an answering machine so if she wasn't home, he could leave her a message. He told her he bought one for him and Livia and set it up on the kitchen counter, right where he could see the light flashing if there were messages waiting.

Usually, Roberto talked about the weather, or a new recipe he created, or a television show he and Livia were watching. He didn't talk for long and ended almost every conversation with "I know you're busy, but I just needed to hear your voice, to know you're okay."

"I'm okay, Dad," she always said. "Thanks for checking. Are you guys okay?"

On the other end, there would be a slight pause, as he was always okay but Livia wasn't and might never be. After Diana died, grief had rooted deep inside Livia, a noxious weed that required no nourishment, no additional tragedy, to flourish. It had overpowered her entire being. He was too loyal to complain, but Angie always knew what the pause meant. Nothing had changed. The one time he'd answered honestly, he simply said, "*Fa niente, carina.* Now the restaurant is our life." It wasn't okay, not really, but Angie was the last person in the world who could help with her mother's grief, so she let it be.

Roberto and Livia had flown out to the East Coast just three times while Angie was in college. Once to drop her off as a freshman, once in early May of her sophomore year, and once for graduation. She knew they would have visited more, but they never wanted to leave the restaurant unattended. They worried employees might steal in their absence—Livia once fired a married couple who washed dishes on nothing more than a suspicion of the wife stealing cash, even though the money was later discovered under a pile of papers—and Roberto didn't trust anyone else to do the cooking. When they visited sophomore year, it was the off-season in Lodgepole and they simply closed the restaurant for two weeks, but when they took a day trip to Boston and Angie showed them her favorite spots in the North End, her father occasionally stopped talking and his eyes glazed over, as if he were back in Lodgepole worrying about the chef's special at DeLuca's.

For every visit and every phone call, Angie erased all traces of Julian. In college, all she had to do was shove the framed photos of him into the back of her closet. Now that Julian was in her apartment every weekend, when she spoke on the phone to Roberto or Livia she made sure Julian was in her bedroom, door closed, so his voice couldn't travel out to the kitchen. She hadn't considered how she would maintain this deception in the future; she only knew it was necessary now.

Julian played the same game with his parents but had recently begun questioning whether it was still necessary. "It was so long ago," he said one morning when Angie walked back into her bedroom after Roberto's phone call. It was Monday and he was packing his backpack, getting ready to head to Columbia for his ten o'clock Criminal Law class.

"What was?" She pulled on a pencil-thin leather skirt over her panty-hose, then stood in front of the mirror on the back of her bedroom door, turning back and forth, admiring the look.

"Everything that happened. Back in Lodgepole." His face reddened. This was a topic they usually avoided. They'd discussed Diana's death once, the first time they reunited freshman year, when Julian had taken a bus from Middlebury to Providence for a long weekend. They cried together, their separation and the reason for it still fresh, clutching each other on the narrow bed of her tiny dorm room. Angie had a picture of Diana in a drawer by her desk and pulled it out. It was a school photo, taken just after the start of second grade, and Diana smiled broadly, two front teeth missing, staticky pieces of her dark bangs sticking straight up, as if she'd just rubbed a balloon on her head. They'd promised to only remember the good things about her life, and Julian sent flowers to Angie every year on February 28, the anniversary of the accident, but they'd never talked about it again. Not until today.

Angie sat down on the bed, blouse still in her hands. "Not that long ago."

"We were different people."

"What does that have to do with anything?"

"I'm just wondering how long we have to keep our relationship a secret. How long you're going to make me hide in your room when you talk to your father." He stood awkwardly in the middle of the small room, a book in one hand and his backpack on the floor.

"My sister *died*."

"I know that," he said sharply. "Don't you think I remember—"

Angie held up her hand. "Don't."

"You can't do that to me. We were both there. Both a part of what happened."

She sucked her breath in sharply. She never understood why Julian and her mother found it necessary to assign blame for Diana's death. Livia acted like it was Julian's and Angie's fault because Diana was her favorite daughter and she had to blame someone, which wasn't fair. Julian acted like it was their fault because they'd left Diana unattended, which was wrong. Angie missed Diana—a lot—and would do anything to change what happened that day, but kids skied alone all the time. Diana could have hit that tree whether or not she and Julian were right behind her. Like most kids, sometimes she skied out of control. Sometimes she skied in the trees, weaving in and out of aspen and spruce. Sometimes she even deliberately skied away from Angie because she didn't like the idea of being babysat by her big sister. Yes, Angie felt guilty about what happened. How could she not? But it felt like everyone was forcing her to relive the pain of Diana's death. "She was *my* sister, not yours."

"But what happened, happened. We can't go back and change it, and you and me—that's not going to change either," Julian said. "I don't ever want you and me to change. I love you. And I know you love me. So why do we have to keep it hidden from our families?"

"Because something can be an accident and still be someone's fault. Our fault. My mother will always blame us—and especially you. She hates you, hates your whole family. She's never going to *not* hate you." She pulled the blouse over her head and tucked it into her skirt, then bent over and slid on bright green pumps.

Julian bit his tongue so hard he tasted blood. *Our fault* meant something different to Angie than it did to him. After all these years, he still didn't know what was his fault and what was hers. He'd kept the truth from Angie not just out of guilt and shame but because part of the reason he hit Diana was Angie's fault. He'd swallowed all the blame so she wouldn't have to, drew it in like a breath and made it a part of himself. He'd never wanted Angie to feel what he felt that day. Now he stood in the middle of the room, watching Angie get dressed, bent over her shoes. He remembered Angie bent over Diana in the snow and the yellow pom-pom in the middle of the trail like a dying sun. Maybe he still didn't know what *our fault* meant for him.

Before he could stop himself, he blurted out, "Has your mother ever heard of forgiveness? Isn't that part of Jesus's whole thing, part of what you Catholics believe? She goes to church every Sunday, wears a cross around her neck."

"*You* Catholics? Since when is it okay to make fun of someone's religion?"

He reddened again, the flush staining even his ears. "That's not what I meant. I just meant—I didn't—I'm sorry. I just mean, how long do we have to be punished for something that was an accident?"

"I don't know," Angie snapped. "But Diana *died*." She folded her arms across her chest. Julian stood in the middle of the room, looking down at his feet, and her anger receded as quickly as it had flamed. She knew he'd done his best to understand her difficult mother, but even *she* didn't understand Livia. Diana's death had faded in Angie's mind: it was a past that mattered and she wished hadn't happened, but it was rooted firmly in her past and firmly as an accident. If and when it faded to a mere accident in Livia's mind, she and Julian could disclose their relationship. But now wasn't the right time. Not yet. She stood up and hugged him.

"We shouldn't be fighting about this. Aren't we on the same side?" he asked.

Her mother was more of an eye-for-an-eye kind of person, not a turn-the-other-cheek kind of person, and Angie was pretty sure Livia still hadn't forgiven her, let alone Julian. Now wasn't the time to deal with the future.

Angie wasn't sure why she'd gotten so angry. Julian was right. They were on the same side. She wondered whether it was her own guilt and grief—feelings she thought she'd put to rest four years ago—because they'd dredged up memories of her sister's accident, or worry, because she knew Livia would hate that she was still in this relationship. And she didn't know why she was defending her mother. Nothing Angie did was good enough for Livia, not the number of visits home, her choice to study art in college or to move to New York. Sometimes she wondered what was worse: her involvement in Diana's accident or her failure to return home to run DeLuca's. Yet her mother was still her mother, and it wasn't Livia's fault that she was the way she was. Something about Diana's death had unhinged her, left her unbalanced, and that was still there, simmering under the surface. Angie didn't want to do anything to exacerbate that angry grief. No matter the reason, they'd argued for so long she was late to work, and she had to spend money, money she didn't have, on a cab instead of taking the subway. She closed her eyes in the back seat and took deep breaths, ten in a row, the same way Roberto taught her to calm down before big ski races.

She was five minutes late, but Idara, one of the gallery's co-owners, barely raised her eyebrows as Angie flew into her seat at the receptionist's desk. Angie was lucky to have this job; Hobbs & Co. wasn't a well-known gallery and the pay was crappy, but Idara treated Angie fairly and said someday she might be able to display a painting in one of the basement rooms. Kerry James Marshall and Judy Rifka both knew Idara and occasionally stopped by on opening nights, and Angie was starstruck every time, too tongue-tied to say anything other than *nice to meet you*. None of her other friends had a job like this, and Angie hated being late, hated the thought of doing anything that might squander this opportunity.

"Great heels," said Idara, staring at Angie's bright pumps.

Angie grinned. She'd never dress as well as Idara, who seemed to pull her wardrobe from a fashion designer's closet, but she'd take the compliment. Idara was tall and thin, as graceful and beautiful as any of the supermodels on the covers of *Vogue*, practically a human work of art. Angie modeled her outfits after Idara's but tried not to seem too obvious about it. She'd found the heels in a thrift store, probably discarded by an actual supermodel after being worn once, but Idara didn't need to know where she'd gotten them. And if Angie's legs would never be as willowy as Idara's—years of ski racing meant she'd built thick quads she could never diet away—at least her feet could.

Angie breathed in deeply; she already felt better. This gallery was like her own private sanctuary. The smooth floors and plain walls soaked up her emotions like a blank canvas soaked up paint, transforming whatever she was feeling into something new. Each painting had its own space on the wall with nothing nearby to crowd it. If visitors spoke too loudly, their voices bounced around the cavernous rooms on the first floor, and thick walls insulated the interior from the city's constant horns and sirens. She signed in visitors and took phone calls and occasionally answered questions about exhibits or artists but otherwise spent her days dreaming of when her own work would be displayed here.

This morning, the gallery was empty except for Idara, chatting on the phone in her office, and three old men in black suits and berets, wandering around and whispering among themselves. They moved as one, shuffling from painting to painting, whispers occasionally traveling through the cavernous room, *the importance of light* and *smooth transition into representation* drifting to Angie at the reception desk. She started sketching out a new painting. Her latest series focused on water—reflections in water, what grows on the edge of water, murky representations of the world reflected back from the Hudson River or a pond that lived in her memory or even of her toes in the bathtub. She liked abstracting out small pieces of reality, visions from a moment in time. She sketched without thinking, unsure of what she wanted the eventual painting to be, not stopping to examine what she'd done until Idara peered over the top of the reception desk.

"I'm headed to a lunch meeting. Back in an hour." She turned Angie's sketchbook around so it was right side up for her. "Moving on to winter, I see?"

Angie turned it back. Idara was right. She'd sketched a series of water droplets in the midst of freezing, reshaping into snowflakes or hail or graupel, an abstraction she hadn't seen until Idara's comment.

"Hunh," she said, scrunching up her nose. "I guess so." She traced the pencil drawing with her finger, the thick paper rough against her skin.

Chapter Eight

Julian planned to spend the flights to Denver and Lodgepole reviewing the files Martine emailed to him, but when the small commuter plane begins descending toward the airport just outside town, his laptop is still closed, tucked in a padded case inside his briefcase. He's been back to Lodgepole only twice, once for Gregory's high school graduation and once for Cyrus's funeral. He was in and out of town within two days each time and slept in his old bedroom in his old house just long enough to confirm the bedroom and the house were no longer *his*. His mind has spiraled for the last hour, wondering what it will be like to spend nights in a room that belonged to a long-gone boy and days acting as the lawyer for Angie's daughter, interacting with Angie, and presumably David, as though their past doesn't matter. And though it should be ancient history, he can't help wondering what will happen if he runs into someone who remembers Diana's accident all those years ago. Livia is no longer an issue—Martine made that clear—and many of the kids he used to know settled somewhere else. But he thinks about the ones who stayed, whether he will recognize them or they him.

November in Lodgepole is his least favorite time of year, monochromatic and somber, the town itself mourning fall and winter's betwixt season, but when he first boarded, a group of tourists filled in most of the seats, including the one next to him. Now they *ooh* and *ahh* as Mount Warren comes into view, its craggy summit towering above the surrounding peaks.

"It's beautiful," the woman next to him says. "We don't have these kind of mountains in Texas." She's chewing gum, snapping small bubbles every so often, craning her neck into Julian's personal space to look out the window. She's young, maybe midtwenties, wearing a cowboy hat and furry boots, and she'll probably start taking selfies as soon as she lands. When she holds her phone against the window, arm stretched across his lap to capture a picture, he clears his throat.

"Is that where you're from?" He feels forced into playing a polite seat-mate.

"Yep. How about you?"

"I live in New York." Julian wishes she would stop talking to him.

"This is where that girl shot her brother, isn't it?"

"I'm not sure," he lies.

"It's a horrible story. My friend shared the Instagram article with me. Some kid used her father's gun to kill her brother, like, a few weeks ago."

Julian angles his body away from her and peers out the oval window. The mountain peaks are covered in snow, but the lower slopes are swaths of green pines and naked aspens. The roads and mesas look clear, strange for this time of year. His mother mentioned an October snow, but it must have all melted.

"I don't get it. How could she have done that? And what did the parents do to turn her into the kind of kid that would do that? I guess she'll be in jail for, like, the rest of her life." The woman chews her gum harder, as though it will help her solve this complex legal issue.

"She has to have a trial first," mutters Julian. The plane touches down and a few tourists behind him clap. This woman is part of why he has a job. He pulls out his phone and checks his email. He hates these kinds of conversations. When he was younger, he'd engage with people like this, talk about the core legal principle that a person is innocent until proven guilty. But these days, once a person is accused, everyone rushes to judgment: guilty until proven innocent. People see a crime on the news, a man arrested for robbing a bank or a woman arrested for killing her boyfriend, and assume guilt. But an arrest is just an accusation—it doesn't make a person guilty.

"Well, yeah, but she *did* it. That's totally messed up. It's not like they'll ever let her out. She needs to be punished, and a crime like that is unforgivable," she says. "Right?" The woman looks at him expectantly, and he realizes he mistakenly spoke part of what he was thinking.

He turns back toward the window without responding. People always say that. All retribution, all punishment. Maybe that arrested woman *is* guilty of killing her boyfriend, but what if he abused her for years? She deserves some measure of mercy, at least a mitigation of her sentence, and once she's served her time, a chance to rehabilitate herself. Everyone has committed wrongs, but everyone needs forgiveness and the chance to make up for those wrongs.

This time he almost says it aloud on purpose: "Sometimes who a person becomes is more important than who a person used to be," but that's something this woman would never understand. Her thumbs furiously tap her phone, the "horrible story" about the girl who killed her brother already an afterthought. She holds her phone in front of her face, camera pointing back at her shiny lips, fluffs her dyed hair, and snaps the selfie. She hasn't even considered that Nora might have been playing with the gun or had a mental health issue, which Martine already suspects. This tourist's mind is already made up, her opinion as fixed as the character she assumes for Nora.

He contemplates shocking her with the irony of their conversation, that his job is to defend people accused of crimes, to defend Nora in particular, but the plane pulls into the gate, one of two in Lodgepole's small airport, and the seatbelt sign dings. Julian massages his stiff ankles—there's too much sitting on these long flights—and stands hunched under the overhead luggage racks. She jumps up, clutching her oversized purse in one hand and phone in the other.

"Have a great trip," she says over her shoulder and pushes her way into the line of people exiting the plane.

When Julian steps outside the airport's doors, his mother is waiting for him on the sidewalk. As a child, he thought his mother was the tallest woman in the world. At five eleven, she towered over the other moms, and with heels, even over Cyrus. *Will I be that tall, Mommy?* he used to ask. *We'll see, little duck*, she always responded. *Drink your milk and you might.* By fifteen, long after he'd banished the nickname *little duck*, he had her beat by three inches. He never reached the status of towering over her, but now for the first time he feels like he has. She looks smaller than she did before Cyrus died, shrunken into the generic figure inhabited by most older people, with rounded shoulders and a puffy abdomen. For the first time, he feels a pang of guilt for holding on to his resentment for so long—she'd only done what she thought was best as a mother—and wraps his arms around her.

In the car, the silence is awkward but not angry. Finally, she says, "Thank you."

"I couldn't say no any more than you could."

"Yes, but still . . ." She hits the left blinker to turn. "And Mayumi? Will she be okay without you for a couple of weeks?"

When he first told Mayumi he wanted to help Martine represent the daughter of his ex-girlfriend, he'd told her the truth—all of it, including what happened with Diana. They were sitting on a couch in the apartment he'd inherited from his grandmother, facing each other. She'd searched him intently, her eyes peeking from behind the bangs she kept intending to get trimmed, then said, "Each of us is more than the worst thing we've done." In one fell swoop, she bestowed a forgiveness on Julian he'd been trying—and failing—to find for twenty-five years. He'd searched for that forgiveness in alcohol, in self-flagellation when he abandoned the sport he loved, and in thousands of hours of free legal work. He distanced himself from his family and ruined his relationship with Angie, and searched again in alcohol. After Angie left, he spent two years getting sober, trying and failing so many times he lost count

of how many different church basements he visited for new AA meetings, too ashamed to return to the old ones and tell them he needed to
start over on his sobriety chip or couldn't complete all the steps because
it was impossible to make amends to everyone he'd harmed. Mayumi's
words erased all those years of searching, and he'd wondered whether he
deserved the forgiveness, whether he deserved her.

"She's bummed I'm missing a birthday party for her nephews," he
only says. "But her therapy practice is overbooked with patients. She'll
work extra hours and catch up."

"Were you able to get your cases covered?"

He nods. "That's the benefit of working in a big firm. Plenty of junior
associates to help while I'm gone. And I can do some of what I need to
do remotely."

Martine pulls onto Main Street and slows down to fifteen miles per
hour, the town speed limit. The Lodgepole police have been sticklers about
speeding on Main Street since Julian was a kid. Back then, Main Street
was a collection of hardware stores, mom-and-pop restaurants, clothing
and shoe stores, and a post office. Now it's lined with shops selling jewelry
and luxury leather, expensive farm-to-table restaurants, and art galleries.

"I want to get right to work," she says. "The DA wants to make an
example of her, and I'm worried his filing to transfer her case to district
court might succeed."

"Why is he going after a thirteen-year-old kid as an adult?"

"Who knows?" She throws one hand up in the air in exasperation.
"Well, that's not true. I do know. It's political. There's an election coming
up, and he's running on a tough-on-crime platform. The woman who
plans to run against him already has a lot of support, so maybe he's nervous. It's ridiculous, though." She pulls into the driveway, pulls up the
handbrake, and steps out of the car.

"He couldn't find someone other than a kid to pick on?"

"I guess not," she says, grimacing. She hesitates, then says, "You haven't
asked about Angie."

"I'm not sure where to start. It's—I don't know. It's weird to be back
under any circumstance, you know that." Other than Mayumi, Angie

was the only woman he ever loved. He has no experience dealing with former girlfriends. How is he supposed to act? What is he supposed to say? "I feel sorry for her, that's all."

There was another thing troubling him he didn't want to say aloud: Why had David been the one to ask for his help? Angie had been so angry with him, all those years ago in New York, that after he heard about the shooting, he didn't reach out to see if she needed help because he was afraid she'd say no. Or worse, not respond, like she'd done with his letter attempting to make amends. He'd laid bare his soul in that letter, admitting to alcoholism, to effectively abandoning her for work, to fucking up their relationship, and even though his AA sponsor at the time had cautioned him that Angie had no obligation to respond, her failure to do so felt enough like rejection that it still stung, even all these years later. But she must have known he *would* help if she asked, and he'd half expected her to give in and contact him. David reaching out was what didn't make sense. They disliked each other in high school, and David never would have wanted his help, knowing he was Angie's ex, knowing—at least Julian assumes he knows—what happened in New York.

He steps into the house. Home, but no longer home. Martine is watching him, evaluating him like mothers do. "And you?" she asks. "How are you? When's your next marathon?"

"I'm taking a little break. My joints have started complaining about all the running."

"You need to take care of yourself, Julian. You've always pushed yourself so hard for sports."

"And I need to slow down at work, sleep more, eat better. I know the drill, Mom." He grins, then heads upstairs with his suitcase to unpack, the black carry-on heavier than it used to be. "I could say the same about you. You're the one who's seventy-two."

"We meet with Nora tomorrow morning, then David and Angie the following day," she calls after him, ignoring his comment. The seventh stair, the one he always skipped as a teen because it got him in trouble when he snuck out, creaks as he rounds the corner of the staircase.

• • •

The detention center is down a long, bleak road filled with potholes, though in fairness, everything in Colorado looks bleak in November. Arid autumn weather withers and browns every tree, bush, and blade of grass until the whole landscape looks like it's been overcooked. Even the blue in the anemic sky seems washed out, ready to be discarded in favor of a new one.

"She's talking again," says Martine. Her hands sit on the steering wheel, at ten and two, where she'd taught him, in another life, to hold his hands. "Angie visited her a few days ago and she spoke."

"What'd she say?"

"That she heard knocking. She was afraid a guard was coming to get her."

"At least she's talking."

"Yes, but there was no guard, no knocking," she says. "She was hearing things. I thought her not talking was shock, maybe a way of processing what she did or protecting herself from the consequences of her actions, but—I don't know. Maybe not."

"I think it'll take some time to figure out. And it could be a combination of those things."

Julian read the psychiatric evaluation last night after Martine, finally admitting to fatigue, went to bed. The psychiatrist said Nora appeared to be experiencing depression, hallucinations, disorganized thinking, and grossly disorganized behavior, including catatonia, could be suffering from psychosis, and may have experienced a break with reality weeks before she'd killed Nico. He stated he needed further visits to confirm her symptoms and a diagnosis because he'd only been permitted to spend sixty minutes with her, and he noted it was difficult to diagnose psychiatric disorders like psychosis in a child of thirteen because they're so rare.

"How did Angie handle the results of the evaluation?" asks Julian, then immediately regrets it. He's here for Nora, not Angie.

"Not well," says Martine.

"You said they can't pay for anything. Who paid the psychiatrist?"

Martine raises her eyebrows and shrugs with her face, that odd way she's always had of admitting something.

"The file said one of the symptoms of juvenile Huntington's disease is depression and aggression. Was Nora tested for HD after Nico was diagnosed?"

Martine nods. "She was. She doesn't carry the gene, so whatever is going on is unrelated."

This detention center doesn't look any different from the ones he's visited for juvenile clients in New York. They're always cinderblock and brick, though this one is newer, its cheery lobby a pretense this isn't a prison. Martine and Julian enter through double doors and check in to an area filled with light from massive front windows. The kids probably never see this lobby; Julian assumes they spend time in their cells, in the pods' common area or bland rooms that pass for classrooms, and maybe in good weather go outside into a yard hidden in the back and surrounded by a two-story chain-link fence topped with barbed wire. In his experience, most juvenile detention centers, regardless of how they look, act like penitentiaries and treat kids like prisoners. They rarely provide appropriate rehabilitation or education.

"Sign here," says the guard at the front desk, then waves them through to the meeting rooms.

Nora is already in the room. Another guard stands outside, scrolling on her cell phone.

Julian nods to the vending machines in the hallway. "Can I grab a candy bar for her?"

"Yeah," says the guard, "but don't take too long. You only get ninety minutes, and that started when you signed in out front."

"M&Ms or Snickers?" Julian asks his mother.

Martine hesitates. "I don't know. I've never brought her any candy."

"Mom, that's not how this works. You need to bring treats, establish a relationship. She's just a kid."

"I bring her paints," says Martine, her voice testy.

Inside the meeting room, Martine sits opposite Nora, but Julian chooses to sit next to her. Every time he meets a new client, he reminds himself how it felt to know he'd just made a terrible mistake, the panicky realization that the rest of his life was forever altered. For just a moment, he tries to put himself in the client's shoes, to bond himself to their guilt, although of course it's not the same because they have to pay for their mistakes, and he never got to.

He sticks his hand out to shake. "Hi, Nora, I'm Julian Dumont. I'm Martine's son, but I'm also a lawyer, and your parents asked me to help on your case."

When she doesn't respond, he hands her a Twix bar and a Coke. She pops the top and sips the Coke carefully, as if she's afraid of what's in the can. She doesn't open the Twix, so he does it for her.

"Your mother told me you like them," he lies. "She said it was your favorite when you were little." He hasn't spoken to Angie yet, so he doesn't actually know what Nora's favorite is. It was Angie's favorite a long time ago.

Dark half-moons underline her eyes, and she rubs her nose, then shrugs. "I guess."

"Are you doing okay in here, sleeping and eating?"

"That's all anyone asks when they visit."

"Are you watching anything on TV?"

"Last night the TV had *Shrek* on it." Her lips are set in an angry line on her face.

"It's nice to hear you talking, Nora," says Martine. "Does that mean you're feeling better?"

"I'm tired. I don't like the new medicine they gave me."

"It's just for a little while," says Julian. "It's to help with—" He hesitates and glances at Martine, who shakes her head slightly, but he doesn't agree with deceiving kids, especially when it's going to come out in court, so he chooses a half answer. "It's to help with the mental health problems you've been experiencing, to get your brain back on track."

"I know," she says. "They give me a paper cup with pills twice a day. I used to take depression medication, but they took that away and gave me new ones. Now it's too many."

"I don't like pills, either," Julian agrees. "But these are important, okay?

You have to keep taking them." He makes a note to check which medication she took previously. No one he knew growing up took depression medications when they were thirteen. This poor kid, depressed before she lived most of her life, before she got to the hard part of living.

"Nora, we need to talk about what happened with Nico," says Martine. "I know it's hard, but it's important."

"There are a lot of flies here," says Nora, swatting at the air. "They're everywhere, even in the food."

"I'm sorry," says Julian. He pushes back from the table. "Are there some in here now?"

Nora looks at him coldly. "Of course there are."

"They'll go away soon. That will get better."

"Maybe," she says and folds her arms across her chest. "I don't remember what happened," she adds. "I keep telling people that."

"That's okay," says Martine. "Do you want to paint again while we talk?" There's understanding in her voice, but her confusion is apparent to Julian, betrayed by the crinkle between her eyebrows, so deep it's visible through the wrinkled skin on her forehead.

Ninety minutes later, Martine and Julian are in Martine's Subaru again, her hands back at ten and two.

"You handled that well," says Martine.

"I've had clients with hallucinations before, so I knew what to expect." He's suddenly aware of their experience difference and feels sorry for her, having to take guidance and advice from her son on a job she's worked at for forty-five years.

"You did better than me," says Martine. "I didn't know how to respond."

They strategize the entire three hours home. They have to proceed with Nora's 911 confession as their base. They have three options: argue Nora was playing with the gun and it went off by mistake; argue "not guilty by reason of insanity"—always a difficult and unpredictable plea; or plead guilty but argue she's less culpable because of her age and mental health, hopefully resulting in a reduced sentence. The mistake theory, pushed by Angie, is wishful thinking. If the gun discharged by mistake, why would all three shots have hit Nico, and why would they have hit him so cleanly, on body parts a person would aim at only to kill?

"And she knows how to handle a gun," says Martine. "David's taken her hunting before."

Julian drums his fingers on his legs, wondering how Angie would have felt about that. The Angie he once knew wore high heels and leather jackets, clinked champagne glasses in New York's finest art galleries, and spent a year as a vegetarian, making it hard for them to eat at some of his favorite restaurants. He gave up hamburgers and pepperoni pizza in solidarity with her, ate falafel and lentils and tofu. He knew why she'd left him—he couldn't ever forget that, couldn't ever forgive himself. But he'd never understand how she returned to Lodgepole or why she married someone like David.

"I think our best option is to negotiate a plea with the DA based on the mitigating circumstances, especially her mental health. The psych eval supports that," he says.

Martine's hands tighten on the steering wheel, and she shakes her head. "I don't know. Gil Stuckey has been clear. He doesn't care about her age or lack of criminal history and said he doubts that she has mental health issues."

The car is silent for a minute.

"I feel so sorry for them," she says.

"David and Angie?"

She nods. "They've basically lost both kids, you know?"

The next day, Julian and Martine explain the legal strategy to David and Angie. The awkward greetings—stiff handshakes, Angie's cold-as-ice hand, no hugs, no *It's good to see you* or *It's been a long time*—were worse than Julian anticipated. He'd once known everything there was to know about Angie, her body as familiar as his own. He knew the way her hips curved when she lay on her side and how long it took her eyes to focus when she woke up. He knew she ate potato chips before lunch but never gained weight. She used to cry easily, especially after watching sad movies or seeing a person perform a good deed. She always fidgeted when she got nervous or upset, twisting her right index finger with her left hand or tapping her foot. She has three chicken pox scars on the inside of her right thigh, one just past her knee, the other two much higher. It was a knowledge so mundane he assumed it would always be a part of him. Now he feels slightly embarrassed by it, as if he knows something profane he shouldn't. They sit at a small circular table in Martine's office, Julian sandwiched between David and Martine, Angie across from him, unable or unwilling to make eye contact, still wearing her coat. She's perfectly still, as if fidgeting might betray who she used to be.

For a long time after she left him, he thought he'd never love anyone else and no one else would ever love him. Then Mayumi came along, the daughter of his old boss's best friend, a blind date he almost skipped, and he finally banished Angie from his everyday thoughts, stopped thinking about his mistakes, her mistakes, their mistakes. But here Angie is, sitting in front of him. Before the meeting, his stomach was so hollow he couldn't eat breakfast or even drink coffee, but now he feels a terrible twinge of triumph. *I ended up okay even though you left me.* The thought rises from that hollow stomach like curdled milk and he swallows again and again, as if he's trying to pop his ears on an airplane when what he really wants is to stifle an emotion he knows he shouldn't feel. Then that's followed by a second feeling: guilt. Because he's better than okay. He has a wife, and plans for children, and he's happy, happier than he's ever been, and Angie's family is crumbling.

They review the possible defenses and sentences, the potential for a plea deal, Angie insisting vehemently, as Martine said she would, that the shooting was a mistake. David interrupts Angie the second time she says it.

"I want to talk about the 'not guilty due to insanity' argument," he says.

"I know it sounds like a good argument," says Julian, "but it's not what you think. The problem is that defense would mean Nora would have to be evaluated by a state psychiatrist in addition to ours."

"What's wrong with that?"

"It's a wildcard," says Julian. "There's no guarantee the state psychiatrist will agree with ours. He might think she has no mental health problems at all, or worse, conclude she's a sociopath who needs to be locked up for life. The DA would have a field day with that."

"She's thirteen," says Angie. "She's not a sociopath."

"That doesn't mean the DA won't go down that road. Even if he doesn't, proving insanity is tough. You have to prove Nora couldn't form a culpable mental state, and courts aren't very accepting of that idea. In some states, you can't even claim insanity as a defense anymore. The national statistics on this defense are bleak—less than twenty-five percent of insanity pleas win. We'd be taking a big risk, and if we lost, the jury might see her as calculating. She could end up with an even longer prison sentence." Julian tries to make eye contact with both David and Angie, and Angie finally raises her eyes to look at him.

Martine adds, "I'm not sure that's the best outcome in Nora's case, anyway. If she's acquitted because of an insanity plea, she'd be committed to a state psychiatric hospital for treatment, and that commitment is indefinite."

"What do you mean, *indefinite*?" asks David.

"She wouldn't be released until the doctors and the courts agree she's stable and safe enough to reintegrate into the community."

"And how long is that?"

"It can be a long time," says Martine, "because Colorado's insanity statute doesn't have mandated timelines for these steps. She'd have group therapy for anger management, individual therapy for past trauma, and meds for the psychosis and depression, at least in theory, but she could be there for decades. The Colorado State Psychiatric Institute in Denver has a reputation for holding on to people for a long time, sometimes longer than they might have been in jail."

"Trauma?" asks David. "What trauma?"

"She'd get treatment," says Angie, "for something that was a mistake?"

Julian doesn't know what to make of Angie and David. They talk over each other, not to each other, as if the other isn't there. He almost wishes they'd disagree, so they'd at least acknowledge the other's relevance. He clears his throat.

"We have another issue to discuss. This morning the DA filed to transfer Nora's case out of juvenile court and into the district court so he can charge her as an adult." Julian twirls his pen on his finger, a habit he picked up in law school.

"But she *is* a juvenile," says Angie, following his pen with her eyes. "She's a child. A thirteen-year-old child. I don't understand." She looks at Julian with an emotion he can't discern. When they were together, he always knew what she was thinking, but that was a different life. Now he wishes he were a mind reader.

"So the sentence we just discussed—a maximum of seven years in a juvenile correctional facility—it'd be more, right?" says David.

Julian nods. "I know it doesn't seem fair, Angie. And it's not. But Colorado law does permit this. In New York, things are even worse. If a thirteen-year-old is charged with murder, they're *automatically* charged as an adult. At least here we have a shot at defeating Gil in the transfer hearing, which is why we'll fight so hard on this. And yes, David, if she's tried and convicted as an adult, the sentence could be more than seven years. She could be sentenced to life in prison, with parole not possible for forty years. And depending on available space, she might have to serve her sentence in an adult penitentiary instead of the juvenile system. If so, she'd be segregated from the general population until she turned eighteen, basically in solitary, so we'd have to fight that, as well."

Angie squeaks like a terrified mouse and covers her mouth with her hand. David's face remains impassive and he does nothing to reassure her. Even when they were kids, Julian felt antagonized by David. He skulked around playgrounds as if he'd been forced to pretend he liked playing, and as a teen, he liked getting Julian in trouble, especially on the ski team, where he reported each of Julian's pranks to their coaches. Now Julian wants to poke a hole in that impassive face to see if it will pop or deflate, or at least to comfort Angie if David won't. He stops himself from reaching out to touch Angie's arm, because it's no longer his place. She's no longer his person and he's no longer hers.

"I know it's terrifying," he says instead.

"What about—this is a capital crime, right? If she's charged as an adult, what about the death penalty?" Her voice is soft but doesn't falter.

"No," says Julian. "Oh my God, Angie. No. That's not a possibility because of her age. In 2005, the Supreme Court banned capital punishment for people who committed crimes before they turned eighteen. She's—she's safe from that."

Angie's crying now, her shoulders heaving in relief.

"Is the timeline in district court the same as it was in juvenile court?" David asks. "Will this still be resolved in six months?"

"No. That six-month time frame is just for the juvenile system." Martine reaches out and touches Angie's hand. "It could take a couple of years, maybe more."

"Years," repeats Angie.

"So the dates you gave me," says David, "the ones I put on the calendar on my fridge?"

Martine shakes her head. "No longer relevant, unless Gil Stuckey loses the transfer request at the preliminary hearing. Like Julian said, we'll have to fight hard."

"If he wins at the transfer hearing and does charge her as an adult, our best option is to avoid a trial by negotiating a plea agreement," says Julian. "We'll have more certainty and avoid any wildcards the DA might throw at Nora. It would be a compromise—she'll definitely serve time—but she's going to prison no matter what. The question is for how long."

The meeting takes over four hours because Angie keeps asking the same questions and Julian answers as best he can, every time, even though David keeps looking at his watch. When they're done, Martine schedules their next meeting and explains that Julian will fly back and forth from New York to handle Nora's case.

"You can call either of us," Martine adds, "but he's the expert here, so you might want to try him first."

Under the table, Julian wrings his hands together, trying to stop them from trembling, whether from anger or annoyance or the strain of being near Angie, he isn't sure.

Julian settles back into Lodgepole more easily than he thought possible. Martine redecorated his room long ago but left some of his old belongings in the closet: hiking boots he outgrew in high school, a paper-mache pirate he made from a water bottle in seventh grade, a shoebox diorama of the Lorax from third grade. The things she kept were oddly comforting, a walking path through his childhood. In town, he meets people's eyes and smiles, something no one does in New York. A few recognize him and smile back or stop to talk, and no one looks at him strangely or mentions the past. Town is filled with new people and new houses. There's a clear divide now between locals, the people who send their kids to Lodgepole High School and have appointments with the town's pediatrician, and the second-home owners, the ones who use their seven-thousand-square-foot houses once a year. Some locals are "new" and moved here ten years ago. When he gets coffee from the coffee cart on Main Street, he can tell the new locals don't know what to make of him. "You're from here?" they ask, raising an eyebrow or looking up and down the street, as if they might find someone to confirm or deny his claim, a librarian who issued him a library card or a postal worker who witnessed him mail a package. The second-home owners see him as one of them. It could be the haircut or his shoes, who knows, but they ask where he's from ("New York"), who he uses as the caretaker for his house (he deflects), and their voices change, just a little, when he says he was born here.

Every day after he buys his cappuccino, he does legal research and searches for Colorado precedent that might help Nora's case, then emails the DA to see if they can meet to discuss a potential plea deal, but Gil Stuckey doesn't respond until two days before the November 17 preliminary hearing. Even then, he refuses to meet. Their phone call is brief and depressing.

"I'm not interested in negotiating," Gil Stuckey says flatly. "Why would I be?"

"Because Nora is a thirteen-year-old who made a terrible mistake, not a hardened criminal. She's never been in trouble with the law, never been caught shoplifting or drinking. She never got in trouble in school. There's no evidence of premeditation, no history of violence. All you have is what happened that night."

"I guess I see it a little differently," says Gil. "In the eyes of the law, she's a cold-blooded murderer who didn't hesitate to kill her brother."

"These kids were basically twins. They did everything together," says Julian.

"That doesn't mean anything. Maybe she got mad at him for stealing an Xbox controller or harbored some jealousy about who the parents loved more. I don't know yet."

"There's no way this was an intentional, premeditated homicide. The shooting was either a mistake or caused by a major mental health issue." Julian tries to disclose just enough to let Gil Stuckey know it will be difficult to convince a jury that Nora's a monster, but not so much it ruins their case. He also wants to head off another line of inquiry, one that's unlikely but he still wonders about: Was this a mercy killing? Gil probably wouldn't consider this because he clearly sees only the worst in everyone, and the impetus for a mercy killing, however misguided, is kindness—wanting someone to avoid pain. But if he did consider it, it would be a disaster: Nico wasn't that sick, not yet, and Gil would see it as an admission of premeditation and intent, making it easier for the first-degree murder charge to stick.

"All I know is she needs to pay for her crime, like every other criminal out there. There's no way I'm going to send a message that we aren't tough on crime in San Moreno County." There's finality in his voice, like the conversation is over, and Julian wishes they were meeting in person instead of talking on the phone, so he could stare down this idiot.

"I think it would be beneficial for us to meet so I can at least give you Nora's mitigation presentation and you can see what I'm talking about."

"Look, Mr. Dumont, I'm gonna be honest with you. While I appreciate that you used to live here in San Moreno County and that your mother still does, you can't actually believe you can show up from the big city and tell me what to do."

Julian hesitates before answering. Gil Stuckey doesn't live in Lodgepole and isn't technically from San Moreno County, either. He's from Denver but bought a ranch outside of Waring so he could claim county residency and get elected as DA. It would be a mistake to aggravate him by calling out his hypocrisy.

"Mr. Stuckey, I would never presume to tell you what to do," he says instead, hoping his voice sounds polite. "I only wanted to meet before the hearing to see if we could resolve this without the court expense for the state and the Sheehan family."

"That's not going to happen."

Julian hears a click and wonders if he's imagining that the DA didn't have the decency to say goodbye. He's looks out on Main Street from his mother's leather chair, resigned to what will likely be initial failure on Nora's case.

The day after the preliminary hearing, Julian and Martine sit at the kitchen table, dejected. Judge Castro held the transfer hearing at the same time and issued both decisions this morning. Nothing unexpected happened. Judge Castro ruled the case had probable cause to proceed and in favor of transferring the case to district court. Angie cried, David stayed impassive, and Julian felt like he'd been punched in the gut. In the 1990s, criminologists and politicians propagated a myth that some juveniles, so-called super-predators, were about to unleash a national crime wave and were so irredeemable that treating them as minors didn't make sense. In response, most states enacted laws that allowed, and sometimes required, young teens, sometimes even children, to be charged as adults and exposed to adult sentences, including life without parole. He's been fighting the legacy of that myth his entire career and thought the country had come further than this.

"Did you think you'd come here and turn the case around in just a couple of weeks, that you'd be Nora's savior?" Martine says it kindly, but Julian feels like an idiot. "You know better than I do it doesn't work that way. Be patient. These cases take time."

"Your DA is awful," Julian says. "I never expected Gil to take his threats this far."

"He wasn't always like this. We were on a bar association committee, years ago, maybe in the midnineties, to put together a continuing legal education retreat for new lawyers. He was—I don't know, just a regular guy. He bought donuts for the staff, joked around, did his fair share of work. Decent enough. We weren't that friendly, but I didn't dislike him. His brother was stabbed in a bar fight, though, and it changed him. He quit showing up to meetings, resigned from the committee, and dropped out of teaching the class he was supposed to teach at the retreat. Now he's . . . he is what he is, I guess."

Julian raises his eyebrows. "He's a little much."

"We'll keep working on him."

"He's everything I've spent my career fighting against. I thought— Jesus, I don't know. The number of kids being charged as adults is declining in most states, but this—"

"Go for a walk," interrupts Martine. She sips her tea, then adds, "Clear your head so you're in the right frame of mind before you meet with Nora tomorrow."

"Come with me. You need to clear your head, too." Julian pushes back from the table and pulls his coat from the closet.

Martine shakes her head. "I'm exhausted. Take Jack to keep you company, and I'll get dinner started." She pushes her chair back from the table, too, but when Julian shuts the front door, she's still sitting and her head is in her hands.

In the cemetery, he visits Cyrus's grave first, because he hasn't seen it yet and he's not sure he has the energy to also visit Nico's and Diana's. Three might be too many in one visit, and even though he should visit Diana's, just to prove the specter of her death isn't as threatening as it used to be, he doesn't want to add shame and remorse to today's emotions.

Cyrus's gravestone is polished and simple, just the way he would have wanted it. No muss, no fuss, he used to say when Julian was little. His life's motto. Sometimes Julian forgets it's less than two years since he lost the man that acted as his father for all but the first year of his life. No matter how angry he'd been with Cyrus for siding with Martine and sending him away, Cyrus was a good father, and Julian wishes he'd let the past go sooner, not just for his mother's sake but for Cyrus's. Now it's too late.

Jack zooms in front of him, running in crazy circles, then stops and lifts a leg on Cyrus's gravestone.

"Jack! Bad boy!" he yells. He rushes at Jack to push him away but somehow trips and ends up on the ground, cursing himself for his clumsiness. Then, though he's not sure why he needs to, he apologizes. "Sorry, Dad. Jack doesn't mean anything by it."

He wanders away from Cyrus's grave, rubbing his elbow, and eventually finds Nico's. Two coyotes skulk in the distance, yipping, and another, invisible somewhere in the trees, responds. Blood drips from the face of the closest one; they must have just killed something.

The dirt mounded on top of Nico's grave is still just dirt. Grass won't grow over it until spring. There's a handprint where Nico's heart would be, as if someone had come and pressed a hand into the earth, trying to feel what's underneath, a heartbeat or a soul or anything other than a casket and a lifeless body. He and Mayumi are struggling to have children—originally the doctors thought it was Mayumi's age, but now they're pointing their fingers at Julian, claiming he has poor swimmers, an athletic insult for the precursor of a child that might never be, and who knows if the latest implanted embryos, this time fertilized with donated sperm, will take—but Angie's grief for her dead son tugs at him and he turns away.

Silence stretches through the cemetery, and Julian realizes he hasn't heard Jack or the coyotes for a few minutes.

"Jack!" he calls. He starts jogging toward the gate, searching for the dog's shape in the distance. "Jack!" His heart pounds, but he hears a whine from the other side of the cemetery and turns in that direction. Shit, fuck, goddamn it.

The whine intensifies, and he speeds up, but his feet are still clumsy, and he realizes he'll fall again if he's not careful, so he slows, then frantically calls Jack's name. If the coyotes ate Jack, his mother will never forgive him. And then, all of a sudden, there's Jack, a bloody bone in his mouth, sitting on top of Diana's grave, whining not in fear but with joy. It's a huge bone, maybe from a deer leg. It probably took the entire coyote pack to bring down a deer, and Jack is lucky they didn't kill him when he stole the bone, although maybe they were more interested in fresh meat than a canine thief.

When he approaches to take the bone away, Jack pulls his lips back and growls, incisors bared, blood dripping down his chin the same way it dripped down the coyote's.

Chapter Nine

Winter hits Colorado hard in late November, temperatures hovering far below normal. Inside the juvenile detention center, cold permeates the cinderblock walls, the cement floors, and the bunk beds' metal bars. There are no soft surfaces in the common room Nora shares with her pod—even the chairs and couches are made of a smooth, molded plastic—and the hard surfaces hold on to the chill long after a girl sits down. After mothers or fathers or guardians walk through the lobby's metal detector, they put their jackets back on and keep them on during the visit. When they return to their car, they turn the heat on full blast, or if they took a bus, sit by the heat vent. At the end of the day, the guards go home and eat soup for dinner or hop into a hot shower. The girls wear their sweatshirts and socks all the time, something they would never do in real life, and bury themselves under their blankets to sleep. The unfortunate girls new to the detention center, the ones who go through intake with the surly female guard who greets every newbie with a frown and furrowed eyebrows, endure the humiliation of the strip search with goose bumps that rise in protest from naked skin. The warden can't seem to get the temperature right, though, because three days later the temperature inside spikes and the sweatshirts and jackets come off, a reverse osmosis of clothing.

When Julian meets with Nora, sweat beads gather on both their foreheads, droplets so small they're almost invisible. Even the Coke cans, chilled from the vending machine, sweat. When he hands her the painting supplies he always brings, she wets the paintbrush by brushing it up and down the aluminum.

"You can paint while we talk," he says. "We have a lot to discuss, so it'll take a while."

Nora nods, probably out of habit. There's always a lot to discuss, only she's never part of the discussion. She keeps nodding and occasionally grunts "uh-huh." She hears "charged as adult" and "jury trial instead of adjudicatory trial" and "still trying for plea agreement," but focuses on getting her owl just right while Julian focuses on figuring out whether or not she's listening. Occasionally he scribbles something on his yellow pad, and eventually the corners of her mouth turn up slightly, almost a smile.

"What's so funny?"

"Your handwriting."

"It's pretty bad," he says. Her hallucinations and catatonia seem to be controlled by medication now—either that or the shock of what she did has worn off—but this is the first time he's seen her amused. "Maybe because I'm left-handed."

"Like Nico," she says. "He was left-handed, too."

"They call people like us southpaws."

"Why?"

He stops and looks up at the ceiling, then shrugs. "Baseball, I think. Something to do with where the left-handed players hit the ball. But I never liked baseball, so I'm not sure. It's just what people always called me." He peers down at her painting. "Your mother says you like Harry Potter. Is that one of the messenger owls from those books?"

"It's just an owl."

"Do you like owls?"

She shrugs. "Not because of Harry Potter. My mother doesn't know anything. They're hunters, good hunters."

"I guess you're right. We just never see them hunt because they do it at night." He twirls his pen on top of his finger, looks at the ceiling again, then adds, "And they mean different things to different cultures. In Japan, owls are said to bring good luck and offer protection from suffering."

"Nico liked them," she says. "He liked falcons more, but he always said owls were smart."

Julian looks at her and nods but doesn't say anything. He looks like he expects her to keep talking.

"He liked smart people, too," she finally says. "That's why he was so sad about getting Huntington's. He was going to end up with dementia like our grandmother. He wasn't going to be smart anymore."

He keeps twirling his pen, back and forth on his finger, looking at her with curiosity, so she leans back over her painting and sketches out tufts of feathers for the owl's horns.

Girls who've been at the juvenile detention center long enough claim memories of life *before* seem like a movie, or a book they've read but can't remember very well. This is as true for Nora as it is for every other girl there. Every day, she wakes up in her bunk bed in a room she shares with three other girls, goes to classes or group therapy, eats runny scrambled eggs or soggy grilled cheese or spaghetti that tastes nothing like what her Grandma Livia used to make. She walks around the yard outside, following the edge of the chain-link fence, and pretends it's not topped with barbed wire. Sometimes a plastic bag blows in, detritus from the outside world. If it makes it over the wire, she watches it float in the air, up, down, and around as though it's a bird playing on a wind current. If an airplane flies overhead, Nora and the other girls stop and crane their necks skyward, following the metal birds carrying people to far-off places, the contrail an elusive and fleeting path to other lives. At the end of the day, Nora goes to sleep in the same bunk bed she woke up in. This routine feels like all there ever has been, all there ever will be.

All that remains of Nora's life before are a man and a woman, a father and a mother, who sometimes visit. They talk about the weather and TV shows, bring her food from the vending machine, then leave. The father smiles, but his face is empty, blank. It's not a real smile. The mother gives her pointers on painting and talks about the detention center's weekly art class as though it's an art class in a real school. They never mention why Nora is here, never speak of Nico. They never talk about the family Nora used to be a part of. It's as though her past no longer matters or has been erased.

Except it *does* matter, because that past is why she's here.

One day when Nora meets with the detention center's psychiatrist, he asks, "How do you feel about your brother being dead?"

He scrunches his face when he says *dead*, as if he's the one who's sad. Trying to act empathetic, trying to care—it's the best he can do most days. He travels between four juvenile detention centers and three adult prisons and barely has time to skim a patient's file before the ten-minute appointment. He never has time to learn their names. It doesn't matter, though, because he's not their therapist. He only has to know enough to prescribe the right medication, and since almost every kid in the penal system is on some kind of medication, he needs only a question or two to help him figure that out.

"When you're dead," says Nora, "you don't have to be afraid."

The psychiatrist looks at Nora and Nora looks at the psychiatrist. He has pasty cheeks and his hair is yellow, not because it's blond but because it's greasy and old like the photos in her grandmother's house, and she folds her arms across her chest.

Strip searches, barbed wire fences and meetings with lawyers, cold beds and wrong medications. How does that change a thirteen-year-old child?

On Thanksgiving, there's a so-called special meal for lunch and dinner. The lunch meal, for parents and guardians, was one of two times a year siblings under eighteen were allowed to visit, except Nora no longer has a sibling. Dinner is exactly the same as lunch, only now it's leftovers and the families are gone. Nora and Jacqueline fill their trays and sit down at their pod's table. Paradise wants to do what she saw a family do on TV, a round of what they're thankful for before they eat, but no one wants to wait for gratitude because the food here is never warm enough and would only get colder, so they just start eating.

At Nora's house, everyone had a part to play on Thanksgiving. David woke early to wash the turkey, sauté the breadcrumbs and sausage and celery and shove it into the dead bird's belly. Sometimes it was a turkey he'd shot on a hunting trip, sometimes it was a turkey from Bea's Market. Angie peeled and mashed the potatoes, then baked the apple pie. Livia played cards with Nico and Nora, Go Fish when they were little and War when they were older. She used to make meatballs and red sauce to accompany the turkey, and cannoli for an extra dessert, but she stopped doing that once she moved to the memory care home. Sometimes Nico and Nora helped with the apple pie, and Nora loved to watch the apple skin's curlicue spiral to the ground and see who could make it the longest. If Nico was in charge of the cinnamon sugar, he sprinkled extra on the crust because Nora loved cinnamon sugar and Angie never used enough. He was like that, especially for Nora. The apple pie here doesn't have any cinnamon sugar on the crust, but Nora eats it anyway, the bites sticking in her throat when she thinks about home too much.

The bites of apple pie stick in some of the other kids' throats, too. This juvenile detention center houses delinquents from all over Colorado's Western Slope, from as far south as Cortez and Pagosa Springs to as far north as Craig, more than twenty rural counties. For some families, drive times can be five to six hours each way. Many struggle to afford the gas for such a long trip, and although some juvenile detention centers bus families to visit on the big holidays, this one doesn't. When Nora's parents visited during the special lunch, eleven o'clock to twelve-thirty, both Paradise and Jacqueline sat at a table with other kids because no one came to visit them. They pretended to not care, but the apple pie stuck in their throats anyway.

For more than a few of the kids, the apple pie simply tastes good.

These are the kids for whom a bed, three meals a day, and special food on Thanksgiving is a treat. Pulling a fire alarm in school for the third time or picking a fight with a teacher was a sure ticket to juvie, and they knew it. Most of these girls talk tough, but for some, juvie is a break from watching a father throw a mother into a wall or caring for younger siblings because their parents are high on meth.

Whether the apple pie is stuck in a girl's throat because it doesn't taste like home or because no one visited today, or isn't stuck at all, by nine o'clock they'll be in the same place they are every night: lying in a bunk bed, waiting for lights out.

In Nora's pod, Maria Elena is gone, and it's just Nora, Paradise, and Jacqueline sleeping in their room. A few days ago, Paradise moved to Maria Elena's old bed and told Nora and Jacqueline that Maria Elena had been sentenced to prison, "the kind of prison you should be scared of, because she had a terrible lawyer."

"Why?" asked Nora.

"Not everyone gets lawyers like you. Her lawyer never visited, not once," Paradise said. Her teeth were crooked, every one of them, and food gathered on the gumline and between her two buck teeth. She picked at something with her fingernail and then examined it.

"Couldn't she get a better one?" asked Nora. If Nora had been here more than once, like Paradise, she might have known not to ask this.

"Shit, Nora. Are you really that stupid? Not everyone can pay a lawyer, and even if she could've had a better one, she's not white, like you. She didn't get special treatment." She flicked whatever had been in her teeth in Nora's direction. Nora shrank back and pulled the blanket up to her chin. Maria Elena snored and sometimes talked to Paradise until late into the night, so Nora wasn't bothered by where Maria Elena was, as long as it wasn't here.

Tonight she stares at the ceiling, waiting for the day to end. After dinner, a guard—one of the nice ones—made popcorn and set up a movie for the girls to watch. They were all excited, except Nora, and she climbed into her bed instead. She can hear their laughter through the open door, and the unforgiving fluorescent lights illuminate flecks of dust hovering in the air. The space above her looks like it's twinkling, a sky full of stars in her narrow, windowless room. When Nora and Nico were little, they used to pretend each fleck of dust in their living room contained a whole world, alternate Earths floating around as though the living room were a universe. They gently blew dust particles to provide them with a specific home in this alternate universe, left toward the kitchen for a world of plentiful food, right toward the bathroom for watery worlds. They populated each speck with flying people and swimming cats, fluffernauts and uniphants, and Nico told stories of their births and deaths, of mothers and fathers and children with superpowers.

Finally, the overhead loudspeaker buzzes, the sign for lights out. The room dims and the dust particles fade. Nora closes her eyes against the darkness, tries to remember what her life used to be, and drifts off to sleep, a refuge from thoughts that clamor constantly in her head.

She almost never dreams. That's something her mother always did, gleefully telling the whole family about the strange places her mind went each night, sometimes good (somersaulting off ski jumps, something Angie couldn't do in real life) and sometimes bad (packing suitcases and finding there were more and more clothes to fit into smaller and smaller suitcases). Tonight, though, Nora falls into a restless sleep, tossed right and left by her brain's memories of dust particles and alternate worlds. When she startles herself awake, the room is still dark, still quiet. Her dream took her back to the living room at home. She could hear her brother laughing, smell Grandma Livia's red sauce cooking in the kitchen with garlic and oregano, and see the worlds on the pieces of dust. Only now she can't hold on to the dream, not long enough, and it disappears before she can reach out and touch Nico. It disappears the way her own world has disappeared, with no warning, and won't return even when she squeezes her eyes shut and promises God she'll be good, if he just gives her brother back.

Three hours away, up the lonely road that leads away from the detention center, through the city of Rimrock Junction and onto Route 52 for over a hundred miles, then up the San Moreno Canyon to the town of Lodgepole, Angie wakes from a dream at the same time as Nora. The house doesn't smell like it usually does on Thanksgiving night, hints of roast turkey still wafting through the house or burned pie crust because she forgot, again, to cover the edges with tin foil. She can't remember what they ate for dinner, but it wasn't a turkey stuffed with gratitude. She's panting, but she doesn't know why. The dream is gone, every detail erased, but she doesn't feel the normal residue of her dreams, no fear or anger or frustration, so she tries to slide back into the sweetness of wherever she was, the only escape she's had from the nightmare she faces in the real world.

The two of them lie in their beds in dark rooms, mother and daughter, bound by DNA and dreams and Thanksgiving, separated by blame and guilt and long, lonely roads.

Chapter Ten

1998–1999

The day of Julian's twenty-sixth birthday, his partner-mentor offered to take all the litigation associates out for drinks, not to celebrate Julian's birthday, which he didn't know about, but Julian winning his first argument in court. It was a small case, nothing important to the firm in terms of money or prestige, so Charlie had let him make opening and closing statements, and the judge ruled in their client's favor.

"A first-year associate, winning his first argument? This kid is going places," Charlie hooted. They were back in the offices of Simpson, Howard & Harrison, standing in the hallway. The firm leased out floors 25 to 43, and Charlie and his criminal defense group occupied the entire forty-third floor. Bland art covered the walls and stern carpet the floors. A few of the other associates and partners stuck their heads outside their offices and whistled.

Charlie play-punched Julian's shoulder, a little too hard, and Julian almost fell over, but he couldn't stop grinning. He couldn't wait to tell Angie.

"I've got conference calls now, but let's leave by five-thirty and head to the Greatest Bar on Earth to celebrate." Charlie ducked into his corner office with its view of the Brooklyn Bridge. The secretaries gave a polite clap before the clickety-clack of fingernails on keyboards started again.

"Which bar around here does he think is the greatest bar on earth?" Julian asked no one in particular. All the attorneys had disappeared back into their offices, but Charlie's secretary smiled at him from her cubicle.

"It's not which bar is the best, hon. That's its name: the Greatest Bar on Earth."

"Oh," said Julian. He was glad no one else had heard him ask that question.

"It's where he likes to go when he's in a good mood," she added, fingernails still clicking on the keyboard even though she was looking at Julian. "It's in the World Trade Center."

"Oh," said Julian again, this time deflated. He'd once promised to take Angie to the restaurant in the World Trade Center, and it felt wrong to go without her, even if it was just the neighboring bar. It was also in the opposite direction of Brooklyn, where he was supposed to meet her for dinner at eight o'clock. The restaurant, their favorite French place, was on Seventh near their new apartment, and he quickly calculated how much longer of a walk he'd have from the bar back to the subway station. If the subways were running on time and if Charlie didn't want too many drinks, he'd make it. He smiled at the secretary and ran to his office to call Angie and leave a message that he might be a little late.

Five-thirty came and went, then six o'clock. Finally, at six-thirty, Charlie opened his office door and shouted, "Time to go" as though he hadn't made everyone wait an hour. The partners had left, but the associates, who had no control over their work hours, stayed glued to their office chairs until they heard him bellowing in the hall. Julian liked Charlie—he never yelled about mistakes and always asked nicely when he made Julian work through the weekend, pretending Julian had an option to say no—but Julian and the other junior associates knew better than to ignore any of Charlie's directives, even the social ones. Recently divorced and in his midfifties, Charlie always forgot his associates had a life outside of work. Julian left one more message for Angie, then sprinted to catch up to the group walking over to the bar. He hoped she was still at the gallery to get it.

The Greatest Bar on Earth was busier than Julian expected, for a Monday night, and swankier than what he expected, for a bar. There was a dance floor and a DJ and a sign that advertised live music—classic funk— after nine o'clock. Charlie ordered double martinis for all seven of them, then clapped Julian on the shoulder again. His shoulder was getting sore from all of Charlie's celebrating, but he didn't mind the attention. Charlie got them a table next to a window, made a speech, then downed his entire martini. Most of the other associates sipped at theirs. Julian gulped his, hoping they would finish sooner rather than later, but Charlie ordered another round before Julian set his empty glass on the table.

"Excuse me," Julian said, "I need to use the restroom." He ran to use the house phone and tried to reach Angie again, this time at home, but had to leave another message.

Back at the table, three of the associates ogled the view, and the others scarfed down an order of french fries in a silver-footed bowl. Julian peered out the window and drank his second martini. A curtain of fog surrounded the building, but it was thin enough that the city lights below shined through in a hazy glow. He almost wished he had a camera to capture it for Angie, even though she hadn't enjoyed the view when they visited a few years ago.

"Julian," said Charlie. "We need to talk about your next case." He grabbed the last handful of fries and put them on his cocktail napkin. "How would you feel about handling a case solo?"

The room was either getting louder or the martinis were stronger than Julian realized. "Did you say solo?"

Charlie grinned. "I did. It's a *pro bono* case in New Jersey, but it'll be all yours. I'll advise when you need help."

Julian finished his second martini and leaned in. "What is it?" The other associates were on the dance floor now, jumping around to a re- mixed Beastie Boys song the DJ had thrown on, so it was just him and Charlie.

"It's a juvenile justice case. Well, sort of. He was a juvenile for the first two crimes, fourteen for the first and sixteen for the second, but twenty for the third."

"A three strikes case?" Julian sat up straighter. He'd worked on a couple during law school, but only on a team for a criminal law clinic. The clinic had worked on both three strikes cases and death row cases, and that work was what convinced him to become a defense attorney instead of following his classmates into corporate law. Three strikes cases involved people who had been convicted of three crimes, usually violent felonies, and were sentenced to life in prison with no parole. The disproportionate sentences were mandated by laws that eliminated judicial discretion for repeat offenders. He supposed it was better his first solo case was a three strikes case than a death penalty case. The stakes were still high, but if he failed, no one would die.

The waitress set down more martinis on the table, and Julian sipped at one, then drank the whole thing. It tasted like water; the bartender must have stopped adding extra gin. He couldn't believe his luck. This was everything he ever wanted as a lawyer: working for one of the city's best litigation firms, defending white-collar crimes during the day and handling important *pro bono* cases in his spare time. He'd spent the summer after his first year of law school at a firm that specialized in corporate law, but the work felt soulless. The second summer, he interned for Legal Aid and worked on criminal cases and housing complaints. He loved the thrill of helping people but couldn't have paid off his loans on that salary.

At Simpson, Howard & Harrison, he got the best of both worlds, and now it was getting even better: he would have a chance to help people who'd been unfairly treated by the justice system. He'd never had the opportunity to see how the scales of justice would have tipped for him after Diana died. The weed was Angie's, and it was her idea to smoke it. The alcohol was his, but Angie was the one who drank it. They were both supposed to be watching Diana, and because neither of them were, he rushed down the mountain to catch her while Angie vomited on the side of the trail. It was dark, and Diana was obscured by the lip he'd jumped. He'd hit her, but did that kill her or did she hit the tree and was that the proximate cause of death? Maybe if someone had weighed his involvement on those scales to see where his culpability landed, he wouldn't have ended up in this purgatory of not knowing, always wondering how guilty he was or wasn't, forced to leave Lodgepole, give up skiing, hide his relationship with Angie, and worst of all, keep the truth *from* Angie. *Pro bono* criminal cases would give him a chance to help someone who'd either been falsely accused, or maybe, because of racism or poverty or sheer bad luck, ended up facing consequences they never deserved. Maybe, by righting other wrongs, Julian could somehow atone for his own.

"Our client, Randall Martin, was convicted of being the lookout on a gas station robbery when he was fourteen. He was with three other people—all adults. When he was sixteen, his second conviction was for assault, though by most accounts it was self-defense," said Charlie.

Julian reached for the olive in one of the spare martinis, then took the whole glass. Angie would understand if he was late. This was important. "Shouldn't he have been sentenced as a juvenile?"

"He was after his first conviction. But he was automatically charged as an adult for the second one, and the DA refused to plead him down to a misdemeanor—which, by the way, would have kept the three strikes law from applying—because he claimed he was exactly the kind of superpredator that should be removed from the streets. He served his time for the assault and was released early for good behavior. The problem is, he was arrested a third time last year, when he was twenty. He and another guy were selling marijuana out of a car, and the other guy robbed and shot a grocery store clerk while Randy was selling pot in the parking lot. Because of the three strikes law, he was convicted and sentenced to life in prison without parole."

"For two crimes he committed as a kid? And wasn't he just selling pot for the third crime?" He heard the slurring in his words and caught himself. Charlie was huge, with a round middle and ruddy cheeks, and hard to keep up with when he took the associates out for drinks. Julian didn't want to seem drunk in front of him.

"Well, the DA claimed he was an accessory to robbery and attempted murder, even though the other guy corroborated that Randy was just selling drugs." Charlie finished the martini in front of him and wiped his upper lip. "It's an appeal. The odds are against Randy, but I think you can argue that juvenile convictions—especially for a fourteen-year-old who was probably coerced by adults—shouldn't be counted toward the three strikes."

"I'll give it my best shot." Julian glanced at his watch. "Umm, I need to go. I was supposed to meet Angie an hour ago for my birthday dinner."

"No shit," said Charlie. "Happy birthday, kiddo. Take off and I'll see you tomorrow."

Julian sprinted to Fulton Street and jumped on the C train, but by the time he got to Jean Marchand, it was almost nine-thirty. He could see Angie through the large glass window, sitting alone in the back at a table for six, not the table for two he'd expected. There were food scraps on all the plates except one, and dribbles of red wine at the bottom of some of the glasses. Three wrapped boxes and a gift bag sat on the other end of the table. He hadn't been late for just Angie. Dread rushed through him, a heaviness that sank down into his fingertips and drowned his prior euphoria. He stepped inside.

"Don't bother with excuses," she said, holding up a hand. Her eyes were red, like she'd been crying.

"Didn't you get any of my messages?"

"That you were going out for drinks and might be a few minutes late? Yes, I got that message. But it's nine-thirty."

"I thought dinner was just you and me?" He gestured at the empty chairs. "I'm sorry. I couldn't say no to Charlie."

"Actually, Julian, you *can* say no, especially on your birthday." She finished the wine in the glass in front of her and stood up. "This was supposed to be a surprise, but Caroline and Isha and Myles and Leela left. They all have work tomorrow. And so do I."

"Please, Angie. I'm sorry." He knew she could hear the slurring in his voice, and he cringed.

Angie sniffed the air and her face soured. "Grow up, Julian. We aren't in college anymore."

He hated that look on her face but grasped her hands. "I'm sorry, I really am. It was a work thing, celebrating my first case."

"You said that in your message."

"I have news about a case I get to handle on my own," he said. "Can we at least talk while I eat?"

"Fine," she said. She sat back down and smoothed her skirt. She only said *fine* when she was really angry. The days after she said *fine* were the days she refused to speak to him and pretended he didn't live in the apartment with her.

Julian kept his sigh to himself and opened the menu. He was sorry he was late, but she didn't understand what it was like to work in a law firm. And he'd won his first case. There was nothing wrong with a little celebrating.

Julian was right about the silent treatment. They spent the next three days avoiding each other, knocking on the bathroom door when they normally would barge in and brush their teeth while the other showered. The more she resented him for being late or for drinking (neither was sure which it was, and it was probably both), the more he resented her for resenting him. Part of the reason he always said yes to just one more drink was to avoid the full import of that look on her face. And the other reason, one he didn't want to acknowledge but couldn't ignore, was that sometimes Angie's face, her whole attitude toward their relationship, was a reminder of the secret he'd now kept from her—for her benefit as well as his—for almost a decade.

They circled round and round, anger building up the pressure inside the apartment like a bloating bubble about to pop. Angie couldn't stop thinking about what had happened, about the ruined surprise dinner, the money she wasted, money she couldn't afford to waste, the friends who sat waiting, but most of all, the nonstop work and the nonstop drinking. She'd never thought about it that way before, as *the drinking*, but once she started, she couldn't stop. She'd done her fair share of partying in college, especially freshman year. It was an easy way to rub away the past, to forget about Lodgepole and waiting tables at DeLuca's and her parents' disappointment that she was studying art in college. And most of all, to forget about what happened back in Lodgepole, so when she took Diana's picture out of her dresser drawer, it wouldn't hurt so much. The whole year had been a blur of cheap beer and hidden joints, fake IDs and grungy bars in Providence that accepted those fake IDs. But somewhere along the way, the ache for her sister lessened and she moved on. Why hadn't Julian moved on?

Idara once said her brother was an alcoholic, that he'd started drinking after a divorce and thrown his life away—he was fired from his job managing a restaurant, lost his apartment when he could no longer pay the rent, and was scorned by their parents, neither of whom drank. Now he crashed on Idara's couch or sometimes disappeared for days in a row, when she assumed he was on a friend's couch or maybe on the streets. Eventually Idara threatened to kick him out unless he started going to AA. He still wasn't sober—he'd tried five times but kept relapsing—and Idara spoke of it only in hushed tones. That was what Angie thought an alcoholic was: someone who'd lost everything.

But Julian hadn't lost everything. He had everything. And yet, something drove him to bury himself in drinking and work, as if he were blind to what he had. The two of them rented an apartment on the third floor of a brownstone that was almost in Park Slope. The backyard was tiny and overgrown, but they could see trees instead of a brick wall from their bedroom, and the kitchen had a full-sized fridge and a four-burner stove. They'd hung her paintings on the walls, and Julian had a closet full of navy suits he bought with his sign-on bonus and wingtips he shined every month and stored in a shoe rack by the front door. He celebrated with her the day she sold her first three paintings, acrylic on micro canvases to an anonymous buyer who saw them in a small show at a RISD alumnae gallery back in Providence, then bought a couple for his office. He was winning cases at work and his boss loved him. He talked about marriage and children and a real Park Slope brownstone with a trimmed backyard and a grill, but she wondered how he'd be able to make it to that future if he couldn't move beyond the past.

By Friday morning, she was tired of their silent apartment. She stood at the door after she slipped on the sneakers she wore so she wouldn't ruin her expensive-looking thrift store heels on her commute and cleared her throat. He looked up from the kitchen table, where he was drinking coffee and scanning the headlines.

"There's an exhibit opening tonight at one of the new galleries on Twenty-Fourth. It's photography, not painting, but I'd like to go. Do you want to come?"

Julian smiled and nodded. She stood awkwardly at the door, holding the handle with one hand. She didn't want to say she was sorry, because she wasn't. But she also didn't want to keep fighting. Then Julian did what he always did, stood and approached her, took her hands in his. They were warm, either from holding the coffee mug or just because he was always hot, always a degree or two warmer than the next person.

"I'm sorry," he said and wrapped her in his big bear arms. "I love you."

"I'm sorry, too," she said.

He grinned, that quick and mischievous grin that made others like him so much, that made him seem like he knew which corner to go around to find the fun trouble. "After the exhibit, we'll make up for real." His hands drifted down her back and began to pull up her skirt, and she swatted him away.

"After the exhibit. After work. After, after, after." She laughed and scooted out the door.

Julian arrived at the Slominsky Gallery on time and sober, and they walked into the first room to admire the photographs. The theme seemed to be discordance, the contrast of urban and rural. The photos were all hard lines and angles, skyscrapers like the Petronas Towers in Malaysia juxtaposed against the tallest trees in the world, redwoods in California and Himalayan cypress in Tibet, and macros of the metal and wood from those skyscrapers and trees. In the corner, a woman stood in impossibly

tight jeans and a purple velvet jacket; next to her, a man with bushy eyebrows and long ears clinked his beer bottle against hers.

"Oh my God," whispered Angie. "That's Andres Serrano."

"Who?"

"Andres Serrano. The photographer. He did that photo *Piss Christ*.
The one that caused so much controversy."

Julian looked baffled, then laughed. "Just hearing the name gives me
an idea of why it was controversial. You better not tell your mother about
that. I think she'd be offended."

"Angie!" she heard from behind. It was Idara, champagne flute in one
hand and clutch purse in the other. Her husband Jamie stood next to
her, six inches shorter but with hair that was six inches longer than hers,
almost to the middle of his back. "You must love this exhibit."

Angie nodded. "I do." She felt bright with excitement, inspired to go
spend the weekend working on her new piece.

Idara knew about their fight but didn't show it. She nodded at Julian.
"How's work?"

"Yeah, how are all the criminals?" asked Jamie.

Idara and Angie grinned. Jamie loved to tease Julian, and Julian almost always bit, eager to defend his clients not just in court but also in
public.

"They're not criminals yet, Jamie. They're innocent until proven
guilty."

Jamie sipped at his champagne. "You always say that."

"You give me a hard time, but both John Adams and Abraham Lincoln were once criminal defense lawyers, did you know that? And the
right to a criminal defense attorney is guaranteed in the Sixth Amend-
ment because our founding fathers thought it was important to not
railroad people accused of a crime. People need to be able to get a fair
trial, a fair sentence for their punishment, and fair treatment in general.
That's not possible without a good lawyer."

Angie stepped backward. She'd heard this banter before.

"He never lets up, does he?" asked Idara.

Angie inclined her head toward the next room and began walking.

"It's important to him. He feels like he's doing some good in the world." Julian talked about it all the time at home. Once, when she asked about his dedication, he'd referred to what happened with Diana, which made no sense, since that was an accident. All they'd done was fall behind; they hadn't done anything *criminal*. He'd looked strangled for a moment, then said exactly what she'd just said to Idara: it was his way of doing good in the world. She listened to his speeches, attended protests with him about conditions on Rikers, and sat at dinners while he and his co-workers complained about overreaching prosecutors. She loved his passion and agreed with the cause, but this night was supposed to be for her.

They stopped in front of a darkened photo that initially appeared to be a series of disappearing lines. All around them, conversations bubbled, including one about recent sale prices for photos in galleries across the city, tantalizing numbers Angie tried to ignore. She loved art, no question, but sometimes at exhibits, self-doubt plagued her. Did her art *matter* the way this work did? Her paintings didn't focus on identity politics or social critiques and it wasn't installation art that made bold statements or photography that inspired political backlash like *Piss Christ*. Sometimes finding meaning in her work felt like writing essays on Shakespeare back in high school. What could she say that hadn't been said before? Would her paintings ever matter to anyone but her? And if she never sold enough of her work to make a living, how could she keep painting?

"Actually," said Idara, "I wanted to talk to you about something else."

"These are aspens, not lines," Angie said, not really hearing Idara. The photo had been taken at night, in a tight grove. Moonlight shone from above—it must have been a full moon to be that bright, but the photographer had adjusted the exposure and the images were shaded so that from far away, it was impossible to tell you were looking at a tree trunk instead of a line. Through the aspens, empty space beckoned, the sky and more distant tree trunks blurred by the aperture into nothingness. There was no sense of scale, no way to know whether the photo was taken on the edge of a steep slope or in a valley, because only the endless aspens were visible. She felt a pang of longing for home, something she hadn't felt since the day she'd left for college, and closed her eyes against the pull.

"It's a brilliant photo," agreed Idara. "Listen, Angie. I have good news. Hobbs called earlier today. He finally agreed to do the exhibit of up-and-coming artists I proposed. He wants to title it 'Thirty Under Thirty.' This is a big deal."

Angie opened her eyes but held her breath. This was a big deal. Hobbs, the primary owner and Idara's partner at the gallery, was always afraid to do anything new. He was a relic from a different era, one who resisted change so fiercely he'd almost tanked his own gallery until Idara came along. He looked and sounded exactly like his name. British, portly, and short. He always wore a suit, regardless of how hot it was or who he was meeting with, his formality too ingrained to disregard. She was afraid to say anything, afraid to hope.

Idara grinned. "He wants to include one of your paintings."

Angie almost crushed the champagne flute with her bare hands. "Oh my God."

"God had nothing to do with this. This is all you and the strength of your work." She hugged Angie. "I'm really proud of you."

"Can I tell Julian?"

"Yes. We'll announce next week, so the news is about to be out anyway."

They found Julian and Jamie in the front of the gallery, right next to the open bar. Jamie was gesticulating wildly and Julian was laughing. They both had whiskeys in their hands; Julian's was almost empty. Angie was too excited to wonder what number this was; she grabbed the glass from his hands, gulped the last sip, and almost screamed the news.

The next morning, she called home after she and Julian had their coffee. They'd celebrated when they got back to their brownstone, drinking a bottle of champagne they bought from the liquor store above their subway stop. Her head hurt from the sweetness of whatever brand it was, so she swallowed two Tylenol and handed the plastic container to Julian as the phone rang on the other end. He shook his head and moved to the couch, where he stretched out with some files.

her from across the room. "And the show will be in early March, the height
of spring break. You'd miss so much business from the skiers."

There was silence on the other end, and the footsteps stopped, then:
"It doesn't matter, *carina*. I'm coming. I'll figure something out."

Angie's shoulders sagged. She couldn't believe she'd let her excitement overrule reason.

On the other end of the phone, her father cleared his throat. "But I have good news, too. In April, after the ski area closes and the tourists leave, we're closing the restaurant for a month to do something we've wanted to do for a long time. We're going to visit Italy."

"Oh, Dad," she said. "I'm so happy for you." She was also relieved, secretly. If they were closing the restaurant in April, there was no way they'd close it in March to come see the exhibit. Livia would never let them close twice in the same year.

"I want to see my brother in person once more, and the whole town will be empty since it'll be mud season here—we won't even miss any revenue."

"That's great, Dad. It'll be an amazing trip."

After they hung up, she felt Julian's eyes on her and knew what he'd say before he said it.

"It's time to tell everyone," he said. "Time to stop hiding. We need to tell our parents."

Two days after the exhibit at the Slominsky, she set her alarm for six o'clock in the morning and rushed to her studio. Early on Sundays, Angie had the place to herself. She shared it with three other painters, but they were night owls and she was an early bird. It was a cavernous, unfinished loft in Gowanus, and when all four of them showed up at the same time, they often ended up sprawled on the mangy couch in the middle of the room, smoking someone's pot, talking instead of painting. Sundays were better because there was no one there to distract her.

She set up quickly, eager to work. The possibility of, no, she reminded herself, *the reality of,* being included in the Thirty Under Thirty exhibit inspired her, and the black-and-white photographs of trees had reminded her she didn't need to avoid painting the natural world forever. She realized now why her abstract water series extracted water from nature and focused on urban scenes. Dissecting each aspect of what water could and couldn't do in the world was a way of separating herself from the natural world, maybe a way of reinforcing her divorce from Lodgepole. She was just as separate from her place of origin as water could be from its own.

Her paintbrush began to move almost of its own accord, bold strokes of raw sienna for the trunk; burnt umber, ivory black, and titanium white for the bark, the imperfections in the tree's skin enhanced by decades of life. Cadmium yellows and reds for the leaves, because maybe it was fall in Central Park, and a swirl of cobalt blue at the top, because the viewer, a seven-year-old girl, looked upward from the tree's tether to the sky. Diana, her forever muse. Angie didn't need to think, didn't need to plan out the next stroke or angle or shadow.

Hours later, the studio darkened and she stepped back and surveyed the canvas. It was still abstract, divorced from reality, but no longer divorced from nature. It reminded her not of Lodgepole but of Julian, and she felt comforted by the image. When they were teens, they loved to lie under the aspen grove off of Wolf Creek Trail. They'd started doing it in ninth grade, when they would ski out of bounds to escape their coach. The first time, they'd ducked a rope off the corner of Big Bend, the edge of the ski area's boundary. They'd been skiing in fresh powder all day, whooping and hollering at fat snowflakes, their coach just as excited as they were, and it was the last run so they knew he wouldn't care if they disappeared. Deep powder slowed their descent on the steep slope, and every so often one stopped to wait for the other so they didn't get separated. Julian, heavier and faster, did most of the waiting. One time, she found him flat on his back, staring up at the trees.

"Did you fall?" she'd asked.

"No, I'm just resting. Lie down with me—it's an amazing view." He pulled her down without waiting for her to bend down herself, and she laughed.

"Shh," he said. "Listen to the silence. Look at the shape of the branches against the sky, the snow falling from nowhere."

Julian was so rarely serious that she'd stopped laughing immediately, stopped joking, and lay her head back in the snow. Pillows of snow coated the branches, outlining the arboreal landscape in white. Fat flakes emerged from the gray sky above as if by magic, hundreds and thousands of them, unique crystals that were part of the never-ending metamorphosis of Earth's water. Mesmerized, they watched until they got cold, then stood up, brushed the snow off their ski pants and jackets, and started down the mountain again. Eventually the ravine spit them out onto a gentler slope just above the meadow by Wolf Creek Falls.

They'd skied the rest of the way down on a hiking trail in the almost dark, and afterward they couldn't stay away, in the winter or any other time. That spot felt like theirs and no one else's, and they started measuring the change of seasons by visits there. They knew from biology class that the grove of aspens was actually a single organism, hundreds of trees linked together by a tangled web of roots. In late spring, bits of red would simultaneously emerge from the pregnant buds, each tree signaling the end of winter in rhythmic unity. In July, they brought a blanket and picnic and stared up at green leaves swaying in the summer breeze. And in the fall, golden leaves colored in the sky and fell on them, rustling and crinkling the whole way down. Each year, fall's rustling gave way to winter's silence, imposed by heavy snowflakes that muffled the whole world, but by spring that frozen world thawed, the *plink-plink* of dripping water a prelude to the forest's summer symphony. The breeze wended its way through the aspens the way the seasons wended their way through Angie and Julian's relationship.

Angie couldn't remember the last time they'd gone there, but it didn't matter, because they continued their tradition here. They visited Central Park or the Brooklyn Botanic Garden and migrated from tree to tree, or sometimes sat on benches and craned their necks upward to stare at the leaves, outlined by whatever show the sky offered that day: serene, angry, or colorful. Julian had recently lost interest, but she didn't want to stop. Those memories were what birthed this painting. It was a part of their shared past they'd brought into the present, and she didn't want to give it up.

Angie looked at the little girl in her new painting and wondered what it would be like to come clean with her parents. Angie knew Julian would always feel terrible about the accident, but he didn't understand the magnitude of betrayal Livia would feel if she knew her daughter lived with the person she believed was responsible for Diana's death. And underneath Livia's certainty about Julian's culpability was Angie's uncertainty about her own, an uncertainty she couldn't shake even now. Had it been her fault, for getting the pot, then pushing Julian to smoke it? Julian's, for not skiing fast enough to catch Diana? Or Diana's, or nobody's? She still didn't know, but she didn't want anything to overshadow her relationship with her parents. It was an accident, something that happened that she couldn't change. It was easier to focus on the present and enjoy what she had rather than get mired down in the past.

She capped the paints, washed her brushes, then stood back to admire the painting once more. It was good, she could feel it. She pushed the easel into the corner, turned out the lights, and left to meet Julian at Oskar's Bar for french fries and a beer.

For the next few months, Angie and Julian alternated between fighting about how to handle Roberto's potential visit and avoiding the topic altogether. Angie spent all her time at the gallery with Idara, preparing for the exhibit, or working in her studio, painting. Julian worked as much as he always had, but his obsession with Randy Martin's three strikes case had hijacked his life.

"He's only twenty," he said to Angie for the hundredth time one Saturday morning in February. Angie groaned and pulled the duvet over her head. Sun streamed through blinds they'd forgotten to close last night, and she wanted to go back to sleep. She wished Julian did, too, so he would stop talking.

"Twenty," he repeated. "Not far from being a kid. He's been sentenced to life, and because he's not eligible for parole, he's basically been sentenced to die behind bars. Did you ever think about it that way? And—he didn't even commit the first or third crimes because he was an accessory!"

Angie rubbed her eyes and sat up. "Fine, I'll bite. How's the appeal going?"

Julian grinned. "I have a new strategy. In addition to the appeal, I'm going to fight his first conviction, see if there's a way to get that overturned, because he was fourteen. I might argue ineffective assistance of counsel, or see if there was overlooked evidence or whether I can argue crimes committed as a juvenile shouldn't count as strikes. Maybe there's a constitutional argument I can make."

"You mean the robbery conviction? The one where he drove the getaway car?"

"Yep."

"Sounds like a good plan," she said. "He's lucky to have you as his lawyer." She kissed him, then got out of bed and went to the kitchen to dump extra coffee grounds into the coffee maker. No matter how tired she was, she was going to her studio today. Her abstract tree painting with the little girl was almost done, and she wanted it to be perfect.

"I'm going to get this kid a new lease on life," Julian said. "I swear. There's no way I'm gonna let him rot in jail."

When the phone rang, the caller ID showed Angie's house and she assumed it would be Roberto, but there was a surprise voice on the other end.

"Mom?" she said uncertainly. Angie spoke to Livia every so often, but Roberto was the one who usually called.

There was hesitation on the other end, then this: "It's your father."

Angie could hear her mother sniffling, then blowing her nose.

"He's in the hospital and didn't want me to call. He woke up this morning and he was *giallo*, like egg yolk. All over."

"That's probably jaundice, Mom."

"No," snapped Livia. "It's more than that. *è cancro*. They scanned him, and the *cancro* is in the pancreas."

Angie dropped into a chair. Cancer. "But is he okay? Is it bad?"

"*Non so niente*, not yet. He's in the hospital all the way in Rimrock Junction, *e adesso hanno detto che lo devono trasferire all'ospedale di Denver perché ha bisogno di uno stent.*"

"A stent? For cancer?" This was more Italian than her mother had ever spoken to her, even after Diana died. More than she could fully understand.

"*Ho già detto che non so niente.* They said it will help with the *giallo. Chiudo il ristorante e vado con lui.* I will call *più tarde, dopo che hanno finito.*" Livia hung up without saying goodbye.

Angie looked at Julian, who'd lost his cocky grin.

"Your dad has cancer? What kind?"

"It's in his pancreas. But they're taking him to Denver for a stent because he has jaundice, so I don't really understand what's happening. Mom spoke more Italian than I know, but I think she's closing the restaurant and going with him."

"What should we do? Can we do anything?"

"I don't know." It sounded like the stent would help with the jaundice, and she wanted to see what the doctors said after that. She dropped her head into her hands, then stood up. "I need to go for a run. I can't just sit around and twiddle my thumbs while I wait for my mother to call."

"But—we need to do something. We should at least go research what this means."

She needed to move, not read about cancer. Her head was spinning, and she couldn't concentrate on anything if she tried. She pulled on leggings and sneakers without answering.

"I can't come with you, Angie," Julian finally said. "Charlie is expecting me in the office in an hour." He looked helpless, and for just a second, Angie wanted to slap him, though she didn't know why. She turned and left, letting the door slam behind her.

Without bothering to stretch, Angie broke into a run and headed toward Prospect Park. More than anything, she wanted to be home running up Wolf Creek Trail, not running in Brooklyn, watching the ground so she didn't step on a crack vial or holding her breath when the smell of urine got too powerful on a particular corner. Normally she loved the city and hated the thought of returning to Lodgepole, but today going home was all she wanted.

Pancreatic cancer. That was bad. She didn't know much about cancer. She didn't personally know anyone who'd ever had it. One friend's mother had breast cancer, and another friend's grandfather had lung cancer. She knew some cancers were worse than others, and that pancreatic cancer was one of the bad ones, but she didn't know what this meant for Roberto.

At Flatbush Avenue, she waited for the Walk sign, surrounded by families pushing strollers with bundled toddlers. At first she jogged in place, anxious to get off street sidewalks and onto the park's less crowded trails, but then she slowed and simply stood there. Something had just occurred to her, and she wondered if it had already occurred to Julian: there was no way her father would come to the exhibit's opening now. It was in two weeks, and while she didn't know much about pancreatic cancer, she knew Roberto would have surgery, then start chemo and radiation. He wouldn't be able to travel. Relief and guilt simultaneously flooded through her, like a muddy delta where a river meets the sea. She and Julian could continue to avoid telling her parents, but what kind of person would feel relief over a reprieve caused by her father's pancreatic cancer? She clenched her fists and sprinted across the street, past the now-blinking Walk sign, her feet pounding faster and faster on the hard sidewalk until her chest hurt and she couldn't run anymore.

Chapter Eleven

In December and January, Martine and Julian shared as many responsibilities on Nora's case as they could, but in practice, Julian ended up making decisions and attending meetings with Nora or the Sheehans, and Martine did the scut work. It was almost as if Julian were the partner and she the associate, even though he'd been practicing for only twenty years and was her son and she'd been practicing for forty-five and was his mother. Still, the arrangement worked, and it left Martine with time for legal research to incorporate into the case. She was grateful for Julian's help and knew she never could have competently represented Nora on her own. Gil Stuckey continued to rebuff their attempts to negotiate a plea deal, and a few weeks ago, she'd discovered why: there's a draft bill making the rounds at the Colorado Bar Association, a juvenile justice reform bill that would limit the ability of prosecutors to charge young teens as adults and create a system of alternative rehabilitation services, and he'd just been appointed the chair of the Colorado Prosecutors Council, the bill's main opponent. Knowing why he was treating Nora so harshly only confirmed he was likely to dig into his position, not back away from it, though. He still said he'd aim for a life sentence because of the brutal nature of the crime and because he claimed her silence immediately afterward demonstrated a lack of remorse.

Julian flew back and forth between New York and Lodgepole three times; he couldn't be away from Mayumi and his actual job all the time, and Mayumi had finally convinced him to see a physical therapist about his joint pain so he could run again. Even more importantly, he had to be there for Mayumi's OB appointments. It was early and still a secret, but Julian confessed the pregnancy after Martine found him browsing for jogging strollers on his laptop. Martine was careful to not ask too many questions and only visited the town's toy store when Julian was back in New York and couldn't catch her. She didn't want to jinx it, but she couldn't help herself—what she really wanted to do was stand on a street corner and yell *I'm going to be a grandmother!*—so she limited herself to amassing a hidden stash in her bedroom closet: four baby board books, a giraffe rattle, a set of old-fashioned wooden building blocks, and a fleece blankie.

People always try to find silver linings in bad things, and having Julian home was her silver lining in the Sheehan tragedy. It was almost like the years of estrangement never occurred. They talked about Diana's death and his departure from Lodgepole only once, Julian interrupting her apology with a shake of his head, then a hug. "It's in the past," he said. "Let's leave it there. I'm just glad we reconnected." Now, when he was home, Martine felt inklings of their mother-son bond again. Maybe it was strange to be united by both the cloud (their fight for Nora's fair treatment) and the silver lining (their excitement for his and Mayumi's pregnancy, a secret he and Mayumi shared with her and no one else because it was so early), but she couldn't ignore the good that had crept back into her life.

One night in February, a night Julian is in New York and she's alone in the house with Jack, she pushes Nora's file aside and pulls out an old family album to remind herself of what her little boys used to look like when they were babies, to remember that distant life when she could still pick them up and dream of what they might become. Gregory and his husband are also trying to start a family, looking at adoption and surrogacy, and she lets herself dream of filling a future photo album with new pictures of little boys and girls, grandchildren of her own after spending so much time thinking that would never happen.

Jack, sleeping next to her on the couch on his back, pink tongue hanging out the side of his open mouth, didn't exist in this old album's world. Back then, the boys ruled her and Cyrus's world. The yellowed photos, shot when retakes were rare because of the cost of film, caught an imperfect but happy family, with blinks, smiles, and scowls. Julian and Gregory, playing in a sandbox in the backyard, Gregory so small that Julian half buried him for fun. Julian, maybe ten years old, trying on new skis he found under the Christmas tree, smiling above his dimpled chin, and Gregory setting up an Incredible Hulk game on the floor under him. In later pictures, Julian and Cyrus, standing over a sink, Cyrus demonstrating how to shave the peach fuzz from Julian's upper lip, and a second picture of Julian, bending over a sink, pointing at the almost nonexistent hairs he thought he saw in the sink's basin. In all the pictures, Julian and Gregory have smooth cheeks, plump with childhood sweetness that used to prompt her to plant kisses on their foreheads, and full heads of hair. Now Gregory's black hair has morphed into salt and pepper, and Julian's blond hair is thinning. She can't help wondering if their metamorphoses on the outside reflect what happens on the inside, whether Julian's thinning hair is a sign of what was taken from him, of things he can never get back.

Jack rolls over and knocks Nora's file off the couch, and when Martine bends over to pick it up, a family picture of the Sheehans falls out, an old one. Nico must have been seven or eight, Nora a year younger. Angie had given her this one so she could remember Nico as he was. "And Nora," Martine had added, and Angie had smiled and touched the picture.

"Yes," she said. "And Nora. All of us." Angie is clear-headed most of the time now, her high-pitched anxiety dispatched by numbness—or maybe she's just acclimated to her new reality—and she said it with sadness instead of frantic desperation.

Nora and Nico are shoving each other in this picture, Nico pinching her belly and Nora laughing. They exude the same childhood sweetness she saw in Julian and Gregory's photos—the same sweetness every child carries before the world damages them or they damage the world—with blond and red hair instead of blond and black. Yet, more has been taken from them than from Julian and Gregory. Much more. She studies the picture carefully, running her finger over Nico's face, and wonders: How would he have grown, who would he have become, if only he'd had the chance?

On her way to bed, she's too tired to avoid the creaky step Julian always skips, her fatigue a constant companion ever since David pounded on her door last October. She closes her bedroom door and turns the ceiling fan on high so she can sleep. If David comes knocking with another emergency, she doesn't want to hear him.

The next morning, Julian calls her cell just as she lets the dog out to pee. It's 5:30 a.m. and she's too tired to take Jack to the cemetery for a walk. She's standing at the open door, hoping the cold air will wake her up, but she's starting to realize this might not be fatigue from Nora's case.

"Gil finally called back," he says.

"And? Any progress?" Standing on the walkway because he's too lazy to walk over to the grass, Jack barks insistently, and Martine peers past him into the darkness. Eyes glow in the field across from her house. Lots of eyes, not just one set of them. Judging by how low to the ground they are, it's not a herd of elk, so she assumes they're coyotes skulking around.

"No. I almost wish he wouldn't have called. At least then I could still hope he might show mercy to a thirteen-year-old girl."

Martine's chest tightens and Julian's words fade, and suddenly she knows: this isn't stress or a reaction to Gil's refusal to negotiate. She feels dizzy and backs up into the house to sit down without answering Julian or closing the door.

"Mom? Are you there?"

She clutches at her chest, grunts, and sags lower in her chair. "My heart," she whispers, then hangs up and dials 911 before she passes out.

Jack scampers inside and whines. He sniffs at Martine, whines again, then trots to the doorway, where he stands to guard Martine against the eyes in the field.

On the other end of the phone, panic rises in Julian, and he almost spills coffee on his latest death penalty file. The breathlessness, the fatigue, the sunken eyes. It's been her health all along, not age or anxiety. He returned home for work and his own medical tests, for something that was probably nothing, and now he's two thousand miles away and can't help her. She's his mother, older than him, more fragile. Why hadn't he forced her to see a doctor, focused on her instead of himself? There's a dial tone on the other end because she's hung up or already died, who knows.

By the time he calls the Lodgepole police to send an ambulance, runs home to pack, takes a cab to LaGuardia, and texts Mayumi about his last-minute departure, two hours are gone. Martine hasn't returned his texts and no one from the hospital has called. So much time has passed since he lived in Lodgepole that he no longer knows anyone's number to call. The only people he knows are Angie and David, but he can't call them for help with his emergency when he's supposed to be helping them with theirs. He finally calls the hospital's general number and is patched through to a nurse who only says, in a terse voice that might or might not be kind, "It's her heart. They're working on her." While he's waiting to board his flight, he calls every doctor friend he knows, and they all say the same thing: don't panic. She could already be dead, but she's not, or they would have told you. Maybe she just needs a stent. *Or maybe*, he thinks, *a bypass or something worse*.

Julian has been through this before with Cyrus, but that second heart attack killed him so quickly he was dead by the time Julian received the call. And Julian didn't remember his biological father—Theodore, now nothing more than a name, was killed when he tripped on the sidewalk and fell into oncoming traffic before Julian's first birthday—so Cyrus's death was his first experience with the pain of losing a family member, the grief of never being able to hug them again. He was sad when Diana died, but she was Angie's little sister, not his, and he'd been consumed by guilt and shame, not grief. There was Angie, of course, but he lost her to his own stupidity, to his failure to recognize that sometimes there's a limit to forgiveness, and he always knew she was still out there, her heart beating somewhere in Colorado. He isn't ready to lose his last living parent.

When the flight descends into Lodgepole, he ignores the view and the skiers' voices rising in excitement and turns his phone on as soon as he thinks there might be service, even though the plane hasn't landed. His phone immediately sounds, a series of dings and chimes he doesn't think to silence until the man next to him gives him a dirty look. Mayumi, his secretary, more of his doctor friends, a long voice mail from the hospital saying Martine is out of surgery. And a text from Angie: she's waiting for him outside the airport.

He pushes the airport door open and steps, blinking, into a winter sunlight reflecting off a glare of snow and metal. That Angie would be here to pick him up never would have occurred to him, but there she is, waiting on the sidewalk, hands stuffed into jean pockets, jacket unzipped.

"Jennifer—you remember her from high school? She's a nurse at the hospital. She called me because she knew from the news that your mother represents Nora." Then she adds hurriedly, "She knew she wasn't supposed to, so don't say anything."

"But how did you know what flight I'd be on?" He feels tongue-tied and awkward in an unexpected way. They haven't been alone together yet, haven't had a conversation that didn't revolve around Nora and Nico.

"I called your office in New York and convinced your secretary to tell me."

"Did Jennifer know anything about my mother?"

"She's okay, Julian. She'll be okay. She's not—She'll be okay."

Tears well up in his eyes, tears he doesn't want Angie to see since her family is not okay. Angie's kindness hits him as hard as knowing his mother isn't dead.

"They put a stent in," says Angie. "She didn't need to have a bypass or anything like that."

Julian tries to swallow the lump in his throat.

"But, Julian—there's damage to her heart. I guess there was something wrong for a long time, and she ignored the symptoms, you know? She has some heart failure, and she'll have to do cardiac rehab and stay home for a few months while she recovers."

She reaches out and hugs him, the thing he's wanted to do for her since that first meeting about Nora but never could, not with David there, not in front of his mother. She's on tiptoes, standing almost as tall as him, her smaller body somehow enveloping his, pulling his head into the crook of her neck. The memory of what this feels like, of a comfort he took for granted so many years ago, floods his dazed brain with emotions.

"I'm sorry, Angie," he whispers. "For Nico and Nora, for what you've been through and for—for everything. I'm so, so sorry." He pulls his head back; tears gather in her eyes, pools above dark circles and below now-deep worry lines. He bursts into his own tears, tears of both relief and grief, and they stand entwined on the sidewalk, tourists hurrying by to start their vacations with wheeled suitcases and overstuffed ski bags.

Martine's room is on the west side of the hospital, the window facing Miner's Peak. By the time they arrive and finish talking to the doctor, the sinking sun drapes her room in a pink glow. She's awake, and her eyes light up when he walks into the room with Angie.

"I thought you'd be—"

"Dead?" Her voice is slow and still a little slurred from the anesthesia, and she smiles ruefully. "You can't get rid of me that quickly, Julian. I'm old, but not that old."

"No," he says, rushing the words, "I thought you'd be asleep, or sedated with pain meds, or—I don't know, on a ventilator or something. Are you okay?"

"It was just a stent, so all they gave me was Valium," she says. "Seems like it should have been more, doesn't it?"

He reaches out and hugs her gently, feeling a rush of relief. There was a time, a time he has no memory of but knows existed, when his mother was his whole world, when it was just the two of them. A time between his two fathers, before Gregory was born, before they left New York. A picture of this time sits on top of Martine's piano. She's on a park bench, jiggling him on her lap, smiling down at him as he reaches for her face. He supposes he was her whole world, too. He sits on the edge of the chair next to the bed, still clasping her hand. "I told you you needed to see a doctor, Mom. No more lawyering for a while. You need to reduce your stress."

She holds her hand up in his face, the same hand signal she gives Jack for *stop*. "We are not doing that right now. Health problems are normal at seventy-two. I know I should've paid attention to this sooner, but I'm here, I'm okay."

There's silence in the room.

"I'm great, actually, because of the Valium," she adds. Her face is wan and the crepey skin around her eyes is tighter than usual, but her mouth is relaxed. "Let's talk about something else."

"I should go," says Angie, backing out of the room. "I just gave him a ride from the airport."

"Stay," says Julian, pulling another chair closer to Martine's bed. "We can talk about Nora, next steps."

"No," say Martine and Angie at the same time, then they smile at each other.

"Jinx," says Angie.

"Something fun," says Martine, closing her eyes in a long blink, then opening them. "You just told me no more lawyering. How's the skiing this year?"

It's Angie's turn to look rueful. "I haven't skied in a couple of years. I'm so out of shape I'd probably crash if I tried anything too challenging."

"Do you remember the year when Julian crashed on the last day of the season wearing nothing but his tiny Speedo bathing suit?" asks Martine.

Angie laughs, the first time Julian has seen her face light up since he started working on Nora's case, the first time she's done anything to indicate she's still who she used to be, and his relief at seeing her this way overwhelms his anxiety about discussing skiing—and crashing while skiing—in this room with these two people.

"Yes! We were sophomores, and the whole team was wearing bathing suits on a dare from the coach. Julian was grandstanding, flying off every jump, doing spread eagles and three-sixties, but he landed wrong. It was a complete yard sale—his poles and skis ended up all over the slope."

"And it was right under the lift," admits Julian. He can still remember how embarrassed he was. People on the chairlifts hooted and hollered as he gathered his poles and the ski closest to him and then skied down on one ski to the other that had slid a hundred yards down the trail.

"You came home with a very bruised ego," giggles Martine.

She's clearly still high on the Valium if she's giggling like a little girl about ski crashes, but maybe the laughter is good for her. Julian wonders something he hasn't allowed himself to wonder in a long time: What would his life have been like if Diana hadn't died? He's learned to live with the sting of her accident and death, but it's been a long time since he thought about skiing. He and Mayumi take vacations to Florida and Japan, and sometimes to Vermont to look at changing leaves, but only in October—never to ski. He runs, Mayumi does Pilates. They go to comedy clubs on Friday nights and brunch on Sunday mornings. Would his alternate life have been this, living in a ski town, his mother and Angie in his life? Laughing, reminiscing about old times, no Nico, no Nora, no David? Martine and Angie are still laughing, going on about another Julian story, some ridiculous prank he'd pulled on a teacher at school. He leans back in his chair, astounded at how quickly the day turned, and almost wishes this mirage would never dissolve.

The route from the hospital back to Martine's house takes Angie and Julian past the DeLuca's building, and Julian is surprised to see a sign out front for Lodgepole Brewing Company. Angie doesn't mention Nora or the trial, and Julian refrains from bringing it up. He knows how hard it is to always have a disaster on the mind.

"DeLuca's is now a brewery?" he asks, turning from the minivan's window toward Angie.

"Sort of. Mom still owns the property, but after she developed Alzheimer's I leased it to help pay for the memory care home."

She takes a small breath, like she's about to say something else, and Julian waits, then finally says, "And . . . ?"

She's silent for a minute, then shakes her head. "And nothing. I was just thinking it's weird to be taking care of the parents that used to take care of us."

"It's weird that we're that old." She pulls into Martine's driveway. She hesitates, then covers one of his hands with hers. "I know today was stressful, more than stressful, but I'm glad she's okay."

Julian suppresses an urge to pull her toward him and kiss her—it feels so familiar, almost as if the last sixteen years have been erased, as if they never broke up, as if he's not here because one of the two children she had with another man killed the other—but she has David, he has Mayumi. Instead, he thanks her for the ride and touches her cheek with one hand, then gets out of the car and shuts the door gently, careful not to slam it.

Julian brings Jack into bed with him that night partly so he'll have a warm body to keep him company and partly because he figures the day must have traumatized the old dog as much as it traumatized him. Martine is back to her usual self: brusque and matter-of-fact. He'd returned to the hospital after dropping his luggage off and checking in at work, and she shooed him away after dinner, claiming she wanted to sleep. He calls Mayumi from under the covers but leaves out any mention of the hug with Angie. It was simultaneously meaningless and meaningful, and it would be impossible to explain without hurting her feelings. Instead, after updating her on Martine's condition, he focuses on her day, whether the morning sickness was better today and how many patients she saw at work, whether she's eating Oreo ice cream or mint chocolate chip while they speak. "Neither," she says, too quickly. Then, "Well, maybe both. But I can't help it."

"What does the baby like the best?" he teases.

She laughs. "It's too early to say. Maybe I'll keep eating until I get a clear answer."

When he first met Mayumi, he worried he might never stop comparing her to Angie, but as time passed, thoughts of his prior life faded—so slowly he almost didn't realize Angie had fallen out of his thoughts, until he woke up one day and realized the man who'd been with Angie was another self, someone he vaguely knew a long time ago. Tonight, after he hangs up with Mayumi, he realizes there's no way to keep that prior self at bay, not while he's defending Nora.

The topic of Nora's trial stayed beneath the surface of their conversations all day while he focused on Martine, but now, lying on the mattress in a dent that's been there for thirty years, a dent he can't escape no matter how he shifts his body, the jumble of what's next resurfaces. He and Angie can't avoid the topic forever, because at the moment nothing is going their way. Nora seems to be stuck in the district court, far from the juvenile system where she might have had a chance to someday have a normal life. If Gil Stuckey has his way, Nora will never see sunlight again, except when it's filtered through a chain-link fence topped with barbed wire.

Angie seems almost normal—not the Angie he used to know, but steadier and less anxious, like she's resigned to a dead son and a daughter who might spend the rest of her life in prison, as if she's already given up the fight. Nora seems just as resigned. When Julian visits, she speaks of friends and art and math homework as if the detention center is where she belongs, as if it's her new home. The normalcy they project must be an act, a coping mechanism, but he doesn't know how to handle it himself. He's seen this before, of course, counseled juveniles and walked their families through the process, at least if those kids had a family or anyone who cared about them, but this is different. He feels a tie to Angie and Nora and Nico he doesn't understand.

He's something more than a lawyer to the accused here. He just doesn't know what.

Chapter Twelve

Angie can't stop herself: she looks up Julian's wife. The curiosity nips at her until she gives in. There's a name for this, she thinks grimly as she types the name into the search engine. Stalking. Julian's not on social media—no Instagram or Facebook, no Twitter, nothing—but Mayumi is. There aren't many posts, but there are enough. They've been together eight years, based on a Happy Anniversary post. Mayumi likes food porn and her nephews. Most of the photos are of them: the two little boys on top of a camel at the zoo, or standing outside a theater dressed in miniature blue suits and ties, or kicking balls at a weekend soccer game. Julian doesn't tower over Mayumi in pictures like he did Angie, so she must be tall. She's pretty but wears no makeup. Her book club always meets with wine, but her food pictures from dinner dates with Julian don't include alcohol. She never posts about work, but Angie finds a separate website: she's a therapist with her own practice, with links to helpful websites and a blog about trauma. She seems like a good person.

Angie never wanted Julian back in her life—it's David's doing, David's fault—but here he is, riding in cars with her, defending Nora for killing Nico. And here she is, helping with Martine's health scare, comforting him. She swallows the past and ignores the bile rising in her throat.

The mountains are inescapable in Lodgepole. The San Moreno Range towers above town on the east, north, and south, walls of sandstone and granite that rise to the sky and hem in residents on three sides, a box canyon with only one way out in the winter, west to Waring and a state highway. In the summer, a rutted dirt road leads out of town to the east, up and over San Moreno Pass, winding past abandoned mines and wooden cabins crushed by a century of snow, but in the winter that road is impassable, covered by avalanches and swirling storms.

Visitors appreciate the isolation because it makes the town and their vacation seem more exotic. The tourists are easily identifiable to the locals: they buy twenty-five-dollar hamburgers and fifteen-dollar beers for lunch in the ski lodge and get sunburned because they don't understand the strength of mountain sun. They wear new jackets with brand names and winter boots that look nice but don't repel snow. After they're done skiing, or even if they haven't skied, they sit in hot tubs until wrinkles puff their fingertips. Everyone stops to take the same picture: the backdrop of San Moreno Mountain rising above town, visible down the center of Main Street. Sometimes the setting sun burnishes the snow on the highest peaks in an irresistible rose glow that begs to be photographed, and they rush into the middle of the street to capture it. None of them know this ephemeral phenomenon is called alpenglow, or the cause—the diffraction of sunlight by the atmosphere in the fleeting moments after sunset or before sunrise—but they'll have something to post, a picture that tells a good story. After their vacation, they go home to California or Texas or New York.

Angie searches for Nico among the throngs of these visitors, unable to ignore the instinctual drive to find her son, the irrational impulse overwhelming her intellectual awareness of his death. When she sees a patch of overgrown blond hair escaping from a ski helmet, her head turns of its own volition, following the hair until she confirms it belongs to the wrong body or wrong face or wrong smile. Outside, she hears his voice in the groups of brazen teens jaywalking across Main Street, skis hefted onto their shoulders as they head toward the gondola at the base of the mountain, either in the crack of a joke or the guffaw after the punch line, but it's never the exact pitch or right tone. Inside, when jackets have been discarded, she sniffs the air like a bloodhound, searching for the scent of his body spray, sweet yet masculine, boyish yet manly. Only when she detects it does she remember: every fourteen-year-old boy in Lodgepole wears the same spray.

She feels his absence as acutely as she used to feel his presence. He was her firstborn, her baby. He clomped through the house the same way he clomped through life, full of mischief and never sorry. Sometimes she thinks if she tries hard enough, she might manifest his being, bring him back into her life the same way he brought Julian back into hers. She spins around in the kitchen or the grocery store, hoping to catch him behind her, watching her cook dinner or throwing cookies into the shopping cart. *I'm still here*, he might whisper. *I'll be with you always.* But it's like her as a little girl, trying to catch her stuffed animals coming to life. Wishful thinking won't make it so.

One day when she's crossing the street, walking home from the library with yet another self-help book, her face hidden beneath a wool hat and sunglasses, a woman asks if she'll take a picture of her family. Angie hesitates—Did this woman single her out because she knows who Angie is, knows about Nora shooting Nico? Or is she just another tourist looking for the perfect family photo?—but she doesn't see disapproval or judgment in her eyes, so she nods. There are two parents and four children but no blond hair, no scent of Nico's body spray, but still, she looks at the mother and thinks, *I could almost be you. I wish I was you.*

"You're so lucky to live here," squeals the mother when she hands Angie her phone. "How much do you ski every year?"

The truth is more painful than she admitted to Martine. The whole family used to track not just days skied per year—and sometimes it was sixty or seventy—but total vertical feet, ten or twenty thousand a day or eighty thousand a week. It was a game. But now? Zero.

"As much as I can," she responds brightly, hoping the false notes in her voice aren't audible.

Two girls, two boys. One boy looks the age Nico would be now, almost fifteen. The mother rushes back to her family, and they all lean in, arms encircling waists. Angie zooms in on the boy who's Nico's age, zooms out, then clicks the photo button three times. She probably caught at least one of them blinking, but she hands the phone back and walks away before the mother can discover the flaw.

At first, the extra nutrition from Livia's feeding tube gave her enough energy to sit up again, to enjoy watching squirrels and birds through the window, to occasionally respond to Angie's questions or hum along to favorite arias. But eventually that manufactured boost fizzles, because Livia's life has simply run its course. By February, Livia has stopped speaking to Angie altogether, not because she's mad at Angie but because she can no longer speak, other than occasional echolalia or babbling. She loses even her Italian, though that's a relief for Angie because she can stop bringing her Italian dictionary to visits. The most Angie gets is a smile when she opens the door to her room.

Today is one of the days Livia smiles, a good day. It's early, only seven o'clock, but this is the best time to visit, because her sleep cycles are upside down; she falls asleep by late afternoon and wakes up in the middle of the night. By noon, sometimes before, she sundowns. Her fingers rub the rosary beads in her lap and she moves her lips silently, opening and closing her mouth without shaping any words, the physical act of prayer as instinctual as breathing. Father Lopez used to assign Angie the task of saying three rosaries as penance after confession when she was a child, but she hasn't said a single one since she left home for college. Her mother's blind faith in, and lifelong reliance on, her rosary is bewildering. Livia once said praying the rosary was mostly meditation, but her persistent hold on the beads, even after her mind has abandoned her body, makes Angie wonder whether it's something more, maybe an eternal penance she's required of herself.

"*Buon giorno, mama,*" says Angie. She won't keep up the conversation in

Italian—it's too hard—but who knows what Livia understands. Maybe greeting her in the language she was born into is comforting. "I brought you flowers."

Angie opens the Bea's Market plastic bag and arranges the daffodils in a small vase. They're too tall, so she pulls them out and snips a few inches off the stems, then stuffs them back in. The yellow petals always wilt quickly here, as if the flowers sense they're in a place where the living are sent to die, but the color brightens the room.

"*Nu-nu-nu-nu-nulla*," babbles Livia. "*La-la-la*."

Nulla, Italian for "nothing." Angie wonders whether the sounds are actually that word or just sounds. Both Julian and Martine have asked about Livia's health, and Angie has been honest with them: Livia is no longer Livia. She can't tell whether they're asking because they want to visit or because they're still afraid of her. They must not have experience with Alzheimer's patients, because it's Livia who would be afraid of them. She either wouldn't recognize them or would perceive their faces as negatively familiar without knowing why.

Angie presses the mechanical bed's up button to move Livia into a sitting position—she can no longer sit up on her own or even hold her head steady—and moves the vase to the bedside table. Nora asked for a picture of her grandmother, and Angie wants Livia to look as normal as possible, for the room to appear as cheerful as it can. It would break Nora's heart to realize how far the Alzheimer's has progressed, to see what the dementia has taken from her.

In some ways, these visits with her mute mother are easier than they used to be. Livia is like the therapist Angie never had. Now Angie has someone to talk to, someone she can trust to hold on to her secrets. Like a powerful vacuum, Livia sucks in Angie's words and never lets them go. Angie can spill any thought or crisis of conscience and no one will ever know. Angie's seeing one of her friends again—Jennifer—but they don't talk about anything real. They do yoga using YouTube videos or go for hikes, but Angie's afraid to say anything about Nora or Nico for fear of a leak to the media. The news reports have stopped, but she doesn't want them to restart. Sometimes the therapy sessions with Livia have taken the form of an apology, but other times they've resembled a confession, something she hasn't done in church in years. The first was the hardest:

"I'm sorry about Diana. That's something I never said out loud. I should have been watching her more carefully. I understand now why you were angry with me. Maybe I always understood but never wanted to admit it because I wasn't ready to accept that it was my fault." She should've said that long ago. "*My* fault," she repeated, mostly to herself, once a question, now a statement.

Livia was awake that day, her milky eyes fixed on something no one else could see, as though she were a soothsayer in a trance. Angie sat next to the bed and held her breath, waiting for Livia to turn her head in Angie's direction, to scream or yell or acknowledge this admission, but Livia only nodded vacantly. Angie wondered, was this what it took for her mother to forgive, the complete loss of her memory, the complete loss of the self?

On a different day:

"Nora killed Nico. I don't how I'm supposed to feel, what a good mother is supposed to do. Does choosing to support one of them mean I've betrayed the other?" Livia blinked three times, in quick succession, and Angie worried that Livia's brain had somehow distilled those words through its tangled neurons. Liquid leaked from the corner of one eye, but it was the same gelatinous nothing that had been leaking for months. When nothing more happened, Angie picked up the lotion and rubbed it into Livia's cheeks and forehead.

And finally: "I stayed with Julian when you told me not to." She said that on a day she was especially angry with David, a day she'd spent wondering about life choices and the alternate lives she could've lived. Angie waited for Livia's closed eyes to open at that revelation, but they didn't.

Livia never interrupts, and as a confessor she's much better than a priest: this version of her forgets to assign penance. She never pushes the rosary in Angie's direction, never raises her eyebrows at the mention of Angie's sins. Still, Angie hasn't confessed everything because some secrets are too painful to admit. Livia the therapist doesn't give advice, but just saying some words aloud feels good. The worst secrets—well, saying those aloud wouldn't feel good.

Livia's eyes are closed again, her smile gone. Angie doesn't have any-thing to confess today. All she wants is a photo for Nora.

"Smile, Mom," she says, and Livia opens her eyes, but this time she doesn't smile. Angie checks the picture on her phone and grimaces, but it's the best she'll get.

After visiting Livia, she sits in the car and looks at Mayumi's website again. When she clicks on the "*Find Advice Here*" link, it says what all her self-help books say: every day, find a positive and acknowledge gratitude for it, even if it's in a memory. She sets aside her annoyance with the repeat advice and tries anyway.

She thinks back to a day when she was skiing alone with the kids. Nico, five; Nora, four.

They must have been the tiniest kids on the slopes. Most weekends in the winter David skied with them, but this particular weekend he was working. Nora, always like a wet noodle, giggled and laughed in a tattered jacket and goggles with bright yellow tractors on the strap, both hand-me-downs from Nico, and pointed her skis in a pizza wedge down the bunny slope. Nico, who thought he knew everything there was to know because he'd already skied two seasons, whizzed past Nora, shout-ing encouragement as though he were the expert. Those goggles still fit him, but he'd told Angie that morning he was a big boy and didn't need tractor goggles. At lunch, Angie pulled a Tupperware full of macaroni and cheese from her backpack and heated it in the lodge's microwave, and the three of them sat around a small table and ate it with plastic forks, then drank hot chocolate from a thermos. They skied one more run after lunch, most other small children long gone but Nico not ready to quit. Nora was tired and cold, and Angie picked her up and skied down the bunny hill, carrying her like a baby.

It was an ordinary day during an ordinary winter. She's grateful she had it, but she'd give anything for just one more.

The minivan's odometer struggles to turn over, sometimes sitting on the same number for hours. Today is one of those days, the glowing lights stuck on 143,984. It's something electrical that she hasn't found the time to get fixed. She used to put things off because she didn't have time, always running here and there for work or Nico's medical appointments or elder-care. Now she has nothing but time, and she puts things off because they need every penny for Nora's case. It's okay, though, because she doesn't need an odometer to know she's driving a lot, visiting Nora three times a week, as much as she's allowed.

When she arrives at the detention center, she practices saying the thing she still hasn't said: "I forgive you." She says it as she sits in the minivan waiting for visiting hours to start, as she crosses the parking lot, picking her way around piles of dirty slush, and as she walks through the metal detectors at the entrance. She says it loudly, softly, sincerely, falsely, over and over again. As a child, she learned how to say "I'm sorry." Livia made sure of that. Angie had to say it to her mother and father, and of course Diana, because Diana was never wrong, at least in Livia's eyes. But Livia never taught Angie how to forgive. She never once said "Don't worry about it" or "I forgive you" after Angie said "I'm sorry." But does any mother teach that? She's not sure. Some people say "That's okay" after an apology, but that's different, and maybe not exactly right. It's not that you think what the person did was okay—you don't—but that you forgive their transgression. The most Livia ever said was "Thank you for your apology."

Angie isn't sure she does—or wants to—forgive Nora, and even if she does, how does she accomplish the forgiving? What does it mean to forgive her? And does Nora need to forgive Angie, too, because hadn't Angie failed Nora as much as Nora failed Nico? If Nora's soul was filled with darkness, so was Angie's.

Every day, she wonders what she could have done differently to change the present. She thinks of things both big and small. There's the gun, always the gun. But that was David's fault, not hers. Where does her fault lie? She can't simply say she was a bad mother, because that doesn't seem specific enough. After Nico was diagnosed, she spent too much time with him and not enough with Nora—David reminds her of that often enough—but what choice did she have?

She read about a theory once, the butterfly effect, the idea that if a butterfly flaps its wings in China, it might cause a tornado in Indiana. The idea that small, seemingly trivial events could have real consequences, that they could impact other events in a nonlinear way, made sense—after all, if she turned left to the 7-Eleven for a quart of milk instead of turning right to the supermarket, thereby avoiding a car crash, that would prove the theory—but also seemed ridiculous. Now sometimes it's all she can think about, certain that if she'd ordered pizza that night instead of serving leftover chili, or returned home earlier from Nico's physical therapy by speeding through the yellow light instead of stopping, or stayed up late to watch TV instead of going to bed—if only she'd done any of those things, she'd still have her family.

And there are days she allows herself the worst thought of all: If she'd stayed in New York, never returned here, or told Julian the truth—what would have happened then?

In the end, the reality of the present always comes back to haunt her. She can't change her past any more than she can change her present. If Livia were still Livia, she would point to her wooden rosary beads and tell Angie these thoughts are her penance, the price she has to pay for the sins she's committed and for the original sin she was born with. She deserves the burden of living with unlived alternatives.

In the same visiting room with the same hard plastic chairs, Twix, and Coke, Angie avoids saying it just a bit longer.

"I just saw Grandma," she says, holding up the picture of Livia on her phone. "She's doing well."

Nora grimaces, then quickly erases the emotions from her face. So like David, Angie thinks, though the blank look on Nora's face probably isn't anything more than a fragile varnish. That's not a good thing, never being able to share an emotion, but maybe that trait protects her in here.

"Are you sure?" asks Nora. "She looks pretty tired. She looks like she's asleep."

Angie spends the rest of the visit dancing around the words she doesn't want to say. She talks about the weather and Nora paints without talking. A regression of sorts. Practicing the words didn't make saying them—and meaning it—any easier.

In the car on the way home, Angie can't help wondering what David talks about with Nora when he's alone with her. They rarely visit at the same time because he's working more and more, taking extra hours whenever they're offered, hiding behind his job the way he always has even though he's been banished to the entrance booth and still hasn't been reinstated as a law enforcement ranger. The next three weeks he'll be in New Mexico, working at a private reserve doing trail maintenance. He has paid vacation days he has to take and thought this was a good time to earn extra money—double pay, he claimed, because while he was getting paid to be on vacation, he'd also be getting paid by this private reserve. He insisted on going even though the pay isn't much more than he'd make bagging groceries. When she'd objected, using visits with Nora as a reason to not go, his eyes flashed with anger. They were standing in the kitchen, cleaning up after another silent dinner, and he whirled around and almost spat in her face.

"Don't speak to me about not visiting Nora. Ever." He jammed his plate into the dishwasher and stomped upstairs.

The emotion startled her, even if it was deserved, but she leaned over the dishwasher, straightened his plate, and swallowed her response. He'd been the strong one right after the shooting, or if not the strong one, the one able to set aside emotion. Now he's falling apart, forgetting to eat, not communicating with her or visiting Nora, and not attending legal meetings, and Angie is the strong one, the one supporting Nora, checking legal bills and cooking dinner.

The one meeting with Julian. She's blocked from her mind the reality of what it means for Julian to be defending Nora.

In her minivan again, searching for positives: I used to be somebody. I was a painter. I created works of art and added meaning to the world. I helped other people see beauty that was otherwise invisible.

• • •

A few days later, Julian arrives at her house unexpectedly, a bouquet of flowers in one hand and his briefcase in the other, and she stands at the front door, wondering why he's here. Martine is still recuperating at home, sticking to her no-stress, no-lawyering pledge, and David is still in New Mexico.

"Are you going to invite me in?" he asks.

She pushes the door open, not sure what to say.

"For Diana," he says and hands her the flowers. In some ways, she sees him as clearly now as she did when they were together. Parts of him feel familiar, like an old habit. His slightly crooked smile, the one that used to light up when he pranked someone. The intense way he always had of examining whoever he was speaking with, as if he were trying to decipher a secret, as if that person were the most important person in the room. The hairstyle is the same, though almost three decades have passed and there's distinctly less of it. No beard. And yet, something elemental has shifted. He jokes less than he used to, but it's not that. His transition into seriousness began long ago, back in New York in his twenties, and there isn't anything to joke about when they see each other now. And it's not the wrinkles or the skin beginning its middle-aged dive. She has that, too. He's probably sober, or he wouldn't have been able to hold on to his job all these years or marry a therapist. Mayumi would have sniffed out the alcoholism and run in the other direction if it were still a problem, though he always was good at hiding it.

"Diana . . ." she says. "You mean Nico."

He shakes his head and looks at her strangely. "It's February twenty-eighth. I mean Diana. I'm in town to meet with a potential expert for the trial, and I just wanted to remember your sister."

She should feel relief—he hasn't brought flowers in a romantic gesture while David is out of town—but instead she feels disappointment. Then, as quickly as she's disappointed, she's guilty. Before he can see her cheeks burning and recognize her mistaken assumption, she walks to the kitchen and makes a show of hunting for a vase. Maybe nothing shifted in him. Maybe the reason she thinks something did is because something shifted in her. Or maybe it's impossible to understand all the in-betweens, the separate lives they've lived.

"You know, this is the first time I've been here since I left Lodgepole," he says. "The house looks good." He's lying, of course, but that was Julian, always polite, always complimentary.

"Thanks," she says. "You know—you've never seen Nico's and Nora's rooms." She turns and walks down the hallway without waiting for an answer.

Nico's room looks the same now as it did the week after his death. Sun shines through the window, highlighting the undisturbed dust specks that cover every surface of the room. The avian inhabitants of the painted tree peek out from behind leaves, blaming her for not taking better care of Nico's belongings. She dutifully bought sheets and a comforter and made the bed after the new mattress arrived, tucking the top sheet in with hospital corners the way Livia taught her, decades ago in a different life, the life when she still had a little sister and parents and a best friend in her third-grade class, a little boy named Julian who grew to be this man in front of her. Other than the dust, the room looks as neat and tidy as if it were in *Town & Country*, the way a real, lived-in room never looks.

"My mother said you painted this tree, that you did it for Nico when he was born." He looks at her like there's something more he wants to ask.

"Yes," she says. She's not sure she feels like saying more, explaining how her life shifted after she left New York.

Julian walks around the house, wandering from room to room. It's like pacing, almost, but with intent. He leaves Nico's room, enters Nora's room, leaves Nora's room, walks back down the hall to the kitchen and the living room. He walks upstairs, through each room, even her bedroom. Oh, how angry David would be if he were here, if he knew Julian was alone in the house with her, alone in the bedroom! The tips of his ears would flame red and he'd lock his square jaw, walking the line toward the rage that had denatured his normally impassive personality in the past couple of years. But then, maybe Julian knows that and only does it because David's not here. Eventually, he walks back downstairs and stands in the living room.

"Where—where is the rest of your work? What happened to your paintings, the ones Idara and I shipped to you after you left?"

What happened to her paintings was life. Livia had added Angie to the deed on the house as a joint tenant long ago, and when Livia moved into assisted living, the step before the memory care facility, Angie and David moved in. Angie moved the plastic crosses with the bloody Christ and the cheap replicas of Italian Renaissance art into the basement and covered the walls with her paintings and art she'd exchanged with friends back in New York. Her paintings never looked quite right in this little purple house, but she loved them. David wanted photos of nature, real representations of mountains and valleys and rivers, not her painted abstractions, but eventually gave in.

She was too busy to paint anything new, between being a mother and teaching, managing Livia's finances and medical care, and assumed she could paint later, that life would get easier when the kids got older. But when Nico was in seventh grade, he started having trouble in school, getting Cs instead of As, sometimes slurring his speech, getting into fights. He fought at home, too, with David and Angie and even Nora. The school psychologist thought it was drugs or alcohol and absurdly recommended counseling and juvenile AA meetings. The pediatrician, stuck on his dumb ADHD theory, recommended behavior modifications and medication. Angie and David did everything they were supposed to, but nothing changed. No matter how hard he studied, he failed tests; no matter how much counseling he got, her gregarious son couldn't seem to stop fighting. That winter, when he started missing gates on the slalom course, sometimes falling for no reason, Angie knew it was something more. It wasn't that he couldn't see the gates, Nico said, he just kept misjudging where they were. Angie and David started on a circuit of specialty doctor visits, and that year was a jumble of misdiagnoses until they finally found a doctor who watched Nico's clumsy, broad-based gait and the tremors in his arms, did bloodwork, and provided the correct diagnosis.

He sent Nico to read in the waiting room while he told them, and was blunt but not unkind. Huntington's is never good news, he said, but juvenile Huntington's is particularly bad. Nico's health would steadily deteriorate and there were no treatments that would alter the disease progression. They talked for an hour, Angie furiously taking notes and David crumpling the medical pamphlets the doctor handed him.

After that, Angie quit her job and devoted herself to managing Nico's health. He didn't need full-time care yet—he was still mostly functional, going to school and trying to participate in his regular activities—but she wanted to be ready when things changed.

But how to explain all of this to Julian, how to explain life after Nico's diagnosis? How to explain the years before that, when she had a happy family and a normal life, with her secret well hidden? How to explain her leaving New York, leaving *him*?

"Being a mother is what happened," she says, answering Julian's question the only way she can. "And once Nico got sick, I had even less time. I didn't want to walk around the house and be reminded of the fact that I couldn't paint, so I moved my art to the basement."

"Your beautiful paintings are in the basement," says Julian slowly. He sits down on the couch, his face almost as incredulous as when she picked him up from the airport and took him to the hospital. "But, Angie—they should be in a gallery, or you should be—I don't know. You don't have a studio in town? Or in a room in the house?"

Hysterical laughter gurgles up in her chest, bitter laughter she can't stop from spitting out, threatening the emotional stability she's worked so hard to rebuild the last few months. "A studio? Do you have any idea what life is like when you have two children and two jobs? And then one child is diagnosed with depression and the other with an obscure fatal disease? The money we spent for Nico's health care and the time I spent taking him to those appointments?"

"Yes, but—"

"There are no buts, Julian. And just so you know, everything I did for the kids—I wanted to do all that. I made a conscious choice to be there for them." The problem was she hadn't known what it would cost her, how much of herself would be lost in that process.

"I wasn't saying you didn't want to, Angie. I know you were an incredible mother. I always knew you would be."

The birds chatter outside, sitting in bushes and trees, darting to and from the bird feeders David insists on keeping filled even though Nico is gone. Angie hates those birds, hates the sound of them. All she wants is a little quiet. "You don't have kids, so you don't know this, but you do anything for your kids. Anything you have to. You would give your life for them."

As soon as she says it, she regrets it. Julian always wanted kids. He'd wanted them more than she did. He asked her to marry him more than once, planned out names—Gabriel and Nicholas and Angela and Grace—for each of the four kids he wanted, stared at families on the playground when they sat on benches in parks. She'd been the one who wasn't ready. He looks down at his feet, the way he always has when his feelings are hurt.

"Maybe you should start painting again," he says, looking back up, out the window in the direction of the cacophony. He pushes himself off the couch with his arms, as if he's too tired to do it with his legs. "Maybe it would help calm your mind. These aren't easy times."

"I'm sorry, Julian. I didn't mean it that way."

He looks at her, pain unfolding across his face, and doesn't say "That's okay." Instead, he says, "I'll see you at Nora's evidence hearing next week." At the door, he hesitates, his back still to her, then keeps walking, pulling the door shut without looking behind him.

Angie, still standing in the middle of the living room, feels frozen to the floor. She never thought she was capable of cruelty, not the way her mother was. But not only had she just been cruel, she'd been cruel to someone she used to love, to someone she's not sure she ever stopped loving. She stares at the door, at the rectangular piece of wood separating her from Julian, covered with nicks and scratches from a lifetime of entrances and exits, and closes her eyes.

Chapter Thirteen

MARCH 2017

O
n the day of the evidence hearing, Ignacio drives Nora from the
detention center to the courthouse in Lodgepole, Ignacio silent
behind the wheel, Nora silent behind the plexiglass partition.
Sheriff warned him not to unlock her handcuffs, but it's a three-hour
drive and he unlocks them anyway. Her wrists look too delicate to support the weight of handcuffs. They also look too delicate to support the
weight of a gun, but he tries not to think about that. There are a lot of
troubled kids in juvie—he won't deny that—but the way the system treats
these kids only makes them more troubled, not less. The judges know it,
the DAs and public defenders know it, and the parole officers know it,
but the world seems to think a child stops being a child the moment they
commit a crime.

"Buckle your seat belt," he says, hoping his voice strikes the right
balance between gruff and kind.

He arrived at the detention center at 5:50 a.m. because the hearing
starts at ten, and he needs to deliver Nora to the Lodgepole courthouse
an hour beforehand to meet with Martine. He's already exhausted.

"Make sure you're on time," Sheriff had said yesterday afternoon as he
walked out the door. "It's a three-hour drive, and if Nora is late because

you hit traffic it'll give her attorney fodder for police misconduct or something like that. Maybe even to get Nora off or reduce her sentence."

"Geez, I've transported prisoners before," grumbled Ignacio.

Sheriff stood there with her hands on her hips, glaring at him.

"I won't be late," he finally said. He left after dinner to drive to Rimrock Junction and spent the night in a Holiday Inn so he wouldn't have to get up at two in the morning.

He spent most of the night lying in the middle of a stiff queen bed, staring at the ceiling and the alarm clock's red glow. He couldn't stop thinking about his own daughter, his own son. Who would have killed whom? He turned off the alarm before it blared, showered, and stopped at a 7-Eleven for a large coffee, then forgot to drink it on his way to the detention center. Now it's cold, but he drinks it anyway. The only sound from the rear of the squad car is the occasional clanking of Nora's belly chain when she shifts positions. Time plays the same trick on him as it does everyone else: the night of Nico's murder seems like forever ago and just yesterday.

Sheriff was wrong about the traffic. The roads are empty and the way back feels desolate. After leaving Rimrock Junction, they pass an occasional light, but it's always hard to tell whether it comes from a rural ranch or from one of the junkyards lining this part of the highway. Lights from oncoming traffic appear as a dot in the distance, blinking if the vehicle hits a frost heave, bouncing up and down, then grow into a spotlight as they approach Ignacio's car, a crescendo of blinding luminescence. Then the light disappears as quickly as it appeared, leaving Ignacio and Nora alone in the car. The darkness of the night sky doesn't lift until almost seven o'clock, when they've driven more than an hour.

With so little traffic, this would normally be an easy drive. This stretch of the highway is on the mesa, flat and straight, but Ignacio is agitated, checking his sideview and rearview mirrors every few minutes, for what he's not sure. Perhaps he's using it as an excuse to furtively examine Nora, the girl in the back seat accused of an adult's crime. When he does, he finds her staring back, and each of them startles and looks away, Ignacio out the front window, Nora out the side window into the gray dawn.

After Ridgefield, they exit the highway and cross over the Silverado Divide on an open, winding road covered in snow. Even when it's not storming, high winds blow the snow from surrounding peaks across the asphalt, leaving bands of ice in their wake. Ignacio grips the steering wheel tightly on these sections, pursing his lips. If he were with his wife or children, they'd be listening to music, talking about the driving conditions or what was happening in school or what summer job his daughter hoped to get, but today the car is silent. When the first fingers of color reach through the distant sky, they're entering the canyon to drive up to Lodgepole. A dull light seeps through the pine and aspen lining the road, but this only makes the road feel lonelier, and he fiddles with the radio, trying to find music.

The loud *thunk* comes out of nowhere for Ignacio, but Nora has been watching the road instead of the mirrors, and when he hits the brakes and mutters, "Shit, what was that?" she answers.

"A coyote."

He looks at her, surprised at the sound of her voice, soft and steady, and pulls to the side of the road without using a blinker. "Damn it," he says, drumming his fingers on the steering wheel, then reverses until the car reaches a furry shape in the middle of the road. The mass moves, and he curses again, then gets out of the car and kneels next to it. It raises its head off the ground and whines, tawny eyes clouded, then drops its head again. Blood covers its twisted hind legs, staining the brown-and-gray fur. The gurgling in and out of its labored breathing is like his grandfather's wheezing when he caught pneumonia, and he strokes the song dog's head, then stands. This coyote is going to die; the question is when. The knowledge of what he needs to do seeps in, and he shivers.

He pulls his revolver from its holster, crosses himself, then turns to the car and says to Nora, "Close your eyes."

Her face is pressed up against the window, an oval of fog coating the window where her breath hits the glass. He knows she won't look away, but when he places the muzzle against the dying animal's head, he looks up at the sky instead of into its eyes.

"I'm sorry," he whispers, then squeezes the trigger. The gunshot echoes off the canyon walls like a boomerang, the shot ringing out again and again, a reminder he has just ended a life. He takes a picture of the dead coyote with his phone to include with the report he'll have to file about the discharge of his weapon, then drags the lifeless body to the side of the road and covers it with fallen pine branches. The birds will pick the carcass dry as soon as they find it, but the boughs might delay their discovery.

When he gets back into the car, he feels like he has to justify himself. "I didn't want it to suffer," he says, but the words feel empty, because it was him who caused the suffering in the first place.

"I know," Nora says.

Their eyes meet in the rearview mirror, each of their gazes steady, the silence in the car overwhelming the ricocheting gunshot.

Chapter Fourteen

2000

In March 2000, Angie flew back to New York to help Idara get Hobbs & Co. ready for that year's Thirty Under Thirty. She'd spent the week in Lodgepole, helping her parents mark the one-year anniversary of Roberto's diagnosis. He'd lost all his hair and so much weight that he joked he looked like a scarecrow, but he was alive and cancer-free, according to the latest scan. The night before Angie left, Livia had made fried artichoke hearts and spaghetti carbonara and the three of them sat around the kitchen table drinking wine, grateful Roberto's stomach could manage something more than soup and plain noodles. For the first time, Angie clung to the hope her father might survive, that her life might return to normal so she could stop flying back and forth to Colorado and focus on work. The theme for this year's Thirty Under Thirty was sculpture, so even though the New York magazine *Inside Art* had singled out Angie's painting for praise last year, her work wouldn't appear in this exhibit, but the weeks before the opening would be busy. Idara had been understanding about Roberto's illness and always found someone to fill in for Angie when she went home, but she expected Angie to make up for the time away when she was here.

When Angie walked into the apartment lugging her suitcase and backpack, all the lights were on and Julian was asleep on the couch, papers spread all over the coffee table, an empty bottle of wine on top of Randy Martin's file. Dirty dishes filled the kitchen sink and blanketed the small kitchen counter, and an empty whiskey bottle was shoved into a corner. Wilted flowers sat in a vase on the end table next to the couch—a bouquet of carnations, baby's breath, and roses—the buds barely clinging to life because the water had dried up. She flicked the light switch on and off when he didn't wake up, then slammed the apartment door as hard as she could, but he only turned over and started to snore. It had been like this for a couple of months now. Every time she left to help Roberto and Livia, she returned to find the apartment a mess, Julian a mess.

She stood in the middle of the room, wondering if this was the normal she wanted to come back to.

When she woke up the next morning, the kitchen was clean and Julian had already showered. He sat at the kitchen table, drinking black coffee and reading the *New York Times*, and smiled as if he hadn't passed out on the couch last night.

"How's your dad?" he asked.

"Good," she said. "How are you feeling?"

He shrugged. "Fine. Why do you ask?"

"Looked like you had a lot to drink last night."

His jaw tightened. "You were gone for a whole week, Angie. I didn't drink it all last night. And we've had that bottle of whiskey for a while."

This was the way all these conversations went. There was always an explanation. He'd told her he was at work most nights until ten or eleven, sometimes later, which meant he *must* have had it all this weekend. She also knew he'd gone out with work friends Friday night and worked in the office most of Saturday, because when she'd snuck away from her mother's kitchen to call him on Saturday, that was where she reached him. He seemed fine, though, so maybe he wasn't lying.

"Come have a cup of coffee," he said. He got up and poured her some, then grabbed the vase with the wilted flowers and set it on the kitchen table. A few exhausted rose petals drifted off the stems and landed next to his mug. "These are for you. February twenty-eighth was while you were gone, but I didn't want to let the day go by without remembering."

She sat down, still annoyed but too emotionally drained to fight. At least he always remembered Diana. The last year had been hard on both of them. She'd been gone a week almost every month. In Lodgepole, she filled in at DeLuca's so Livia could spend more time at home, did the restaurant's accounting—something Roberto had always done—then cared for Roberto when Livia was in the restaurant. She wanted to be there, wanted to help, but could never stop worrying about her 25 percent pay cut or what Julian was up to. Then, when she was in New York, she worked constantly to make up for being gone and spent her free time worrying about her father's next scan or how sick he'd get from the next chemo round. Even though she'd reconnected with a high school friend in Lodgepole, a guy named David who'd also been on the ski team, and he'd volunteered to stop by DeLuca's and occasionally check on her parents in case they weren't being honest with her, she still felt guilty when she wasn't there. The year had been a never-ending conveyor belt of guilt and worry.

"All the more reason to tell them about us, so I can come help," Julian kept saying, but now wasn't the right time. She still remembered the night after Diana's funeral, her mother's chafed hands as she cleaned up the kitchen, swiping cake crumbs off the counter and gathering half-empty paper cups of whiskey or coffee. All the visitors were gone, even the priest and the church ladies, and the three of them struggled to bear the weight of the house's silence. Roberto went upstairs to bed, his eyes red and swollen, but Livia grabbed Angie by the shoulders, lips pursed. She was a tall woman, with broad shoulders and a thick middle, and looked down at Angie. Her eyes weren't red; they were angry. She'd locked up her sorrow deep inside, and in its place was hate.

"I know *that boy* did this. Whatever happened was his fault," Livia had said flatly. "Do not see him again. Do not speak to him again, and do not speak to his family, or you will no longer be a part of this one."

Angie hurt too much to argue, and her mother shook her shoulders, hard enough that her neck cracked. Livia had an uncanny ability to ferret out the truth, like a bomb-sniffing dog or a rat trained to find treats in a maze. She did it with Angie, with employees at DeLuca's, with anyone who crossed her. And once she did that, she was ruthless about imposing retribution. What had happened wasn't just Julian's fault, it was Angie's, too, but if Livia was this angry at something she only suspected of Julian but couldn't prove, she couldn't imagine how Livia would react if she knew Angie had been involved. Keeping her mouth shut was the best option.

"Do you hear me?" asked her mother. She'd seized Angie's cheeks with her huge palms and squeezed, her pincher-like grip so tight it made Angie's eyes water. After Angie nodded, Livia gave her shoulders one last shake, then turned and climbed the stairs to bed.

In the years since, Angie watched her mother avoid everyone in the Dumont family no matter the circumstance. The anger had never dissipated, and Angie didn't want it directed at her. It was easier to keep her lives separate and avoid the confrontation. This past year, she'd felt trapped between two worlds: the one she'd grown up in and the one she'd made for herself. Traveling back and forth between them, always keeping her new life separate from her old one, was exhausting. She wanted to move on, to move forward.

"Thanks," she only said now to Julian. "They're pretty."

He snorted. "*Were* pretty. I worked so much last week I forgot to give them extra water. They look tired now."

Like me, thought Angie.

"I saw you had Randy's file out," she said. "How's that going?"

"Not great. One of the cases I was relying on for my appeal was just overturned, and now I have to restructure part of my argument. The filing is due in a couple of weeks, and the case isn't nearly as strong as it was."

"Are you going to tell Randy?"

Julian got up and dumped the rest of his coffee into a to-go mug. "I don't know. I feel like he needs hope, you know? I don't want to destroy that if I don't have to."

He kissed her on the forehead. "I need to go. Are you leaving now?"

She shook her head. She wanted to call her father first. Today was his first day back in the restaurant full-time, and she knew he'd be excited.

Once Angie settled back into her old routine—working in the gallery, running with Julian on the weekends when he wasn't working or she wasn't painting, no more rushing to pack a suitcase for a monthly trip to Colorado or squeezing four weeks of work into three—she felt like she could breathe again. The Thirty Under Thirty was a huge success again, with another article in *Inside Art* and a bigger crowd on opening day than last year. When she saw the article, pangs of jealousy and regret pricked at her even though she couldn't have been included in a sculpture exhibit. On Saturdays and Sundays, she woke up early so she could work in the studio without the distraction of the other painters' clouds of weed, then left before they arrived in the late afternoon.

She bought her first cell phone and gave that number to her parents so Roberto could continue his morning calls. Sometimes he called when she was walking to the studio or the gallery, and he'd say, amazed, "Are those birds in the background? Are you walking outside while you talk on the phone?" She'd given them a cordless phone for Christmas a couple of years ago, and he'd extended his telephone pacing from the kitchen all the way to the front door, but if he walked outside, the connection got staticky and cut him off. He thought cell phones were a marvel and only for the rich.

"Yes, Dad," she'd say. "You can talk on a cell phone anywhere. There's no cord, no need to be home. And they're not that expensive, not anymore." He was less amazed when ambulances or fire trucks drove by, or when it was windy, because he was hard of hearing and the background noise made it difficult to pick her voice out from the other sounds. On those days he'd hang up quickly and make her promise to never buy him one of "those things."

She gave the cell number to David, too. She told herself it was so he could reach her any time, in case he noticed something wrong, but the real reason was she didn't want him calling the home phone, where Julian might answer. Julian wouldn't understand why she was relying on David, of all people, to check on her parents. Most of her childhood friends had moved away, but a few still lived in Lodgepole, and she probably should have called one of them, but something about David's offer of help had comforted her, and she'd taken it. He seemed different now, the same way she supposed she was, and when he'd first approached her in DeLuca's she almost hadn't recognized him. He'd filled out, his skinny legs and arms thickened into muscles he probably developed as a park ranger. He spent his summers working as a temporary education ranger for the crush of vacationing tourists—a job he hoped would someday become permanent so he could get benefits—and the rest of the year maintaining trails, clearing fallen trees or the occasional rockslide, and the work agreed with him. His red hair had darkened into auburn, so he no longer looked like a carrot-top, and he often sported scruff on his cheeks that made him look like a Scottish warrior from a movie she'd seen once. He stopped by every Thursday night for takeout, and whenever Livia saw him talking to Angie, she nodded approvingly. One day she'd said, "David Sheehan, right? He's a good Catholic boy." Angie almost said *I'm already taken* but remembered in time and stopped herself.

"I'm focused on my career right now, Mom." Then she'd added for good measure, "I'm pretty sure he's Buddhist, anyway. He has prayer flags in the back of his truck."

David never called the cell—she'd accepted his offer to report on her parents' well-being, but "only if something was wrong"—and her parents sounded good, so Angie's normal routine in New York returned to exactly that: her normal routine.

In July, she and Julian found a cheap flight to Paris and went on their first vacation since Roberto had gotten sick. He showed her the building where he lived when he studied there—an ugly apartment block where they shoved all the foreign exchange students—and his favorite neighborhood restaurants but gave up speaking French once he realized he'd forgotten most of it. They ate and drank their way through those restaurants, walked until their feet had blisters, and did what every other tourist in Paris does: climbed to the top of the Eiffel Tower, saw the

Mona Lisa, and locked a padlock to the Pont des Arts railing and threw away the key.

At dinner one night, the waiter asked, "Where is home for you?"

"America," said Julian. "New York City."

But was New York home? Angie wasn't sure. Home was Lodgepole, where she'd grown up, where Diana was buried and spaces in the ground waited for Roberto, Livia, and Angie. Home was pine and spruce in the winter and golden aspens in the fall, a clear sky that stretched 360 degrees into infinity when viewed from the top of a fourteen-thousand-foot mountain. Home was watching dawn tint mountain peaks with its gentle rose hue, or the full moon illuminate the world with reflections on snow bright enough to be daytime, if not for the desolate shadows cast by the upside-down light. But home was also her art, and the life she'd built with Julian in New York, his smell on the extra-large T-shirts she slept in when he was away on business, the Indian and Thai restaurants they explored every weekend. She let Julian do the talking and only smiled.

Angie's return to normal was short-lived. By early September, Roberto's cancer had returned. She was sitting at the gallery's reception desk when she got the call, and the ring startled her. It was her cell phone, not the gallery phone. The number that flashed wasn't one she was familiar with, but it was a 970 area code, from Lodgepole.

"Hello?" she said.

"It's David," he said. "David Sheehan."

"Oh. Oh, no." Her heart sank. He'd seen Livia with swollen eyes in the restaurant, sitting in a booth with a fat yellow binder filled with printouts organized by tab. Angie knew that binder: it was the one full of research on pancreatic cancer, treatments, and diets to follow. She'd created it when Roberto first got sick.

She listened and thanked him, grateful she was able to hold it together, then called her mother, who lapsed into a barrage of Italian Angie struggled to understand. There would be no surgery this time, only palliative chemo and radiation, because the cancer had metastasized. The doctor said if Roberto was lucky, he might live another six to nine months.

"I'll come help," promised Angie. "This time, I'll come for two weeks a month."

The option to not go, or go for less time and avoid upending her and Julian's lives, didn't occur to her. She walked to Idara's office, took a deep breath, and asked for more time off. It wasn't just that she owed her mother after everything that happened with Diana, though that was part of it. All these years, she'd worked to put Diana's accident behind her, to live life as though it never happened, but she knew her mother hadn't and probably couldn't. Roberto's death would leave Livia alone in Lodgepole with a restaurant that had been his dream, not hers. Not the kind of empty nest people dreamed about. Still, it was more than guilt that compelled her to return home. If Livia once had a favorite daughter, then Angie had a favorite parent. She loved both of them—they were her parents—but she shared a bond with Roberto she was terrified to lose.

When Roberto got sick the first time, Idara hadn't hesitated to give Angie time off. This time, her "Take as much time as you need" morphed into a worried "Okay." Her brows crinkled together in a line on her forehead. "But two weeks a month means you'll only be half-time. I'll need to hire someone to take your place, and I don't think Hobbs will be happy. I won't be able to convince him to hold your job for long."

This job was everything Angie had ever wanted, and she couldn't imagine losing it, but she also couldn't imagine losing her father, so she nodded, said thank you, and went home to tell Julian. Not helping, not going home—that wasn't a possibility.

Julian responded by getting up and hugging her, his embrace stiff and quick, then pouring himself a glass of whiskey, something he usually tried to hide.

"I'm really sorry," he said. He pressed his lips together and looked down at the table. They were having dinner, eating pad thai straight from the take-out container. Angie had forgotten to specify Thai hot and someone at the restaurant had forgotten to add the crumbled peanuts and fresh cilantro and neither of them was enjoying the bland rice noodles. He downed half his whiskey in one gulp.

"That's all you're going to say?" asked Angie.

"I'm sorry," he repeated, "that your father's cancer came back, but you knew it would. That's what happens with pancreatic cancer. But how am I supposed to feel about you telling me you'll be gone half of every month to take care of him?"

"What else am I supposed to do?"

"For starters, you don't have to go for half of every month. What about your job, your painting?" He circled the rim of the glass with his finger, then added, "And most of all, you could tell your parents about us, so we don't have to be apart this much. I've been ready to do that for years now."

Angie had expected more sympathy. How could he not understand she was about to lose her father? She pulled the Styrofoam container closer to her and stabbed a piece of chicken with her fork. She felt betrayed by his failure to understand, his failure to care. "I happen to love my parents, unlike you. You treat your parents like distant relatives you barely have an obligation to. The only person in your family you talk to is Gregory. That's not how families are supposed to work. I have to go help. I can't *not* go help."

"What about your obligation to us?" He finished his drink and set the glass back on the table, almost but not quite a slam.

"This isn't about you, Julian. It's about my father."

"I agree that it's about your father. But it's also about *us*. I could be helping you. I could come with you. We should be helping your parents together, as partners."

"Have you forgotten about Diana? Your role in her death, and how my mother feels about that?" She wished she could take the words back as soon as she said them. She'd always known, on some level, that Diana's accident took more from him than it did from her, but she'd never understood why. Her memory of what happened was filed away in her head as a tragedy that happened to her, not an accident she'd caused, but Julian's was filed away as a wrong he'd committed, a crime. He looked down at the floor for a minute, hurt.

"My role," he finally said. It wasn't a questioning voice. "I've never forgotten *my* role. I never will. I'll think about it every day for the rest of my life. I still wake up with nightmares about it. But it seems you've forgotten *your* role, forgotten we were both there."

He walked over to the door and put his shoes on.

"Where are you going?" asked Angie. She'd long ago come to terms with the fact that she should have been with Diana on that ski slope, but her guilt was circumscribed by the very nature of skiing. People died every year from hitting trees or crashing, sometimes six or seven a year in Colorado. The details of that day were hazy now, as if an artist had deliberately blurred the precise imagery and intense emotions she once felt, but one thing she still remembered clearly was sitting across from Julian in the hospital's waiting room. He rested his head in his hands, as though it was too heavy to hold up otherwise, and she'd felt sorry that he'd been the one to discover Diana's body, that he hadn't skied fast enough to stop her from hitting the tree in the first place. This was the first time— ever—he'd pointed a finger back at her, and she felt her cheeks flushing, burning with surprised shame.

"For a walk," he said. "I need some fresh air."

"Fine," she snapped. He was probably headed to a bar. "I'm going to pack. I'm leaving tomorrow." She turned and walked into the bedroom, and the front door and the bedroom door slammed, one after the other, the syncopation inaudible to Julian and Angie.

When Angie's flight arrived in Lodgepole, her mother was nowhere to be found. Instead, David Sheehan waited at the curb, standing in front of his pickup, hands stuffed in his jeans pockets.

"Are you meeting someone here?" she asked, looking right and left for Livia.

"You," he said. He hoisted her suitcase into the cargo bed and opened the passenger door.

Angie stood on the sidewalk, still hesitant. "My mother is coming to pick me up."

He shook his head. "She asked me to come so she could get ready for the lunch rush. I don't have to work today, so it's no problem. I'll just drop you off at the restaurant."

Angie settled into the front seat and smoothed her pants with her hands. She thought back to the time her mother said David was a good Catholic boy and laughed, for some reason more charmed than annoyed.

"What's so funny?"

"I don't think she really had to get ready for the lunch rush," said Angie. "Or if she did, she could've found someone to cover. I think she's trying to set us up." She felt a little guilty her mother—and David—thought she was single.

He raised his eyebrows. "I think she's just overwhelmed."

"You don't know my mother," said Angie. Then she sobered, not sure why that, of all things, had caused her to momentarily forget her father's cancer and last night's fight with Julian. "But I guess you're right."

David kept his eyes on the road. "She's pretty broken up. Usually she has a stiff upper lip, you know? At least, when I see her at the restaurant, she seems to."

"The prognosis isn't very good."

"I know."

Saying the prognosis wasn't very good was an understatement. Death was certain—the only question was when. She focused on the trees on the distant hillside, the aspens just beginning to turn, the first shudder of fall. In high school biology, on a field trip to one of those hillsides, she'd learned about abscission, the natural process of separation in the cells of plants and trees. Abscission, the teacher had explained, was an aspen preparing for winter by halting the work of the leaves' chloroplasts, preventing photosynthesis and causing the leaves to yellow and then drop. She remembered the first call from her mother, when Livia said Roberto had developed jaundice and turned "*giallo*, like an egg yolk," and wondered what her father's body was doing to get ready for its death, what her own head was doing to prepare for that eventuality.

She felt a warm hand on her own, a light squeeze. "We're here," David said gently. "You seem lost in another world."

Outside the car window, the cursive letters on the awning beckoned: *DeLuca's Authentic Italian Cuisine*. She shivered but held her tears inside. She would not cry.

"You should get outside while you're here," he said. "Go for a hike, spend time in the fresh air. It'll help with the stress."

He grabbed her suitcase from the back and handed it to her. "Call if you need anything."

She stood on the sidewalk and watched his pickup disappear around a corner, then turned and walked under the awning and into the restaurant.

The weeks and months blended together. Each part of her life held its own routine. In Lodgepole, she chopped vegetables, waited tables, or reconciled the books—whatever her father or, increasingly, her mother— told her to do. She called Julian from her cell phone late at night or early in the morning, when she took walks around the block away from the house. If Roberto had a bad day, she stayed home with him while Livia worked at the restaurant. If Roberto had a good day, he came to DeLuca's and answered the phone or placed orders for supplies, and sometimes seated people while Angie helped Livia in the kitchen. The nausea from the chemo prevented him from cooking and the smell of onion and oregano made it worse. In New York, she worked at the gallery every spare moment, once again trying to make up for lost hours and hoping the half-time replacement Idara hired wouldn't become permanent. The extra hours left little time for painting, but sometimes she and Julian found time for a run together or a dinner out with friends. They'd entered into an uneasy truce about her travel schedule, and he worked longer and longer hours because he was inexplicably drawn to death penalty cases and three strikes cases—not just Randy Martin's—that detracted from the paying clients he needed to make partner. He claimed he couldn't say no when there was so much injustice in the world, and since Angie was never home herself, she couldn't complain about his hours.

She felt unmoored in Lodgepole and aimless in New York. She imagined herself as a marionette controlled by strings in the sky, strings that were attached to her arms and legs but not her head, which swirled with emotions and desires she couldn't pin down, all of which surfaced in frustrated and peevish dreams. Both Livia and Idara had admonished her for snapping at customers, their own voices testier than she'd ever heard, and she couldn't help wondering whether everyone in her life was actually being crabby or whether it was just her.

One day in October, David called and asked if she wanted to hike up Miner's Peak, while the aspens still held some color.

"I can't," she said. "I have to help in the restaurant."

"We'll go early and I'll have you back by ten. It'll be good for you, I promise. Maybe make the rest of your day better."

Angie didn't know why she said yes, but she did. And the next morning, when she tied the laces of her hiking boots and filled a water bottle for her backpack, she didn't know why she didn't call to say *no, never mind*, but she didn't. She told herself it wasn't a date, but she knew he was being more than just nice.

It was cooler on the hike than Angie thought it would be, and when they headed up a shady part of the trail, she shivered. David took off his fleece and handed it to her.

"Put it on," he urged. "The higher we go, the colder it will get."

"But what about you?" she protested.

"I'm used to it. I'm not cold."

And he wasn't; his hands were warm when they touched hers. He avoided the topic of her father's health—they already talked about that every Thursday when he dropped by for his takeout, though sometimes he now ate there and sat in a booth until closing, chatting with Angie as she helped clean up—and instead asked about life in New York, her apartment and the gallery, how much a taxi cost and how it felt to walk on sidewalks surrounded by hundreds of people.

"I don't mind the people," she said frankly. "That's what makes it special. All those people contribute to the culture—the art, the museums, the food from all over the world."

"But there's life here, too. Real life, not life in a concrete zoo," said David. "I don't think I could take that many people at the same time. And all that stuff—it just isn't my cup of tea."

"Don't the parks get crowded in the summer?"

He shook his head. "Not like New York. I went there as a kid, and I felt claustrophobic the whole time, always surrounded by two walls: a wall of people and a wall of buildings. If it gets crowded in the park, all I have to do is look up at the sky or a mountain to know there's plenty of elbow room. There's nothing in cities for me."

At the summit, a thousand feet above the tree line, the aspens, the spruce, and even the scrubby juniper bushes replaced by lichens clinging to gray boulders, she heard only wind and the occasional marmot chirp. When they sat down on a rock to rest, David took a couple of apples from his backpack and handed her one. He leaned back on his arms and closed his eyes, tipping his face toward the sun. Angie wondered what it would be like to touch his skin, whether the skin underneath his beard would feel like Julian's—sandpapery if he'd forgotten to use lotion too many days in a row, but always warm and smoothed out by his gentle touch when he nuzzled her neck—or whether she'd never know because that skin was untouchable, shielded by the bristly hair.

When another couple appeared, David jumped up and handed them a small camera to take a picture of him and Angie. Just before the woman said "Cheese!" he put his arm around Angie and pulled her in close, and she leaned into the crook of his arm as if she'd done it before.

After another hike, they got coffee at Katie's Breakfast Cafe in town. They drank mugs of coffee sweetened with flavored creamer and compared memories of high school teachers and college professors. He'd gone west, not east, to forestry school in Oregon and was fascinated by her time in art school, by the idea of living in a dorm with elevators and sleeping in a room the size of a shoebox, and by classes she'd taken for her art major that were, in his words, weird. She was fascinated by his time in Oregon, by classes that met in the woods or near lakes: Pest and Wildfire Control, Hydrology, Land and Wildlife Conservation. They laughed at how different their experiences were, polar opposites even though they'd both started in Lodgepole.

When she was with Julian, he talked incessantly about his latest cases, hashing or rehashing every detail of some intricate law she'd already heard about too many times, but David talked about the beauty he saw every day at work and at home. A family of bobcats—a mother and three cubs—slept under a pine tree behind the cabin he was living in, and he hoped the cubs would make it through the winter. He'd just put away his hummingbird feeder for the season and he'd miss seeing the birds zoom in and out from his kitchen window. He watched the bobcats from that same window—you're lucky it's bobcats and not a mountain lion with her cubs, she interrupted—and his face lit up as he told her about the mother bobcat swatting away a cub when it playfully pounced on her one too many times and about the runt of the litter, the one who pranced by with a chipmunk dangling from its mouth just last week, head held high with what might have been its first kill. When they reached for the creamer at the same time, he smiled and pushed it toward her, and she forgot about her father, just for a moment.

It didn't feel like cheating, not at first. Angie told herself David was a high school friend who watched out for her parents, a friend she sometimes saw when she was home. But she knew he assumed she was single because that's what her mother and father thought, what the few friends she had left in town thought. Part of her liked pretending she was single, liked the feeling of being wanted, and being with him was easy. There was no need to hide the relationship or worry about Livia pinching her cheeks and disowning her for spending time with the person she'd always blame for Diana's death.

Angie knew David expected—and wanted—more than a friendship, and one day in December she gave it to him. He'd eaten late that night at DeLuca's, the way he now did every Thursday, and helped her close up after Livia and Roberto left, Roberto complaining of fatigue. She often walked home because her parents' house was less than a mile from the restaurant, and the cold air helped expel the pungent garlic odor that permeated her clothes after a day in the kitchen. David hung around until she turned off the lights, double-checked the kitchen burners, and locked the doors, then drove her home. When she turned to him in the pickup to say good night, he reached out and cradled her cheek. She couldn't tell if the flush on her face stemmed from the heat of his hand or the thrill she felt, and she reached out and cradled his cheeks back. He leaned in and kissed her, his lips as warm as his hands, and when she pulled away she kept her hands on his face and he kept his on hers. They sat like that, searching each other's eyes in the moonlit truck, until he finally laughed.

"You're a surprising woman, Angela DeLuca," he said. "But I like your surprises."

One other time, long ago, David had called her Angela. It was just after Julian's sudden departure from town, and she was in the hallway, walking from biology class to art. She'd heard a voice from behind: "An-gel-aaa!" and whipped her head around before the third syllable, because David had pronounced the first two syllables "Angel." Angel was Julian's pet name for her in grade school, and she half expected to see him walking down the hall, even though it was David's voice. She hadn't known whether he was trying to take Julian's place or simply mark his mysterious disappearance, but fury had risen up inside her. "No one's called me Angela since fourth grade," she'd snapped, then sped to the art room. This time it felt natural, as if he were simply repeating what he heard Livia yell when she wanted Angie in the kitchen, and she laughed, too. He probably didn't even remember that time in high school.

"Only my mother calls me Angela."

"I know." He grinned. "You don't really seem like an Angela, but I thought I'd try it." He kissed her again, harder this time. His hands lingered on her neck and he crooked his finger under the neckline of her sweater. She felt like a teenager, making out in a truck like this. It felt easy and natural, as if there was no Julian waiting back in New York.

Blue light shone under the living room's closed blinds, and Angie knew her parents were in there, watching the eleven o'clock news, Livia in her easy chair, Roberto dozing on the couch.

"I have to go," she said, squirming out of his embrace.

"To be continued," he called out the window as she walked toward the front door.

Her mother looked up at Angie from her easy chair. Worry had cemented her thin lips into a hard line. Even if she were smiling, it would be hard to tell. "Was that David's pickup I heard outside?"

Angie nodded. Now she felt even more like a teenager, being interrogated after a night out with a boy. There'd only ever been one boy in high school, though, and her mother knew that. Angie knew it, too, and for the first time that night, guilt tapped at her conscience, asking her what she was doing and why she was doing it.

"He's a good man, Angela. Maybe it's time you settled down, stopped living alone in New York, trying to be an artist, and came home." Her mother pushed herself up and out of her chair. "I'm going to bed. Will you help your father when you head up?"

Angie nodded again, not wanting to speak, afraid her emotions would betray her, uncertain of what her emotions were.

Roberto opened his eyes when she sat down and started clicking the remote, looking for something other than news.

"*Ciao, carina*," he whispered. "How are you? How was your night?"

"Everything was good, Daddy. I locked up, turned off all the lights, checked the burners."

"That's not what I meant."

Angie blushed. So they had been peeking out the blinds, or at least wondering when they heard the diesel puttering of David's truck.

"Mom already interrogated me."

"Do you have fun with him?"

"It's hard to have fun right now, when I'm so worried about you, but he helps me relax," she said.

Roberto closed his eyes for a minute, then reopened them. Light from the television reflected off his face, illuminating the whites of his eyes.

"Choose wisely, *carina*. You want someone who will always be there, who will never stop lifting you up when you fall down."

She nodded and waited to see where this was going, whether he was warning her about David or all men or something else entirely. She'd deflected his questions about dating for years now, ticking off lies about being too busy with her career or the difficulties of finding the right guy. Roberto sometimes spoke in riddles, his advice so opaque and gentle that Angie wasn't sure what was advice and what was something more. She almost missed the sharpness of Livia's tongue because at least it was offset by the comfort of knowing exactly where she stood.

He raised himself up on one elbow and looked at her intently. "I've spent all the years since Diana died trying to lift up your mother. She is not an easy woman to lift. She can be angry, mean, and vindictive. You know all those things."

"I don't know how you've dealt with it."

Roberto's jowls sagged, the extra skin hanging down from his cheeks. "The thing is, it's easier to be angry than it is to be sad. Some people eventually forget the difference."

"Like Mom."

"Yes, like your mother. But she can also be kind, caring, and loving. She works hard. She overcame a lot from her childhood. And she gave me you and Diana. I love her, and I'll be there for her as long as I'm alive. And when I'm gone, you'll be there for her."

Angie nodded. The last part wasn't a question. This wasn't mere advice. "I promise, Daddy."

"There needs to be someone for you, Angie. Someone who will always lift you back up, even when you're not the person you used to be. Make sure whoever you marry someday will do that for you."

Livia had been judging Angie for as long as she could remember, but the judgment implied by Roberto's words was new. She wasn't sure what it meant or what he knew. Livia and Roberto lived by different moral codes—her mother would never forgive her for staying with Julian, whereas Roberto would never forgive her for being a cheater. And that's what she now was. She drew in a breath and tried not to shrink under the intensity of Roberto's gaze, or under the weight of her own burgeoning guilt.

"And most of all," he added, "make sure you know how to do it for yourself." He laid back on the couch and closed his eyes again, the television's light still flashing on his face.

Now Angie kept her cell phone tucked away in her purse, ringer off, so that when she was in Lodgepole, David wouldn't see Julian's texts or hear his phone calls and when she was in New York, Julian wouldn't see or hear David's. She always found a way to speak to, or text, the man she wasn't with, and because she had a dying father in Lodgepole and a job in New York, both men were more understanding about her absences and unavailability than they should have been.

Everything about David was slower than Julian, but that wasn't necessarily a negative, not in Angie's mind, because it also meant he was steadier. The speed at which Julian lived his life—skiing in high school, drinking, and working—and the way he attacked his passions was maddening. She liked this slower pace, the way David sometimes went cross-country skiing instead of racing downhill, or sometimes spent Friday nights at home cooking, making venison stew from a deer he'd shot during hunting season instead of drinking in a bar with work friends. He never had more than one beer and didn't like whiskey. He was always there for her, always able to take time off from work when she visited, always knew when she needed to quiet her mind with a hike or help closing the restaurant. And yet, he was a pale shelter from the storm engulfing her life, the tug between family and Julian that was tearing her apart. Maybe he was Julian's antithesis, and Lodgepole was New York's. She wasn't sure she minded the change.

Sometimes in Lodgepole, when she was talking to Julian on her cell, walking the dark streets on her way back from DeLuca's, she struggled to recall the sensation of touching his skin, of tousling his hair or being enveloped by one of his bear hugs, because it was almost as if he didn't exist except in New York. And sometimes in New York, even though she could almost hear David poking fun at people's fancy clothes or complaining about taxi and bus fumes, she wondered if he existed outside of Lodgepole.

When exhaustion from living in two worlds set in, she wondered

whether it was the strain of loving and betraying two men simultaneously—if she even loved either of them—or the strain of Roberto's sickness, the abiding awareness he would not get better.

On one of those phone calls to Julian, late at night in Lodgepole and
even later in New York, an owl swooped over Angie's head as she walked
home. Its silent wings stretched close to five feet across, almost as wide
as Angie was tall, and its talons hung down loosely. The gliding shape
was over her head and in front of her before she realized what happened.
It was March, the time of year when owls start nesting, preparing for a
family that doesn't yet exist. Roberto had surprised everyone, including
the doctors, and was still living, frail but fighting.

"Jesus," she said.

"What?" asked Julian, concern in his voice.

"A great horned owl almost thought I was his dinner. I must look like
a rabbit tonight."

Julian was silent on the other end when he usually would have laughed,
his breaths the only sound.

"Julian?" she asked.

"We got a ruling today," he said. "On Randy." He slurred his words a
little, and Angie didn't know if it was because he was drunk or crying. A
quiver in his voice told her the news wasn't good.

"What happened?"

"We lost. We lost on everything."

"So the life sentence stands?"

"Yes."

"Isn't there anything else you can do? Someone else to appeal to?"

"This *was* the appeal," he snapped. "You know that."

"I only meant—I don't know what I meant," said Angie. "It seems so
unfair that I don't know what to say."

"We've talked about this before. It's partially because it's a bad law,
but it's also because Randy is Black. It's almost impossible to fight all
the racism in the system. Haven't you paid attention to any of our conversations?"

"I'm sorry, Julian. I really am."

Julian sighed. "Tomorrow I have to tell a kid he's going to spend the rest of his life in jail. How am I supposed to do that?"

"I don't understand," said Angie. "You told me he didn't do the robbing or the shooting. And that he was fourteen for the first strike. How did he end up with a life sentence?"

"When are you coming back?" asked Julian. He sounded plaintive, like a little kid.

"You know when," said Angie. "It's the same as always, two weeks here, two weeks there." There was silence, again, and then she heard him swallowing.

"Are you drinking?" she asked.

"You can't just leave me like this forever," he said and hung up.

The phone's silence droned in Angie's ear, and she flipped it shut and kept walking. She felt the same worried fury she always did about his drinking, but she could no longer feel virtuous about who was being wronged in this relationship. She didn't need to be here two weeks a month. Returning early to comfort Julian would be the right thing to do; she just didn't want to do it. The full moon brightened the inky sky but obscured the night's constellations, and all she could think now was, *If that owl comes back, it will have an easy time finding me.* She laughed, the sound bitter in her ears, and kept walking.

On the other end, Julian slammed the phone into its cradle. The flowers he'd bought for Angie on February 28 sat in the same vase he'd used last year. He'd carefully watered them, but they looked as lonely as he felt. The rosebuds drooped, the flower on each stem hanging as if connected to a broken neck even though the bud itself looked perfectly healthy.

The power of the grief engulfing him was a surprise. He felt like he'd failed Randy, failed to right a wrong. He knew better than most people that tragedies resulted from a convergence of circumstances, a set of facts and actions that aligned in an unforeseen way and synthesized into a result no one could have planned for. Yes, Randy had committed crimes, but a young man, just barely older than a kid, spending the rest of his life in prison for a series of decisions he made when he wasn't ready to make decisions—that *was* a tragedy.

But the grief he felt wasn't just from losing Randy's case. He felt the loneliest he'd ever felt, lonelier than when his parents expelled him from Lodgepole. Lonelier even than Thanksgiving this year, which he'd spent by himself because Angie had flown home to be with her parents even though he and Angie always spent Thanksgiving together. He couldn't criticize her for choosing to spend it with her dying father, but he also couldn't quell his bitterness. If she'd only disclosed the relationship, he could have gone with her. He told his family what he always told them: he was too busy with work to get together. He spent the day in the apartment, sleeping on the couch in front of football games he didn't care about, then finally left to have a burger and some beers at Oskar's, where he sat at the bar sandwiched by two other lonely men.

Something key had shifted within Angie recently, something he didn't understand. Attributing it all to Roberto's cancer seemed wrong. He'd seen Angie after Diana's death, seen her grief and sorrow, and through it all she'd still been the same person. This was different. This wasn't just Angie grieving Roberto's impending death. This almost wasn't Angie at all. It was as if she were someone else, and he didn't know what to do about that.

It felt like he was living in his own tragedy, one that began the moment Angie bought the joint from that idiotic liftie. He marveled at how quickly that one moment in his life had happened, how each choice had led to the next, how they'd all gathered together, the weight accumulating and gathering force. There'd been no way to avoid the consequences, like an overloaded truck with lost brakes speeding downhill. No way to stop or turn around or veer off that course. But he knew then, and still knows now, he couldn't go back in time to change it. He supposed the same was true for Randy. Probably not just for Randy. For all his clients.

He walked into the kitchen and poured himself another whiskey, realized the bottle was almost empty, then poured the rest into his glass rather than recap the bottle. He sat back on the couch, staring at the dying flowers, and wondered what he could have done to make them last longer. His mother used to dissolve sugar into water to feed her flowers. There was no sugar in their apartment—Angie hated to bake and saw no reason to stock things she'd never use—but he looked at his drink thoughtfully, took one last gulp, then dumped the rest into the vase. If the human body turned alcohol into sugar, maybe flowers could do the same. The brown liquid plopped into the water, the thick stems tamping the slosh into a satisfying trickle, like rain dripping through the canopy of a tree.

Chapter Fifteen

In most criminal cases, Julian spends weeks poring through the evidence disclosed by the prosecution. But after Nora's evidence hearing in March, he realizes the evidence file is surprisingly thin. He and Martine—she's back to work on this case, at least a little, because she claimed she might die of boredom if all she did was recuperate—sit at the dining room table, documents spread in neat piles across the dark wood, spring sun blazing through the bay window. He pushes away from the table and tilts on the chair's back legs. This puts them in a better position than he thought.

"Julian," says Martine, her eyebrows raised.

He knows that look; he just thought he would have outrun it by now. He leans forward until the chair is on four legs again, smiling, then says, "Well, that hasn't changed." He's heard this same chastisement about the dining room chairs since he was a kid.

"It's old, and the legs aren't that strong. Besides, that digs into your father's family carpet." She smiles back at him.

"Based on Gil's bluster, I thought he had more evidence," says Julian.

"He has more than enough to convict her."

"Yes, but he keeps harping on her lack of remorse and on supposed violent tendencies in what he claims is one of the most horrific crimes he's ever seen. The last time we spoke, he tried to argue that kids like her are the reason school shootings happen." Julian forgets and tilts backward again but quickly brings the chair down before his elderly mother can chastise him.

"He's a big proponent of gun rights, Julian. Every time something comes up nationally, he's out there repeating that slogan: *Guns don't kill people, people kill people.* He wants to ensure he can blame this on Nora, not the gun."

Julian grunts. "He didn't find evidence of Nora being violent anywhere, so he's going to have a hard time proving that her violent tendencies are a reason to convict her of first-degree murder." After everything the cops took from Nora's room, the months of collecting information and researching the case, the DA's case rests on just a few things: Nora's 911 call, her prints on the gun, the fact that she knew how to use a gun because she'd gone hunting with David, and the bloody clothes she wore when Colin and Ignacio arrived on the scene. Enough, to be sure, but no one ever questioned whether or not she did it, so that wasn't surprising, and Gil found no diary outlining plans to kill Nico, no references to guns or violence on social media or in texts, nothing violent in her paintings. Gil's refusal to negotiate a plea had led Julian to expect he possessed hard evidence supporting his thesis that Nora was violent and the shooting premeditated, but other than her history of depression, there was nothing to indicate Nora was anything other than a regular kid. The worst he could come up with was his unsubstantiated claim that her silence was proof of a lack of remorse.

"I still think this is part of his political agenda," says Martine. "But in the end, all he really wants is a conviction."

"I wonder if he's already asked for his own psych evaluation. Every time I bring up mental health, he brushes me off, and that could be because the results match ours and he doesn't want to admit it, or because they didn't show any psychosis and he plans to accuse her of malingering and use that against her," says Julian.

"We won't know until we get to trial, so there's not much we can do

other than speculate. And if the state's evaluation says something different, at least we have ours to counterbalance it."

Julian nods, then pulls the pile of police interviews of Nora toward
him. There are four, one from that night, the next day, the following
week, and a final one two weeks later. Each resulted in almost no information. Either she hadn't been speaking at the time of the interview or
she simply said what she always says: she didn't remember. But there's
one thing in the file that might help them. On the night of the shooting,
when Ignacio and Colin questioned Nora, they did it without her parents or a lawyer present.

"So?" asks Martine. "Why does that matter?"

"She's under eighteen. A minor can't waive her own rights for questioning," says Julian.

"But it wasn't formal questioning," says Martine. "It was informal,
at the crime scene. The police can informally question a kid. They can
informally question anyone."

"Yeah, but she was sitting in the cop car. That makes it a custodial
interrogation. No kid would have felt like they could leave without answering questions."

Martine shrugs. "But she didn't answer any questions, because she
wasn't speaking. After the 911 call, she didn't speak again for more than
two weeks, so it's not like their interrogation led to a confession that is
now tainted. I'm not sure that detail matters."

"Maybe not," says Julian. "But it might open the door for Gil to finally negotiate. The optics of questioning a thirteen-year-old girl stuck
in a cop car without her parents aren't good."

"We could try getting the media involved. Convince someone to do
an investigative report on the sloppy tactics of the DA's office." Martine
shifts in her seat and tilts back the same way Julian did ten minutes ago.

This time Julian raises his eyebrows.

"Old habit, I guess." She laughs, not even a little embarrassed, and the
chair thumps back to the ground.

"Maybe we can change the narrative out there and start portraying
her as what she was, a kid suffering from a mental health crisis. If we

get the media on our side, that might persuade Gil to stop focusing on a made-up motive—killing Nico to get back at him, or whatever his theory of the moment is—and acknowledge it wasn't premeditated. That might push him away from the first-degree murder charge."

The problem with this plan is the media has relentlessly focused on the *why*. Some articles in the news supply their own answers and side with Gil: Nora was a violent kid, the product of violent video games and movies, and must have snapped after arguing with Nico. Others aren't convinced and assume no thirteen-year-old could do this unless she had a mental health issue. After seeing the psych evaluation, Angie and David perseverated on the cause of her psychosis—What triggered it? Depression? The medication for the depression? Drugs?—but legally, the cause is irrelevant. He's told them this now several times: the law will account for the existence of the psychosis but disregard the cause. Its existence simply means they can try for a "not guilty by reason of insanity" verdict, which Julian still thinks is too risky, or argue it's a mitigating factor to reduce her total prison sentence.

And then there's the angle he considered last fall, the idea of a mercy killing. Nora once said Nico was terrified of Huntington's, scared he'd end up like Livia in a nursing home, and though she didn't say it, it was clear she was scared, too. Nora might have convinced herself—or the voices she was hearing convinced her—this was an act of mercy. But that *why* wouldn't help with her defense. Killing a person isn't legal even if it's merciful. Some states allow physician-assisted suicide, but this was nothing close to that. And Nico might have lived another five or ten years, so not only is that something they can't use for her defense—he still thinks Gil would see it as an admission of premeditation and intent—but it's something he hopes the public will never raise, because he doesn't know if they'd be sympathetic.

But maybe all this wondering is pointless: if there's no obvious answer to the *why*, and as long as Nora isn't a violent predator threatening the community, maybe the public wouldn't need to know *why* in order to sympathize with her. Maybe he can turn people's attention away from the question of why to the matter of what the police had done wrong by questioning a child without a lawyer or parent present.

It was at least worth a shot.

When Mayumi calls later that day, her voice is bright and cheerful, the way it always is. She's between patients, she says, and just wants to say hi.

"Hi," he says back. "I miss you." He imagines her sitting in her office with its green plants and gray couch, a couch not so uncomfortable that patients feel uneasy but not comfortable enough for them to want to stay beyond an hour, a box of tissues on the end table for the criers, and a wire wastebasket to throw away tissues full of tears—or, for the non-criers, to throw away tissues ripped to shreds by fretful hands. At the end of each day, she walks around her office, dictating notes or making phone calls, trying to get in the steps her smartwatch forces on her. He actually *is* walking, up and down Martine's driveway, looking at his own fitness tracker and wishing he could go for a run up Wolf Creek Trail, but he has too much to do and his joints have ached recently even when he's not running. "How's Mayumi Junior doing? Is she marinating in BBQ sauce or olive oil and lemon juice today? Or just ice cream?"

"Not Mayumi Junior," she says. "I don't want to name the baby after me! I'm not having this conversation again."

"Fine," says Julian. "How about something old-fashioned, like Josephine? And Mayumi as a middle name."

"Maybe." She laughs. "And if it's a boy, Julian Junior, JJ for short?"

"Okay, okay. I see your point. JJ doesn't sound exactly right. If it's a boy, Bernard, maybe. Or Cyrus or Theo."

"Maybe," she says again. "We have to see the baby's face first, so we know what she or he looks like. And who."

"Yeah." He's silent for a second—the sperm was donated; the baby can't look like him—but he knows that's not what she means and he can't raise this fear again, anyway (*We're having a baby, it doesn't matter how!*). They've talked about this. He doesn't care that the baby won't genetically be his; after all, Cyrus wasn't his biological father and that never mattered to him or Cyrus, but sometimes he feels like he and his bad sperm failed Mayumi. He only says, "How, exactly, would a baby Bernard differ from a baby Cyrus?"

"We'll know when we see the baby," she says. "That's the whole point."

"How? It will have a little wrinkled face that looks like every other baby!"

She demurs by changing the subject. "How's your day going?"

"Better, maybe." He tells her about Nora being questioned by the cops without her parents and that it might give them enough ammunition to force the DA into negotiating.

She's happy for him, he can tell by the tone in her voice, but changes the subject. She won't say it aloud, because she's empathetic and generous to a fault, but he knows she's tired of him being here and not there, tired of hearing about this case, and would rather talk about something else. And he understands—how could he not, when he remembers how hard it was when Angie traveled back and forth to care for Roberto. He's now acutely aware that Angie's travel was what enabled her to start an affair with David, to choose another man, a whole other life, over him. All these years, he'd never realized Angie cheated, but one night as he re-read Nora's file, he figured it out: Angie married David just two months after leaving him, got pregnant, and had Nico soon after. And Nico's birth was no mistake, because Nora came less than a year later. All those times Angie said she didn't want kids because of her art career had been a lie. She wanted marriage, she wanted kids. She just didn't want them with *him*. It felt like a punch in the gut, even fifteen years later.

He would never cheat on Mayumi the way Angie cheated on him, ever, but he wonders if Mayumi wonders. And although Mayumi understands why he has to work on Nora's case, he feels guilty being in Lodgepole so often, and worse, focusing on it when he's back in New York and should be paying attention to his life there.

"I'm going to dinner at my sister's tonight," she says now. "The twins won an award for best history project at school and we're celebrating with pizza and ice cream."

"What are they, third grade?"

"Yes," says Mayumi. "They're growing up fast."

"So is this best in their class, best in the whole third grade, or best in the school?" He suddenly feels irritable, even though he should be excited for them. He's missing time with Mayumi, missing time with their nephews. Missing out on pieces of his own life to help an old girlfriend who cheated on him and left him. He swallows his resentment over being forced into working on this case.

"Best in anything is exciting when you're in third grade," she says.

Julian spends part of the afternoon scrolling through the district attorney's website, hunting for inspiration. Gil's picture looks nothing like the man Julian usually sees on the other side of the courtroom. In his official headshot, glasses perch on his nose, as if the lenses will make him smarter, even though when he's in the local paper the glasses are absent. It's a small DA's office, covering a six-county area in this rural part of Colorado. Besides Gil, there's only one assistant district attorney and two deputy district attorneys, all three virtual clones of him, just twenty years younger. When Julian clicks on the website's "News and Media" link, he finds an almost laughable list of crimes that have been prosecuted, at least compared to what he's used to seeing in New York. A guilty verdict two months ago for distribution of twenty grams of methamphetamine (*Twenty grams!* he thinks. *What about twenty kilos?*), an indictment four months ago for assault in a highway bar, a warning from last summer about an illegal camper near a popular trail who had rifles and a crossbow laid out in view of passing hikers, and a notification that no charges would be filed in the death of a man who fell off a cliff while fleeing a police officer outside of Waring. On the home page, an image of a herd of deer standing in the snow sits above the mission statement: ***"We seek justice for the victims of crime and pursue justice for our communities through fair and ethical prosecution of those who commit crimes."*** The first tab on the home page is "Victim Information," with links to information about victim rights, victim resources, and victim compensation.

Julian studies this thoughtfully. Maybe Gil hopes prosecuting Nora as an adult will, in addition to bolstering his opposition to the juvenile justice reform bill, improve his "News and Media" page, make it look more serious, as if he's more than a big fish in a small pond. Martine is right: if they go to the media with the cops' blunder—a custodial interrogation with no parents present to waive Nora's Miranda rights—that could undermine Gil's quest to be taken seriously. But they may have something else: this mission statement proclaiming victim rights are paramount. Nico, the first victim, is dead. But Angie and David stand in as victims because they're his parents. Gil, by refusing to negotiate a plea deal, something Angie and David want because Nora is their daughter and they want this ordeal to be over, is ignoring the victims' wishes. Maybe they also take this to the media. And maybe not just to local media, but to Denver media.

He goes back to Martine with this plan, but she has a better idea.

"No," she says. "Don't take it to the media right away. Angie and David don't want this in the news any more than it already has been. What you need to do is threaten Gil with both things: the cops' blunder and ignoring the victims' wishes. We'll end up with the best of both options if it works: a plea deal for Nora and no more painful media coverage for the Sheehans."

"Good point," says Julian. "That's a better way to handle it."

"See? Even mostly retired, I'm not useless."

You never were, thinks Julian. *It just took me a while to get over the past.*

Julian doesn't bother to call or email Gil Stuckey in advance. He drives sixty minutes to Waring and shows up unannounced so Gil can't weasel out of meeting with him. The brick building housing the DA's office is topped with a clock tower, and the clock hands inform the world it's 9:00 a.m. even though it's actually 2:45 in the afternoon. If he were back in New York, he'd be halfway through his workday, maybe on a conference call or headed to Rikers to meet a client. He has four clients there now, one woman and three men, only one of the men isn't a man; he's a boy. Terrence is sixteen, just barely, charged as an adult for assault after he fought with a friend about a girl. Julian visits Terrence more than he has to because he can see the abject terror in Terrence's eyes when he looks at the other prisoners in the cavernous visiting room. The terror isn't unfounded: when Terrence's uncle was in Rikers three years ago, a gang leader forced him to participate in a fight night, and he ended up in a coma and had to relearn how to walk and talk. Rikers Island is in its own special category for brutality, beyond what Nora might be subjected to, but Julian doesn't want Angie's daughter to end up as terrified as Terrence.

Inside, he marches past Gil's gatekeeper, a woman so old she may have worked as a secretary under every DA for the past seven decades. She raises a hand with gnarled knuckles as if to wave him off, then lets it float back to her desk when she sees he's already opening the door to Gil's office.

Gil stands up behind his desk when Julian enters.

"Can I help you?" he asks. His voice is saccharine and smooth, exactly the same as it sounds over the phone. In court, he injects a sincerity into his voice that's entirely absent here.

Julian holds his hand out. "Good afternoon, Mr. Stuckey. It's nice to see you."

"Do we have an appointment, Mr. Dumont?"

"We do now." Julian doesn't wait for permission to start talking. He summarizes his position: the violation of Nora's rights by subjecting her to a custodial interrogation without her parents, the violation of Gil Stuckey's own mission statement by ignoring the victims' wishes.

"Nora didn't say anything when they questioned her in the police car, Mr. Dumont. She wasn't speaking. And we wouldn't need that statement to convict her, anyway. She confessed she shot her brother on the 911 call, and almost every judge I know will admit that into evidence because it wasn't a custodial interrogation."

"Maybe," says Julian. "Or maybe the illegal questioning will lead the judge to question even the 911 call, meaning you'd no longer have a confession, making your prosecution that much harder."

"This is all to be litigated in the upcoming trial, Mr. Dumont." Gil crosses his arms across his chest. "Why are you here?"

Julian pulls a piece of paper from his briefcase and hands it to Gil. "It's a press release."

Gil scans it, his eyes narrowing, but doesn't say anything.

"I know you like to project a tough-on-crime attitude, and I know you're using Nora as an example to bolster your opposition to the juvenile justice reform bill—"

"That bill is bullshit and will never make it out of committee," says Gil.

"Spare me the rhetoric," says Julian.

"Have you ever considered that not everything in the criminal justice system is black and white? This is a gray area, and sometimes it's as hard for me to walk those lines as it is for a defense attorney. I'm upholding Colorado law in a system that's already working the way it's supposed to."

"That's not—"

Gil holds up a hand. "The system *is* working. We already have appropriate alternative programs for juveniles—and because of those, criminal filings against them have dropped almost fifty percent in the past fifteen years—but you know as well as I do that your client wouldn't qualify for those anyway because she committed murder. And that juvenile justice bill? Have you noticed the provisions that would shift some responsibility away from the child and onto the parents by subjecting them to a child neglect case if their child doesn't follow the guidelines in those alternative programs? That shift is premised on the assumption these kids have neglectful or abusive parents, and that's not always the case. Kids make their own choices. Would you want Nora Sheehan's situation to be made worse by charging her parents with neglect?"

"The poster child for your argument doesn't need to be Nora Sheehan," says Julian. He shifts his weight from one foot to the other, because he's standing in front of Gil's desk to project his "tall and imposing" look, and one of his feet has fallen asleep even though he's in the middle of an inane argument. "She's thirteen. How has that number not made an impression on you?"

"She committed murder." Gil's voice is flat.

"Thirteen," says Julian, pointing at the press release. "That makes me certain the media would eat this headline up: *Small-town DA and cops botch investigation into thirteen-year-old girl.* And then, the same small-town DA harasses the victim's parents by dragging out the trial and preventing them from moving on with their lives, even though your own website proclaims the paramount importance of victims' rights. That's not an example of the system working the way it's supposed to."

Gil hands the press release back to him.

"Oh, no, Mr. Stuckey. That copy is yours. Unless, of course, you'd like to talk about a plea deal." Julian balanced the pros and cons of this bluff the whole way here, but he and Martine are desperate to avoid a trial. Nora could end up with an unfriendly jury and a life sentence just as easily as a friendly jury and a shorter sentence. They don't want to take that risk if they don't have to.

Gil stands there, motionless and silent.

"It's been a pleasure, Mr. Stuckey," Julian says. "Think about it and let me know how you'd like to proceed." Julian turns to go, wondering if his gambit has failed.

"Fine, Mr. Dumont," snaps Gil. "I'll talk to you about a plea."

The ancient secretary appears at the door, unsummoned, holding an old-fashioned paper calendar in one hand and a pen in the other. It's not just her knuckles that are gnarled; beneath her dress, two knees poke through nylons like eyes protruding from the bark of a quaking aspen.

"I'm going on vacation tomorrow," says Gil. "Make an appointment with Nancy for early April."

When Julian and Martine eat dinner that night, it's still light out. It's the spring equinox, and the sun now sets at the same time as in September, a time of year he halfway associates with summer. In the middle of winter, the sun sets in Lodgepole at four-thirty but disappears behind the steep mountains on both sides of town even earlier, sometimes at three o'clock, rendering every afternoon dim and dusky even when the skies are clear, and he's glad that time of the year is past. While he met with Gil, Martine had cooked a *tahchin*, baked rice with lamb and spinach, and she sets a large helping on Julian's plate, then pulls the window blind all the way up to enjoy the sun. She's mostly followed the doctor's orders to stop working and reduce stress but seems to have transferred her energy into cooking instead. She tried, a few times, to accompany Julian to meetings, but now that they've reconnected he doesn't want to lose her, and this afternoon he made her stay home.

"It's a good celebration dinner," she says. "I can't believe he finally agreed to discuss a plea."

"It's almost unbelievable, especially coming from Gil Stuckey," says Julian. "Hey—not to change the topic, but are you resting enough? All this cooking? Being on your feet this much? You have to be in good health for when the baby comes."

"I'm doing exactly what the doctor ordered," she says. "Not working too hard and relaxing by doing the things I love to do, like cooking."

"It's delicious," mumbles Julian, halfheartedly covering his mouth with his hand. A drip of turmeric-colored yogurt falls from his fork and he scoops it up with his index finger. It's been a long time since he had this Persian treat, and he can't help himself.

"This was Cyrus's favorite," she says. "I never make it anymore because it's too much work for one person."

"You still miss him, don't you?"

"We were married for a long time. He was everything to me." She takes a small bite, then sets her fork down. "I hope someday it won't hurt so much."

"How long did it take after my first father died?" He doesn't remember Theodore or having anyone but Cyrus as a father. He's talked to Martine about what traits he inherited from Theodore, what he was like as a person, but never asked how *she* felt after his death, and he recognizes now the selfishness of his younger self, never thinking of his mother.

Martine looks out the window. "It's been more than forty years since he died," she finally says. "We barely had any time together, in the grand scheme of things. I had a lot more time with Cyrus. But I haven't forgotten how much it hurt when Theo died. All the men in his family died young, but I never thought he'd follow in their footsteps. It was a shock, but I had you to worry about, diapers to change and a job I needed so

I could pay our bills. I met Cyrus a few months later, and life started to make sense again. He became your father—and my everything—and we moved here not long after that."

Julian puts his fork down and reaches for her hand. The edge of Lodgepole Ski Area is visible through the bay window, the white trails carving across a swath of pine and spruce trees. Maybe her marrying so soon after Theodore's death was like him quitting skiing. A way to forget, a way to move on. And maybe, in some strange sense, it worked, but he wonders, not for the first time, what his life would have been like if he'd made different choices. He and Angie had wondered about that, and fought, in the rare times Diana pushed into their conversations, but if he brings up regrets in his current life Mayumi chastises him. Wondering what might have been is one of life's greatest burdens, she says. She'd tell him that now, if she were here.

"It's strange, isn't it?" he says.

"What's strange?"

"How something that was so important to you can just . . . fade away. I thought I'd ski in college, maybe go on to coach—" He doesn't mention the whole other life he'd planned, a life in New York with his first love, a brownstone, and four children.

Martine looks at him thoughtfully. "And marry Angie."

He wonders how much she knows. He always thought he kept his relationship in New York with Angie a secret, but maybe she'd figured it out, or known all along. Maybe he should have admitted to it long ago. Or maybe she's just remembering how he felt in high school.

He picks up his fork again and shovels another bite into his mouth.

Chapter Sixteen

When Angie calls the next day, Martine assumes it's about the plea negotiations, but it's Livia. *Of course*, thinks Martine. *Of course Livia would choose to die now, during this difficult time for Angie.* But Angie doesn't seem upset.

"It's a relief, to be honest. I know that sounds bad, but she hasn't been herself for a long time. You know how Alzheimer's is." Her voice is matter-of-fact.

"Yes," says Martine. "It's a cruel disease."

"I probably shouldn't have agreed to the feeding tube," says Angie. "If it were me, I wouldn't have wanted it. But I was supposed to do what she would have wanted, and she was a stubborn son-of-a-bitch."

Martine doesn't disagree, but she just *mm-hmm*s.

"Anyway, I know this might seem strange, but the funeral is next Thursday, if you want to come. She—" Angie hesitates. "She was angry, after Diana died. But I know you were friends before then."

"Yes," says Martine, "but if we're talking about what she would have wanted, I'm not sure I'm the right person to be there."

"It depends which version of my mother you're talking about. The one you were friends with before—she would have wanted you there. You don't have to come. I just thought you might want to."

In the other room, Julian rustles papers and his fingers tap his laptop keyboard, preparing for the plea negotiations with Gil Stuckey next week. He's flying to New York on Thursday to spend the weekend with Mayumi, then back here Monday. He'll have a good excuse to avoid Livia's funeral. Martine is certain no version of Livia would have wanted Julian at her funeral: dead Livia, Alzheimer's Livia, post–Diana's accident Livia, or pre-accident Livia.

"I'll come," she finally says, even though she'd rather not. There's a children's consignment store around the corner from the church, and maybe she can sneak into it after the funeral. Her secret stash of baby toys is big enough, but maybe she can find something for the baby for next winter, a hat or a puffy bunting for cold walks.

Spring in the mountains is Mother Nature oscillating wildly. Every time a snowdrift begins to melt, exposing a lost ski pole or dropped pair of goggles, winter rushes back in with late storms, rebuilding that same snowdrift and the hopes of skiers, then melting again into a torrent of mud. When Martine walks Jack in the cemetery, his yellow fur blurs into brown, and every time he returns to the house, she has to wipe his feet so he doesn't track paw prints everywhere.

The aftereffects of the heart attack still wear on her. The effort of getting dressed every day, walking up and down the stairs, or acting happy on days when she feels grumpy weighs more than it did in her youth. She has to adjust to the reality of being old. Some parts of aging were gradual: skin wrinkling, first requiring more moisturizer, then different and more expensive moisturizer, finally triggering an out-of-character desire for Botox; eyesight worsening, requiring stronger and stronger lenses until she was forced to admit to the DMV that she drove with glasses; family disappearing, either because they had their own lives or their life was over. This last shift—confronting the mortality of family members—was sudden, not gradual, but it taught her something. She's no longer afraid of her own health problems because no matter what, being old with health problems is better than being dead.

And another thing: she thought she wanted to retire—that was the plan before Nora's case—but now it seems like all she ever does is cook for Julian, walk Jack, and wipe Jack's feet. And attend funerals she doesn't want to attend. She misses work. She misses the structure, the brain-work. She misses the gravitas it provided to her sense of self and the excuses it bestowed on her social life: *I can't come because I'll be at work, I can't come because I'll be in court.*

She wonders what she's going to say when Nora's case is over and people ask, *What do you do?* What will she say when she's no longer a lawyer? Will *I'm a grandmother* be enough?

At St. John's, the crowd is bigger than at Nico's funeral, but only be-cause no one was invited to his. Angie and David sit in the first pew, and behind them are two rows of seventy-and eightysomethings, mostly women, mourning another expected death but chatting loudly before the service starts, happy it's not their body in the open casket. On the other side of the aisle, a few couples, Angie and David's age, sit quietly. The only funerals they attend are for parents of friends; they're not yet accustomed to having their own friends die. The women Angie used to walk with, the ones who still stride by in their fluorescent sneakers while Martine spins in her office chair idly contemplating retirement, sit among that younger group, probably trying to make up for missing the funeral of Angie's son by attending the funeral of Angie's mother.

Livia was seventy-eight, not very old but not young, either. Not young enough for this to be a tragedy, to be anything other than what's expected. Most of Livia's friends were older than Martine, women Mar-tine knows, but not well. She sits in the second of the blue-hair rows, on the edge of the pew next to the aisle so she can escape if she needs to. The reality that she didn't have many friends had hit hard after Cyrus died. She knew men died first—that's life—but she hadn't expected *her* man to go so far in advance, to leave her widowed for the second time. And when you're in your seventies in a town this size, new boyfriends are few and far between. The irony of worrying about what not working will be like is that she simultaneously wonders if she would've had more friends if she hadn't worked, if she'd stayed home like so many other women in her generation. She should have made time for friends, she knows that now, but *now* is too late. Until Nora's case brought Julian back into her life, sometimes the loneliness of being a two-time widow ballooned inside, straining her willingness to endure.

Martine smooths the wrinkles in her black dress, then presses her palm on her thigh to calm her jiggling foot. At the lectern, Father Lopez is Our Father–ing and Hail Mary–ing, and just in front of him, Livia's skeleton-like hands clutch her rosary beads like a claw, forever devout yet forever unforgiving. A woman to Martine's left blows her nose, the sound like an elephant's trumpet in the quiet church, and Martine shrinks into the hard wooden bench, hoping no one thinks it's her. Father Lopez must be hungry, because when he gets to the eulogy, he spends all his time on Livia's food at DeLuca's and none on Livia herself. The taste of her red sauce, her bread, her eggplant parm! The red wine! The aroma of garlic roasted with olive oil and oregano and the tang of her fried artichokes! The red wine! He stops when he realizes he said red wine twice and the audience titters politely.

After the service, she stands in the receiving line to give her condolences. David, in the same suit he wore to Nico's funeral—Martine remembers the missing button from his left cuff, and maybe a national park ranger only owns one suit—stands next to Angie. He occasionally puts his arm around her shoulders, but Angie doesn't need the comfort. She's wearing navy blue instead of black and chats with each guest. David's Irish skin is pink and peeling—Angie mentioned he'd been doing trail maintenance on a temporary job in New Mexico—and Martine's first thought is that he should wear more sunblock to protect himself from cancer, but that's an inappropriate thought, especially for a funeral, so she shoves her judgment to the back of her mind.

"Thank you for coming." David, holding a casserole dish the last mourner plopped into his hands, turns to set it on the table as he says this.

"I'm sorry for your loss," responds Martine automatically. There's no one left in the DeLuca family to blame Julian for Diana's death, yet the closure she expected eludes her. Maybe while Livia was still alive, she should have looked toward Livia's grief, not away from it. Her fear of Livia's potential reprisals caused her to make a decision—to send Julian away—that she'd felt guilty about ever since. Would she do it again? "Julian wishes he could have come"—that's a lie, of course—"but he had to be in New York for work."

"It's okay, Martine," says Angie, reaching out to hug her. "I understand. I really do."

The thing is, everyone has a skeleton in their closet, something they feel guilty about, something they blame themselves for. She ticks off her own, ranging from dollars snatched from her mother's wallet when she was a kid to leaving her younger brother alone when she was supposed to babysit to cheating, just once, on a high school sewing test. Helping Julian evade responsibility for whatever happened to Diana. Worst of all: falling in love with Cyrus just months after Theo died. It was a betrayal she never would have thought herself capable of, but Cyrus was an oxygen mask in the middle of a firestorm, the only thing that saved her from suffocating in sorrow, that enabled her to breathe and care for a newborn that howled anytime she tried to shower or eat.

"Yes," she says to Angie now. "I know you do."

Martine isn't sure Julian learned to bear his share of the burden from Diana's accident—Gregory once told her of Julian's alcohol struggles, and she hopes he's past that because she hasn't seen him drink since they reconnected—but they don't talk about it. She hopes they can, someday. Maybe being here would have been good for him. Or not. He's always held the secret of what happened to Diana that day close. Maybe what he didn't tell her is what's been hurting him all these years. She has no real way of knowing what he's been through.

Martine hugs Angie again, struck by the frail frame under the navy dress, her arms like matchsticks, shoulders almost as bony as the body in the casket, then heads toward the side door so she can sneak away and avoid the post-ceremony cookies and tea. Nora, too, would need to learn to live with guilt, but that wouldn't be possible until she acknowledged—to herself, at least—having committed the murder. Her future would be marked by a dark cloud until she did. So far, she's protected herself under the banner of memory loss, and they've all assumed the diagnosis of psychosis is correct, but there are two other possibilities. Gil's argument, that Nora was an angry and violent kid—which isn't supported by the evidence and she didn't believe—and something else entirely, something Julian raised a few nights ago: this was a mercy killing to save Nico from a certain, horrible future. It doesn't matter, though. Knowing why she did it won't lessen Nora's guilt or Angie's pain. Martine looks back over her shoulder at Angie, her life like a face in a Cubist painting, eyes and nose and lips barely held together by a hodgepodge of glue and tape, ready to disintegrate in the slightest puff of wind, then gently pulls the church's side door closed.

Chapter Seventeen

Nora and Jacqueline have bottom bunks now. They've been here longer than the other girls in their pod and all new girls sleep on top bunks. They—like Paradise and Maria Elena—have the unlucky distinction of being charged as adults so their cases take longer to resolve. Paradise left months ago, just three days after Christmas, a day she made everyone in the common area sit by the television tuned to a Yule log while they ate the nice guard's popcorn again. She said she'd won in court and was only sentenced to twelve years. The first five would be in a Department of Youth Services correctional facility in Denver, far from here and even farther from home, because the correctional facility attached to this building is full. Her aunt can't visit there because it's too far, but she shrugged about that. She seemed happy about twelve years, but Nora and Jacqueline thought it was a long time for dealing meth.

"After I turn twenty-one, the other seven will be in regular prison, but I might be out on parole by then," Paradise said as she stuffed one picture and two books into a small plastic bag. She wasn't allowed to take any toiletries, so she left those in her bin and shoved it back under the bed, then stood between the two bunks, looking around as if there were more to pack. Nora and Jacqueline stood by the door, and the guard waiting in the hall tapped her foot.

"Do you know anyone there?" asked Nora. "In the DYS in Denver, I mean."

Paradise shook her head. "But people get moved, all the time."

Jacqueline reached out and hugged Paradise, and when she was done, Paradise hugged Nora, then walked out the door.

"See you there, maybe," she called over her shoulder.

They waited until Paradise's footsteps faded down the hall, then pulled out the bin to take the toiletries she'd left behind. They split the pads—the guards never gave anyone enough to get through a whole period, and it was hard to know why Paradise had extras stashed away—and Nora took the toothpaste and Jacqueline took the soap.

Those extra pads are now long gone, and Nora is back to rationing hers, using each one until it overflows with blood, washing her underwear in the sink at night. Since Paradise left, seven other girls have come and gone. The two newest—Zoey and Ximena—decided they hate each other and lie on their mattresses, each facing the opposite wall, whenever they're in the room. Zoey was yanked off her medications when she got here because the state psychiatrist was on vacation during intake. When she's not throwing up from the withdrawal from the Suboxone used to treat her opioid addiction, she's crying because of the withdrawal from her depression meds. Her crime? Truancy. She wasn't attending school because her family lived in a car and didn't have an address to register her. Ximena was arrested three times at her middle school in Rimrock Junction, twice for vaping pot and once for a fight that put another girl in the hospital. None of this is new for her: she was only nine the first time she was handcuffed, by a white SRO who told her she was headed down the wrong path, straight to jail. She thinks she'll be released on probation by next week and says she can't be bothered to make friends with anyone, even though she tells her story to anyone who will listen. Because she keeps starting fights, the guards have placed her in a Wrap twice now, the second time with a spit mask that made her feel like she couldn't breathe. She talks about being wrapped with a fear that belies her bravada, but no one makes fun of her for that. Being placed in that full-body straitjacket is all their worst fears, other than extended time in the seclusion room.

Julian still visits Nora every other week, and one day he talks about a meeting he'll have with the DA that might avoid a trial. He chooses his words carefully, repeating the meaning of *plea negotiations* and other technical terms so she'll understand what he's saying, but it's clear there's something else on her mind: she asks why everyone else is always coming and going and she's always staying.

"I don't mean people visiting me. I mean the other kids. I have new roommates, again."

They've talked about this before, but he reminds her it's because kids only stay in juvenile detention until their cases are resolved. After sentencing, they're transferred to a correctional facility, or the ones who've already served their time or committed less serious crimes are released to the custody of their parents or to a group home as part of a juvenile diversion program. When he says that, *released to the custody of their parents*, hope shoots across her face, a star falling from heaven that most people could wish on.

"Could I be . . . ?" she asks.

His jaw tightens, sending rippling lines across his cheeks. "No. I'm sorry, Nora, but your crime was too serious." Julian is never unkind, but he doesn't dance around things with his clients the way he sees parents do. "We've talked about this before. You won't be going home for a long time, but I'm working as hard as I can to make sure it's not forever. Ten, twenty, thirty years is what it will probably be, although I hope it will be closer to ten than thirty. That's what the plea negotiations are for."

They *have* talked about it before, but all those numbers, all those decades—that *is* forever to Nora. Forever to any child in this facility. She looks down at her hands and bites her lip. She remembers more of that night than she's willing to admit, but the whole truth—a horrible truth—is buried deep inside. For the first few days after Nico died, she couldn't stop remembering and wished she'd died, too. The only way to go on, the only way to survive, was to forget. But twenty years is more years than Nora has been alive. Thirty years is more than double her age. How can she keep her cache of memories hidden for that long?

"What if it's true?" she blurts out. "What if I did it?"

"Are you saying you didn't?"

"I don't remember," says Nora. She's not ready to unbury this truth. "I still don't remember."

Julian sets his pen on the table. Most girls would have opened up to their lawyers by now, some with the truth, others with concocted stories they think might exonerate them or reduce their culpability. Nora is not most girls, though, and there are some questions he no longer wants answered. If the plea negotiations fail, he might want her to testify, but she can't testify if he thinks she'll lie on the stand. The buzz outside the room, of people talking and shouting or slamming doors, softens. "Do you think you ever will?"

The words come out in a whisper. "I don't want to."

"Why not?"

Nora fidgets, then sits on her hands.

"You don't have to tell me if you don't want to, Nora. It's okay."

"What if—what if that other lawyer is right?"

Julian raises his eyebrows.

"Mr. what's-his-name, the fat one," she adds impatiently. "Mr. Stuckey. He thinks I'm cold-blooded and violent. What if I am what he—what everyone—says I am?"

Julian drums his pen on the table, then spins it on top of his finger, a trick Nora tries to copy but has yet to master. He's thinking one thing, Nora another. Neither wants to say what they're really thinking. "The evidence says you did it, and you confessed in the 911 call," he says. "But I don't think you're cold-blooded. I think your brain went haywire. And I think every human is, or can be, different than what other people say they are. You did a bad thing, but that doesn't make you a bad person."

"But I can't undo the bad thing." Nora—and in this she is like most other girls here—wishes she could take back what happened that night, do or say something different, anything to undo what she did. Learning to live with consequences is a hard lesson.

"No," he says. "You can't. None of us can undo the bad things we've done. All we can do is learn from our mistakes."

Nora doesn't answer at first, but she eventually nods.

He adds, "You need to become the person you want to be instead of the person who did the bad thing."

Nora looks back up at Julian. "But how am I supposed to know who the person I want to be is? And how am I supposed to find her in here?" She pulls her hands out from under her legs and looks down at them, raw and wrinkled.

Jacqueline is the only girl Nora started with that's still here. For some reason, rumors of what she did never followed her into juvie, but one day she shares her secret with Nora. She stabbed her father with a butcher knife from the kitchen. "It was easy," she says matter-of-factly. "He drank so much he passed out, so he didn't fight. He did that a lot— drank, I mean. And then he'd wake up in the middle of the night and come for me."

Nora doesn't say anything. Who is she to ask questions about something like that?

"The night before I stabbed him, he went after my sister instead of me, and she's only ten," Jacqueline says. "So I had to. And I don't feel sorry."

Jacqueline looks at Nora, her eyes unflinching, and Nora holds her gaze.

The regimented schedule at the detention center is purposeful. Wake up at 5:30 a.m., make your bed, get dressed. Breakfast, 6:00 a.m. Classes, 6:30 to 10:30. Lunch at 11:00, dinner at 4:30. Group classes—like anger management therapy and PE—are not optional, whether or not you need the therapy (most do) and whether or not you like to play basketball (only some do), and are in the afternoon. Quiet time, when everyone must be in their cell with the door closed and locked from the outside, is scheduled regularly but also imposed unexpectedly if the detention center is short-staffed. Deviations from that schedule, breaks in the routine—those are avoided because they make it more difficult to control the girls.

Anger management therapy is where Nora is when a guard sticks his head in the door. Every head in the room turns toward him in unison: the kids are relieved to have a break from the monotony of learning to control uncontrollable emotions, and the therapist, the third to rotate through since the first of the year, is relieved she can stop trying to teach anger management when all she feels today is anger.

"You have a visitor," he says, and looks at Nora.

"But it's not visiting hours."

He shrugs. "The warden told me someone needs to see you."

A couple of the girls whistle under their breath.

"You're in trouble now, Nora," catcalls one.

Nora's cheeks flush, and she looks at the therapist for permission. The therapist nods, and Nora scampers out behind the guard.

In the visitors room, Angie paces back and forth but stops and wraps her arms around Nora when she enters, squeezing so tight Nora coughs.

"Why are you here?" asks Nora, pulling away from the embrace. "Everyone got mad that I left group."

Angie sits down and pats the chair next to her. "Why don't you sit down?"

Nora crosses her arms across her chest. "I don't feel like it."

"I have bad news, sweetie."

"Go away," Nora says. "I don't want to talk to you."

"I'm sorry, Nora. I know this is hard to hear." Angie pulls on Nora's hand, trying to make her sit down, but Nora jerks her hand away, banging Angie's hand into the metal table.

"Ow," says Angie. "That hurt."

Nora backs away, into a corner of the room, and Angie follows and tries to hug her again. Nora shoves her away, hard, as if she suspects what Angie is about to say and doesn't want to hear it, then slumps into a chair, overwhelmed by a ballooning prescience she cannot understand.

"Grandma Livia—well, she died."

After the words come out, Angie returns to the chair on the other side of the table and wonders if her daughter is trying to land on the right feeling. Sadness, because her grandmother died, and death is always sad. Relief, because Livia wasn't her grandmother anymore, wasn't anything other than a sack of bones with a funny smell she had to work hard to ignore. Shame, for pushing her mother. All those feelings would be fair feelings, feelings any child would feel in this situation.

Angie has pictures, not of Livia but of the church and the flowers. She speaks gently of the funeral, friends that were there, friends with names that mean nothing to Nora because they belong to other grandmothers, and what the priest said. Nora listens because she has to, nods when she's supposed to, but doesn't cry. That's something she no longer does.

On her way out, Angie hands Nora a letter.

"It's from Michelle's daughter. I always forget her name."

"Hannah," says Nora and grabs the letter and stuffs it into her pocket before her mother can ask what it says.

Later, she sits on her bed and tears open the envelope.

> Dear Nora,
> My mother told me about your grandmother, that she died of Alzheimer's. I'm very sorry, and I hope you aren't too sad. I remember you telling me you loved to do puzzles with her, and to make cookies together. I guess you miss her a lot. School is the same as always. I still hate art, but I bet you still love it. I'm starting lacrosse team in a couple of weeks.
>
> xo, Hannah

Hannah added two eyes and a smile to the O. Nora leans against the wall and closes her eyes. This is the first time she's heard anything from or about anyone at school. They aren't allowed to use phones or social media here, no Instagram or Snapchat, and the computers they sometimes use for classes have controls so no one can secretly log in.

Hannah used to be a good friend. Before everyone at school stopped talking to Nora (or was it Nora that stopped talking to everyone at school?), a group of them used to hang out at Hannah's house. Sometimes even at Nora's house. Two of the girls in that group once had crushes on Nico.

Did Hannah's mother make her write this? Maybe she didn't. Maybe Hannah wrote it to be nice. Nora refolds the letter carefully, puts it back in the envelope, and stores it in her plastic bin under the bunk bed.

Later that night, Nora sits on her bottom bunk with crisscrossed legs, facing the wall. The wall is one of the few ways girls here can control their access to privacy; perhaps she doesn't want anyone to see her struggling to write back to Hannah. After all, Hannah wrote about lacrosse and school and Nora's dead grandmother, but what can Nora say?

Dear Hannah, Thank you for your letter. She crosses that out and throws it away. Too formal. She sounds like a teacher.

Dear Hannah, Is lacrosse fun? I always wanted to try it. That's awesome that there's finally a girls' team to join. She throws that out, too. Perhaps it dawns on her: she, Nora, would never get to play lacrosse because she'd never go back to school in Lodgepole.

Dear Hannah, I do miss my grandmother. I didn't get to go to her funeral, which was a bummer. Garbage can, again. The reason she didn't get to go to the funeral was because she's in juvie for killing her brother. She's a murderer. She didn't deserve to go.

She bites her lip. If they've earned enough good behavior points, their pod gets to watch *Friends*—some old show from the nineties—on Friday nights, and they're working through DVDs from the juvie library. She likes it more than she thought she would and can finally laugh at the dumb jokes without feeling quite as guilty about the fact that she's laughing. Can she write about that? Not the laughing part, but what she's watching?

Dear Hannah, Thank y—

Nora stops again, recaps her pen, and puts Hannah's letter back in the plastic bin. She can't write back to Hannah.

Maybe Nora worries Hannah will use Nora's letter against her, screen-shot it and post it on Instagram to make fun of her, or is afraid to disclose what it is that she does in juvie, since she can't play lacrosse or go to her grandmother's funeral. Or maybe Nora simply doesn't know how to write a letter because no one of her generation writes letters. It's the only com-munication she's allowed with the outside world—visitors are restricted to attorneys and her parents—but she crumples up the last piece of paper she wrote on, anyway. Nora has kept all of her thoughts, memories, and feelings buried since the day she shot her brother. Everyone wants to know what's going on in her head, because no one knows. When she tosses the last piece of paper into the garbage can, it swishes silently.

Chapter Eighteen

On the way home from visiting Nora, Angie's minivan turns itself into the church's parking lot. Angie has ups and downs, grief and anger rising then receding, a sense of normalcy within sight and then gone again, but Nora's almost-slap of her hand, the shove, the refusal to cry about Livia—it jarred her, and she is adrift in a sea of emotions, in need of a mooring. Her hand opens the door, her feet settle onto the pavement. The feet, seemingly of their own volition, walk down the path toward the front door, wait patiently for her arms to pull the heavy wood slab and make space to move inside. There's some hesitation, equivocation—what does this mean, why is she here—then a shift in the breath.

As a child, everything inside the church seemed heavy to Angie, the rows of wooden pews on either side of the cavernous room, the dark lectern front and center where the priest stood in his black robe and white clerical collar, sometimes speaking, sometimes listening. The candelabras holding the prayer candles, the thick Bibles, the kneelers she struggled to raise and lower. The slow walk to the front of the church where Father Lopez dispensed communion to the herd of people waiting in line. The gold chalice that held Christ's blood and the cross on the wall with nails through Christ's hands. Even God felt heavy, especially his decision to allow his own son to carry that cross.

God, and Livia, made that younger Angie sorry for her sins once a week, so sorry she had to say Our Fathers and Hail Marys on the stiff kneelers until her knees ached. That felt heavy, too. Livia took penance after confession very seriously and never let Angie skip a week. Roberto's God, the one he claimed watched over Angie when she made snow angels, was lighter, more comforting. When she stared up at the sky from within a newly formed snow angel's body, snowflakes landed gently on her cheek, and he said those were a message from God, telling her *she* was the angel. Angie never believed in Livia's God, an angry God who only sometimes doled out forgiveness for original sin, a sin Angie hadn't committed. She preferred Roberto's God, the one who kissed all of humanity with divinity and love. But somewhere along the way—maybe after Roberto died and she left Julian—she stopped believing in any God. David didn't approve of religion, so it was easy to abandon her belief without guilt and attend church with Livia only as a dutiful daughter.

So if the church only weighs her down, and if she doesn't believe in God, why did her feet lead her here? Though she's not sure, she allows them latitude, and they walk her down the aisle, left at the lectern toward a confessional. Father Lopez holds confession hours for penitents three times a week, and this is one of those times. There's no one waiting outside the wooden booth on the parishioner side, but she hears shuffling on the priest's side. She's here because she wants to be here. She needs someone to talk to, now that Livia the therapist and Livia the confessor is gone.

She steps inside the confessional and kneels, and at first the words come automatically.

"Forgive me, Father, for I have sinned. It's been—" She suddenly realizes she doesn't know how long it's been since her last confession and stops. The oppressive air inside the cloistered wooden booth shrouds her breath, and she fights the urge to push the velvet curtain aside and escape to her minivan.

On the other side of the privacy screen, Father Lopez rustles, then slides the screen open.

"I know it's you and you know it's me." He smiles, and Angie nods uncomfortably. "You can just say it's been a long time, Angie. It's okay."

"I don't know where to start," she says. "With my sins, I mean."

"You can start anywhere, my child. God won't mind."

"God isn't even here," says Angie bitterly. "So why would he mind?"

"I understand you might feel abandoned," says Father Lopez. He pulls on a bushy strand in his eyebrow, then adds, "God goes silent on all of us. It doesn't mean he doesn't love you."

What good does love do, she thinks. *Love doesn't change what happened. It doesn't change anything.* She sits silently, eyes downcast. The minutes pass the way they always do these days, slowly. She holds her hands in her lap, one atop the other. She counts her knuckles, one, two, three, four, then the spaces between her knuckles, one, two, three. Once, those knuckles were how she knew which months had thirty-one days and which didn't. She's procrastinating, putting off confessing as long as possible. There's too much to say; she's committed too many wrongs. Her entire family has been disassembled. Is that her fault? It is her fault, it must be her fault, in so many ways she can't count them all.

"Nora might go to prison for the rest of her life," she finally blurts out. She's angry with Nora, so angry she can't figure out how to forgive her, and she misses Nico every minute of every day, with a deep and thudding ache, but Nora is still her flesh and blood, and she longs for her daughter as much as she longs for her son. "There's a chance she'll be sentenced to life, that she won't be eligible for parole for forty years. I know she did something terrible, but they won't give her the chance to change, to make up for what she did. It's not—none of this is—fair."

"My child," Father Lopez starts, then stops and bows his head. "Angie. You're not wrong. It doesn't seem fair."

She runs her fingers along the ridges of her knuckles again, then says in a low voice, "When did we decide a person can't change?"

He's silent for a moment, eyes still downcast, perhaps staring at his own knuckles. Finally, he clears his throat and says, "I don't have a good answer for that. The criminal justice system doesn't really allow for forgiveness, for much other than punishment and retribution. But you can't control what happens in that system. You're being the best mother you can by supporting her through the process."

Tears, stubborn and fat, gather in the corners of Angie's eyes, and she wipes them away with the back of her hand.

"I suppose there's one thing you can control," he says. "Ask yourself if you're different than the criminal justice system." He looks her in the eyes, and now she bows her head and looks down at her hands again.

"I don't know how," she whispers. "How can I forgive her? And how can I forgive her when I still don't know why she did it?"

"God doesn't attach conditions to forgiveness," says Father Lopez, "and neither should you."

Oh, but he does, thinks Angie bitterly. *Doesn't he?*

"I don't really think it's me you need to be talking to, but I'm always here."

Angie nods, afraid to speak.

"I absolve you from your sins in the name of the Father, the Son, and the Holy Spirit," says Father Lopez.

"Amen."

"Give thanks to the Lord, for he is good," he says.

Angie doesn't remember this part, so she says nothing, and then Father Lopez says, "You would say, if this were an official confession, 'His mercy endures forever.'"

I would, thinks Angie, *if it were*. "Yes," she only says.

"Go in peace, my child. You—" He stumbles, then clears his throat. "Everyone needs peace."

Angie crosses herself and backs out of the confessional, then rushes outside to gulp the fresh air, buoyant and luminous. She realizes too late she didn't confess any sins.

Angie replays what went wrong at Nora's visit over and over. There was her own failure to forgive, of course. Maybe she could have broken the news differently, or been more honest on prior visits. She always downplayed how far gone Livia was because she hoped Nora might be released before Livia died. It was an unrealistic hope, but hope is always unrealistic. Now it's clear that was a mistake because her good intentions resembled a deception. She supposes Nora would have been even angrier if she'd known Livia died alone, that her last moments were in the middle of the night in a dark and empty room. Angie had lied about that, too, telling an elaborate story of Livia dying as Angie sat by her bedside, holding her hand. She said Livia had a peaceful look on her face, almost a smile, and now she wonders whether Nora knew that was a lie, that death is always ugly, even when it's not violent, even when it's expected. Livia fought death the way she fought everything in life. There was no peace in her passing, no smile on her lips. When Angie arrived that morning, Livia's mouth was ajar and her bony face distorted by its struggle to break free of the flimsy, translucent skin.

Angie feels more practical about Livia's death than Nora, as a child, could. She was sad, of course, and angry with herself for not being there for Livia's last moments, but it was time, past time, and Livia had no kind of life left. The last few visits, she'd been shocked to see how little of her mother remained, not mentally—that was long gone—but physically. The muscle and fat between Livia's skin and skeleton had melted away, and even the cartilage on her nose sagged. Livia's jaw and cheekbones stretched the skin so tightly Angie thought it might rip. Her breaths came slow and ragged, and every so often her lungs stilled, as though that breath was the last, but something inside of Livia kept forcing her lungs to rasp in, then rasp out again. It was painful to watch.

Livia certainly had not been kind to Angie after Diana's death, but they'd reunited over caring for Roberto years ago. And no matter what, Livia was Angie's mother. She cared for Angie in her own way, loved her the way a mother was supposed to, and Angie had loved her back. Livia had bandaged her knees, bought her watercolors, helped with homework. And most importantly, even if she hadn't completely taught Angie how to be a mother—Angie hoped she'd been kinder to her own children than Livia was to her—Livia had at least taught her she wasn't destined to fail as one.

Without her mother, Angie might not have made it through Nico's second month. Six weeks after Nico was born, Livia dropped by the small townhouse Angie and David shared. Angie lay on the couch with Nico on her chest, staring at the flickering screen of the TV. A cartoon echoed out from the square box, a cat chasing a mouse, a mouse outsmarting the cat. She hadn't showered in four days and her left nipple was hot and swollen even though she was shivering. The townhouse had more rooms than she'd had in New York, yet she felt the walls constricting around her. She kept wondering if the alcohol she drank before she knew she was pregnant had harmed Nico; the decision she'd made to leave Julian haunted her; and she felt hollow when she looked down at the little life she was responsible for. She sometimes sobbed at sappy commercials, often felt irritable with David for no reason, and wondered why anyone ever had children. When she nursed the baby, she felt like an angry mother bird, forced to regurgitate her own food—food she needed for herself. She loved and resented the tiny life at the same time and couldn't figure out why.

Livia took one look at her, went to the kitchen, and came back with a pot of hot water and a washcloth.

"This is normal," she said. She pulled Nico from Angie's chest and placed him in the bassinet, then dipped the washcloth in the hot water. "Put this on your breast. It will help get rid of the infection. Go see the doctor this afternoon, get antibiotics, then come to DeLuca's. You need to work. You can't stay inside all day."

Angie turned over and faced the back of the couch.

"Get up," said Livia. "You can't take care of your child if you're acting like one." She tugged Angie into a sitting position.

Angie slapped the hot washcloth on her swollen nipple and glared at her mother.

"I expect you at the restaurant by four o'clock," said Livia, her voice brisk and matter-of-fact. "I need help in the kitchen. You can put Nico in that fancy baby carrier while you work. You're going to come every day this week."

Angie sniffled. "I didn't know it would be this hard." The heat on her breast felt better than she'd thought it would.

Livia stood with her hands on her hips and looked around the messy room. "Who told you it would be easy?"

That felt like a trick question.

"Stop feeling sorry for yourself. This happens to everyone." She shooed Angie away. "Go take a shower, and I'll watch Nico."

For the next three weeks, Angie stirred red sauce in the back of DeLuca's with Nico attached to her in the baby carrier. She could finally breathe again. Livia's tough love was what she needed. She didn't know it yet, Livia didn't know it yet, but Angie was already pregnant again, and when Nora was born a month before Nico's first birthday, she'd need toughness to survive.

Without Livia, Angie never could have transformed from a person who only took care of herself into a person—a mother—who only took care of others.

Almost every time she visits Nora, Angie paints with her. She got the idea from Martine and Julian, something to do other than talk. She teaches Nora a new technique, or plants an idea in Nora's head about images to focus on. After leaving New York, Angie had only painted what time allowed: rainbows and stick figures with finger paints when the kids were toddlers, then basic painting for them and her high school students, landscapes or dogs or cars. Nico's wall, of course, but never anything for herself. Now Angie's regular painting with Nora has triggered a lightbulb in her mind, illuminated a part of herself she pushed aside while she mothered.

She pulls out Nora's watercolors, the ones she's been taking to the detention center. Her own paint supplies, shoved into a basement corner, dried up long ago. Within days, she realizes something. This is good for her. Better than all the self-help books. Better than silent therapy and fake confessions with Livia or actual confessions to a God she's not sure she believes in. Better than running, even. Painting had never been just a hobby. It was something elemental that gave her life. Maybe it can be again. She drives to Waring, drumming her fingers on the steering wheel in time to music, buys acrylics, new brushes, and a few canvases, and jumps back into the minivan. It's all on a credit card. She'll figure out how to pay for it later.

At home, hours fly by. She forgets to eat lunch or cook dinner for David. Faces or trees or both emerge on the canvas. Muscle memory in her hands and fingers returns her to abstraction, the idea of an eye in an aspen tree, the scar formed when the tree self-prunes and drops a smaller branch that doesn't receive enough sunlight. Two trees, two eyes. A rock for a nose. Not quite a landscape, because the trees and the rock are almost invisible, but not quite a face. Something like a smile emerges on her own face.

Even if her life is falling apart, she is still this: an artist. She creates beauty; she finds beauty. She is not defined only by her failures.

Angie now runs two or three times a week, whenever warm weather pokes through winter. Wolf Creek Trail is snow-packed in the shade and muddy in the sun, but the Sunday after Livia's funeral she digs out her Yaktrax and decides to run it anyway. Skiing feels like too much work right now and it's something she associates with Nico and Nora.

"Can I come?" asks David.

Angie can't tell if his face is hopeful or already disappointed. "Sure," she says, unsure of her own feelings. Since he's been back from New Mexico, they've existed in an uneasy detente. When they talk, they talk about the weather, or the next legal meeting, or the tip for Father Lopez at Livia's funeral. Not Nico, even though his absence gnaws at Angie like an insatiable rat. David only seems to care about Nora's absence, as though his mourning for Nico ended the day of the funeral. She doubts he looks for Nico each day the way she does, finding pieces of him in other boys on the street, in the cookie aisle of the market, in the window of a passing car. He let go of Nico too easily, as if he'd opened up his fingers to let a melting ice cube escape without trying to hold on to it, to capture and contain it for just one moment more. The implication of this flickers above her occasionally, the full import amassing, waiting to reveal itself, but most days she reassures herself there's no way he could know the truth. She's hidden it too well.

She waits by the front door while he disappears upstairs to change, wondering if they'll talk on the run. A gradual acceptance of the circumstances has blunted both her high-pitched anxiety and David's anger, a blanching of the extremity of their emotions, but she can still feel his blame and perhaps he can still feel hers. Every night, they climb the stairs to their bedroom together, brush their teeth, and peck each other on the lips. In bed, they face away from each other. She wishes—but only sometimes—they could let their hearts break together instead of apart. He always falls asleep first, and once she hears his deep, rhythmic breathing, the muscles she holds stiffly as a preemptive rejection of any embrace finally relax.

"Let's go," he says, reappearing in shorts and a long-sleeve T-shirt.

"Aren't you going to be cold?"

"I'll warm up once we start running."

Within moments of stepping outside, his legs are covered in goose bumps. Halfway up the trail, though, it becomes apparent he was right as well as wrong—they're both sweating and breathing hard.

"I'm out of shape," he huffs.

"Me, too," she says, stepping carefully as the mud thickens in rivulets of water running down the trail from the melting snow farther above.

"How are you feeling today?"

"I'll make it to the top."

"No," he says. "I mean, about your mother's death, the funeral. It's a lot to take in."

Angie almost stumbles, then regains her footing. David was helpful with the funeral, hugged her at the right times, stood in the receiving line, froze the casseroles proffered by friends, drove the flowers to Livia's memory care home and gave them to the residents. This is the first he's asked about her feelings. She's not sure she can explain how she feels, or whether she should admit to it if she can.

"Okay," she finally says. "Relieved, maybe." Then, giving in, "Actually, if I'm being honest, more than relieved. *Glad* isn't the right word, but I guess I feel like I can move on because she's moved on."

They come to an icy patch, on the steep uphill just before the falls, and slow to a high-stepping walk, grabbing on to tree trunks to pull themselves up.

"You're allowed to say that. Maybe she feels relieved, too."

Contrary to Livia's original assessment of David as a good Catholic boy, he's about the least religious person Angie has ever known, and she looks at him, surprised. He still has Buddhist prayer flags in the back of his pickup, but it's because he likes the idea of living in the moment, not because he's actually Buddhist. He only agreed to the kids' baptisms to keep Livia happy and said he never felt bad about that deception because religion itself is a deception. "Are you a believer in the afterlife now?" she jokes.

He slips on the ice and barely catches himself. "Only if it will save me from wiping out."

He's smiling, the first time she's seen him smile in months, and she smiles back, surprised at the two of them.

"She was my mother, and I loved her, but it was hard to be her care-taker for so long," says Angie. "I know that's selfish, but I can't help it. Half the time I didn't even know if I was doing anything to make her life better, you know?"

"I understand," says David.

"The worst part is I don't feel sad. And it's not because I didn't love her—"

"I know you loved her," he interrupts. "Everyone loves their mother."

Maybe, maybe not. Angie thinks it's more complicated than that. David has never been estranged from his mother, but they're not par-ticularly close. Julian was basically estranged from Martine but now has a close relationship with her. And for years she resented Livia, even if she did love her, because of everything that happened after Diana died. "I did," she finally says, "but no matter what, it was time, and I already mourned her when she was first diagnosed. And she was a hard woman to have as a mother."

When they reach the open meadow below the falls, they finally get a break from the mud and ice because the trail there is bathed in sun all day, freed from the shade of aspens and pines, and they sprint across the dry dirt to the waterfall. It's half-frozen, the cerulean ice not quite ready to crack, still clinging to the cliff face supporting its weight. When the shade of a passing cloud covers the natural sculpture, the hue pales momentarily, then shines again when the sun reemerges.

They turn around and start back down the trail, picking their way slowly on icy parts, running again in the mud. By the bottom of the trail, brown speckles cover their legs.

"Let's get a coffee," suggests David. "From Cowboy Coffee Cart on Main. If there's a free bench, we can sit and drink it outside."

The unexpected day, the unexpected conversation—it breaks from the anxiety and sadness of the last six months. She doesn't know what it means, or whether it means anything at all, so she nods.

While she saves a bench in the sun, he waits in line, and eventually brings over two cappuccinos and some napkins. She wipes the worst of the mud off her leggings, then sips the hot coffee. The bench is across from what used to be DeLuca's, and David nods at the building.

"Doesn't the brewery's lease come up for renewal soon?"

She feels her face tense and makes herself relax her cheeks. She has a secret about that building, but it's one she's not ready to share, even after this morning. It feels wrong to lie, though, so she just shrugs.

"What will you do with the building now? Sell it?"

"I don't know. It was hard enough to watch the space be converted into a brewery. It would feel strange to sell something my parents cared so much about. My father poured his life into that restaurant." That much is true.

"It would sell for a huge sum, especially given this location."

"I guess."

"Or you could extend the lease," he suggests. "The extra income would give us some financial breathing room next year while we figure out what to do with the building."

She ignores the lease extension comment and wonders at the *us* and the *next year*. She's living day-to-day, still waiting to find out what Nora's life will look like, for the time when a day like today—a run up Wolf Creek Trail, coffee on Main Street—feels normal. Still wondering who David will be to her in that future, who she'll be to him.

"Or you could reopen DeLuca's," he adds.

"An Italian restaurant was my father's dream, not mine."

"Have you thought about what you want to do now that—"

She shakes her head quickly, before he can say *now that you don't have any children to care for*.

"Maybe you can teach at the high school next fall."

"Maybe," she says.

"I only bring the lease up because if you want to terminate, you need to give ninety days' notice," he says. "I didn't know if you remembered that."

Angie sips her coffee instead of answering. She gave notice back in January. She already knew the lease payments wouldn't be needed for Livia's care much longer, and planned to sell the building to fund Nora's legal expenses. She hadn't told David partly because the building wasn't hers to sell—Livia wasn't dead then, not yet, and Angie wasn't sure about the legality of her plan, even though she thought she could borrow against her future inheritance—and partly because she wasn't sure she wanted his opinion on the matter.

And now the building *is* hers, or will be once the estate lawyer finishes the paperwork. It's the last thing left from Livia's life, because Angie emptied her room a few days ago. She cleaned out drawers full of stretched-out underwear and bras, old pajamas from Roberto that hung on Livia's thin frame but kept her calm. Drawers full of shiny objects, coins and paper clips and Hershey's Kisses foil wrappers, objects normally found in a thieving raven's nest or a raccoon den but also hoarded by Alzheimer's patients. Two pairs of slippers and one pair of new but unused sneakers. An empty bottle of peppermint lotion. She donated the sneakers and coins to Goodwill and tossed everything else, except the empty bottle, which she keeps on the fireplace mantle.

Her inheritance—that building—is something real, something solid.

Although she feels guilty thinking about her own future when Nora's isn't settled, for the first time since moving back to Lodgepole, she allows for the possibility that painting can still be a part of her life. Since Nora's case might be resolved by a plea bargain instead of a trial, maybe Angie doesn't have to sell it or keep leasing it to a brewery. There's a third option. She can keep the old DeLuca's building and use it for something other than an Italian restaurant. There are only two art galleries in town, and there might be room for one more—her own.

Chapter Nineteen

2001

Angie's father died in August 2001. His health stayed steady through May, defying his doctors' predictions, and started to decline in June. Livia attributed the temporary reprieve to God, but Angie thought Roberto was too worried about abandoning Livia to die. After the funeral, she stayed and helped with the restaurant, Roberto's estate, and Livia's grief. She returned to New York in early September after the late summer crush of tourists left Lodgepole. Idara had given Angie an ultimatum: return to work or her job was gone, and when Julian heard that, he'd breathed a sigh of relief. He pretended to sympathize with Angie—when she complained she needed a few more weeks, he said "uh-hunh" in all the right places—but secretly wished he'd given her an ultimatum long ago. She had plenty of time with Roberto, plenty of time to help Livia. It was time to recommit to New York, to him. She couldn't live in both places. She either lived in Lodgepole or in New York, and as far as Julian knew, there was nothing left for her in Lodgepole. Her favorite parent there was dead. Her job was here. He was here.

Angie's first day back at work was the Tuesday after Labor Day, and by that weekend Julian felt like life was getting back to normal. Friday night they had dinner with friends, and he was careful to drink only seltzer. Saturday morning, Angie said she didn't feel like painting, so they went for a run. It was sunny but not hot, the air cool and crisp the way it was supposed to be in September. It reminded Julian of back-to-school weather when he was a kid. At the end of every summer, when he was out buying new notebooks and pencils, he always complained the weather was too nice for school to start, but by the time school actually did start, the air in the mornings was exactly like this. A fresh-start air, his mother called it. The chance to start over, to get all As in his classes and impress his teachers with newfound maturity, to stop pulling pranks and stay out of trouble.

"It feels good, doesn't it?" he asked. They were headed to Prospect Park to run what used to be their usual route, though Angie hadn't run with him in months because she was always too busy working at the gallery or squeezing in painting on the weekends. "The fresh air?"

Angie nodded but didn't say anything. She was unusually quiet, but Julian knew she was still feeling conflicted about Roberto's death, so he tried to do her share of the talking by filling her in on two new *pro bono* cases he was working on, both three strikes cases. Randy Martin's life sentence still ate away at his conscience, and he was determined to make up for that loss by finding other people to help.

Since she'd returned, whenever he asked how she was, she had the same response: *I'm sad he's gone but relieved his pain is over.* It was a stock answer, something anyone who lost a sick parent might say, but he had no right to criticize Angie. His parents were both still alive. He was just glad she was here again.

At the corner across from the park, a delivery truck idled in front of them while waiting to turn, and Angie coughed. "That's disgusting," she said and sprinted across the intersection in between cars before the Walk sign turned white.

"Angie!" called Julian. "Watch out!" He started across, thought better of it, and waited until traffic was clear, then ran across and caught her in the park.

"What the hell?" he asked. "You could have been hit."

"I couldn't stand the exhaust," she said. "The air at home is so much cleaner. There's no way running through that is good for the lungs."

"Well, getting hit by a car wouldn't be very good for the body," Julian muttered, but he let it go, out of breath from hustling to catch up. She was breathing easily even though she hadn't been running when she was with him, and he stopped talking so he could run at her speed without appearing breathless.

"Were you running in Lodgepole?" he eventually asked. "You're kicking my ass."

"A little," she said. "Hiking, too. For the stress relief."

"It must have been more than a little. I can barely keep up."

"It's just the altitude advantage. I've been living at eighty-five hundred feet, so running at sea level feels easy, you know?" She wiped sweat from her forehead with the back of her hand and checked her watch. "Should we do intervals on the way back?"

Julian gritted his teeth and nodded.

That night they had dinner with Idara and Jamie, celebrating Angie's full-time return to the gallery and New York. They were at a French restaurant Idara suggested, and the table was littered with their empty plates and breadcrumbs, but Jamie kept ordering more wine and the four of them kept emptying the bottles. Julian halfheartedly put his hand over his wineglass a few times when Jamie moved to refill it but stopped when he realized how much Angie was drinking. It was as if she were trying to excise the demon of her father's death, either by drowning or poisoning it.

"You have to show me your latest work," Idara said. "You'll only qualify for the Thirty Under Thirty for another two years, and I'd love to get you in once more."

Angie's mouth tightened, then relaxed, a telltale sign—at least to Julian—she was about to lie. "I can't wait."

If Idara heard the false enthusiasm in Angie's voice, she didn't show it. "We'll do the show in March again, but I think Hobbs plans to decide who to include earlier, like this fall, so you'll have to be ready, okay?"

Angie hadn't shared what she was working on in months, and although she always said she spent her free time at the studio, Julian wondered whether she was lying about the excitement of being in another show or lying about working on a new painting. Had she been running while she was supposedly painting? Was that why she was in good shape, even though they hadn't run together in months? Or had she been sitting on that ratty couch, smoking pot with one of her studiomates? Maybe the last few months had been harder on her than he realized.

She was quiet the rest of dinner, but when they got back to the apartment she tugged off his shirt before he'd even locked the door. She was looking at him with an intensity he didn't understand, searching for something in his eyes, something in him he wasn't sure he had. She pulled him into the bedroom, tore off both their pants, and for a moment, with his hands on her body and her hands on his, he stopped and thought, *This is how it was, before, but before is not the same as now.* It was clear she didn't want him to stop and think, so he capitulated when she pushed him onto the bed, his head swimming and numb from the wine and predinner martinis.

When he finally came, he shut his eyes for a moment, then opened them again to watch her on top of him, riding him the way she always did, to see the way her body curved and her skin shone, but instead of looking back at him, her head was turned sideways. She stared out the window, the blinds only half-closed, a tear running down her cheek. She looked like she was a million miles away.

"Angie," he whispered. "What happened?"

She turned her head back to him, her eyes glassy. "Nothing," she said. "Nothing happened." She rolled off him and walked into the bathroom, and he passed out before she finished peeing.

Tuesday morning, Livia called Angie. She was shouting, and Julian could hear her hysterical voice even though the phone wasn't on speaker.

"Slow down," said Angie. "I can't understand when you speak Italian that quickly."

She listened intently, then said, "A hundred and fifty pounds of prosciutto? Why would you order that much?"

Angie sat down on the couch and sighed. "The difference between a hundred fifty pounds and fifteen pounds is a zero, Mom. You just didn't double-check the order."

The pitch on the other end of the phone increased, the words coming so fast Julian was glad he couldn't understand. Angie covered the mouthpiece and whispered, "She made a huge mistake with an order, and it was delivered late yesterday. I need to stay here, because it's going to take a while to figure out how to fix this."

Julian shrugged and waved goodbye. He stepped outside to a bright blue sky to walk to the subway and saw smoke coming from somewhere in Manhattan but was too distracted to care. Something felt off with Angie, and he wasn't sure what it was or why he even felt that way. He only knew it was something more than her dead father. Even worse, he'd broken his promise to himself, for the sixth or seventh or eighth time—he couldn't remember now how many times he'd tried—to stop drinking. Sometimes he wondered why he tried, because the only person it bothered was Angie, and the reality was he felt calmer when he drank. It quieted an anxiety he couldn't shake, an anxiety he'd shouldered since Diana's accident. Every time he took a sip of alcohol, he felt relief course through his whole body, almost as if someone had injected him with a sedative. He didn't want to give that up.

When the subway stopped just after Bowling Green, he looked at his watch in annoyance. Five minutes passed, then ten, then fifteen. There was no way he'd make his meeting if the train didn't start moving soon; it was already 9:20. More minutes passed, and people started murmuring about a plane and the World Trade Center.

"What happened?" said Julian to no one in particular. He was standing, holding a pole with one hand and his briefcase with the other. He dropped his hand from the pole.

A woman a few seats down looked at her cell phone and said, "I don't know, exactly. There's no service down here, but my husband texted just before I got on and said a plane flew into the World Trade Center. NPR reported it was a small private plane."

The train jerked backward, catching Julian by surprise, and he grabbed the pole again. The conductor muffled an announcement, reversed into the last station, and announced all subway service was suspended. Until Julian got to the street he thought he'd be walking to work, but at the street level chaos assaulted his senses. The smoke he'd seen earlier had mushroomed into a cloud that billowed black and gray. All around him, people stood in silence, looking up at the smoke. Sirens wailed past, more fire trucks, ambulances, and police cars than he'd ever seen, and a cop tried in vain to clear the area. He pulled his cell out to call Angie, but every other person in the crowd was doing the same thing and he couldn't get through.

"What happened?" he asked again. "Is all this from that small plane?"

A man looked at him like he was an idiot. "Haven't you been watching the news? It wasn't a small plane. It was a commercial jet, two of them. One hit each tower." The World Trade Center was blocks away, hidden behind the concrete buildings in front of him, and he wondered, for a moment, how something like that was possible. It didn't seem real.

"Evacuate the area," the cop yelled again. "Now."

Julian tried for service again, this time to call his grandmother.

"They're saying it's a terrorist attack," said the same man. He said something else, but sirens blared past again, muting whatever it was.

"But I have to go to work," said Julian. The words came out automatically because work was all he did right now, but what he really wanted to do was talk to Angie and make sure she stayed at home.

"Didn't you hear what I said? Go home. No one's going to work today."

The mass of bewildered people started to edge away from the smoke, and Julian followed, frantically dialing Angie every few minutes as he headed toward the Brooklyn Bridge to walk home. He finally gave up and sent four texts in quick succession, *stay in brooklyn, I'm coming home, RU OK? pls text.*

On the other side of the East River, Angie was walking to the subway when she first saw the smoke. By then it was no longer the lone spire Julian had seen in the distance, so thin he'd believed the woman who'd said it was a small plane. She'd spent so much time talking to her hysterical mother about the extra 135 pounds of prosciutto that she hadn't seen the news—no *Today* show, no radio, nothing—and this was before she'd received Julian's text. People on the streets hurried in a way they didn't usually hurry: instead of walking with purpose, they walked with fear. There was a line at an ATM machine, fourteen or fifteen people, and when she stopped to ask what was going on, she listened in disbelief as they explained what they knew. One tower had collapsed, and all of lower Manhattan was now engulfed in choking smoke and ash. A swell of emotions overwhelmed the numbness she'd been using to suppress her confusion about Julian and David, New York and Colorado. She felt fear, an automatic and visceral terror for herself, Julian, and the entire city, then anger. Her head swirled, and she forced herself to take ten slow breaths to quell her rising panic, but Roberto's old self-calming advice was useless. She was in the middle of her own firestorm, a personal one, and now this?

Her cell rang—only later would she realize how lucky she'd been to have a call come through, when lines were jammed all over the city— and it was Livia, hysterical again, this time about what she'd seen on the morning news. The barrage of Italian she'd endured this morning was nothing compared to what she heard on the other end now, and she answered in Italian, hoping to calm her mother. "*Sto bene, Mama. Non sono dove sono gli edifici.*" She thought the words out in English, making sure she'd said the right thing: *I'm fine, Mommy. I'm not where the buildings are.* But then she realized: Julian was.

Her phone cut off, and she hesitated before deciding to try Julian instead of calling her mother back, but no matter how many times she dialed or texted, nothing went through. Her heart raced. His office was blocks away from the Twin Towers, but where had he said his meeting was this morning? Someone tugged at her elbow and she jumped, her nerves frayed.

"*Scusi, lei parla Italiano?*"

It was an old man, his shoulders hunched under a sweater vest. His hands, covered in brown spots and sallow skin that betrayed years in the sun, clutched the handle of a stroller and worry knotted his face. An old woman stood next to him; she looked like women in Roberto's family photos from Italy, dressed in a midcalf skirt and sensible shoes, with a heavyset middle from years of sausages and pasta and lips pulled into a frown by her jowls. Angie nodded. "*Sì.*" Normally, she would have qualified it—Yes, I speak it, but not very well—but her phone dinged with a text from David: *Are you ok?*

The man grabbed at her hand, his large hand fully covering the phone. "*Cos'è successo? Non capiamo perché sono tutti così sconvolti.*"

His accent was harder to understand than her mother's, but it wasn't hard to know what he asked: *What's happening? We don't understand why everyone is so upset.* She answered him in halting Italian and tried to explain.

They were lost, he said. They were visiting from Italy and watching the baby—sucking on an Elmo pacifier in the stroller below, blissfully unaware of the swirling emotions above—while her parents, the couple's son and daughter-in-law, worked. Angie looked down at the baby, tiny and brand-new, unscathed in life except for a trip through her mother's birth canal, and thought, *This is what I don't want, to bring a child into this world, a world where people can fly planes into buildings, a world where even if that doesn't happen, she'll have pain and cause pain and never be at peace.*

The woman opened her purse and handed Angie a creased piece of paper, an address just a few blocks from where they were. Angie nodded. She would take them there, she said. *Aspetta tuo figlio lì.* Your son will be back soon, she promised, even though she had no right to make that promise. Her phone dinged insistently, another text from David, and finally, one from Julian. Relief flooded through her. She answered both, her fingers slower than usual on the tiny buttons, then led the couple to the address they showed her. They walked painstakingly, at a pace more halting than her Italian. They wouldn't be able to babysit once the baby started to crawl; if they couldn't hurry in the midst of this chaos, they'd never be able to keep up with a child. All around them sirens blared, headed in the direction of the cloud of smoke that had doubled in size.

By the time Julian crossed the Brooklyn Bridge with the mass of humanity fleeing Manhattan, he was hot and thirsty. Everyone was. Some women had taken off high heels and walked in bare feet, and men in suits carried their jackets. Wet circles lined the armpits of shirts and everyone smelled, though it was hard to tell whether the smell was body odor or fear or acrid smoke. Bodegas handed out free water to people trying to get home, but every time Julian grabbed a bottle he found someone else to give it to, so he was still thirsty. Angie was okay, his grandmother was okay, he was okay, but he could feel the pulse pounding in the vein in his neck and in his hot, swollen fingers, a rhythmic, frantic beating of his heart.

When he passed Oskar's, the door was propped open with a rubber stop. He couldn't recall the exact moment that day when the anxiety had started coursing through his body—the terror started small and built as he understood what was happening—but his chest felt like someone had punched it and he had to make the pounding stop, just for a moment, before he got home to Angie. He would not drink in front of her, not tonight. It would be too upsetting. The cable TV above the bar blared as the media replayed the jets slamming into the towers, the towers collapsing in a pancake, and blood-and ash-covered people running. Four men sat on barstools, glued to the disaster, and the bartender stood unmoving behind the counter, a dishrag in hand. Just one drink, so he could be steadier once he got home. He could almost feel the rush of relief, the numbness fanning out through his body. He glanced at his cell, but it was dead. He hesitated, then stepped inside.

As the hours passed and the streets emptied, an eerie silence blanketed Brooklyn. Everyone was home, glued to the news if they had cable. Everyone except Julian. As Angie watched the news coverage, she alternated between abject terror, anger, and confusion and kept her finger on the remote, flipping the cable from station to station to see if anyone on NBC knew anything they didn't know on CNN, or if anyone on CBS knew something they didn't know on Fox. No one knew anything, not really, except that both towers had collapsed, and thousands, or tens of thousands, or maybe more, were dead. Every few minutes, she checked the streets or tried to call friends on the landline to see if anyone had heard from or seen Julian. Angie dialed her mother until she finally got through and reassured her she was okay. She called Julian's cell, but even once the call went through, it went straight to voice mail. David texted her, three, four, five times. *I need to hear your voice*, he begged. She sat in front of the news, watching the same chaos she'd just experienced in real life, expecting Julian to walk in at any moment, but finally texted David: *At a friend's, will call soon*. When Julian didn't show up even after the streets had emptied, she looked down at her cell and dialed David's number. She knew Julian wouldn't come home and discover her on the phone with another man because she'd slowly realized where Julian probably was. He'd texted he was okay, but that was when he was all the way in Manhattan, before the second tower fell. Then he texted from the Brooklyn Bridge. Then nothing. Julian was fine—probably—he just wasn't home. She spoke to David and calmed his nerves, then walked the few blocks to Oskar's, where she knew she'd find Julian.

The next few days, as the entire country sat at home, stunned, Angie quietly began cleaning and organizing the apartment. Julian didn't notice; he probably thought she was keeping busy while they watched journalists, politicians, and generals figure out what happened and why. Their TV was never off, and no one else's was, either. Sometimes she'd hear the same news story coming from the first-or second-floor apartment of their brownstone, leaking out a neighbor's open window and into their own, the newscaster's voice echoing the way the information echoed, the same thing over and over. Friends without cable dropped by so they could watch the news, but those visitors trickled to nothing once the networks started broadcasting again.

She didn't say anything to Julian, not yet. She didn't want to make his world crumble when he, and everyone else, was still rewatching the towers crumble, over and over. She owed him that much. Focusing on her own life instead of all the lost lives around her would have been wrong—mean-spirited and contemptible when leaving Julian was already those things—so she pretended everything between her and Julian was normal even though nothing was normal right now, and nothing in her world had been normal for a long time. Maybe normal hadn't been, and couldn't be, possible after Diana's death. Or maybe there was no such thing as normal. For now, they ate meals, slept, had sex. She felt like a robot, as if she were on autopilot and had no say over what would happen next, even though she'd made the decision in a heartbeat, the moment she'd walked into Oskar's and found Julian. His arms were on the counter and his head was in his arms, turned sideways toward the news, glazed eyes flickering back and forth in time with the images blaring from the TV behind the bar.

It wasn't just the alcohol. He complained about her absences from New York, but he was absent even when he was present. His preoccupation with work, especially his *pro bono* cases, had become an obsession. His crusade to right all the wrongs in the criminal justice system was all he could talk about, all he could think about. She couldn't remember the last time he made her laugh or joked around. All the fun, all the joy in their lives—it was gone. Everyone always said relationships could be hard, but shouldn't there be good along with the bad? And she didn't want a life in New York anymore. She kept hearing David's voice, critical of the fancy clothes people wore and all the cultural pretense. *Why does anyone care about that*, he'd said. She'd felt like a bug that had been stomped on, and he rushed to clarify he didn't mean art, he meant the rest of it, but maybe he was right. Maybe there was nothing for her here, not anymore. It was time to fulfill the promise she'd made to her father to be there for her mother, time to go home.

Sometimes she and Julian wandered the city, walking but not running. A sea of American flags and missing person signs had flooded the city, unifying its normally ambivalent inhabitants. At first no one was allowed downtown, but they walked through Brooklyn and Queens, took the ferry to Staten Island, and a week after it happened walked over the Queensboro Bridge into Manhattan. They sat on a bench in a small park overlooking FDR Drive and the East River and watched cars whiz by. People had to work because they had to keep living, and traffic had started to move through the city again. She closed her eyes, leaned back onto the hard bench, and listened to the wounded city limp back to life. She wasn't sure that was how she felt—wounded—because this city was no longer her city. The city wouldn't even notice when she was gone. Julian was walking to check on the city, to take its pulse and temperature, while she was walking the streets like a tourist, seeing them one last time because she never wanted to come back.

When she opened her eyes again, the black wrought iron fence in front of the bench marred her view of the East River, and she wiggled up and down, trying to find a position where her line of sight landed above the top bar or between the top bar and the rest of the fence. For the first time, she considered how much fencing there was in New York. It was everywhere: in parks, surrounding the courtyards of expensive buildings, barbed wire around abandoned parking lots or construction sites, on bridges to keep people from jumping and cars from plunging into frigid water after crashing. Even the lucky people in the city, the ones with balconies—they, too, were hemmed in by bars or glass or fencing, trapped like prisoners.

It was obvious to Angie, even if it wasn't to Julian, that the two of them no longer comprised a singular unit, no longer equated to a *they*. She wondered how a *they* fell apart, whether the *y* was the first to go, leaving *the* available for *the* boy and *the* girl, *the* man and *the* woman. Once the *y* left (in her case, without leaving an obvious answer to the question that was the letter's corollary), it left behind two separate beings where once there was a unity, a single word that encompassed the entirety of them as a couple, years of time lived together.

A seagull landed on the wrought iron, squawking for food or maybe a real beach, then crapped. She looked at the white splatter on the chipped black paint and realized she'd only be leaving one thing behind that truly mattered: her paintings. She supposed they were her children, in a way. Some complete, some incomplete, some yet to be started, only a seed in her mind. She'd cared for them like a mother would a child, curating and cleaning and nurturing. She'd groomed the canvases with a brush, fed them with paints. Yet they would be easy children to abandon, because they were nothing more than cloth stretched thin over wooden frames.

She sat up straight and glanced at Julian. His eyes were still closed, perhaps against the reality of what she was about to tell him.

Some of the defining moments in life are nothing close to moments. They are instead the accumulated debris of personal history that reaches a tipping point, debris that weighs too much and topples over, or extends too high in the sky and simply falls back to the ground, brought down by gravity or hubris or simply the knowledge that this is the wrong place in the universe. A week after the FAA cleared airlines to fly again, Angie sat on a plane in LaGuardia waiting for her flight to take off and expelled air from her lungs in a calm breath. What had happened to the towers was not a defining moment for her but the culmination of what was already going to happen in her own life. The man on her left stared straight ahead, clenching his jaw, and the woman on her right wrung her hands. The plane was eerily quiet, except for a toddler fussing somewhere in front of her. In the face of all the terror and sorrow, she felt only relief, grateful to be moving home, to be escaping this concrete zoo that had come to feel like a prison, but she didn't feel guilty about that. She wasn't grateful people had died, but she was grateful her relationship had.

For other people, defining moments are exactly that: a moment in time they look back on and see—or believe they see—a bad choice, a good choice, or simply a change. As the flight attendants closed the door to Angie's flight, Julian, who didn't know about her deception with David, stood at their kitchen sink hating himself and regretting every sip of alcohol he'd ever taken. He dumped out the whiskey he'd hidden in his underwear drawer and the vodka from the top shelf of the linen closet, the shelf Angie couldn't reach without a step stool. *You won't, or can't, stop drinking. But that's not the only reason. Maybe it's not the reason at all. This*

isn't the place for me. I don't belong here. I'm going home. He'd protested—
You are home—but she'd simply turned away from him. *No, I'm not. This
is not my home. My home is not with you.* The city was still quiet, still
shell-shocked, and so was he. He dug out a box labeled "Randy Martin" from another closet and pulled out what was really inside: three
small paintings he'd purchased anonymously from an alumnae art show
at the Rhode Island School of Design. He'd fabricated a business trip
to Providence for the sole purpose of purchasing those paintings, all so
Angie would think someone wanted her work and have her own spending money. He ran his fingers over the painted canvas and vowed to fix
this, to go after her when he was sober, but it would take years for him to
sober up and even longer to make it through all twelve steps, especially
the one that involved making amends.

Julian's and Angie's mothers, the ones who'd created and then divided
them, were across the country, still not talking to each other, unaware the
division they thought they'd imposed after Diana's death had taken this
long. Livia bustled around the DeLuca's kitchen. She was sorry about
the terrible thing that happened in New York, but that was thousands
of miles away. She had a life to live, meals to cook, and prosciutto to use,
and Angie would be arriving soon. Martine sat at her desk in a black
leather chair, one that Cyrus had bought to celebrate the completion
of her office's renovation, and signed onto her computer to draft a lease
agreement for a new liquor store in town. Martine's mother and Julian
were both safe; it was Gregory she had to worry about, off chasing the
latest news story related to the towers.

Three weeks later, Angie sat in her car in a parking lot in Rimrock Junction. Her appointment was in fifteen minutes. The car, a forest-green
Subaru, smelled like her father used to, slightly garlicky. When she'd
returned home, Livia handed her the keys and the title and said firmly
he didn't need it anymore. Now the smell comforted Angie, even though
she had no idea what Roberto would have thought if he knew what
she was about to do. She kept hearing his voice but couldn't discern the
meaning of his advice, the path he'd recommend she follow to escape

this moral quandary. Livia would never speak to her again if she found out; she'd think this was no better than being involved in Diana's death, maybe even worse.

Angie reclined in the seat, not ready to go in. She didn't know if she was starting a new life in Colorado or picking up her old one. Home wasn't exactly what she remembered, and memories she no longer wanted to relive pulled at her. She would have to reinvent herself, reinvent what home would be. Behind her, cars whizzed by on the service road, the whine almost constant. Occasionally, the whine slowed and turned into a putter as a car pulled into this strip's parking lot. Most people parked their cars a few spaces down and headed into the liquor store or the Subway. Only one parked next to her. Angie followed the driver with her eyes but didn't sit up. There were no protestors here, no one to harass her, and she was a three-hour drive from Lodgepole, but she didn't want to risk running into anyone she knew. The woman kept her head down and scurried inside the same building where Angie's appointment waited for her. The door slammed behind the woman and Angie closed her eyes again.

How had she let this happen? She'd been careful for so many years, more than any other woman she knew. But somehow, in her last weeks in New York, her crumbling world had distracted her, made her less careful. Or forgetful, maybe. In the days after the towers fell, engulfed by personal and national grief, she'd turned to cleaning and organizing. She tossed rotten food from the fridge and expired medication from the medicine cabinet, set aside too-small clothes for Goodwill and alphabetized the CDs. She put everything in its place so when the planes started flying again, it would be easy to pack, easy to leave. Easy to never look back. Julian's failure to come home that day—essentially an abandonment—was the final straw. It was far from the only straw, though, and she never wavered, never stopped preparing for her departure. In her organizing frenzy, she'd packed her birth control pills into a travel cosmetic bag and zipped it inside a suitcase. When she finally told Julian she was leaving, she dug out her suitcase and there they were. The round disc of pills glared at her as if each plastic hole were an angry eye, the unswallowed pills the pupils. She'd missed seven days. She took one, stuffed the pills back into her cosmetic bag, and continued packing. By then, all she wanted to do was leave.

It didn't take long to realize there were real consequences to her forgetful grief. She'd been sitting on the toilet in the bathroom at DeLuca's a few days ago when she looked down at her clean underwear. She tried to remember when her last period was, counted backward, counted forward, counted again, and said, "Shit." The test she bought at the drugstore confirmed it. Two things were certain: it was too soon to be David's, because he'd been out on trail maintenance the first couple of weeks after she got back, and she still didn't want children.

Now she was here, alone in a parking lot in front of a nondescript clinic, with ten minutes to go before her appointment. It was time to go inside, time to check in. There was another person who would object to what she was about to do, but she blocked his voice from her head. Her failure to consider what he would have wanted was no worse than his failure to come home on a day when home was the only place he should have been, his failure to stop drinking no matter how much she'd begged.

Five minutes to go. She got out of the car, locked it, and walked toward the blue-and-white sign. The colors in the sign were muted, as if they didn't want to draw attention to what happened inside. Her hands shook, and she shoved one into her pocket. With the other hand, she reached for the door's hard metal handle.

Chapter Twenty

Gil Stuckey's secretary stands when Julian and Martine enter the small reception area, though Julian wishes she wouldn't. Her knees wobble as she wordlessly waves them through to Gil's office. Gil, on the other hand, doesn't stand. He waits a few seconds to look up and notice them.

"Set yourselves down." Gil motions to the two chairs in front of his desk.

"Shouldn't we be in a conference room?" asks Julian. "It might be easier to spread out so we can give you the mitigation presentation for Nora."

"That won't be necessary," says Gil. "You can do it right here."

Julian meets Martine's eyes and she shrugs, almost imperceptibly. It's what we expected, she seems to say. He hands a tabbed notebook to Gil. They hope to plead Nora down from first-degree murder to manslaughter. In between the two—second-degree murder—could still involve a sentence of up to twenty-four years, and if they went to trial, doubled to forty-eight years if the judge implemented enhanced sentencing. If they can get Gil to agree to manslaughter and consider the mitigating circumstances—her age, her mental health—it might be a lot less. She might even serve out her entire sentence in the juvenile system.

"Let's start at tab one," says Julian, clearing his throat. "I'd like to discuss why first-degree murder isn't appropriate. As you know, first-degree murder requires intent and premeditation, and while you're charging Nora as an adult, it's important to consider that she's thirteen—"

"Basically fourteen," says Gil. "She has a birthday coming up."

"We're talking about her age at the time of the crime and you know it," snaps Julian. He takes a steadying breath. Gil Stuckey gets under his skin every time they speak, more than any prosecutor he's ever dealt with. "At any rate, proving intent and premeditation for a thirteen-year-old will be difficult because at that age a child's brain isn't fully developed."

"Let me stop you right there, Mr. Dumont. I know your next argument will be that second-degree murder is also too much, but there's no way in hell I'll allow anything less. This shooting was intentional, not merely reckless, so it'll never be manslaughter"—the secretary walks in and sets a chipped bowl filled with Hershey's Kisses on the desk, and Gil continues after giving her an almost imperceptible nod—"but I might allow second degree instead of first degree, if you can give me a good reason why."

Julian answers as carefully as he can. The truth he and Martine can't avoid is Gil has a pretty good case for second-degree murder. Although there's no evidence of premeditation, there's an argument, even if it's not solid, that Nora knowingly caused Nico's death, because she shot Nico three times. "Nora has no history of violence, no criminal history at all. And she's a thirteen-year-old girl with a mental health crisis."

Gil picks up two Kisses, peels off the red and green foil—Christmas leftovers, apparently—and pops them in his mouth, his cheeks working like a baby sucking on a pacifier. "Maybe she's having a mental health problem, maybe not. Maybe a state psych evaluation shows something different than yours. After all, other than a bit of depression, there was no evidence of anything that would qualify as insanity prior to the crime. Her behavior after the shooting could easily have been malingering."

"She's not malingering. She's thirteen. How would she know how to fake it?"

"TV," says Gil. "Obviously. There are enough shows out there that she could have—"

Julian, his irritation growing, can't help himself and interrupts Gil. "You've already done Nora a disservice by charging her as an adult, Mr. Stuckey. The state penitentiaries for adults impose penalties not meant for youths, and she's much further from being an adult than most juveniles. She'd be better off in the juvenile justice system, which is designed not just to punish but also to provide education, medical treatment, and activities focused on rehabilitation."

"Well, now," drawls Gil, as if he were a sheriff in a movie, and all Julian thinks is *fucking idiot*, but then he stops and hesitates.

"Well, what?" Martine looks irritated, too.

"Look," Gil says, his voice sincere for the first time, and hope shoots through Julian. "I understand our criminal justice system isn't perfect. I do. And there's a reason we have a different system for juveniles. But Nora committed a crime youths don't usually commit. She killed her own brother, and there's also a reason states have different rules about charging a juvenile as an adult when they've committed murder."

"Again, she's suffering a mental health crisis—" Julian begins.

"I'm tasked with enforcing state law," interrupts Gil, "and that's what I'm doing. There are consequences for Nora's actions."

Julian can tell Gil's moment of sincerity is gone, and he reframes his argument. "All across the country, reforms are being enacted to reduce the number of juveniles charged as adults, because putting kids in adult prisons transforms them into worse criminals. You won't be getting a criminal off the street, you'll be creating one. And Nora will emerge from prison shackled by a felony conviction that will create lifelong barriers to housing, jobs, and benefits. The deck will be stacked against her ever succeeding."

"Are you here to pontificate or negotiate, Mr. Dumont? Nancy, can you bring us some coffee?" He hollers his request in the same breath, as if coffee and the plea negotiations are equivalent, his guard back up. The only response from the other room is silence, but Gil seems to take that as a yes. "Leniency for serious criminals, including juveniles, only emboldens them to commit more crimes. I'm not going to create an arrest, release, repeat cycle in my county. And another thing, I'm fairly certain if I asked for enhanced sentencing, I'd get it."

Martine sighs dramatically. She used that sigh on Julian all the time when he was a child. "That's a wildcard, Mr. Stuckey. This is all a wild-card, and you know it. You're trying to stir up a fuss about a violent criminal, but if you get the wrong people on your jury, they may feel pretty sympathetic toward this young girl because of her age and mental health."

"And vice versa. It's a wildcard for both of us."

Nancy hobbles in with three Styrofoam cups and a pot of coffee. She sets the pot on top of one of the files on the desk, then tosses packets of powdered creamer next to it.

"Coffee?" asks Martine, looking at Julian. He shakes his head—his hands have been trembling for a few weeks now, from stress or too much travel or who knows what, and he doesn't want to insinuate he's nervous—and she doesn't offer any to Gil.

"Look," says Julian. "We can agree that we disagree on Nora, but it's also clear we agree the trial is a wildcard. How about you let her plead down to manslaughter, with a sentence of six years served in the Department of Youth Services?"

Gil shakes his head. "No chance in hell. Second-degree murder is as low as I'll go."

"You're forgetting one thing, Gil." Julian's irritation gets the better of him and he slips away from the formality of *Mr. Stuckey* purposefully. "Section 24–4.1–303. Prosecutors are required to consult with the victim regarding plea deals. And doesn't your website proclaim how important you think victims are to this process?"

"The victim is dead."

"His parents, who are also her parents, could easily stand up and give a victim impact statement that they don't want their daughter impris-oned for life. The judge would hear that—heck, the media would hear that—and take that into consideration."

"Second-degree murder," says Gil stubbornly.

"Fine," says Julian. "If you allow a sentence of fifteen years, served in the Pinyon County Juvenile Correctional Center until she turns twenty-one, with the possibility of parole after seven years, I'll accept second-degree murder." This case will dog Nora for the rest of her life—it's been in the news so often that anyone who searches for her online will always discover what happened—so whether it's called manslaughter or second-degree murder isn't as important as how long she has to spend in prison and where she spends that time. If Nora gets paroled after seven years, she'll never have to move to an adult penitentiary, and that's what matters in the immediate future. He holds his breath while Gil ruminates on the other side of the desk.

Finally, Gil stands and thrusts his hand across the desk. "Deal."

"Fifteen years," says David. "Fifteen."

He seems dumbfounded instead of pleased. Julian wishes he could share the sentences of his juvenile *pro bono* clients in New York. Mostly Black and Hispanic, all poor. The system rarely cuts them slack. Fifteen years is what they serve for assault or selling drugs, not murder. What he really wants to say to Angie is, *Remember Randy Martin? Nora's lucky compared to him*, but he bites his tongue. It would be unprofessional to make those comparisons. He looks out Martine's window and forces himself to count to ten. Storm clouds have obscured the San Moreno peaks all day, and now low-lying clouds have sunk into town, sometimes spitting out fat snowflakes, and others, when the temperature rises slightly, a constant, dreary drizzle.

"This is good," says Martine. "This is a positive result, given the circumstances."

"I thought you could do better," David says bitterly, glaring at Julian. "I thought because of the psychosis she'd go to a psychiatric hospital."

David's square jaw hasn't changed at all since high school. Mountain man scruff—at least that's what Julian calls it when he jokes to Mayumi about the men in his hometown—shades his cheekbones, the beard sprouting two matching patches of white on either side of his mouth, whiskers betraying his age or the stress of what's happened or both. He has Nora's ice-blue eyes, or Nora has his, and a nose that's too perfect, but the skin under his eyes is puffy and his shoulders sag. He seems like a decent father. He showed up to Nora's court dates. He visited her as often as he could, researched mental illness and the potential side effects of antidepressants, and sent article links to Julian in the middle of the night. Yet Julian still feels remnants of the contempt he felt for him in high school.

"We talked about that," says Julian. "Remember, we decided, together, not to pursue an insanity defense because the risk of that defense failing is always high, and because the DA's expert could have submitted a psych eval that didn't show any mental illness. If we lost, Nora could have been convicted of first-degree murder and sentenced to life in prison. And even if we won, Nora would have been committed to a psychiatric hospital for some indefinite period. The hospital might have held her for much longer than fifteen years."

"It's not fair," says David. "She's just a kid."

David—and Angie—had done their best and loved their children; how is any of this fair? But then again, how is any of life fair? Suddenly, Julian feels irritable again, unreasonably angry even though he knows how hard this kind of case is on a parent, and he spits out the comparison he'd tried to hold in. "It is fair. If she was a client of mine in New York, a Black teen from the Bronx who'd killed her brother, she'd be headed to prison for much longer than fifteen years. Nora is lucky this is all the time she'll have to serve. She's *lucky*."

Angie sets her lips in a tight line. "He's right, Dav—"

"You," says David. He jabs a finger at Julian. "This plea deal is a joke. I thought you'd do better than this, but I should've known not to hope. What you've done will just cause more pain to all of us. More pain than you've already caused."

"Jesus, David," says Julian. This is what he gets for helping Angie? An accusation that he's caused pain? He wonders, again, if David knows about his collision with Diana. But not even Angie knows; no one knows except Mayumi. So what is he talking about? "Everybody hurts, all the time. We all have pain. You just can't see it because everyone hides it. Your pain, Nora's pain—you'll have to learn to live with it."

Martine puts her hand on Julian's shoulder, a light touch to let him know his angry voice is out of line, and Julian expels a sharp breath. It's normal for parents to be upset when they find out a child's sentence, but usually he's better at not letting them push his buttons. His irritability and annoyance with not just David but everyone has skyrocketed. He needs a vacation.

There's silence in the room, then David speaks again. "You know, Nico was a special kid." His voice is calmer now, but something in it makes Angie straighten her shoulders, something Julian used to see her do when she was in trouble with Livia.

"I wish I could have met him," says Julian. It's the automatic, polite thing to say. He's said it before, when Angie or David reminisces about Nico.

"I mean he was unusual. We got calls all the time from doctors after he was diagnosed."

Julian sets his pen on the conference table. "What do you mean? Because HD is so rare?"

"No. He was special even in the Huntington's community. Most of the time, it's inherited from a single affected parent. Other diseases, both parents have to be carriers to pass on the gene."

Julian nods.

"The doctors assumed one of us was the carrier and said that carrier would develop Huntington's, so they suggested genetic testing." Angie turns her head and looks out the window, and Julian turns to see what she's looking at. The snowflakes are rain now, big drops plopping on the window. Across the street, two women he remembers from high school stride by on the sidewalk, swinging their arms underneath raincoats. Angie's jaw clenches as David continues, "Apparently, though, testing for HD when you're asymptomatic is an ethical dilemma."

"An ethical dilemma?" asks Martine.

"There's no treatment, so there's no upside to knowing. And it's devastating to know you have the gene because of what the disease does to you. Angie thought we shouldn't get tested, because of that and because if we came back positive, we'd have a preexisting health condition and never be able to get health insurance."

"And the tests were expensive," adds Angie nervously.

"We got tested, anyway." David locks eyes with Julian, and Julian wonders at his intensity. "We knew we had to get Nora tested, because we thought she might be symptomatic. Depression and irritability are some of the first signs of Huntington's for a kid, and she had those. And since she was getting tested, it made sense for all of us."

"I understand. It would be hard not knowing," says Julian.

"We were negative." David folds his arms across his chest and leans back in the chair. "Nora's depression was just depression, and Angie and I aren't carriers. None of our parents were either, because people with Huntington's typically develop it by their late forties, and none of them ever did. And since usually the father is the carrier, I was relieved it wasn't my fault."

Julian feels confused. "So that was good news, right? Because none of you will get it?"

"Yes," interjects Angie. "Nico just had bad luck. So, special in an unlucky way."

David keeps his eyes locked on Julian's and ignores Angie. "The doctors claimed Nico's was a spontaneous mutation of his DNA, which is pretty rare. They called it idiopathic."

"That's terrible," says Martine.

David shrugs and looks out the window, finally breaking eye contact with Julian, then turns back to them. "The doctors were the ones who thought he was special. Special medically. They wanted to study Nico to see why he had this spontaneous mutation." He puts an arm around Angie and squeezes her in a side hug, smiling in that bland way of his, a smile that's neither insincere nor real; it's nothing at all, not even a muscle twitch.

Angie is stiff as a board, her shoulders tense and square, and she's staring at David intensely, eyes wide. Julian thinks back to when they were together, to how she'd act when he'd done something to anger her. He'd ask how she was, she'd say "fine," and then he'd know he was in for the silent treatment. Right now, her whole body is screaming "fine"—and maybe something more—and Julian knows he'll never understand how this life she chose was better than the one they could have had together.

"Anyway," says David, "we wished he'd never developed it at all, obviously, but at least Nora isn't a carrier and can have children—when she's released—without worrying about passing on the gene. And Angie and I aren't responsible for giving a terrible disease to Nico. The genetic fault is not ours."

A show of emotion peeks through David's face, some measure of self-satisfaction, like he knows he's won a game of poker even though everyone else is still analyzing their hand, and Julian wonders at it only briefly before a sinking dread lands in his stomach. When he first realized what Nico's date of birth was, he'd wondered whether Nico was his—how could he not?—but then dismissed his concerns when he found out Nico had been premature and because he knew, or he thought he knew, Angie would never do that to him. Now he doesn't want to believe what he suspects, doesn't want to believe Angie would have deceived him this way, so he packs his papers into his briefcase and closes it, hands shaking and sweat gathering in his armpits. What he's thinking can't possibly be true. The symptoms of Nico's juvenile Huntington's, the symptoms of adult Huntington's. All the men in Julian's biological father's family who died young. His own recent clumsiness, the strange tremors, his irritability, even in this meeting—

"I have to go," he says. "I have a conference call for another client. We'll let you know when the sentencing date is." He walks out of the conference room, out of Martine's office, and stands in the rain on Main Street, dazed, as the building's door thuds behind him.

Later that day, Julian and Martine receive notice that the court has set sentencing for the third week of April. They're at the dining room table, finishing another Persian meal, eggplant *kuku*. Martine cooks one of Cyrus's old favorites every time Julian is here. She says it makes her miss

Cyrus a little less, but sometimes when she tells a story about a meal, serving eggplant *kuku* for an anniversary or forgetting baking soda in the pistachio cake for Cyrus's fortieth birthday, tears well up in her eyes. She always pretends nothing is wrong and says her runny eyes are just allergies.

"I'm going home," says Julian. "There's plenty of time before the sentencing, and I have things to take care of." He leaves out that one of those things is seeing a doctor. Though he spent the afternoon in his old bedroom googling Huntington's, he struggled to focus on what he read. One minute the terror of a fatal diagnosis paralyzed him, the next, thinking about what Angie had done provoked intense fury. For years, he punished himself for hiding the truth about Diana's death, for wrecking their relationship, but she'd done something as bad. Worse. She never told him he had a child—a son! Never told him he was a father. She stole his opportunity to know his own son. And she kept that secret even after discovering Nico had probably inherited a fatal disease from Julian, a disease that would also be fatal for him. *How could she?*

"Of course you do. And you need to see Mayumi." Martine looks at him from across the table. "You know, these past few months it's almost been like your home is also here. It's been good."

He breathes in through his nostrils and focuses on that word: *home.* The hours he logged at this table added up in the last few months. As a teen, he sat here every night to do homework. The chairs were different then, covered with 1980s velvet instead of the tan linen Martine reupholstered them with, but the imprint in the chair he's sitting in fits his body just as perfectly as the imprint he created back then. The table's familiarity is a push and a pull. He has his own home, his own life in New York, but he wishes he hadn't kept his life in Lodgepole at arm's length for so long. Now it might be too late.

He reaches for her hand and squeezes, trying to shelve his fear. He won't know for sure until he's tested. And several websites said people diagnosed late in life have milder cases and can live twenty to thirty years after their diagnosis. He could live to almost seventy-five. There are new medications, especially for those with milder cases. Severity of symptoms and the speed with which the disease progresses worsen with each generation, and juvenile Huntington's is the worst of all, so it was natural that Nico's disease would have been worse than his. Or maybe Nico wasn't his son. Maybe David was wrong. "I agree. It does feel good."

"Maybe when you come back you can bring Mayumi?" she asks hopefully. "Now that we're basically done with Nora's case?"

"I'll ask." He's avoided calling Mayumi all day, sticking to texts so she can't sniff out his emotions from the tenor of his voice. Another website confirmed what David said: Huntington's is usually inherited from a father, not a mother. This meant he, Julian, would have inherited it from Theodore and not Martine, so Gregory is safe. Martine is too old, anyway: if she were a carrier, she'd already be sick. And the baby, his and Mayumi's miracle baby, will be safe because they used donor sperm. The thing that used to keep him up at night, all his inane worry about failing Mayumi because his bad sperm caused their fertility problem— that will be what saves the baby: not being genetically related to him. *Pay attention to your mother*, he tells himself. *You don't want her to suspect; you don't want to scare her.* "If she doesn't come with me for the sentencing, we can visit in May. She'll be six months pregnant, so she can still fly, just barely. I can show her all my favorite spots in Lodgepole, and if it's warm enough, we can eat some of these amazing Persian dishes out on the deck and reminisce about Dad."

She smiles and looks out the window toward the mountains.

The day of the sentencing, Julian sits with Martine, Angie, and David in the back of the wood-paneled courtroom, waiting their turn. David jiggles his foot nervously, shaking the whole bench, and Angie whispers, "Stop."

Angie's nervous, too, but she's better at hiding it. Maybe she's better at hiding things in general. She swishes her hair over her shoulder, and the scent drifts over to Julian: sweet, like lavender, the same shampoo she used when they were together. After she left him, he bought some of his own, used it for a week, then dumped it down the drain. He tried calling her, texting, but she only responded once: *please don't text again.* Years later, when he finally got sober and worked his way to the ninth step, he wrote her a letter to make amends and mailed it, with no return address, to the only address he had: DeLuca's. She never answered, which seemed out of character, but he assumed she was still angry. He remembers the satisfied look on David's face and realizes she probably never received it. When he first saw Nora's file and realized Angie's quickie wedding meant she'd cheated on him, he'd been angry but got past it. Now he can't stop remembering their last days together in New York, the time they spent mourning the people who'd died, the wreckage of their city, the threat to the country. Shock had overwhelmed them, and they barely ate and slept, but every night they took solace in each other. He reached for her, and she responded, more than any other time in the last year of their relationship. But Angie went far beyond just cheating on him. How is he supposed to get past that? For Nora's sake, Julian swallows his fury, but he wants to reach out and punch David or throttle Angie.

"Can the judge change the sentence?" David jiggles his foot again and Angie lets out an exasperated sigh. They look more like acquaintances than husband and wife.

"He won't," says Martine. "Judge Castro is fair."

"This is mostly a formality. We've already agreed to the plea deal. The judge just needs to approve it." Julian makes what he hopes is a reassuring face for David and Angie. David ignores Julian and cranes his head left and right, perhaps searching for reassurance from the room.

There are four rows of wooden benches in the courtroom, almost like church pews. In front of the first bench is a low partition—a gentle precursor to the coming prison walls because it's only waist-high—dividing the room between the unlucky participants waiting their turn on one side and the legal professionals and judge on the other. Judge Castro sits at a raised desk facing the room. A white shirt collar peeks out from underneath his black robes. He listens carefully as an assistant district attorney, one of Gil Stuckey's clones, presents each case, meth possession then child neglect then robbery, from a desk on the right side of the room. The judge speaks occasionally, asks questions, checks the file in front of him. The real Gil is nowhere to be seen.

A court recorder sits at a small desk below the judge and a bailiff on the side of the room, next to a door. Some defendants, the ones currently held in jail, appear from behind this door, escorted by the bailiff, hands and feet shackled until they join their defense attorney at the desk on the left side of the room. Others, the ones being processed for less serious offenses or the ones who could afford bail, rise from the benches and walk slowly forward to join their attorneys. Some appear before the judge without an attorney, representing themselves. Each is evaluated and dealt with efficiently and quickly, like sheep being herded in and out for a shearing.

The stillness here lightens the room compared to the criminal courts in New York. There's more chaos there, the stridence of yelling or arguing or sometimes just harsher voices. Certainly the crimes tend to be worse, though perhaps that's because more people are squeezed into that one metro area than into all of Colorado, than Colorado plus Utah, Wyoming, and Montana. But the stillness won't last. Yesterday, Julian and Martine received a copy of a media request made to Judge Castro to cover Nora's proceeding. Only one still camera and one video camera are permitted under Colorado law, but it will be enough to disturb the peace of the courtroom, and certainly enough to disturb Nora, Angie, and David. Even though there won't be much to cover—the sentencing shouldn't take long—Julian wishes the judge had denied the request. The cameras are already in the room, held in the laps of two men in dark shirts. One of them looks back at David and Angie twice, snapping a not-very-surreptitious picture each time.

They arrived early because Martine hates to be late, and still it's not Nora's turn. Julian stifles a groan when a wild-haired man accused of starting a five hundred acre fire in a state park is brought out by the bailiff—the photographer also takes a picture of him—and then finally the judge calls Nora's name. Julian and Martine walk to the defense attorney's desk and settle in, and David and Angie sit on the bench in the row directly behind them. The bailiff disappears behind the side door, then reappears with Nora. She shuffles past, hands and feet shackled to a belly chain, a hint of hope on her face, eyes wide, looking at her mother and father. Perhaps she hopes for a hug, though she should know by now those are forbidden for defendants in the courtroom. The belly chain, large for her birdlike frame, rattles and the bailiff unlocks her handcuffs once she sits down between Julian and Martine. Gil is here now, his cloned deputy relegated to sitting silently by his side.

Nora takes an oath, her "I do" soft but audible. The camera clicks from the other side of the room and she flinches.

Gil Stuckey asks her questions:

"Do you understand the charges against you?"

"Have you discussed the charges with your attorneys?"

"You are pleading guilty to murder in the second degree."

Gil stops and shuffles his papers. The camera clicks again. While Julian understands the posing and the desire to make a splash for the media, he's always eschewed courtroom drama and he sighs, anxious for the proceedings to finish. Nora hasn't moved since she sat down, except to answer yes or no to Judge Castro's and Gil's questions. When Judge Castro asks questions, his voice is kind yet severe. Nora keeps her eyes focused on her hands, and her head and neck roll forward from her thin shoulders and rounded back, a turtle venturing out from her protective shell.

"The maximum sentence for this crime would be forty-eight years, but your attorney and I have agreed that upon entering your plea, you will be sentenced to fifteen years in prison. Does that accurately reflect how you wish to proceed?"

Nora answers yes to all the questions, sometimes looking to Julian for assurance, and he nods each time. When he, Angie, and David met with Nora to get her approval and rehearse what would happen today, her reaction surprised them. Instead of expressing fear about a fifteen-year prison sentence, she only said, "I just want this to stop. I did it."

Angie looked at her in surprise. "You remember that night?"

"That's my voice on the 911 call, my fingerprints on the gun."

"But do you remember it?"

"I'm almost fourteen, practically a woman. I make my own decisions. My brother is dead and I deserve the chair."

"Where did you hear that?" asked David. His voice was agitated and sharp and he turned to look at Julian, then back to Nora. "That was never a possibility."

"I just know," she said.

"Your father's right. That was never a possibility," said Julian. "And no one deserves that. No one. And you are—Nora, you are more than the worst thing you've ever done." As he repeated Mayumi's words, he wondered how much Nora believed them. He thought of what he'd done to Diana and what Angie had done to him. How much did he believe those words, himself?

Nora didn't look at her mother or father when she finally said, "I accept the punishment." She looked only at Julian and sounded more like a child accepting a grounding than a murder defendant accepting a plea deal.

Sitting here now, it's hard to imagine what's going on in her head, whether she understands what's being asked of her, whether she's listening or her mind is elsewhere, remembering her brother or any part of that night she won't admit to remembering. She's as much of a mystery to Julian now as when they first met. He stifles an urge to turn and see Angie's reaction to Nora's answers and instead focuses on the next questions.

"Has your attorney advised you of the consequences of your plea?"

"Is there a factual basis for this plea?"

Nora's shoulders slump a little at this question, but she answers in the same clear, soft voice. Yes, yes. She coughs into her elbow, and Julian pats her back, then hands her a glass of water, the camera clicking all the while. He assumes the video camera has been running the entire time and wonders whether this will appear on the local news. Hopefully the national media has had their fill of this story and will ignore it.

At the end of his questions, Gil turns to the judge.

"Your Honor, I recommend that the plea, as agreed on by me and Mr. Dumont, be accepted by the court."

The judge nods. "Before I move forward with the court's acceptance, are there any victim impact statements?"

"No, Your Honor," says Gil.

"This court hereby sentences Nora Sheehan to fifteen years in a state penitentiary," the judge says. "However, until she turns twenty-one, she'll serve those years in Pinyon County Juvenile Correction Center. Before I dismiss you, Miss Sheehan, do you have anything to say?"

Angie sniffles, the sound reverberating as if the room is a canyon throwing it back at her. Somehow, today Nora seems like the most innocent member of her family, maybe the most innocent person in this room. Nora nods and stands, says "I'm sorry," and sits back down, so quickly and quietly Julian isn't sure anyone other than him heard. Whether her words are empty or full, she's said them aloud. Those are words he never got to say after Diana's death, and now there's no one left for him to apologize to. The judge turns to the bailiff and nods, then pushes away Nora's file and pulls a different one toward him, calling out a new name.

The bailiff stands in front of Nora, and she holds her hands out to be shackled again.

"Wait," says Julian. "Can she have a hug from her parents, just one, before you take her?"

The bailiff looks at the judge, who agrees with a curt nod, and Angie and David lean over the partition to awkwardly hug their daughter, wrapping her in a warped embrace.

Chapter Twenty-One

I n May, the cemetery's grass wakes up, poking green tendrils through the dirt, pushing away dead thatch left over from autumn. The caretakers spread seed on the cemetery's three new graves earlier in the spring, including Nico's, and those graves are the greenest, free from the work of breaking through the matted old grass. Elk sprinkled their scat liberally among the gravestones over the winter, and the extra fertilization speeds along the new growth.

The day before David moves out, he and Angie walk through the cemetery, heading toward Nico's gravestone. Angie carries a packet of blue columbine seeds in her left hand, and her right hand swings free. When hers accidentally bumps his, neither of them reaches to grasp the other's hand.

"Sorry," murmurs Angie, and she moves the seed packet from her left to her right hand.

"No worries." He veers away, almost imperceptibly, and they keep walking.

She hasn't figured out how she feels about their new arrangement, partly because she's not sure if it's an arrangement or simply the next step on a path with no clear end. He said the memories inside the purple house were eating him alive and signed a lease on a house down valley, in a town with a ramshackle post office and a gas station that sells worms in the summer. Angie knows the house: it's nestled between the road and the San Moreno River, just barely visible when you slow to thirty-five miles per hour to drive through town. It's white instead of purple, a ranch instead of an old Victorian. It's twenty minutes closer to Nora, twenty minutes closer to a job in Waring he's interviewing for—a job with a land conservation nonprofit that doesn't pay any better than the National Park Service but won't involve him carrying a gun. Although he didn't say it, maybe the memories of working as a ranger were eating him alive, too.

He didn't ask her to move to the white house, maybe because it would have led to a discussion about their future, a discussion neither of them is ready to have. He did tell her the key to the front door is in a fake rock on the ledge above the porch light—those exact words, that exact cadence—the same as the purple house, but his face was as inscrutable as always when he spoke. Once, she thought, maybe they both thought, things between them could go back to the way they were before Nora shot Nico, back to normal. But that life wasn't normal, because Nico was already sick. And before then their life, their marriage, that wasn't normal, either. She'd realized it in the meeting about Nora's plea deal. David knew—had known for a long time—Nico wasn't his. When she'd confronted him, he told her everything: he'd intercepted a letter to her from Julian and realized she'd been with Julian at the same time she was with him. He'd reexamined Nico's birth weight, date of birth, and the sonograms, and double-checked the dates he was out of town when Angie returned from New York. He burned Julian's letter in their charcoal grill and thought he could live with the way things were, but it was harder than he thought it would be. And he didn't love Nico less—after all, it wasn't his fault—but he did love Nora more. At least, that's what he said.

Another thing he didn't say, but she wondered: Did he love Angie less?

She's tried to parse it out, which of them hurt the other more, and whether a premeditated intent to hurt another person made the hurting that much worse, like the difference between first-degree and second-degree murder. If so, David wins. He hurt not just her but Julian, too, by bringing him here to defend Nora. Two birds with one stone, that's what he probably thought. She'd never have believed he was capable of that level of vindictiveness, but he probably never would have believed her capable of deceiving him about Nico's true paternity. It was wrong to make David believe Nico was his—she always understood that—but she did it to avoid hurting him, to prevent him the pain of knowing she was with Julian at the same time as him. Parsing out blame now won't help, though. It won't bring Nico back, won't free Nora from jail. It won't magically make Angie and David love each other again.

David didn't say *no* when she asked him to see a marriage counselor, but he didn't say yes, either. He said *I'm not ready*, the look on his face as indecipherable as it always was. She still doesn't know what he meant, whether he wasn't ready to forgive her, or to love her again, or simply for the counseling. She doesn't know whether that door is open or closed, but that's okay. She's not sure how she feels about him, either, and she has something else to focus on for now. It's time to do something for herself.

The brewery vacated the old DeLuca's building more than three weeks ago, the owners angry but resigned, and she's converting the space into its next reincarnation: an art gallery. Her art gallery. Part of the gallery will be for her paintings. The rest she'll dedicate to local artists, and twice a year to a show for incarcerated juveniles, juveniles she plans to teach and mentor if the state will let her volunteer in the detention and correction centers. The front of the building will be a cafe, with coffee and pastries in the morning and wine and tapas in the evening. Not exactly an Italian restaurant but close enough that Roberto would be proud. Maybe she'll even throw an old DeLuca pasta dish onto the menu.

They reach Nico's grave and kneel. The air is filled with the croaks of ravens and the cheeps of sparrows, their excitement to mate synthesizing into a cacophony that overwhelms the usually silent cemetery. Over the past few months, Angie has taught herself to not ask *why*. Asking why only led to imagining the answer, then the circumstances surrounding the answer, the night itself and all the possible ways the shooting could have played out. She could not bear to go on living, or to love Nora, if those images took up permanent residence in her mind, so she banished them as well as a human being can banish a bad memory. She learned to forget and she learned to remember, and now she can focus on finding the right place in her mind for the good memories of Nico and Nora, on filing each memory in its proper place so she can access it when she needs to.

She places her hand on the grass above where Nico's heart would be and presses down, wishing she could will the thump of his heartbeat into existence. "Do you have the spade?" she asks.

David pulls it from his backpack and begins turning the soil at the edge of Nico's gravestone, and she stretches her fingers past the silent heart and up to the stone to trace her fingers along Nico's name, his date of death, date of birth. June 11, 2002, seems like forever ago and just yesterday, all at the same time.

When she'd gone to the clinic in Rimrock Junction all those years ago, she couldn't go through with it. She went inside, registered, then went into the bathroom while they processed her paperwork. She looked into the mirror and her reflection glared back at her, taunting her with the image of a child that might be, then she turned around and left.

She worked out a plan as she drove the three hours back to Lodgepole. A few days later, when they were walking David's dog in the park, she told him her period was late, and she wanted to keep the baby. When he plunged to the ground, weight on one knee, the other knee, the marry-me knee, wobbled like the spindly legs of a new foal. She did the only thing she could and nodded, not trusting she could say the words. He jumped up and lifted her into a twirl, spinning her legs outward like swings on a carnival ride. She heard clapping in the distance and was dimly aware those spectators wanted to celebrate a happy moment, but her heart stood still, anchored like the center pole of that carnival ride, stuck in place. Telling Julian would have been a betrayal of David and telling David would have been a betrayal of Julian, so she closed her eyes against the dizzying whorl of aspen trees, saw a door close, and turned toward a new one.

She told him the due date was six weeks later than it was. She planned for a home birth so there wouldn't be any doctors to fuss about the size of a baby supposedly born six weeks early. When her true due date approached, she planned for a ten-day trip with David, their last trip as a couple, and hoped the baby would be born away from the prying eyes of nosy, small-town Lodgepole. They drove to Santa Fe and stayed in a bed and breakfast with a heated pool and free cookies in the lobby. In the mornings, David hiked in the desert or the Sangre de Cristo Mountains and Angie sat by the car in a chair under an umbrella, painting surreal pink landscapes that shimmered in the sand and didn't remind her of New York. In the afternoons, he followed her from gallery to gallery, only a little grumbly, as long as she agreed to try a bite of spicy Tex-Mex at dinner.

Every night she tried a bite, then pretended she didn't like it. She was doing everything she could to avoid an early or on-time delivery, including avoiding spicy foods and sex, because she'd researched every old wives' tale she could find and was doing the opposite of what each one said would precipitate labor. Avoiding sex was harder than she planned, but she got around it by showering David with blow jobs.

When the day finally came, Angie was nine days past her true due date and four and a half weeks early for the due date she'd told everyone else to expect. Her water broke in the lobby of the Georgia O'Keefe Museum, dripping down her legs like a leaky faucet, nothing like the cascade of fluid she'd seen in the movies. David was terrified, but Angie had done her homework. She had the address of a local birthing center and David drove his brand-new pickup faster than she'd ever seen him drive, his normally placid demeanor shaken. He ran stop signs and took every corner on two wheels, or at least that's what he would say later, when he told the tale of Nico's early arrival.

"How'd you know where to go?" he said as he ran one of the stop signs.

She'd made arrangements months ago, and was just lucky the timing worked out, but between contractions she groaned, "I looked it up right before we left. Better safe than sorry."

There was one problem with a birthing center instead of a hospital: no epidural. Angie was reminded of her deception with every contraction, every push. She'd always sworn she'd never choose a natural childbirth—Why? she always said to pregnant friends in New York. Why go through that pain if you don't have to?—but David didn't know that. He thought she was brave for wanting to experience childbirth the way Mother Nature intended. She gritted her teeth and figured it was an even exchange: pain for a buried truth.

After the final push, Angie held her breath, waiting to hear the baby cry, to hear it was healthy, to hear the doula's voice when she announced the baby's weight. Angie had been a small baby, less than seven pounds, and she hoped that what she'd read—daughters often take after their mothers during pregnancy—was correct. If the baby was too big, his size might lead to questions about his true conception date.

"It's a boy," yelped David. He was holding Angie's hand, rubbing her forehead with a washcloth, and Angie wanted to celebrate, but she was waiting on that last detail, the detail that would ensure her deception's success.

He weighed in at six pounds ten ounces, small for his gestational age but big for a baby supposedly born early. A happy medium for her plan. "Very healthy for a baby that's five weeks early," the doula said.

"Four," said Angie.

"He's a good weight. You must have eaten well during your pregnancy." The doula placed Nico on Angie's breast and helped him latch on to her nipple, then looked Angie in the eyes. The woman was in her sixties, with curly gray hair, the achromatic color that said she didn't care what anybody thought about her. She wore jeans and a long-sleeved Grateful Dead T-shirt. Her eyes were sharp and focused, but her square jaw was relaxed.

She knew. Angie knew she knew. But she didn't care. This woman wouldn't say anything. It was easy to rationalize: women have deceived their husbands since the time of Christ. Before then. Since the Greeks or the Egyptians. Angie wasn't the only woman to ever do this. Maybe it was harder now, because men sometimes go to OB appointments and ultrasounds can predict gestational age, but Angie had made appointments with midwives, avoided ultrasounds, and made it easy for David to miss appointments. She'd been lucky Nico arrived late, so it seemed he was only four weeks early, not six, but her mother delivered both her and Diana two weeks late and Angie had known there was a good chance she'd do the same.

Now it's hard not to wonder if everything that's happened is her fault, if it's all karma coming back to get her. She looks over at David, digging a hole in front of Nico's grave for the Columbine seeds, and wonders if he suspected before he intercepted the letter from Julian, when Nico had blond hair instead of red, was tall instead of short, brown-eyed instead of blue-eyed. If he ever wondered whether his suspicions were correct after the letter, it was clear when Nico developed Huntington's and she and David proved not to be carriers. She had agreed to the genetic test because it only tested for the Huntington's gene—it wasn't a paternity test—and knew it was possible, even if rare, for it to develop on its own. She'd argued against it to the extent she could, but David stood firm. He wanted the test. She gritted her teeth and finally agreed, knowing that if this was the way he discovered her deception, it would be her penance, a punishment far worse than saying Hail Marys on hard wooden pews. When the doctor said the test results meant Nico's case was idiopathic, David didn't question his assessment, and she'd breathed a sigh of relief. Now she knows he already had all the proof he needed in the letter he intercepted from Julian. David, the erstwhile Buddhist, always says karma is just another name for bad luck, but she's not so sure that applies here. Her justification for hiding Nico's true paternity was always the protection of David's or Julian's feelings, but on some level the deception was also selfish: she'd never stopped loving Julian, not really, and Nico had been more than just her son. He was a link to her past, a link to Julian. How could that kind of deception *not* have blighted Nico's life? How could it not have blighted her own?

A raven sits on the gravestone next to them, watching intently. His sooty feathers ruffle in the breeze, then settle, and his croaks reverberate through the now-quiet cemetery. Nico always liked ravens because of their tendency to pull pranks, and she wonders if this one sees something to steal: the empty seed packet, the shiny spade, or the seeds themselves. She kneels down and pats the dirt with her hands to make sure the seeds are buried deep enough to protect them from this potential thief.

Angie doesn't know if fifteen years is too much or not enough, if she's angry with David or Julian or the past or herself, or instead ready to move on, move forward. When she wakes up every morning, she only knows if she stops to think, she might not be able to start again. She marches onward. She helps David box his clothes, books, and guns and pack them into his pickup. She waves goodbye. She takes the calendar off the fridge, the one with Nora's trial dates if she'd stayed in the juvenile system, crumples it, and tosses it in the garbage. She runs up Wolf Creek Trail to the falls once a day, regardless of the weather. Sometimes on her way back, she sees tourists slowing down in their car to take a photo, as if the house or the crime or the people that used to comprise this family are nothing more than a curio that belongs in a museum; she keeps going and jogs past her driveway as if she doesn't live there. She donates Nora's and Nico's clothes. Nico will never need his; Nora will outgrow hers over the course of the next fifteen years. Angie keeps a couple of their favorite T-shirts, folds them into tiny squares, and hides them in her dresser. She still hopes to catch Nico sitting at the table behind her when she turns around in the kitchen—maybe with his chin resting in one hand while he studies a book on falconry, or working through a math problem—but he's never there. She wonders at how a child, a person she loved, a person who was part of her very essence, could have disappeared so quickly. One day she scrapes away the last remnants of the crime-scene tape from a crack in the doorframe of Nico's room, digging out yellow bits with the tip of a screwdriver. Another day, she finds a baseball bat in Nico's closet. It's junior-sized, from the year he played, and hated, baseball. She fingers the smooth wood and marvels at how untarnished it is. No dents, no smudges. It looks brand-new, because even though he'd begged to play, he decided he hated the sport two weeks after the season started.

Outside, the birds continue to engage in their sex-infused warbling frenzy. She stands and wanders into the yard, bat in hand. When David left, she offered him these bird feeders—after all, he installed them—but he didn't want them any more than she did. "Shoo!" she says to the birds, and they scatter to the sky. She grasps the bat tightly in her hands and stands in front of one of the feeders, then swings. It's like swinging at a birthday party piñata, only no candy will fall to the ground after she breaks it. Her joy suffused with sorrow, she swings again and again, harder and harder, until the plastic splinters, releasing the seeds.

Standing there, looking at splattered seeds on the ground and scattered birds in the sky, she weighs one child in her left hand and one in her right. She'll never know if fifteen years is too much or not enough.

She names her art gallery and cafe the only thing she can think of, Angela's Art Cafe, because that's exactly what it is. The name isn't as sophisticated as a New York gallery's would be, but she doesn't care. This place is hers and no one else's. Whatever else she's lost, she has this. She paints the sign, then hangs it out front with the help of a local handyman her mother often hired after Roberto died. The handyman is older and grayer now but no less handy, and he helps with other odds and ends to ready the space for a Memorial Day opening. Roberto always stressed the importance of being open every day during the high seasons—Memorial Day through the end of September and then December through March—and she needs to follow that advice to be profitable enough to make this work. The loan she took out against the building will be enough for her living expenses, the property taxes on the purple house, and Angela's Art Cafe to last a year, maybe two, but Roberto and Livia would hate that the building is mortgaged again, and she plans to pay it down as soon as possible. If she needs to, she'll stay open every day of both the high and low seasons. And if it's successful, when Nora gets out she'll have a place to work, a way to live a normal life. Her record as a felon won't matter.

The day they finish the final touches, she writes the handyman a check from her makeshift desk at a table in a back corner, then props open the front door for fresh air.

When she hears footsteps behind her, she doesn't look up from the ledger she's staring at on her laptop. "I'm sorry," she calls over her shoulder. "We aren't open yet."

"It's a nice place," a voice says. "The culmination of all your dreams."

It's Julian, and her heart races as she turns around.

"Hi," she says awkwardly. "What are you—Did we have a meeting about Nora, something I forgot about?"

"No," he says. "No meeting."

"Is Martine okay?" She searches his eyes, but instead of meeting hers he glances around, takes in the space.

"Martine is fine." He walks around the edges of the room, pausing at some of her paintings, bypassing the work of local artists. He stops at the shelves she's set up to sell local mementos for tourists: stationery made from prints of Angie's mountain paintings, a cookbook with DeLuca's recipes, and glass jars labeled "Livia's red sauce."

She's tried not to think about when she'd next see Julian, but she hasn't been able to keep him out of her head. Every day, she has imaginary conversations with him. She explains why she kept Nico from him, even after the Huntington's diagnosis, or apologizes for David's behavior, or starts over with the truth, all the way back in New York. In some of the conversations, her cheeks burn with shame. In others, she's angry and defensive, the buried truths justified. In all of the conversations, he's forgiving and generous, the way he's always been. But she doesn't know how to talk to him about this in real life.

"Is this your mother's recipe?" He's holding a jar of red sauce.

"Yes," she says. "I'm selling it to make extra money."

His hand trembles, shaking the jar, and he sets it back on the shelf. It's not the first time she's seen the tremor, but she's always told herself, firmly, it was only nerves related to Nora's case, that he seemed healthy enough, that maybe Nico's Huntington's really was a spontaneous mutation. The truth is now unavoidable, and she takes a deep breath.

"Julian—what's wrong with your hand?" she asks. He looks at her, then continues to walk around the edge of the room, his fingertips brushing up against some of the canvases on the wall. When he doesn't answer, she adds, "I mean, are you okay? You look like you lost weight."

"If you want to know why I've lost weight, why I have a tremor in my hand, ask me about the medical tests I had done recently."

Angie's heart sinks.

"Or never mind, don't ask. Let me tell you. I've been in and out of doctors' offices all spring, Angie. For joint pain, irritability, fatigue, tremors. At first I thought it was stress, but my balance is off, and my muscles keep seizing up."

Angie squares up her shoulders and takes another deep breath, but she can't bring herself to look Julian in the eyes. The burning shame is back.

"I know you do your research when medical issues come up. I remember what you did for your dad. And because I know that, I know these symptoms sound familiar."

She nods, barely able to move her head. His voice is quiet but hard, a prelude to what she thinks will be a storm of anger, and she girds herself.

"Yeah," he says. "You know, when I first read Nora's file and saw your wedding date and realized you'd cheated on me with David, I was hurt. But it was in the past, and I tried to leave it there. And I believed the story about Nico being premature when my mother mentioned it. But when David talked about Nico's diagnosis in that plea deal meeting, I thought about the strange health issues I was having, and suddenly everything clicked, so I went home and got tested."

"I'm sorry," she whispers. "I'm so, so sorry."

"About what? That I have Huntington's? I'll be fine, or mostly fine. My symptoms aren't that bad, and the doctors think it will progress slowly because I had such a late onset. And my disease isn't your fault, anyway. But—" He stops walking in front of Angie and stares at her, forcing her to make eye contact. He's breathing heavily now, but when she searches for the anger, that's not what she sees. "Maybe what you're really sorry about is that you never told me Nico was mine, never told me you were pregnant after you left me? Sorry you never told me that by defending Nora, I was jumping into an ethical and moral quandary? Do I need to explain how wrong it was for me, the father of the victim, to defend Nora?"

When Julian showed up to help on Nora's case, Angie had pushed her deception to the back of her mind, able to focus only on how to survive Nico's death and what would happen to Nora. She never would have voluntarily brought Julian back into their lives; this was David's doing, and she'd resented it from the day he first told her he'd asked for Julian's help.

"I wasn't the one who asked for your help."

"You let it happen," he says flatly.

"I didn't know what else to do." Her voice breaks. She's told herself the story of Julian's betrayal for so long, his alcoholism and his abandonment of her on 9/11, that she always believed she was justified in choosing David over Julian. And keeping Nico's paternity from Julian wasn't just protecting David, it was protecting Julian, the man she'd loved since she was a child, from knowing she'd cheated on him. Hurting him was the last thing she ever wanted to do. She wonders now whether she'd been protecting Julian or instead protecting herself. Whether he betrayed her or she betrayed him.

"For years, for my entire life since the day Diana died, I've carried around the guilt of being responsible for her death. I almost drank myself to death because of it. But you know what, Angel DeLuca? We're even. We are even. And we're done."

"Do you want money? Do you want me to pay you for the legal work?"

Julian looks stunned, his jaw slack, like he's just been punched or taken a hard fall in a race he was supposed to win. "That's what you think of me, after all this time? That I came here for money?" He turns away and starts pacing the room again.

Angie drops her face into her hands for a moment, then looks at him again. "My whole family is gone."

"You stole my chance to be a part of Nico's. I was his father." His voice catches and Angie realizes he's crying, something he didn't do even when she told him she was leaving New York, leaving him. The only time she's ever seen him cry was after Diana's death.

"I'm sorry," she says again.

He's back at the shelf with the red sauce and the DeLuca's cookbook, and he picks up a jar again, turning it over in his hands. "You knew how much I wanted children, knew how much I wanted a family, and you kept my son from me. I deserved better than that."

"I named him Nico because I knew you wanted to name a son Nicholas," she says stupidly, immediately regretting her words. What she really wants to say is she loved Nico because he was Julian's, because she still loved Julian, she would always love Julian.

Splotches cover Julian's face. Grief spills from his eyes and voice into his hands, which are trembling again, and he lets the jar slip from his hands. It happens as easily as melted water drains through splayed fingers, and when it hits the ground, the glass shatters and red sauce splatters everywhere, on the wall, on the floor, on her closest painting. He watches the sauce drip down, then turns and walks out of the gallery.

Angie feels glued to her chair. *Now* would have been the right time to go after him, to apologize again, but *before* would have been the right time to tell the truth, to admit she'd been wrong, he'd been wrong, they'd been wrong together. But there was no *they* anymore, and there hadn't been, not for a long time.

The silence in the gallery echoes, a lonely ringing she's getting used to. By the time she stands to clean up the mess, the red sauce on her painting has dried, and she runs her fingertips over it, feeling the texture. It could almost be mixed media art, a work of beauty created by her in this new life, but it looks like a crusty scab that will leave a scar.

Chapter Twenty-Two

Since the sentencing, Martine has done her best to put Nora's case behind her. She fully retired, vacated her office, and stuffed boxes of documents into a corner of her basement. The old black chair from Cyrus sits in a corner of the dining room. It takes up too much space, but she's not ready to part with it. Jack likes sleeping on the soft leather and can spin himself around by taking a running jump into it. That's as good of a reason as any to keep it there.

The media attention faded quickly. The national news only ran one story, short and to the point—the crime, the punishment, Nora nothing more than every other discarded juvenile delinquent, perhaps because the media realized the criminal justice system's sentence was merely confirmation of a judgment the public rendered long ago. The local paper ran a small piece after the sentencing, then a story on the importance of mental health, then nothing. The sentencing article praised Gil for his important plea deal and the delicate balance he struck when handling the case, and Martine burned that day's paper in her fireplace.

Her life now is both less and more exciting. Without an office on the second floor of a Main Street building and a black leather chair to perch on and watch the world pass by, her ability to observe the Lodgepole world from above has disappeared. She's limited to what she can see from the bench in front of the local coffee cart. It turns out watching the world go by, even right there on the street, isn't as much fun as chatting with other people grabbing their morning coffee. Some are young, returning from a morning run or on their way to work. Others are old, like her, back from something gentler, a hike or a dog walk, and not on their way to work. Everyone talks, young and old. She's made friends with the regulars and plans to go on a hike with a man named Tim who's new to town. It's almost a date. Retirement isn't as scary as she thought it would be, and she wishes she'd done it sooner.

One morning, she sees Ignacio ordering an iced mocha cappuccino for his daughter and a black coffee for himself. His gruff face breaks into a smile when he turns away from the counter and sees her. "Mrs. Dumont, how are you?"

"Good, good. And you?"

"This is my daughter, Natalia. She just had a dentist appointment, and this is how she celebrates, with a sugar-filled drink."

Natalia looks up from her phone and half smiles, then looks back down. Her thumbs are working furiously, and Ignacio is holding her drink.

"She's addicted to her phone," he says. "I'm sorry."

"They all are," says Martine. "It's okay."

"Are you on your way to work?"

"I retired," she says. "That sounds strange, doesn't it? Almost like I'm old."

His smile grows wider. "Congratulations! I'd shake your hand, but I've got coffees."

"I'm gonna be late," his daughter says, tugging at him.

"See you around," says Martine. She orders, then stands off to the side to wait. Ignacio's and Natalia's backs are to her now as they walk down Main Street, presumably to the high school. Ignacio is in his uniform, his gun in the hip holster. He must be on break from work. Natalia looks like she's older than Nora—maybe she and Nico were in the same grade, maybe they dated or did a biology lab together or ate lunch—

and Martine can't help wondering what she knows and thinks about the Sheehan siblings, whether the shooting is forgotten gossip or fuel for learning or simply an event that now lives in her past. Even retired, it's hard to fully banish Nora and Nico from her own head, but she's not sure she should do that, anyway. This is a grief she shouldn't—and won't—look away from. So, she smiles anytime she sees Ignacio, plans to visit Angie's new gallery, and will say hello to David if she sees him on the trail by the river.

Julian and Mayumi are here, visiting for an entire week. It's the first time they've visited since they married eight years ago, and the most time she's ever spent with Mayumi. She's smart and funny and good for Julian, and Martine loves her. She lets Martine feel her belly when the baby kicks—it's a girl—and treats Martine like she's her own mother. She gushed over the crib Martine set up in Julian's room and said Martine could babysit anytime she wanted to. Martine hasn't disclosed the hidden stash of toys or growing pile of clothes because she doesn't want to scare Mayumi off, but she's pretty sure Mayumi wouldn't be one of those overly sensitive daughters-in-law, anyway. She's just waiting for the right time.

They're out hiking Miner's Peak because Julian is determined to show Mayumi everything from his childhood. They left before dawn so Mayumi could see sunrise from the summit, and will meet her here for coffee. Julian's health problems still aren't resolved, but he told her the doctors think the trembling is Parkinson's and will be easily controlled by medication. That makes sense, sort of, but something seemed off about what Julian said. He had a quaver in his voice—that same tell he's always had—but accusing her forty-four-year-old son of lying probably wouldn't be productive, so she's trying to be patient and wait for the truth.

One of the baristas calls her name—Martin instead of Martine—looks at her, looks at the name on the cups, then apologizes, her cheeks flushed.

"Don't worry about it," says Martine. "I'm going to be a grandmother," she adds, as if that explains why she doesn't care about being called Martin, and takes the three cups to a sidewalk bench to wait. When Julian and Mayumi come walking down the street, they break into broad smiles. Jack trots next to them, tail waving. They hike farther and higher than she usually does, and Jack is exhausted every night, but his tail is a window into his soul, and these days it never stops wagging. She snaps a quick photo of them like that, Main Street and San Moreno Mountain in the background, because she plans to make a photo album to remember this week. They look like they belong here, with their backpacks and hiking boots. Even if they don't, even if their home is in New York, at least they belong to her. That's her son, her daughter-in-law. She has a family again. *I'm going to be a grandmother!* she wants to shout at the sky, in the supermarket, on the street, every minute of every day. She doesn't want to tell only the barista.

Last night she pulled out her mother's old photo album. The yellow on the pages deepens each year, shading even the black-and-white photos with a sepia-toned nostalgia. It's organized by decade, all the way back to the early 1900s in Paris, where her mother's mother was born. It's more of a family tree than a record of memories and candid snapshots, but Martine wanted Mayumi to know all of her family. Martine appears in a white christening gown in the pages dedicated to the forties, along with two sisters and two brothers; her youngest brother appears in the pages dedicated to the fifties, held by their mother, looking at her newly baptized baby with dazed eyes. A test of a mother's love, Martine figured, to have six children.

When she flipped to the seventies section, there was Julian, smiling in his grandmother's lap, reaching for her dimpled chin with his chubby fingers. Those pictures, by then color instead of black-and-white, have their own hue, their own tone. Julian wore mustard shorts and brown socks up to his knees and Martine ached as she tried to remember his sweetness, what it felt like when he clutched at *her* chin or tugged on her hair, what it was like to giggle with him or read his favorite bedtime story. What it was like to kiss his knee and make it better when he fell down, to quiz him before a spelling test or make cupcakes for his birthday parties, to cheer him on during ski races or soccer matches. She can no longer fully remember the pleasure of hearing the word *Mom!* when he crashed through the door at the end of his first day of school. Memory can be cruel, and only old home movies can conjure the sound of his little-boy voice.

Mayumi giggled at that old photo, the seventies hairstyles and clothing, then confessed, "My pictures are worse, though. I had buck teeth and braces and my mother once tried to give me a perm. I look horrible in every picture up until college."

"That's not so," protested Julian. "You only looked terrible until eleventh grade."

Mayumi whacked him on the arm, and he laughed, then she snorted, then he laughed harder. Martine smiles now thinking about the two of them dissolving into giggles like teenagers. They seem happy together, as happy as she'd been with Cyrus.

A few times she's caught Julian staring into space, his jaw tight and grim, and she wonders whether it's still hard to return here, even after the last few months, or whether he's worried about running into Angie with Mayumi, or something else entirely. One night, when Mayumi was talking to her sister in another room, Martine pushed Julian to open up to her, but he'd only closed his eyes. When he reopened them, his face was peaceful. "I'm still trying to recover from the Sheehan case," he said. "I've had a hard time not thinking about Nora and Nico, about the tragedy of the whole thing."

"I understand," she said. "But you're done with that case, and it's time for you to focus on your current life." She looked at him with fondness— she'd never forgotten how much she loved him, only he had forgotten that—and more than a little concern. She was his mother, and she knew when something was wrong.

"I'm trying."

"Promise you'll keep trying."

"Pinky promise."

She's stopped wondering why Nora did what she did, because it doesn't matter, not anymore. The crime-scene photographs in Nora's file provide scaffolding, a before and an after, but what happened in the middle—and why—is, and may always be, an unsolvable puzzle. Gil Stuckey believed Nora was an angry and violent young teen. David and Angie first were convinced the shooting was a mistake, then certain it had been caused by psychosis and intent on discovering what triggered it. They would probably never know, but Martine imagined the devastation of the Huntington's diagnosis, what it meant for two kids who loved each other, perhaps combined with the effects of a mental illness that ruptured the essence of who Nora was. She pictured the loading of the gun, the pointing, the shooting. The 911 call.

And maybe an unsolvable puzzle isn't remarkable. Maybe the question of *why* is a question everyone asks, all the time. The steps and decisions that combine to form a life, a choice, an action—maybe they don't add up, like a mathematical equation, to a knowable sum. Maybe they can't. It's better, Martine has decided, to focus on the *what* than the *why*, because the *what* is always right in front of you. And what is in front of her right now is her son and daughter-in-law. Their hands are linked by their pinkies, swinging between the two of them. When Jack sees her, he breaks free and jumps into Martine's lap. She hands Julian and Mayumi their coffees, and they sit down on the bench to show her pictures of this morning's sunrise.

Chapter Twenty-Three

On Nora's birthday, May 10, she's still in the juvenile detention center. She's lucky, a guard told her, because she gets to stay in Pinyon County. She's going to be transferred from the detention unit to the correctional unit. A spot will open up in June when another girl is released, and between now and then, the state won't spend the money to move her somewhere else.

She and Jacqueline are sitting on their bunks, facing each other. Jacqueline sang "Happy Birthday" to her this morning, quietly, in a voice that kept cracking because she couldn't hold any notes, and they laughed about how bad she was, but what Nora really wants, what every girl in here wants on her birthday, is a slice of cake. Nora's mother used to make a chocolate cake with white frosting and decorate the top with chocolate chips and candles; some of the other girls got yellow cake or tres leches cake. A few got nothing.

"Have you ever seen the prison part of this place?" asks Nora.

"No. It's just for kids who've been sentenced. Once you move there, you don't come back here." Jacqueline braids and rebraids a strand of hair on the left side of her head. Her case is scheduled for trial next week, and the braiding is new, a nervous tic she can't control. Nora reaches out to hold her hand once she's finished the new braid so she doesn't start all over again, but Jacqueline jerks her hand away.

Nora makes her face blank, then says, "I'm just wondering why it's lucky that I get to go there instead of somewhere else."

Jacqueline shrugs. "Who knows. I guess your parents can still visit. If you'd gotten Denver or Pueblo, your parents would've had to drive for, like, forever, to visit. Like eight hours or something. They'd probably never visit if it was that far."

Neither Jacqueline nor Nora knows if that's true or not true. Jacqueline is just guessing. No one ever visits her, except her grandmother, one time. The grandmother took the bus from Denver, then said she couldn't come again because it was too far and too expensive, so maybe Jacqueline assumes it would be too far for everyone. But maybe Jacqueline is deflecting, jealous that Nora receives a visitor almost every time there are visiting hours.

"Will there still be school?"

"Don't know."

Nora watches Jacqueline chew on her braid. Most kids feel older just knowing they can say "I'm fourteen" instead of "I'm thirteen." At thirteen, they were only a year away from being twelve. Fourteen is a year closer to being sixteen, to getting the driver's license that will jumpstart their path to freedom. Most kids. She stands up, anger flashing across her face.

"I thought I'd feel better," she says and starts pacing back and forth, five steps in one direction, five in the other.

"What do you mean?"

Nora gestures at nothing, but because the room is so small, her hands end up pointing at the ceiling. "It's done. Everything's been decided."

"But it's not done," says Jacqueline. "It'll never be done. You killed someone."

"I don't—"

"Don't say what you're about to say. I know you remember what happened. Everyone does, eventually." Jacqueline looks at Nora expectantly. She shared her secret with Nora long ago.

Nora squares her shoulders. If she did remember, there's only one person she'd tell, and he stopped pressing her about that night once he realized the answers might not help her case. The truth is that most of the significant and fact-specific memories would only confirm what everyone already knows, whether or not she admits remembering them to Jaqueline or herself or doesn't remember at all. She opened the gun safe, punched in the combination she always saw her father use. Took out the gun, closed the safe. Walked to Nico's room, opened his door, and pulled the trigger. Called 911. Those aren't the memories Julian fears.

Would admitting to possessing memories about the insignificant parts of that night do anyone any good? She remembers before: the chili for dinner—how she hated that chili, the beans and peppers and hamburger all jumbled together, every bite goopy and slippery, and her mother always served it two nights in a row, sometimes three, but at least her father baked cornbread to go with it—the Xbox game she played before bed, handily beating Nico, and deciding not to brush her teeth that night. And she remembers after: her mother crying, then stoic. The smell in the house, still sweet from the cornbread, and the bitter bile threatening to erupt from the back of her throat.

But then there is this: a memory of a feeling, a memory that belongs in the "after" category but not the "insignificant" category: the regret, immediate but stubbornly immutable, because she knew she hadn't done the right thing. What seemed like a good idea, something to help, to save Nico from the dark cloud of a future that had already arrived, that had diminished him and altered their family, wasn't. Nico would never get to go to his falcon camp, never get to finish high school or even just ninth grade. Never get to go to prom—he'd asked a girl, that was the rumor at school—and never get to kiss that girl. He would never ski again. All those nevers were her fault. And all those nevers and all that regret thudding in her stomach, she'd always remember that.

"It changes you, you know," says Jaqueline. "Killing someone. I can't forget, no matter how hard I try, and I hated my father. It doesn't seem like you hated your brother."

Nora doesn't understand it herself. One day she's sad, the next angry, the next she doesn't care. Numb is how she feels. Numb and sorry. The other truth is that she's not ready to remember all of it. The facts of that day sit on the outskirts of her memory, there but not there, locked out until she's ready to confront the consequences of taking a life. If she were to offer to tell Julian the truth, all of the truth, he would tell her that memory and truth are twisted sisters, and perhaps she has known that all along.

"Your trial is still next week," Nora says. "What do you know about how I feel?"

Jacqueline slides her braid out of her mouth, stands up, and walks out of the room and into the common area.

Nora lies down and faces the wall. "Today is my birthday," she whispers to herself. "This will be the worst birthday I ever have. By next year, I'll be used to this. That birthday will be better. I'll turn fifteen and be as tough as Paradise was. Maybe even as tough as Maria Elena."

The month before Nora shot Nico was September. It used to be her favorite time of the year, because the tourists started to leave town and it was less crowded than summer or winter. Main Street belonged to the local kids, and they walked to and from school in packs. Her mother's birthday was in September, and her father always baked jumbo cupcakes, yellow ones swirled with fudge. Nora and Nico used to sneak into the kitchen and eat them in the middle of the night, and Angie never understood why they disappeared so quickly. When Nora was little, her grandmother would say fall was the time of year to start cooking winter foods like lasagna. But by September of last year, Livia was gone, locked away so she'd stop wandering outside in the middle of the night. Angie and David were gone, too, or at least they were gone from the house, because they were always at doctor's appointments with Nico. After school, Nora painted in her room alone.

The week before she shot Nico was October. Angie almost forgot David's birthday and had to buy a last-minute premade cake from the grocery store. Nico was always in a bad mood, and when he wasn't being mean, he was sad. Angie stayed at the kitchen table to help with his homework because she worried about his grades, but most of the time he just sat there, watching birds. He knew, by then, he couldn't race anymore but still thought he could go to his falcon-hunting camp. Nora found his summer camp pamphlet in his room, and one day when everyone else was at the doctor's, she snuck into Nico's room and tried to help make the painted falcon fiercer by adding a miniature leather hood, but it looked nothing like the one from the pamphlet.

The day before she shot Nico was October 12. It was no one's birthday. She and her mother visited Livia after school, and Livia yelled at Nora for interrupting her TV show even though it was just a commercial, then called her Angela even though everyone knows Nora looks like her father and not her mother. Nora was supposed to love her grandmother, and she did, but that day she felt undone by the smell in the room and the unkempt white hair and the drool dribbling from the side of Livia's mouth. That person wasn't her grandmother, not anymore.

The day she shot Nico was October 13.

For months and months, Angie has tried to unearth good memories, at least one a day, but on Nora's birthday, driving in the failing yet faithful minivan to visit her daughter, a different kind of memory rises to the surface.

Nico, fourteen; Nora, thirteen.

His last summer. He was five ten, and it was clear his genes had plans for him to be tall, but it was also clear his genes had disease on their mind. His spastic chorea had worsened and the new weight loss, bradykinesia, and gait ataxia, fancy names for a body in decline, meant Angie and David needed to have a direct conversation with him. They wanted to comfort him—there were medications to help control the disease's unusual body movements—but they also knew they had to be honest about the progression of his symptoms and what it meant. If they weren't, he'd search for answers online, and those answers could be wrong, right, or misleading. One night, with his bedroom door closed so Nora couldn't overhear, they had that hard conversation. There were no tears and no questions, probably because he'd googled everything long ago, but the next day he caught Angie off-guard. David was at work, Nora was in her room painting, and Angie was in the kitchen, preparing lunch.

He cleared his throat before he spoke, a warning not just of his presence but of the importance of what he wanted to say. "Mom. I have a question. I thought of one."

The air in the room, in the house, in the entire town, sat stagnant, throttled by a massive heat dome sitting over Colorado that raised August temperatures to levels rarely seen in a mountain town. There was no air conditioning in the house—who needs it when you live at 8,500 feet?—and Nico wore only athletic shorts. His bare chest was almost concave, and Angie kept her eyes on Nico's and away from the bodily evidence of the disease.

"Okay," she said. "Ask me."

"What's it like to be dead? You only talked about what would happen while I'm still alive." His eyes were wide, not with fear but with curiosity.

That was something she didn't have an answer for. She, like everyone else—except maybe Father Lopez—could only guess or hope. What was it like for Diana or Roberto or the fire chief who died four years ago? She sat down at the kitchen table, pulling him with her, and tried to sound like she did know.

"Peaceful, I think," she said.

"Will you be there?"

She laid her hand on his heart—it was warm and thumping and there was so much more than just an organ under that concave chest—then placed his hand on her heart. "I'll be here. I'll always be in here," she said. "And you will always be inside mine."

They sat like that for a moment, and she drew her breath in shakily.

"But, Mom," he finally said, "that's not—I still don't know what it's like, and I don't know if I believe in Heaven."

She'd read a pamphlet on how to talk to a child about death—what else was the mother of a dying child supposed to do—but the guide was for young children, and she felt lost, more lost that she'd ever felt as a mother. A choking feeling rose in her throat, and she repeated some of what the pamphlet said, trying to buy herself time—*when you're dead, there is no suffering, you won't be in this body any longer because it will have stopped working, and you won't sleep or eat or feel pain*—and then she noticed Nora watching silently, standing under the doorframe. She opened up her arms and pulled them both in for a hug, then wiped the tears from her cheeks once she thought they couldn't see her face.

When Angie finally arrives, it's late in the afternoon, the last visiting hours of the day. She has brand-new paints, paints she's not allowed to leave with Nora but that she'll bring every time she visits so Nora can continue to paint while they talk. She buys a Hostess chocolate cupcake with white icing and a Sprite from the vending machines. Visitors can bring painting supplies into the visiting room for prisoners to use during the visit but not homemade food, even on a birthday, and Angie is muttering to herself about this senseless rule when she bumps into the guard stationed outside of the visiting room.

"Pardon me," she says, but he barely looks up from his phone and Angie pushes the door open herself.

Since Nora's sentencing, a strange peace has descended on Angie, maybe more of an equilibrium than a peace, neither of which she understands, but she knows she must focus on creating new memories and new lives for her smaller, reshaped family. In the meantime, there's one thing she still has to do for Nora, and she's going to do it today.

David isn't with Angie, but he sent a pink card that says "You're FOURTEEN!" in blue letters on the front. He hand-wrote an extra message on the inside in neat, square print. The message is short—*Happy birthday, dearest Nora! I love you and will visit soon*—because he doesn't want to explain where he really is: attending a full day of interviews for the land conservation nonprofit. At the same moment Angie walks into the detention center, he sits in a conference room across the table from a man and a woman. *We're sorry, but we have to ask*, they've just said. They lean forward slightly, as if to better hear. They are kinder than he expected, and they've already told him this final day of interviews is a mere formality, that everyone in the organization wants to meet him, and yet he's tongue-tied. His gun was locked in a safe, right where it was supposed to be. He didn't do anything wrong. But he cannot account for his failure to do more. He cannot account for his failure to safeguard his family. He cannot account for his failure to want to return to the purple house or his old job carrying a gun.

Nora notices her father's absence immediately, and her heart thuds in her chest, not an angry pounding but a heavy acceptance. She sees the paints, the plastic-wrapped Hostess cupcake, the card, and her mother. The same table, the same orange chairs. Her eyes follow the guard leaving the room, but her father isn't in the hallway. The door slams behind the guard and she looks at Angie.

"Where's Daddy?"

"He couldn't come. He wanted to, he really did, but he has something for work." The new paints are already spread out on the table, and Angie gestures toward them. "Happy birthday, Nora. These are for you."

"I wanted your cake, not that." Nora picks up a paintbrush, starts to paint, and doesn't look at Angie.

"I know." Angie says this gently. "But this is the best I could do."

Nora scratches at the paper with her brush, tentatively at first, and then a picture shapes itself seemingly out of nowhere, the same way Angie's paintings do. It's a scene Angie has watched her daughter paint repeatedly. A river in the foreground wends away from a mountain in the background. The mountains and the vertiginous horizon blur together in a haze. The craggy edges of the peaks are visible only because Nora tints them with alpenglow, but it's impossible to know whether the rose flush is sunrise or sunset. An aspen grove lines the trail next to the river. Angie and Nora sit in silence, mother watching daughter, daughter ignoring mother. After a long while, Angie speaks.

"Daddy and I never talked about Nico with you because we weren't supposed to—that's what Julian and Martine told us. They were worried you might say something unexpected and then we'd have to testify as witnesses against you." Angie shifts in her seat, because she's not sure she's strong enough to be the kind of mother she needs to be, but she takes a deep breath and keeps going. "But now that there won't be a trial, now that you've already been sentenced, we can talk about anything. And I want to say that I know you miss Nico, and I know you loved him."

Nora looks up from her painting, biting her lip the way she does when she concentrates, like a freeze-frame from a video. She searches her mother's eyes, then looks back down. Blood gathers on her lip and a drop falls onto the paper, hitting the mountain in the picture. A blond boy on a river trail walks toward the mountain, his back to the viewer.

"I miss him, too," says Angie. "But I also miss you. And I love you."

Nora nods, her eyes full of tears.

"I forgive you," says Angie. She reaches out and touches the back of Nora's hand. "Even though I miss him, I forgive you."

The small room amplifies the meaning of her words, not just the sound of her voice, though maybe that's only in Angie's and Nora's imaginations. Nora looks back down at her painting and runs her fingers over the boy. The still-wet paint smudges, and she lifts her fingers. Tears spill from her eyes onto the smudged boy, but she doesn't cry aloud, and her silent tears resonate as loudly as Angie's words.

Angie walks around the table and gently pulls Nora out of her seat to hug her. Nora's shoulders sag into the embrace, then her whole body collapses into Angie's. She begins to sob, her chest heaving, and the weight and force push Angie to the floor. Nora falls into her lap, wailing now, and Angie wraps her arms around her daughter as if she's a little girl, home sick from school, the two of them resting on the couch together. A rush of warmth floods through Angie, and astonished, she realizes: this is forgiveness. Forgiveness was never a goal for her to reach as part of a process; it wasn't something she had to figure out how to do and then practice. It was a gift that was given. And the gift didn't come from *her* at all. It was a gift given *to* Angie, not from Angie. It's nothing like what she thought it would be. She feels a strange sensation, like a hot drink on a cold day, or a kiss on her forehead from Roberto, or the blue columbines finally blooming on top of Nico's grave. Holding Julian's hand under the aspen trees in their secret grove when they still loved each other, his warm skin absorbing the beauty above and conducting it to Angie as though they were a part of the tangled web of roots linking each tree. The potential weight of the key to David's white house in her hand. She wishes she could extract this sensation and bottle it for later.

The sublime, freeing feeling radiates through her, and Angie knows Nora feels it, too, because it transcends her prior failure to forgive, and even the actions that precipitated the need to forgive. Angie's mind wanders back to a different time, to that day in Mexico when she and Nora lay on rafts in the ocean, at the mercy of rising and falling waves, drifting together under the vast sky. They'd linked their pinkies to keep the rafts from drifting apart, but every so often Nora's tiny finger slipped from Angie's and she would giggle and paddle furiously back. Time and circumstance and gray impenetrable walls separate them from the sky now, but Angie squeezes her arms around Nora tighter, then strokes her hair in wonder and awe, and they sit on the hard floor, their synchronous breaths undulating like the long-ago mother and daughter floating on the swells in the sea.

Acknowledgments

The inspiration for *Penitence* arose from my own experience with being forgiven and forgiving others. Getting to forgiveness is often hard, but it can also be profound and even beautiful. For a long time, I searched for a way to articulate that feeling. I first noticed an account of fratricide in 2017, and filed it away in my head (and on my computer) as a tragedy, but after seeing an uptick of similar stories, I realized fratricide might provide the right framework for a novel about forgiveness. Fratricide is as old as history—Romulus and Remus, Cain and Abel, siblings in countless monarchies—but it's equally common in the modern world. My research found that while some circumstances varied (age, weapons, reasons), others were eerily similar (many perpetrators, especially the younger ones, called 911 themselves, and many incidents occurred while the victim slept). But no matter the circumstances, my thoughts always returned to the parents. Would they be driven toward or away from forgiveness?

This is not true crime; these characters and events are fictional. As I wrote into the characters and story, I actively avoided real people and events, but if in trying to avoid one person's reality I accidentally worked my way into another, I apologize. Lodgepole, Colorado doesn't exist, though some readers may recognize southwest Colorado's topography.

The Pinyon County juvenile detention center also doesn't exist, but

I hope it realistically illuminates certain broken elements of America's criminal justice system. Though I used to be a lawyer, I knew little about it when I began the novel. In my research, the following were especially helpful: *Just Mercy* by Bryan Stevenson; *Redeeming Justice* by Jarrett Adams; *A Closer Look at Juvenile Homicide: Kids Who Kill* by Katelyn A. Hernandez. Mayumi's statement "Each of us is more than the worst thing we've ever done" is a direct quote from *Just Mercy*. I read articles and reports from the New York Times, the Denver Post, www.5280.com, the Sentencing Project, the Juvenile Sentencing Project, and the Pew Charitable Trusts. I watched documentaries on life inside juvenile detention centers and reviewed the Colorado's Division of Youth Services' *Guide for Colorado Families* and *Youth Handbook*; the Office of Colorado's *2019 Child Protection Ombudsman Investigation Report*; the Colorado Child Safety Coalition's *2017 Report: Bound and Broken*; and the Colorado Attorney General's *Roundtable Report on the School-to-Prison Pipeline*. As I wrote, I was conscious of not telling a story that was not mine to tell, but I also wanted to accurately portray the juvenile justice system and its shortcomings, and I hope readers will be inspired to pay attention when journalists highlight these issues.

Thank you to Gail Hochman, my absolute champion of an agent and a firecracker of a human who is always there for me—and who I will always want on my side—and Deb Futter, my incredibly insightful and kind editor with a keen eye and the ability to keep this process fun even when I feel first-time jitters. Gail and Deb took a chance on a debut author and saw this novel for what it could be, and their wisdom and guidance helped steer *Penitence* to its best self. A dream agent and a dream editor. They and their amazing teams (including Marianne Merola at Brandt & Hochman and Rachel Chou, Melissa Churchill, Jennifer Jackson, Margaux Kanamori, Christine Mykityshyn, Jaime Noven, Anne Twomey, and Emily Walters at Celadon) care deeply about their authors and work with unparalleled dedication and talent. I'm lucky to be one of those authors.

Lynn Steger Strong's spot-on guidance during a year-long class helped shape my writing. Classmates Xian Chiang-Waren, Ben Constantino,

Deena Drewis, Lacey Dunham, Sonia Feldman, Ben Izzo, Sarah Kasbeer, Jean Kawahara, Shari MacDonald Strong, Peter Mayshle, and Nicole VanderLinden were (still are!) a godsend. Life works in funny ways: if I hadn't randomly checked my junk email, I wouldn't have seen an almost-expired acceptance to Sewanee. At Sewanee, I met Laura Spence-Ash, who recommended Lynn's class. Laura and I are now agency-and publisher-sisters, and I'm grateful for her constant advice. Serendipity reigns.

Many terrific teachers and classmates (at Lighthouse Writers Workshop, Aspen Summer Words, Sewanee Writers Conference, New York Summer Institute, and Boulder Writing Studio) contributed to my writing growth. A special thanks to Lighthouse, a Colorado literary institution and a huge support for writers. Claire Messud gave generously of her time and shared especially good advice early on. Mary Beth Keane's confidence in the novel's first pages helped me keep the faith. Angie Kim's and Brad Meltzer's advice on querying was invaluable. Long ago, Shannon Costello-Duster's invitation to a writing group gave me community when I needed it most. Allison Kingsley Snyder gave helpful comments on southwest Colorado's topography. Delaney Koval provided insight into the mind of a thirteen-year-old. When I first started writing, Ali Kokmen—whom I stood next to at high school graduation—gave me his perspective on the writing world.

I'm grateful to criminal defense attorneys Hannah Seigel Proff (who read two drafts to ensure I got the nuances of criminal law correct and allowed me to watch one of her trials), and Ann Roan (who spoke with me early in my writing process). They patiently answered technical questions and guided me to helpful resources. My friend Julie Talano, M.D. helped me find a childhood disease that would work in the context of the novel and referred me to *Nelson's Textbook of Pediatrics*. Thank you to a certain guy (mentioned in ways more profound below) for confirming my internet research about heart health and Alzheimer's. Any legal or medical mistakes are entirely my own.

Thank you to my dear friends Cathleen Kendall and Winston Berry, and to my late friend Hilaree Nelson. Our walks and talks sustained me throughout the writing process.

My parents Bea and Bernie taught me to love reading—and only sometimes teased me when I was so immersed in a book that I failed to hear them. I'm lucky they made me, loved me, and raised me. My brother Jay and his dear family always asked about this project of mine called "writing" that may have seemed unproductive for many years. Janie and Jim and Joe, thank you for your curiosity about how things were going and your constant support. Thank you to my sons, for their belief: Alex, the original never-give-up guy with full faith that I would someday see my work in print, and Nicholas, the guy who was always interested enough to be my first reader, even when he should have been doing homework. Above all, my husband. When I decided to leave the law, I was afraid to admit I wanted to write. J.P. gave the best advice I've ever received: I needed to own it so I could fully dedicate myself. We left on vacation a week after I walked out of my law firm for the last time, and when he signed us into the hotel guest register in Cartagena, in the blank space for my occupation he wrote "Writer." His love has always given me strength.

About the Author

[TO COME]

CELADON
BOOKS

Founded in 2017, Celadon Books, a division of
Macmillan Publishers, publishes a highly curated list
of twenty to twenty-five new titles a year. The list of
both fiction and nonfiction is eclectic and focuses
on publishing commercial and literary books and
discovering and nurturing talent.